ZODIAC ACADEMY

BEYOND THE VEIL

CAROLINE
PECKHAM

SUSANNE
VALENTI

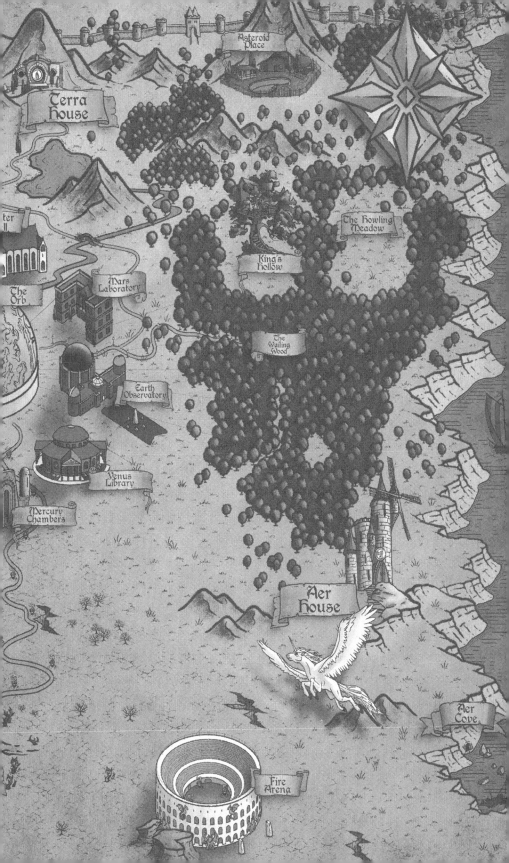

This book is dedicated to all those who wait for the living to join them beyond The Veil, watching ever on, and to all those they left behind. May you be brave enough to follow the longings of your heart to far-flung places, adventure into the unknown, take leaps of faith and dare to dream bigger than the moon.
Be brave, be hopeful, be you.
And give them the show of a lifetime.

This is a bridging book which takes place beyond The Veil (in the land of the dead) during the events of book 8 in the Zodiac Academy series. It should be read after book 8 to avoid spoilers for that book and holds the answer to what takes place for the characters who are held within the clutches of death by this point in the story, as well as vital clues to the conclusion of this epic series.

WELCOME TO SOLARIA

Note to all Fae: Lesser Orders will be sent to the Nebula Inquisition Centres if seen using Order gifts aggressively. All traitors of the crown will be sentenced to death in the palace amphitheatre, and their executions will be televised as a warning to insurgents.
King Lionel Acrux has pledged to make Solaria powerful once more and has vowed upon the stars to protect the loyal, honourable Fae of the nation at any cost.
The King's United Nebular Taskforce will be watching.
All hail the Dragon King

DARIUS

CHAPTER ONE

Death struck me like an anvil to my chest, my soul hurled from my body to collide with the afterlife so hard that the crash of a gong rang out, making The Veil itself rattle with the force of my passing.

I leapt to my feet, my fist colliding with the closed gate which had trapped me here, and I bellowed Roxy's name as my path to her was cut off eternally.

My fist hammered against The Veil so forcefully that for several minutes, I didn't even notice the silence in my own chest, the lack of movement where my heart should have been pounding.

I sucked in a sharp breath as I stumbled back, my hand pressing to my stomach as I found a silk shirt where my armour had been, the silvery fabric unblemished and my hands clean of blood and grime. A golden cloak hung from my shoulders, a circlet falling across my brow as death dressed me in the clothes of a warrior, hailing me as some hero in the moment of my greatest failure.

I refused to accept it. Any of it.

I hurled myself against The Veil and fought harder, bellowing my refusal at death, demanding the ferryman take me back across the raging river which I could hear but couldn't see. Time turned to nothing as I raged against the truth of what I'd lost, of my failure, of all I'd left behind in life.

This wasn't happening.

It couldn't be happening.

"Darius?"

My blood chilled as I took in that voice, the soft, gentle embrace of it wrapping around my name as I realised what must have happened if she was here too.

I didn't want to turn, didn't want to look at her and confirm this unspeakable truth, because if the two of us were here, then my departure from the land of the living would have destroyed so much more than just Roxy's life.

Her hand landed on my shoulder, and I almost broke as I recognised the feeling of her presence close to mine, the memories I'd once let myself forget resurfacing. I remembered her holding me in her arms as a child, crawling beneath the sheets in my bed and whispering stories to me in the dark. I remembered curling up in her arms and feeling safe beneath those sheets, a world hidden away from the fear I didn't even fully understand in my father's presence.

"Mom?" I breathed, my voice cracking as I forced myself to turn, to look into the depths of her tear-lined eyes as she peered up at me.

Her hand moved to my jaw, those tears spilling over as she broke in the face my death, her own passing not even seeming to register with her, and I just had to watch her shatter before me. My beautiful, brave, mother, broken by the monster who had destroyed her life all over again.

"You had so much to live for," she whispered, and somehow, I saw what she meant, like her memories were playing out for me within my own head, shared between us as she opened the gates of her mind to me.

I was running through Acrux Manor with Xavier at my side, giggling as I grasped his pudgy hand, and we sought out somewhere to hide from her in our game. I was growing year after year, feeling the love and pride and pain she had experienced as she was forced to stand back, as she watched Lionel beat and brutalise me in an attempt to make me into the creature he desired. And she feared he might succeed.

I saw myself with Roxy, saw the way she looked at me when I wasn't paying attention, how she let her walls crack sometimes and the love she felt for me spilled through. I saw my mom's heartbreak when she found out we were Star Crossed, felt her unending hatred for my father and what he had cost me. Then I felt her explosive joy when we'd defied the stars despite it all. I felt the pride she'd experienced when watching me turn against my father, the love consuming her as she saw me soaring over the battlefield.

It was endless, her love for me, only matched by her love for Xavier too. Xavier who had been left behind, all alone without either of us now, the truth of that a horror I couldn't bear to accept.

"How?" I gritted out, unable to face any of the other questions ringing inside my skull.

"Xavier was wounded," she breathed. "He was running, fleeing the battle along with the other rebels, and someone had to hold the way clear for them. Hammy and I…we chose to give every drop of our magic to shield the retreat for as long as we could."

At her words, I lifted my head, finding Hamish beyond her, his hand on her shoulder, that gleam of death clinging to him too as he looked to me with utter heartbreak in his eyes.

They had been redressed in death just as I had, my mom wearing a gown of shimmering silver which swept down to her feet and made her look like an angel come to comfort. Hamish was dressed as I was, a warrior laid to rest with a golden cape pinned over his shoulders.

"We used all of our power to stop that cretinous turd from following our dear children," he swore. "We gave everything so that Xavier and Geraldine might stand a chance at survival."

"And they got away?" I demanded, looking around us, spotting more and more people, though there were no others who I recognised close by. The landscape surrounding us was coated in a golden haze, buildings and mountains just visible through it but nothing substantial enough to hold my focus as I hovered on the precipice of death.

"They did," Hamish confirmed, and Mom nodded, her thumb sweeping across my cheek as she tried to contain her grief over seeing me here too.

"We gave all we had until there was nothing left for us to fight with," she swore to me. "And when Lionel came, we only had our Orders, but we knew…we knew that we weren't a match for him and those who followed on his heels in their shifted forms."

"I would have fought him to the last breath," Hamish snarled fiercely. "But I wouldn't risk him taking my sweet Kitty for his own ever again."

I crumbled at those words, understanding the choice they'd made, the sacrifice they'd taken upon themselves. Because they were right, my father would have taken her if he could have. He would have taken her and punished her and committed all kinds of horrors before he ever let her find relief in death.

"Thank you," I gasped, reaching for Hamish as my chest shook with emotion, and I drew the two of them into my arms, holding them close and finding some small measure of solace in the fact that neither of them could ever be hurt by him again.

My mom's slender frame was dwarfed by mine and Hamish's, and I swallowed a thick lump in my throat as I felt her tears falling against my chest, her fingers coiling in the fabric of my shirt.

"You shouldn't be here," she sobbed, and the weight of my own failure crushed me as I nodded my agreement, my eyes meeting Hamish's over her head.

"Your queen will be most tormented by this loss, my boy," he said, clapping my arm bracingly as he tried to offer me some comfort, sensing the grief of his own passage from this world pressing down on him. "Fate has been cruel indeed this day."

Something tightened in my chest, the feeling of true sorrow clinging to Hamish on my behalf overwhelming me. He was hurting for me, for my death and the pain it would cause those I loved. He was disappointed, and yet he wasn't looking at me like I was a failure.

"I re-watched the battle and saw you fighting your father when I arrived here," he said roughly. "I saw it all and I…you should have won. Fate was a wicked thing in that moment, and I cannot fathom the thoughts of the stars when they saw fit to take you from life and the love of your dear queen. It was a brave and honourable sacrifice you endured, and it was not without meaning. Xavier lives because of you. And many more besides him managed to flee the battle when the tides turned, making the most of the time you bought them to escape, ready to fight another day. You gave all you had."

"But it wasn't enough," I replied, my words hollow, vacant, the unending need in me for another outcome to this fate more than I could bear.

"Never think that you are not enough," Hamish growled, his grip on me tightening, and he took my jaw in his hand, locking his gaze with mine as he seemed to peer directly into my soul. "You fought with all you had, unflinchingly and without fear, giving yourself entirely to a fight that could have righted the world. You fought for love and justice, and you should have won. I am endlessly proud of you, dear boy. Endlessly, utterly proud of the man you proved yourself to be."

Words abandoned me at that declaration, something inside the hardened steel of my chest caving at the pure honesty he was offering me with those words. The man who had sired me had never once been proud of me like that. His pride in any accomplishment of mine had been purely a reflection of his own ego, any talent he saw in me something he simply claimed as his own doing.

Lionel Acrux had never cared what kind of man I was, nor what kind of honour I claimed, he only ever saw me as an extension of his own achievements, a puppet he could trot out to bolster his own self-worth. And even if he had been proud of me in my own merit, it was all too clear now that I never would have felt anything like the emotion I was experiencing from Hamish Grus's declaration. He made me feel like I was a man worth knowing, worth following, worth something far more important than my name or any title I might claim.

"Roxanya Vega was right to deny your bond when it was offered," my mom added. "Because it was the push you needed to find yourself, to become the man I had always known you could be. You set out to prove yourself worthy of her love, but in finding what was needed to do so, you became so much more. I have been proud of you from the first moment I held you in my arms, but I am honoured to have been there to watch you step into your destiny as fully as you did."

I shattered then, held between my mother and the man who she had found such brief and pure love with. I broke between them, for all I had failed to do, all I had lost and all the life which had been waiting for me beyond that moment on the battlefield.

Fate was a wicked mistress to have stolen all of us from the embrace of life, and I bared my teeth against the injustice of it all, letting myself fall apart.

I gasped as I felt the power of the woman who I had pledged my life to whipping out with such ferocity that it could be felt even here, beyond death.

I looked up, expecting to see her as I released my mother and Hamish, instead simply hearing the words which tore from her, the pure, undeniable power of them making the entire world quake.

"I will tear the heavens apart for this," Roxanya Vega snarled, the curse of a true queen lashing across the heavens and scoring them with her conviction. "I will shred your world to pieces and rip your hold on destiny from your fucking fists with blood and fire and vengeance for this," she screamed at the stars, her power making the ground beneath me tremble, magic unlike any I'd ever felt before burning its way between the realms as she forced the stars to take note. "On my life, I curse you. On his life, I curse you. And for our fate, I'll end you!"

The power which blasted through The Veil pushed me to my knees, and I turned my face up towards the heavens too, a snarl on my lips as I joined her in that curse and made a vow of my own.

If she refused our fate, then I would too. I would fight with whatever power remained to me and use whatever I could to see an end to this injustice. If there was any way for us to reunite our souls once more, then I would give all I had to do so.

There was only her.

My one, my only, my wife.

HAIL

CHAPTER TWO

I clung to the golden railing that ringed the great orb in The Room of Knowledge, watching Roxanya break over the loss of her one true love, upon a battlefield of decimation, while my other daughter fled to the mountains, bound to a curse so dark I had never seen the likes of it before.

"Merissa," I rasped. "There must be something we can do."

My wife's hand wrapped around mine, our fingers threading as a sob of grief left her. She no longer possessed any gifts of The Sight here, those powers tossed to the breeze of mortality. In this eternal palace of death, we were little more than observers of the world. I was no longer allowed to fight in wars nor shift the tides of destiny, but I could not let go of this.

There were many souls in this room, watching that same giant orb, seeing living Fae through the eyes of the stars themselves, witnessing their fates play out like a show on a screen. There were some who never left here, those who crept up to sit upon one of the gilded seats of this circular room which, at its heart, was little more than an auditorium for the living. Those who never left their perches were enraptured by the living, destroyed by all they'd lost. They watched until they became husks of themselves, barely distinguishable as Fae, their bodies nothing more than flickering shadows, but their eyes…. those ever-watching, never-blinking eyes remained. The remnants, we called them. Most of their kind watched the living from the privacy of their own rooms within the Eternal Palace, fading away without anyone even knowing they were gone. The door to the beyond crept up on them then, no doubt, when they were almost entirely lost, its silent hinges swinging open, a promise of oblivion beckoning them into its embrace.

I'd watched Fae pass straight through that door to the supposed sanctuary and solace promised beyond it, each of them satisfied with their death and at peace with the lives they'd left behind. But for those whose ties to the living were as strong as mine, passing on into the embrace of eternity was not an option.

I assumed that was why some souls remained here rather than staying in the privacy of their own personal sanctuaries within death. The Room of Knowledge was open to all, meaning the door would have to approach them in front of any who might be present, giving them a better chance at resisting its lure. So long as they latched onto something in life, they could keep their grip on this eternal palace, even when their features blurred and they all but forgot who they had once been.

"We cannot change fate," Merissa said, her grief slicing through her beautiful features. Her deep bronze skin near glittered in this place, and her ebony hair shone like starlight. My wife had been a vision in life, and death had immortalised that beauty, the stars always seeming close to her, like she was their prized possession beneath their eternal roof. Though even they could not lay a claim to her that was deeper than mine. They could admire her all they wanted, but they could only envy the king who she had chosen as her keeper.

I accepted her words, aching to step out of this place more than I ever had before, to return to the living and destroy the man who had caused all of this. Lionel Acrux was the root of the pain in my family's lives and the lives of so many others. If I had only seen it sooner, if I had stopped him while I still reigned on earth...

The orb was a great ball of silvery light which twisted and shifted like a pool of fog-drenched water. It used the power of the stars to show those of us lingering in death what was occurring within the realm of the living. It was enormous, taking up the centre of The Room of Knowledge, which was effectively an amphitheatre, countless gilded seats ringing the orb and rising up all around it on every side. Each soul who sat watching it could view their own heart's desire at once. Golden arches swept overhead, grand awnings hung between them to shelter those who sat on the seats, but directly above the orb itself, a hole in the roof let the stars look down upon the glistening ball of power. The sky there was ever dark, the stars bright within it, their strength echoing over us at all times.

The Veil hummed with the power of so many battle-worn souls spilling through it at once, and I bowed my head, knowing what was coming. We had watched as Catalina and Hamish made a final stand against Lionel, and now it was time to greet them after so many years apart. There was freedom in their deaths, and it had not been in vain, I had seen that much, but it still pained me to know more of my friends had fallen.

Them, I could face. I could handle it, but it was the other man who was moving this way that I could not stand to greet. The one who should have remained in the realm of the living with my daughter, bound to her, protecting and loving her.

"Is there no justice left in the hearts of the stars?" Azriel Orion's sharp voice drew my attention to my left where he stood watching reality play out, his dark hair unkempt as always and worry lines etched across his forehead. He reached for the orb with shaking fingers that curled tightly into a fist, his own grief potent.

In our rooms, we all had access to a window which gave a view of those we had loved and left behind in the living realm, but here we could see more, we could widen our view to watch something as all-encompassing as a battle as it took place. So here we had gathered. Here we had watched as the rebellion our children had spearheaded had fallen to ruin and Lionel Acrux had once again triumphed where he had no right to.

I pressed my hand to Azriel's shoulder, drawing his focus to me.

"What have you seen in the great orb?" I asked, wishing to share his burden with him in hopes it might lighten the load a little. So much was taking place at once, and it was impossible to keep track of anything more than the fates of my own children.

"Lavinia has taken Lance hostage. He has offered himself to her in payment for Gwendalina's curse," his voice cracked. "He made a Death Bond on it, Hail." There was pride shining in his eyes, but fear most of all, and a weighted sigh left me.

My mind sifted over this new fact. There was hope in this offering his son had made, a chance for Gwendalina to escape the binds of her curse, and my gratitude to Azriel's boy spilled forcefully through my chest.

Azriel's daughter, Clara, stood just beyond him, her gaze still riveted to the orb. Her dress was silver and flowing, her eyes bright as they reflected the swirling glow contained within the sphere of knowledge. She looked a little younger than the age she had truly died, her brown hair cut to her ears and the freckles dusting her nose looking as though they had seen the kiss of the sun recently.

I squeezed Azriel's arm. "Your son's love knows no bounds, and I know well that he would die for my daughter. But he is no fool. He would not make such terms with no hope in sight."

Azriel swallowed thickly, nodding to me, distress written into his features.

"Dad," Clara croaked, turning away from the orb and pressing her face to Azriel's chest. "She's going to torture him."

Azriel held her tight, and I turned back to Merissa, who was lost to the orb's offerings again while tears tracked silently down her cheeks. To see her like that was another knife in my unbeating heart, and rage took root in me, climbing up through my chest like ivy growing beneath a baking sun. I may have been long dead, but my wrath was as robust a thing as it had been in the Fae realm.

"I will not stand for these fates," I snarled, moving closer to Merissa. "Keep watching over them, I will go to the stars."

I turned my back on the orb and made a path for the arching doors, hostility decorating my face.

"Hail," Merissa called after me, her voice so full of grief it broke what was left of my restraint. "Bargain with them. I will offer anything to free our children from the curse of the stars."

"Of course, my love," I replied, then shoved the doors wide and made a few souls stumble aside from the ferocity of my sparking aura.

Merissa knew well I would do as she willed, but we had tried countless times to offer anything to the stars to break the curse laid upon our daughters by Clydinius. The fallen star, a creature who had not followed its rightful path once it had tumbled from the heavens long ago, twisting the laws of old and changing fate. It should have released the power within, offering it up to the world as a final gift as was decided by the ancient stars themselves. Instead, Clydinius had thwarted nature and unbalanced the true path, setting a curse upon my family for generation after generation with the deal it had offered my ancestor.

The broken promise had taunted me so deeply in life, and now it remained to taunt me in death. I knew its truth. It was the second truth I had perceived within the afterlife, finding the memories of all that had happened in the lead up to my demise and watching them play out from the sanctuary of my room in the Eternal Palace, the first being that of Lionel's Dark Coercion over my mind.

The bitterness of that terrible day still laid deep within me, and I did not believe it would ever be put to rest until Lionel's soul passed into the eternal fields of chaos, hurled through the Harrowed Gate, or tossed down into the raging river which led to that place. Only pain awaited him there.

He deserved that, but far more besides. I would see him through the boundary of The Veil myself, I would walk him on his final path and lay him at the feet of the one they called Crucia. A being of death designed by the stars themselves to inflict unimaginable torment upon the souls of the wicked for all of time. That creature possessed blades forged from agony itself, able to cut apart the essence of a Fae and bind them in infinite suffering.

Only then would my soul find peace.

I moved across the landscape of The Veil, pacing through the picturesque valley beyond the palace, bathed in the golden glow of the sun above. A tower lay to the east of the Eternal Palace, its shadow long and its gaze perpetual. The Stars' Spire, where starlight lived within the walls and moonbeams danced like living creatures across the ornate floor. The whisper of the stars themselves carried on the wind that swept through its glassless windows, the taste of destiny colouring the air.

I didn't pause as I reached the stone archway which led into the tower and stepped onto the stairwell where few Fae ever dared to step, climbing the spiralling stairs that rose up and up forever, the structure as white as purest sunlight and almost blinding to look upon.

I climbed ever on, the power of the beings above pressing in as I approached the entrance to the Halls of Fate. I would not be permitted there, but a king of the living still held sway as a king in the afterlife. They listened to me even when it meant nothing, but at least they would hear me. And today, they would do more than that, I was determined of it.

I made it to the door that stood weightlessly at the peak of the stairway, nothing below and nothing above. It was a simple door forged of something dark, like the absence of light between stars, and the space around it was foggy, the strange clouds made of a lambent, sparkling light.

I pressed my hand to it, the forces in the air trying to make me retreat, to turn me away from this need of mine. All wants faded in The Veil, that was what they'd told me when I arrived. Eventually, I would want for nothing, because I would either possess everything, find peace, and move on, or I would become a remnant. One of those lost souls with their ever-watching eyes, clinging to the living and losing grasp on true death. The stars often told us to seek solace, find acceptance, embrace harmony. Then we would truly rest. We would feel the call of the Destined Door, and we would walk through it into bliss.

There was no resting for me, and I would not become one of those ruptured beings who had forgotten their own name. I would remain Hail Vega and stand at the side of my wife for all of eternity. But while my daughters remained in peril and Lionel Acrux still walked the world, I would always be afflicted by their suffering, and I would not bow to the whims of the stars while my family were in danger.

"Open this door," I commanded, my voice ringing through the air with all the conviction of a monarch. I was power embodied, and they would not keep me out this day. They would hear me and my demands, and they would damn well answer them too.

"Father of the flames," they spoke, but they did not open the fucking door. *"We know what it is you seek. But fate lies not in our hands."*

"You are the stars!" I boomed. "If it does not lie with you, then what are you worth? Are you nothing but false gold? Gleaming prettily with no true value at your core?"

"You know well that we cannot intervene. Clydinius holds their fates in his grip."

"He is but one star!" I roared, my voice echoing out into the strange clouds around this door. "How can you not have the might to take on just one of your brethren? What greatness do you truly possess if you cannot do this?"

"Once a star has fallen, it is beyond our intervention. All that lies in the living realm can only be influenced by our power, not ruled by it."

"Then send another star down there to destroy your brother," I commanded.

"Clydinius has broken the laws of old. When we fall, we must release our power. No other star would dare do what he has done and defy the Origin. It has already led to a mighty unbalance. Chaos cannot be righted by more chaos. Now rest, regal soul of the eternal, this is not your fight."

"It is my daughters' fight, so it is mine," I snarled.

"It is not your fight," they repeated, and I felt their presence withdrawing, leaving me with no answers nor solutions.

But I was not even close to done. I would find a way to send word to my daughters, my children, and tell them what the broken promise was. I'd learn how to push deeper into the barriers between worlds and offer them the truth that the stars continued to keep from them.

If the stars truly wanted balance, they would tell my children the truth of the promise so that they might keep it. But I knew why the stars held off; I had sensed it when I'd questioned them on it once. Even stars could feel fear, it seemed. And the last thing they wanted was for Roxanya and Gwendalina to choose to raise Clydinius into Fae form, the power he could wield then would be some unimaginable terror. But the stars had just confirmed there was no other way. So I would make it my duty to force them into relinquishing that truth to my children.

DARIUS

CHAPTER THREE

This place was ever changing, a song whispering answers on the wind at the merest hint of a question whenever it had crossed my mind.

I had been here and there, somewhere between while caught in the embrace of my mother and Hamish, but with a yank which felt like I was cast through a sea of starlight and darkness, I found myself standing on that hillside where I had felt the last furious beats of my heart before death had stolen me away.

It was instantly obvious why fate had delivered me to this place, the power of Roxy's curse on the stars summoning me to her in her moment of earth-shattering grief.

I fell to my knees beside her, my own body sprawled in the dirt beneath her as her wings created a cocoon over it.

The shock of seeing myself there should have been more than enough to break me, but I was ruined by the utter devastation which lined every inch of Roxy's bruised and bloodied body.

I was there but not. The wind which lifted tendrils of her ebony hair did nothing at all to me while I remained beside her, a ghost without substance. Looking down only confirmed what I already knew; there was nothing of me here. I was observing this, not living it. Her grief and need for me must have summoned this wretched piece of me back to her, and my pain in our separation was only multiplied by the forced confrontation.

"I'm here," I told her, reaching for her arm, but neither my words nor my touch could cross The Veil for her to behold them. I was here, but I wasn't.

Roxy lay prone across the blood-stained chest of the body which had once seemed so intrinsically mine, her entire being trembling and tear stains carved through the dirt on her cheeks.

I sucked in a breath as I took in the jagged cut to her palm, understanding it as the knowledge of what she'd sworn for me. The promise that had radiated through the foundations of the realms themselves.

There were eyes on us now. All-seeing, all-knowing eyes belonging to creatures which seemed to be holding their breath, watching, waiting, wondering…

I didn't have to wonder though. My beautiful, broken, warrior of a wife was no mystery to me. Those words she had spoken had been full of truth and purpose, the power of them casting ripples through the fabric of fate. Destiny was shifting, uncertainty reigning, and I would be ready to fight on from beyond The Veil in whatever way I could.

I shifted closer to her, my knees in the dirt beside hers, and yet I couldn't feel it, couldn't feel anything aside from the soul-crushing grief which surrounded her. I wasn't able to do anything here, wasn't able to comfort her in any way, to show her that I would never truly leave.

"I'm here, Roxy," I growled more forcefully, reaching out to brush my fingers through her hair, but my touch met with nothing, and she didn't so much as blink in my direction.

Pain shredded the fragments of my heart as I was forced to watch her shatter for me, her silence this piercing, soul destroying thing which ate into me and made me bleed for her while she just lay across my vacant body, willing the world to change its mind on our fate.

My gaze shifted to the dagger which had stolen me from her world, the mixture of her blood and mine on it humming with a power so ancient it felt like the air was trying to recoil from it. There was menace in the oath she had sworn upon that blood, a dark promise which coiled from it into the very fabric of all that existed around us and beyond.

She was still bleeding from the wound she had carved into her own palm, her pain making me suffer while I was forced to simply observe it.

Power roiled within me, a deep and unending well of it stirring with so much more than the depths of my flames and ice. There was a purity to my magic which I had never noticed before crossing into death. But now that I had, it was like a song whispered into the corners of my mind.

I needed to return to her, needed to get back to her and draw her into my arms, banish that most powerful hurt which I could see destroying her from within.

"I'm right here, Roxy," I insisted, louder now as I pushed to my feet, that power rising within me, churning and roaring and begging for a way out of this fate.

I reached for her, my entire being radiating that power as the air around me hummed with it, a clang of magic echoing against the walls of death which contained me, a roar resounding through the air as the force of it bucked, and I threw everything I had into fighting this path.

Someone started calling my name, the desperate plea on their lips rocking the foundations of my fracturing soul. But I ignored them and the truth of what I was now.

I couldn't be in a place without her. I couldn't go back on the oaths I'd made to her so soon. She was mine and I was hers. We weren't destined to be apart. I refused it.

Roxy cupped my body's cold jaw in her hand and found my lips with a kiss so bittersweet that it stole the breath from my lungs. My eyes fell closed as I felt the press of her lips against mine, the ghost of me almost tasting her as her tears dripped against my cheeks before she drew back.

As she released her hold on my still body, the sensation of her abandoned me entirely, a strangled cry escaping me as I was abandoned on this dark path, the space between us so thin, yet completely impenetrable.

"Your soul is bound to mine," she breathed against the unmoving lips beneath her, and the pure, potent energy which made up all that I was now stirred in reply, the heart and soul of me needing her to know I agreed with those words more deeply than she could ever know. Goosebumps prickled her skin and her spine straightened as if she might have been able to feel that, and her words were rougher as she went on. "And I won't rest until I make every star in the heavens fall for trying to cleave us apart."

"Yes," I growled, all the power I owned ratcheting up within me, blazing with a need for an outlet, my desire to touch her making everything surrounding me quake. I reached for her bleeding hand, urging her to feel me, to know I would never truly leave her.

Roxy looked down at the cut on her palm, seeming to feel that raw energy which had connected us from the very first time I laid eyes on her. Her blood knowing mine, her power aching for my own.

She curled her fingers closed around the wound, her limbs trembling as she stood, the fatigue and pain which so clearly held her in its deathly grip making me ache to reach for her, to hold her in my arms and lend her my strength.

Roxy looked down at my broken body and I could feel her love for me in the ferocity of her heart-breaking gaze. It passed through The Veil with ease, that feeling so far beyond any barrier that might try to part us.

My warrior queen. The last one standing on a battlefield so drenched in blood and ruin that none but the stars themselves could have ever foreseen it. It was a tragedy beyond measure, the blow struck against our rebellion so harshly that I feared what it would mean for the war as a whole. But one look at the face of Roxanya Vega as she surveyed that blood strewn battlefield made it clear to me that this was no end play. This war was not won, the fight not over. I had never once seen that girl back down from anything, and even here, in the midst of defeat, her husband's blood staining her hands and her whole world shattering around her, she still stood tall and defiant, daring the world to come for her.

A breath left her in a cloud of vapour which rose and then dispersed as she surveyed the devastation of the battlefield, a hardness sinking into her skin which made my own flesh prickle. That girl had been born with a wall of iron surrounding her heart, gilding her spine, and edging her tongue, but I watched as that iron turned to steel before me, her walls becoming impenetrable, her pain sinking deep within her until she was using it as a foundation for her very soul.

She wasn't going to break. She was rallying herself for the fight of her life, and I was right there beside her, urging her on.

Roxy picked up her sword, her own blood mixing with all that already stained it as the wound on her palm continued to bleed in honour of the oath she'd sworn on it.

I watched as she faltered, the weight of all she'd fought for and all she'd lost pressing down on her so heavily that I knew any other would have buckled beneath it.

I moved closer to her, wrapping my hand around hers where she gripped that sword, even if she couldn't feel it, pushing whatever strength I had into her, offering up whatever remained of me at her service.

"You can do this. You were born to wear the crown, and you can bear the weight of it no matter how heavy it becomes," I swore to her.

Her jaw tightened and I growled my approval.

"Fate has never forced you to bend to it before," I said, a phantom tarot deck appearing before me as I spoke the words, The Lovers mocking me from the top of the pile, blood splattered across them, a flame scorching the stiff card on which they'd been painted.

I took the deck and held it before the woman I loved as her eyes fell closed, her resolve hardening. I cast The Lovers aside as I felt her will pressing in on me, followed by Five of Swords who whispered of defeat, then the Death card, King of Pentacles, the King of Swords, Roxy's will shoving them aside as she ignored their whispered words, as if she could somehow tell which card was being drawn, as if she could feel their power even here beyond The Veil and refused to hear their words. More and more cards tumbled to the mud and blood by my feet until finally, The Chariot met with my fingers, and I fell still. Vengeance, war, triumph.

Roxy's lips tightened as she latched onto that meaning, like she'd been the one to shuffle the deck, her will alone forcing the result she required as she chose her own fate.

"Defy the stars," I said fiercely, willing her to do so with all I was and all I had.

She released a breath and forced her eyes open once more, the divide between us growing as she did so, The Veil fluttering between us, parting us despite how desperately I fought to remain there with her.

She sheathed her sword in the filthy, bloodstained scabbard which hung from her hip, her chin high as she looked out across the battlefield, her beautiful features void of all emotion, that fire which ignited her soul all but snuffed out in the face of her loss.

The devastation surrounding her was unreal. Charred and blackened ground circled her, the last stand of the Nymphs reduced to nothing in the face of her terrible power.

She was trembling, her body spent, energy sapped, and I could see how thin her resolve was. The grief that consumed me was compounded for her; all she could see of me a dead body on the ground. She was so alone. And all I wanted was for her to know that I was still here, that I would never truly leave.

Whether it had anything to do with the strength I was battling to offer her or not, Roxy straightened. Shivers wracked her body, and she curled her right hand into a fist, the blood dripping between her fingers from the deep cut on her palm as she set her eyes on the far side of the battlefield and that strength in her eyes flared brighter at last.

"I'll be back," Roxy murmured to my corpse, the pain that promise caused almost dropping me to my knees. This couldn't be it for us. I couldn't be cursed to simply watch over her from this moment on, never able to pass through The Veil which divided us, never able to hold her in my arms again.

Roxy flexed her wings and for a moment, it seemed like she would take off, but she banished them instead, a heavy sigh escaping her as her Order form retreated, making her seem so much smaller than before, so much more alone.

She strode away across the battlefield, and though I tried to follow, the heavy fall of my feet met with resistance, my boots scraping over the dirt inch by inch, weighted manacles seeming to wind their way around my arms.

A defiant roar escaped me as they tightened, pulling me back, the strength of my will the only thing keeping me standing there, my boots carving ruts into the dirt, my muscles bulging with the force of all I was.

But it was no good.

With a final bellow ripping from my throat, I was hauled back, the distant figure of my one love stolen from sight, my spine colliding with a hard surface and all sense of her disappearing entirely.

HAIL

CHAPTER FOUR

Darius materialised before me, almost fully corporeal once more, as the stars dragged him away from the world of the living and deposited him in the great hall of the Eternal Palace where all souls found a home beyond The Veil.

They didn't much like when we did that, but it was impossible to fully control the desperate yearning of lost souls to return to those they'd left behind. Those who remained in this place, refusing to move on, were full of strife, the Fae realm still holding answers, hopes, truths, and loves that none of us could let go of.

The huge room opened out around us, souls coming and going, the vaulted ceilings painted with points of time when fate had turned and changed everything. Some of the images detailed here were so long forgotten that it was impossible to say when they'd been or what had happened in that moment which had once been so important. Others were fresher, the hall expanding to include them, moments from my own life and the lives of my children now marked there among countless others. Points of time that seemingly mattered, a ceaseless story woven from the Fae's very first ancestors right up until now.

I folded my arms as I came eye to eye with the man who had sacrificed himself out on that battlefield in the name of all he cared for. I knew him. I had watched him long enough, seen the poor choices he had made, witnessed the stubbornness of his soul. And all in all, I was still undecided on whether I liked him or not.

"Hail," he breathed, no submission in his eyes nor bending of his back, nor any use of my former title.

"Darius," I said curtly.

"Roxy is-" he started, sweeping toward me with passion in his eyes, but I cut over him in a baritone voice.

"I believe she prefers her friends to call her Tory."

His jaw tightened. "I think I know what my wife prefers. And I am no mere friend."

A growl rumbled in my chest, and he raised his chin, all challenge. Little did he know, I had been waiting a long time to pick this fight.

"Darius." Merissa's voice came at my back, sorrow washing through her tone. She swept past me, wrapping her arms around him, and he stiffened in surprise.

"Merissa," I growled. "Have you forgotten what he did?"

"He offered up his life for those he loves, including our children." She whirled on me, gaze full of fire. "He has redeemed himself in my eyes."

"I believe he has balanced out the scales, returning him to ground zero," I said.

"We don't have time for this," Merissa hissed. "We need to help our children."

"We can't help them now," Darius said darkly. "What good are the dead to anyone?"

"Do not wallow in self-pity any longer, there is much we can do." I twisted around, finding Catalina Acrux standing there at the side of Hamish Grus.

Grief closed around my heart, and I did not want to accept that some of that pain belonged to the man who now stood at my back. But I could let it be seen when it came to these two noble Fae.

"Well bless my gollywobbles," Hamish stammered, jaw opening and closing as he stared from me to Merissa, then fell down to his knees with a wail. "All hail the Vega line!"

Catalina gazed at me in disbelief, then shook her head in apology. "Forgive me for all my ex-husband did to you. I never knew, I swear it."

I frowned, the tightness of my chest speaking of that shame of mine. "And the same to you," I said, dipping my head a little as we shared in this dark truth. Both victims of the same tyrant, both helpless to escape him during our lifetimes, though I supposed she had come closer than I ever had.

"I'm so sorry you had to see your son cross over before his time," Merissa croaked, descending on Catalina and hugging her tight, and Catalina released a sob that was laced with heartache, her eyes latching onto Darius over my shoulder.

"It was my failure that led me here," Darius said bitterly. "But my time would have come to an end soon enough either way. Dying in battle was preferable at least."

I glanced back at him, my shoulders tight, fury daggering through me, but fuck, I couldn't deny the pain I felt at his words. I turned from him again before he could see any glimpse of it on my face, retreating behind a wall of duty. "We must make a plan."

"Anything, sire." Hamish sprang back to his feet. "I am at your service like a walrus in a dinghy, oar grasped a-tight in my flipper."

"You are not in service to anyone now, Hamish," I said. "My crown lays in The Palace of Souls, awaiting my daughters' claim upon it."

"Hamster bear, is that you?!" a warbling voice filled the air that was laced with sorrow, and I found Florence Grus bounding towards us with tears streaming down her cheeks, her light brown hair flowing out behind her like a cape. Her black dress was covered in purple wolfsbane flowers, and she held her large breasts as she ran to stop them from bouncing.

"Well bless my bachelor's button," Hamish gasped just before Florence collided with him, leaping up to kiss both of his cheeks. She was a tiny woman, barely past five feet in height, and Hamish was a tower of a man. I had known both of them in life, had seen their love for one another burn with all the wildness of high school passion, and had always admired the purity of it.

Catalina broke apart from Merissa, wiping the tears from her cheeks as she eyed Florence with uncertainty.

"Oh, Hamster," Florence cried, grabbing his hand in her tiny one with a loud sniff. "I have waited upon this day for eleventy hundred years, it seems. Yet I could never have fathomed it to come as soon as it has, nor as wickedly for it to fall upon your bodacious brow." She turned to Catalina, letting out a high-pitched shriek that made me wince, then she grabbed her hand too. "Lady of the new dawn, I saw you rise from the scaled nightmare who imprisoned you like a whelk in a rusted boat bottom. I have wept in your moments of pain, I have rejoiced in your moments of glory, and I have fallen for you almost as deeply as my big Hamster has."

"Oh, wow, um…" Catalina looked to Hamish, lost for words before opening her mouth to speak again, but Florence barrelled on.

"If friends could be lovers, you would be mine," she hiccupped. "We shall be the merriest of Madelines. And don't you worry your Petunia about my dalliances. My days of wiggling the wango stick are long gone, and even if they weren't, I would have no mind to pursue the past."

"Florry, my dear," Hamish rasped. "I am so deeply apologetic to walk into the land of the dead with my heart in the grasp of another, and yet, at the very same time, I cannot apologise at all, for my love for Catalina is as true and as desperate as ours once was."

Florence nodded, smiling through her tears and bringing Hamish's and Catalina's hands together between hers before releasing them and stepping back. "Time is a taddler of a teapot, Hamster, isn't that what you always said?"

"Yes, Florry," he croaked before looking to Catalina and drawing her close. "A taddler indeed."

Catalina smiled at Hamish, her love for him so clear, it made the air glitter. Without true, corporeal bodies, it seemed our aura spilled from our souls more easily here. Perhaps that was why everything seemed to shimmer with a faint golden fog. I hardly remembered a time when the world hadn't appeared as such around me.

"Forgive me."

I turned at the familiar voice, finding Azriel Orion there with urgency in his eyes as he looked between us all. "Catalina - it's your son. Your, uh, *other* son. He's in great peril. On the verge of death."

"Xavier," Darius gasped.

"What can I do?" Catalina ran to Azriel in terror, and he turned, beckoning us after him.

Merissa hurried to me and I gripped her hand, her fingers sliding between mine, and I found a fortress of pain housed in her eyes.

"We will do all we can," I said, raising my free hand to carve my thumb along the line of her cheekbone.

"I cannot bear to see another person we love walk through The Veil," she whispered, her features pinched in stubbornness like she could will it not to be so. And knowing my wife, she would do just that.

"Come," I said, and we hurried to follow the others, moving through the Eternal Palace, the walls barely tangible in places, revealing only shimmering stars beyond, like a view into a ever-present night sky.

We stepped out into the golden glow of the ethereal landscape within The Veil, and Azriel led the way down the curving path which led to The Room of Knowledge. We climbed the stone steps, then moved through the arched entrance where we all crowded close to the swirling orb, surrounding Catalina as she gazed at the reality of Xavier's fate within it, her knuckles blanching as she gripped the golden rail.

"What is this place?" she breathed.

"Simply think of Xavier and you will see him here," Azriel explained, motioning to the swirling orb.

She nodded, Darius moving to grip her hand as she did as instructed, and the space before her shifted, revealing Xavier.

He lay prone on his back, his features pinched in pain and his face terribly pale. Geraldine stood at his side in her giant Cerberus form, offering him the anti-toxins in her saliva, the power of it so fierce I could almost taste it here in the land of the dead. Catalina became less visible, her soul reaching for Xavier's, and suddenly we could see her in the glimmering orb, standing at her son's side, laying a hand on his arm. I reached for Catalina's soul, offering her the power that still thrummed within me, and Darius hurried to follow, slipping away into the space between realms to lay his own hand on Xavier.

Merissa's power joined mine, then Hamish's, Florence's, and Azriel's followed. Together, we gave what we could and watched as minutes turned to hours, time like water here, one drop flowing into the next, but finally Xavier's features grew less taut, and a flush of colour returned to his skin.

Catalina and Darius came back to us, and the power my soul harboured withdrew into this false body of mine. Elemental power didn't exist here, at least not in the way it had in the living realm. We were pure energy, and the magic of our souls could not be stripped from us.

I moved to take a seat in the ring of stands which circled this room, swiping a hand over my face before settling my gaze on the shimmering orb and seeking out my daughters and son.

I found Roxanya first, the light of dawn brightening the dark hollows of her eyes as she stared across thousands of soldiers who had fought in the battle.

"Glory is an accolade coveted by so many," she called to them. "It is what a lot of us expected to claim when we faced our enemies on the battlefield at last, and yet it is not what many of you feel you found. What glory can be found in defeat after all?"

Silence stretched out and I sat up straighter, my daughter's voice commanding all attention, and Merissa moved to join me. We'd felt the power of the curse she'd placed upon the stars when she had found her husband dead on that battlefield. Every soul in this place had felt that, and I was on edge because of it.

Never had I heard of a living soul affecting the space between realms with their power like that, never had I heard of any arrogant enough to curse the stars themselves. But she had done it, and if the fire in her expression was anything to judge by, she had no intention of going back on that promise.

My gaze strayed to Darius whose attention was now on her too, his hands tight around the railing as he stared at her, the power of his emotions undeniable, the need in him to return to her palpable. But that wasn't a fate they could claim, no matter how desperately they may have wished for it. Roxanya continued to speak, and I gave her my full focus once more.

"What glory can be found when standing shoulder to shoulder with men and women you don't even know while united against oppression and persecution? What glory can be found when standing firm against a tide of tyranny so all-encompassing that you feel like a grain of sand trying to resist an entire ocean? What glory is there in seeing Fae you love cut down and butchered by monsters weaving shadows and creatures born of darkness? What glory can you claim when you fight against a leash which has already tightened around your throat? When laws are written against your rights and a false king dons a crown and no one manages to knock it from his over-inflated head?"

Roxanya's face was laced with pain and all the loss she had faced, leaving me with the burning need to wrap her in my arms. But I had long lost the chance to comfort my little girl. I had only ever been able to watch as she struggled through all the pain life had offered her, never able to offer the embrace she had so often needed.

"What glory is there in fighting a losing battle? In standing with blade in hand and magic burning fiercely through you, against a force far bigger than your own, without fear ever once making you flinch? When even the stars won't help us, and the night turns dark with shadows? What glory is there then, I ask you?"

Roxanya gripped the pommel of her sword and went on, her voice full of spirit and ire.

"Every one of you standing before me and every Fae who fell on that battlefield fighting by our sides knows the answer to that question. Because we don't need glory. We only need to know that we are fighting for what is right. We are fighting for freedom from oppression and the end of a tyrant. We are standing up and saying no more. And Lionel Acrux may have sat his scaley ass on my father's throne, but he is nothing but a serpent perched on a pretty seat. I don't bow to him or his false crown. Do you?"

A deafening roar of defiance met her question, and a dark smile curved her lips that was worthy of my own.

"No war is won in a single battle," she went on. "No kingdom claimed with one fight. And though we may have bled for our cause on that field of chaos and carnage, they bled for it too. We cut them in that fight. We made them bleed for us and a thousand tiny cuts can kill just as surely as a single blow to the heart. So I say we keep cutting Lionel Acrux and his shadow bitch bride in every way we can. We cut and slice and carve them up and we keep fighting and fighting them until the bitter end, when I know in my soul that we will claim more glory than any of us ever dared wish for!"

Darius shoved away from the railing at the edge of the orb, smoke spilling from his lips as his Dragon stirred and Catalina went after him as he stalked off into the palace.

Pride spilled through me, and Merissa laid her hand on mine, her expression echoing my own feelings. Then as one, not needing to say anything at all, we sought out our other daughter in the orb, finding her in the belly of a dark cave with a cloud of wicked omens clinging to her.

My pride gave way to terror, and I stared helplessly at my flesh and blood, not knowing how I could help her.

"Gwendalina," I called to her, aching for her to hear me through the space between realms, to think of me and draw me close so that I might remind her she was not alone. Oh to hold her in my arms now, to promise everything would be alright.

"You can fight this, my darling," Merissa called to her, and the world shifted, tilting on its axis as we were drawn to her through our desperation alone.

I fell to my knees before my little girl, her face pinched in pain, eyes shut as shadows shifted and wriggled across her body. Though I knew it wasn't her own agony she lamented, but of those she had left behind on the battlefield after the violent beast of shadow had forced her to kill time and again.

"You are not that creature," I growled, reaching for her, and cupping her cheek. She blinked at that very same moment as if she could just sense the warmth of me.

"We're here," Merissa promised, kissing Gwendalina's temple, and brushing her fingers into her hair, though it didn't truly stir beneath her touch. "You possess the blood of the Phoenixes, but not just that. You possess my blood too. The blood of the Voldrakian royals. Generation after generation of warriors who fought and bled for each other. This beast is your enemy and yours alone. You will defeat it, darling, I have no doubt."

The air shuddered and The Veil forced us to release our grip on her, stealing us away where I found Merissa looking to me in agony.

"She has faced down each of her demons and come out victorious," I said with passion. "This will just be another mark of her greatness once she overcomes it."

Merissa blinked back tears and her jaw tightened as she latched onto the truth of my words. "They are fighting battles we should have raised them to face. They should have been far more prepared for the grim days they have endured."

"Then we must marvel at how well they have navigated the evils laid at their feet without us to raise them," I said, and her eyes brightened. "I know that Gwendalina will overcome this one in ways we cannot yet foresee."

"When one falls to the dark, the other shall be their guiding light," Merissa murmured with a frown, those words familiar to me.

"What is it?" I asked in concern, laying my hand on her knee.

"When they were born, those words were whispered to me by the stars," she said.

"Yes, I remember now," I said, nodding slowly. "It must mean they balance one another. A harmony forged of fire and ice. Between is where they find true peace."

"If they cannot find their way back to one another, I fear what will happen. The balance starts with them, but it does not end there," she said mysteriously, and I realised what her mind had moved to.

"The Zodiac Guild," I said.

We had discussed it countless times, but it was Azriel who truly led the charge on that front. His hunt for the Guild Stones had not ceased even in death, and the importance of them was unfathomable – if his and my wife's predictions were correct. And Marcel's of course.

As if summoned by the thought of him, Marcel appeared, the tall man walking through the crowd of souls gathered around the orb. Irritation stirred within me at the sight of his handsome face, his resemblance to my son too stark to ignore. He had his black wings in place as always, bronzed chest bare and a look of all-knowing about him that already had my teeth grinding.

"We were just talking of the Guild Stones," Merissa called to him, and his eyes slipped our way, frustration pooling in my chest at her inviting him closer.

"Ah, yes. I have *seen* more glimmers of fate hinting towards the reformation of the Zodiac Guild," Marcel said as he arrived.

He no longer held any access to The Sight here, but both he and Merissa were capable of seeking glimpses of the future in the orb, their power too great for even the stars to stop them finding truths now. "That path seems far from easy to claim, however."

"Yes, Lionel's reign makes it less likely than ever," Merissa agreed, rising to her feet and I got up, coming face to face with Gabriel's biological father. "But where there is possibility, there is hope."

Marcel inclined his head, then his brows lowered. "Gabriel is in grave danger," he said thickly, terror crossing his dark eyes. I had witnessed my son be taken by Lionel Acrux, had roared to the stars to see him freed, to be given a new fate. But their silence was as damning as Gabriel's current path was, and my fear for him knew no bounds.

"I shall do everything in my power to protect my son," I said fiercely.

"As will I," Marcel said, nodding to me. "I foresaw his life long ago, and

I know him intimately."

"Not so intimately as the man who raised him," I said coolly. "You may have had pretty visions of his life, but I know his truth."

"I have seen him take many paths. I have known him as he is and as he could be. Some would say, there is no greater knowing of a person than that," Marcel said, but before I could start an argument, Merissa interjected.

"We must do what we can for our children," she said firmly, gripping my arm. "And while we cannot change their current fates, we can stoke the flames of the fire that will blaze a path towards a better future for them. The answer lays in the greatest weapon known to Fae kind. Knowledge. The whereabouts of the Guild Stones and the truth of the broken promise. If we can find a way to provide these to our children, then we will be handing them knives fit to carve fate and shape it into something blissful."

She swept away from us towards Azriel, and I hurried to follow, feeling Marcel close at my back and clenching my jaw as he shadowed my movements.

"I can take it from here," I told him, but he brushed past me, his wing slapping me in the face, causing me to stumble a step so that he reached Azriel before I did.

Azriel turned to him with fear clouding his expression for his own son, and I let my frustration with Marcel ebb away as I focused on the task at hand. If finding the final Guild Stones could help my family, then I would break the heavens apart to find them, and once I had handed them to my heirs, I would find a way to reveal the broken promise and help my daughters break the Vega curse once and for all.

DARIUS

CHAPTER FIVE

I strode through the huge doors of a palace without end, a growl ripping free of my throat as I stalked down pristine golden hallways where the half visible forms of dead Fae loitered as if looking for something to occupy them.

Smoke rolled up the back of my throat, the Dragon in me desperate to break free of my flesh but as the shift threatened to take over, I felt a rupture spilling through me. A feeling so alien that it stole my focus, the need to shift overwhelming me and forcing me to give in.

I gasped, buckling forward and taking hold of the closest wall. Instead of transforming, my Dragon broke free of me, racing up and out of my body, roaring ferociously as it took off, leaping from a huge stone balcony and tearing away from the palace towards the stars beyond.

"What the fuck…" I stared after the enormous golden Dragon, my mouth falling open as I watched it race away from me, fire billowing from its jaws as it roared loud enough to rattle the walls of the ethereal palace around me.

Another roar answered it, a purple Dragon leaping over my head, the force of its wings lifting my hair as it passed, and I had to resist the urge to duck. I watched as it raced after my Dragon, the two of them blasting fire at one another, dancing through the sky in a symphony of wings and fire, not quite fighting, more like playing.

"Scared the shit outa me the first time that happened," a deep voice said behind me and I whirled around, power balling in my fist, expecting to see my father there then falling still as I found a stranger instead. But that voice…

"Don't you recognise your own uncle?" the man asked, rolling his shoulders back and lifting his chin.

He was a big motherfucker, clearly a Dragon Shifter like me, and now that he mentioned it, there was something familiar about him. He had a look of Lionel about him, that same blonde colouring to his hair and something around the nose, but this man was bigger, his chin squarer, brow more prominent and he looked to be around my age.

"Radcliff?" I guessed, wondering how many of these little reunions I was going to have to endure in this place. I may have been glad to have the opportunity to speak with some of the dead, but an uncle who had died before my birth hadn't been high on my list of priorities.

"In the flesh. Let's get a look at you then. I'd say you're almost as big as me now…"

Radcliff Acrux, the man who had been born to become the Fire Lord, sauntered closer, swirling a glass of liquor in one hand, a red smoking jacket seeming to unfold itself over his body, the twin of the one my father favoured. I eyed him with interest, uncertain what to expect from this stranger who shared some of my blood. In all honesty, I had no further interest in my Acrux heritage. I was happy to leave all claims to it behind in the taking of my wife's name. I was a Vega now.

Radcliff stopped before me, raising a hand to the top of his head before moving it towards mine. He angled it upward so his palm brushed my hair, making up for the few inches of height I had on him, then grinned.

"Yes. A dead match. And you're nearly as broad as me too." He indicated his chest and I glanced at him. He was big, yeah, but bigger than me? Not so much.

"Look, I'm not really interested in some drunk, muscle-measuring-get-to-know-my-uncle shit. It sucks you got stung by that mosquito and died and all, but I really have more important-"

"It was a wasp," Radcliff hissed and for a moment the golden light wavered, a darkened room appearing around me, Radcliff immobilised in his own bed, his younger brother smiling down at him as he held the jar containing the norian wasp to his chest.

Lionel's eyes were bright with glee as he watched his brother die, there was a heat to his expression which only ever awakened with cruelty and violence. I knew it well.

"Now there will be no question over which of us is destined for greatness," Lionel hissed as he murdered his own flesh and blood like a coward.

"If we're swapping stories about whose life that motherfucker ruined more then I'm pretty sure I win," I said flatly, waving my hand so the room disappeared, flashes of beatings, Dark Coercion, what Lionel had done to Roxy and finally my own death at his hand surrounding us until we were drowning in the horribly tragic reality of my life.

Radcliff sighed, wafting the memories away like they were nothing but a fart on the breeze, and we found ourselves standing on the stone balcony once more, our Dragons darting through the air beyond.

"Well, I had to put up with the little runt stealing my life, watching him connive and wheedle his way into power from this golden palace of nothing while I just lingered here, never changing, witnessing all the ways I would have prospered where he failed," Radcliff griped.

"Maybe you should move on," I suggested, turning away from him to look up at my Dragon again. Longing filled my chest as the need to be at one with it consumed me. "Seems like all you've done with your afterlife is obsess over that bastard. I think you need a new hobby."

"Says the man whose eyes are full of revenge," Radcliff scoffed. "Mark my words, Darius, you'll be stood here in another twenty years watching him, hating him, wishing all the worst on him while unable to do more than fuck with things he doesn't even care about."

"My obsession doesn't lie with the man who sired me," I dismissed, my heart aching for all I'd lost. "If I end up trapped here, that won't be what I'm stood here watching."

Even as the words left my lips, they cost me something, the admittance that I *might* be stood here in twenty years' time watching someone at all. The idea that I wouldn't find a way back from this fate was a wound I couldn't let fester.

"But I won't be here at all," I added darkly.

Radcliff blinked at me then barked a laugh. "Oh, I do love it when the dead refuse to accept their fate," he said, clapping a hand down on my shoulder. "But you aren't the first who swore to return, and you won't be the last. I'll tell you what you will be though, son."

"What?" I growled, not liking his patronising tone.

"Disappointed. The sooner you get comfortable here, the better. Because there is only here or what comes after, should you wish to pass beyond." He glanced to the side, and I followed his gaze over the edge of the balcony to the sweeping lawn below, an arch climbing up out of the shadows there, mist twisting through vines which grew around it, and a door of glimmering light forming in its centre. There were whispers coming from within it, soft and peaceful, promises of more, of an ending which was utterly complete.

Radcliff shuddered, barking a command for the door to leave us be and it spilled away into grains of sand as if it had never been there at all. Yet somehow, I knew it was still close by, waiting for us to summon it again, knowing its time would come.

Radcliff gripped my shoulder and drew my focus back to him. "Nothing that came before will ever be yours again unless it steps through The Veil and joins you here. And even then, unless fate is kind and sends them soon, they won't miss you the way you ache for them. Time heals and grief fades. People move on. Your pretty bride will likely find a new husband in time and when she passes over, she won't be looking for you anymore."

"Fuck you," I snarled, shaking his hand from my shoulder but he caught my arm, refusing to let me leave.

"I'm not telling you this because I'm a son-of-a-bitch like your daddy," Radcliff growled and there was something in his eyes which stopped me from striking out at him again. A deep sadness laced with the kind of pain I didn't want to understand. "I'm telling you because it's true. Right now, you still feel connected to them the way you were when you died because it's fresh. They think of you all the time, they grieve you and the power of that pain, that connection, it draws you back. It might even let you slip into their world from time to time and let you be with them again. Except you aren't with them. They can't see you or feel you – hell, you'll be lucky if they feel strongly enough about you to allow you to a flip the page of a book. That's what it is, see?"

"No, I don't see. It sounds like you're rambling," I growled, and he huffed out a breath laced with smoke.

"Them. Their pain, grief, love, whatever you want to call it, but the power of what they feel for you is what lets you go back rather than just sitting here staring into the great orb in The Room of Knowledge like a forgotten spectator, or lingering alone with your memories in your room here in the Eternal Palace. So for now, especially right now, while it's fresh and their love for you burns with the agony of your loss, you'll be able to step back and see them clearly, maybe stir the wind around them, drop a flower in their lap if they care enough to look for you, but that's it. And while you fight to hold onto them, they'll be working to let you go, to move on, to…fucking live their lives without the constant pain of your loss. So in time you won't stir the wind, they won't react if you try to brush your hand over theirs. When you go to them, the details surrounding them will start to fade, get fuzzy, until one day – poof. You're sitting on your ass watching from out here instead of over there. Their need for you will fade as they find a way to move on, to cope with your loss-"

"You're saying I won't be able to visit them like that once they start dealing with their grief?" I asked, a frown furrowing my brow.

"One by one," he replied. "One by one by one, they'll move on. Your bride will likely be the last, but I've known folks whose spouses are the first to forget them and push them out into the cold. I don't say it to be harsh, I say it because no one told me. I had to figure it out on my own, watching from further and further away as my girl grieved, then found a way to deal with it and finally moved on. She married someone else, she has her own family. I feel the pull whenever she thinks of me, but it's less and less often now. And I can't cross back to see her anymore. Haven't been able to do that in years. It's not a bad thing, not for them at least, and for us I guess it's a sign that we should just move on ourselves, cross over, let it be done."

Radcliff sighed, stepping back, and swiping a hand over his face, a sadness clinging to him which bit into me. I'd never given much thought to this man who had died before my birth. Never really wondered about him or the life he would have led, aside from speculating whether things might have been different for me with Lionel if I hadn't been the direct Heir. Then again, knowing my father, he would have groomed me to challenge for the position of Heir anyway, likely putting even more pressure on me than he had. Though I doubted there was ever any future for Radcliff available once Lionel had decided to take his place. He clearly hadn't believed he could win in a fight with his brother Fae against Fae, so murder was the obvious path. And if Lionel hadn't succeeded in that then I likely wouldn't have been born at all.

"Sorry," I said roughly, making myself look at the man before me, the uncle who should have been well into his fifties yet stood before me frozen in his twenties, his life ended before he'd had a chance to really live it at all. I guessed we had that in common.

"For what?" he asked curiously.

"For my father being a total cunt."

Radcliff snorted. "Yeah. Well, I'm sorry too."

"For my father being a total cunt?" I guessed and he grinned.

"Yeah, that'd be it. Looks like he fucked us both over in the end. If anyone had told me Lame Lionel would end up here, seizing the throne of Solaria for himself, placing a crown upon his head, and seeing almost all of those more powerful around him dead in the quest for it, I would have laughed in their faces and told them to go check the cards again. But here we are. He won. By cunning, deception, and unFae tactics, but he won all the same."

"Not yet he hasn't," I refused. "The Vega twins are rising. They'll hunt him down and gut him before this is done."

"*Seen* that in a vision, have you?" Radcliff asked with a low scoff, and it was clear he didn't believe it would come to pass, but I knew better.

"I don't need to. I've seen it in my wife's eyes. And I can tell you now,

47

that nothing in their world or this one will ever stand in the way of those twins. They were born to rule. And I get it, you've been here a long time, forced to watch while Lionel rose to power, taking down every obstacle in his path by whatever means necessary, and you've lost hope that anyone can stand in his way-"

"He saw the Savage King dead, boy," Radcliff growled. "Hail Vega was the most powerful Fae of our time-"

"That time is done," I replied firmly. "But the time of the Phoenixes is beginning now. They *will* rise to power. And I *will* be there to help see it come to pass."

I turned and stalked away from my uncle, the golden Dragon bellowing in the skies above before racing after me, diving straight from the air and slamming back into my skin again, making me whole once more.

I didn't slow my pace, trying to forget his words as they carved their way deeper into my skin. The people I loved wouldn't simply mourn me and move on. They wouldn't forget me. They wouldn't give up. Roxy had sworn a curse upon the stars, promising to change our fate and I wouldn't be convinced to do anything other than help her in that quest. So I needed to figure out how I could defy the stars from within this place.

I didn't know where I was headed, only that I needed to do something to keep that vow, and as the palace warped and changed around me, I found myself stepping out into a garden thick with flowers, the air filled with the rustling wings of a million butterflies as they swarmed overhead. They danced and shifted, creating unnatural shapes with the combination of their bodies.

I thought of her, my heart aching for the night we should have had together, celebrating our wedding, consolidating our union. I wanted to hold her in my arms and have our first dance, but instead I found the butterflies twisting themselves into her shape, burning wings beating hard on her back.

I could almost feel the wind rushing through my hair and as I pushed into that sense of her, the world fell away once more, The Veil retreating, letting me push back through until I was with her again.

"Roxy," I breathed, but she didn't react at all, her face set with determination, her wings beating hard as she flew, a net of air magic towing Geraldine along with her through the sky.

With a thought, I shifted, a Dragon's roar escaping me as I fell into the body of the beast, no longer separate but whole, as we should be, though no answering echo replied from the valleys below. I was there with her, but I wasn't.

The sun was rising, illuminating the land bit by bit as the shadows lifted and I blinked as I recognised the landscape stretching out below us. Acrux

Manor lay just over the next rise. I'd flown these skies a million times, knew this land better from the air than I did from the ground. What was she doing here?

Roxy wheeled to the side, putting the sun at her back so she would approach the manor in the thick of its light, shielding her from view of anyone on the ground.

"Oh, in the valley of the fruit of my loins, sweet Petunia shall rise and claim her salmon," Geraldine called, swinging her flail aggressively while she was propelled through the air with Roxy's magic. She looked completely insane and at least as terrifying, the armour she wore glinting in the sunlight, the pointed tips on her breastplate looking sharp enough to cut.

With a jolt I realised why they must have been here, my shock over my own death having pushed all thoughts of my brothers from my mind, but I'd left them here not long before my death and one look at the manor below showed the pulsing shadow rift still very much in place in the courtyard outside.

"No," I gasped, my body yanking away from Roxy and Geraldine, dissolving then reforming in the centre of that courtyard. Horror gripped me as I took in the sight of the other Heirs and their families, each of them tethered to the shadow rift, their magic rolling into it from their bodies while they were forced to replenish over and over again.

I ran to Caleb whose jaw and chest were coated in blood, his fangs bared and desperation in his eyes as he looked towards the others.

They didn't know I was gone yet. They hadn't been grieving me so I hadn't felt the pull towards them from their side of The Veil, but now I knew what had become of them after I'd abandoned them to save Xavier, I couldn't help but rage against the stars for cursing us even further.

"Cal?" I reached for him, gripping his arm in a fierce hold and he turned his head towards me, glancing at the place where my hand lay almost as though he had felt it. "I'm here. Roxy's almost here too, I-"

I turned from him, looking up toward the sun, just about spotting her and Geraldine in the sky. But the wards were still up, the power my father had channelled into them over years upon years still standing, keeping them out.

I spared a glance for Seth who ran endlessly on a turning ball of stone, and Max whose face was crumpled with the pain of Fae who were being tortured by Nymphs beside him as he was forced to feed on their suffering, then I broke into a run and leapt into the sky.

The Dragon tore from my limbs, and I flew hard for the dome of magic that I knew surrounded the manor. Roxy plummeted from the sky overhead, her sword drawn, Geraldine right beside her, the two little more than a streak of light descending from the heavens.

"For honour and death and the true queens!" Geraldine cried, her words finding me as I summoned all the power of everything I was and everything I had been, tearing up to meet them as little more than a blur of raw energy.

Roxy held her sword up, Phoenix fire bursting along the length of it as she hurtled towards the wards. She swung it with a ferocious cry, a bird of red and blue flames erupting from its tip.

Power blasted from her, and I threw myself and all the power I had into the wards from below just as her magic struck it from above, colliding with it so hard that I broke apart in the explosion that followed.

The world fractured and spun around me, and I fell in and out of The Veil, flashes of reality coming too fast for my mind to fully comprehend.

Roxy and Geraldine were fighting with the ferocity of feral beasts, my brothers crying out warnings from their positions chained around the stone altar, blood spilling, Nymphs screaming. Geraldine in Cerberus form, Nymphs swarming my girl, an eruption of ice then an explosion of fire hotter than the pits of hell itself.

I materialised in the Acrux Manor courtyard again just as a shield of solid ice broke apart, a great wave of water crashing across the soot-stained stones and broken altar, revealing my queen standing among a pile of ash beyond it, panting, wounded and utterly devastating.

I stared at the beauty of the woman who had claimed me for her own, my soul thrashing with the desperate need for her to see me too, to turn my way and meet my gaze with the blazing fire in her eyes.

The closest wall of the manor was in ruins. The house which had been home to so much pain for me, my mother and brother, now falling to rubble at her back while the Heirs found themselves free of the hellish fate that had befallen them.

She was hurt, a jagged wound carved into her side, frozen with ice to stem the flow of blood though she was in desperate need of real healing. I moved to her with little more than a thought, my presence here entirely my own, no other Fae aware of me in the slightest, and I was surprised by the sharpness of the pain that carved into me at that realisation.

Radcliff's words burned into me as I looked between the people I loved most in this world, wondering if he might have been right, if this might be the closest I ever got to them in this life again.

The thought alone was enough to close my throat over, my chest heaving with a panic I refused to feel.

No.

I wouldn't accept that fate. I'd find my way back to them. Whatever it took, I'd do it.

"My daughters have been forged in a fire far hotter than any a Dragon might hope to tame."

I flinched at Hail Vega's voice, turning to look at him as he moved between the flashes of reality which were swirling around me. I wanted to stop and experience what was happening with the people I loved but time seemed to be leaping forward in sudden jerks and gasps, flashes of what they were doing appearing then fading just as fast.

"Why is it like this?" I asked, reaching for Roxy as she strode towards the house I'd grown up in, her jaw set with determination, her power making the air crackle around her.

She passed straight through me, not pausing or flinching, simply heading inside with Max, Seth and Geraldine closing in around her.

"The Veil doesn't follow the rules you lived by when you were on that side of it," Hail replied, waving a hand towards Roxy and the others as they moved into the house, leaving us outside by the broken altar and the destruction the battle had wreaked. "Our desire isn't what draws us to it, it's their need for us which allows us to step close, to experience time the way they are. When their grief or need is sharpest, we can experience it the best, our reality drawing so near to theirs that we can even reach between the two, press through The Veil and influence certain things around them. But we can never truly be with them. We can never really change anything."

"I need to go back," I said, turning my back on the damaged building and it all fell away as I did so, leaving the two of us standing in a grand hall, banners hanging from the walls which glowed with that golden hue, depicting a Hydra bellowing to the stars.

Hail sat and a throne appeared beneath his ass before he could fall to the floor, with gilded Phoenix wings sprouting from the back of it, one blue and one red. He reclined into the throne like it was as natural as breathing to him, his legs spread wide, his arm hanging loosely over one side.

"Sit," he commanded, a nod of his head making a grubby three-legged stool appear for me.

I arched a brow at it then sat, not really giving a shit if he offered me a throne or a toilet to sit on, I only cared about figuring out how I was going to keep my promise to his daughter.

"You've been here long enough to know how this place works," I said, resting my forearms on my knees, keeping my tone level despite the sneer on his lips. "I need to know how to get back."

"Back?" Hail snorted. "You think if there was a way back, we wouldn't all have taken that path?"

"I made a vow," I said, ignoring his sneering. I didn't really care if he liked me or not, I just needed to know where to start looking for the fate I intended to seize.

"Which vow was that?" Hail asked. "The one where you swore to chase my daughters out of their academy? To rid them of their birth right and inheritance in one fell swoop? The one which drove you to make them relive their worst fears and ended with you near drowning my-"

"The one where I swore to love and protect your daughter with all that I was for all the time I had in that world and the next. The one that I joined her in when she vowed to change our fate at the cost of the stars if that was what it required. She has sworn to defy destiny in the matter of my death, and I have sworn to do all I can to defy it too. So will you help me, or would you rather allow your distaste for me to leave her grieving and alone for the rest of her life?" I demanded.

Hail sighed heavily. "I preferred the blonde one," he grunted.

Merissa clucked her tongue as she appeared suddenly, stepping out from behind the throne as if she'd always been there. She looked more like the twins than Hail did, her features reminiscent enough of theirs that it hurt to look at her for too long.

"You mean the Vampire who threw Roxanya off of a roof and broke her spine in a blood frenzy?" she asked sweetly. "Honestly, Hail, next you'll be saying you preferred the mortal who drove her off of a bridge and left her to drown."

Hail straightened at the reproach, his attention shifting from his wife to me once more. "I did rather enjoy watching you beating the shit out of that son-of-a-bitch," he said to me, and my lips lifted in a grim smile.

"I'd have killed him if I didn't know Roxy would have castrated me for it. She deserves her own chance to kick his ass one day if she wants it."

"Regardless of who might like to kick whose ass, it's safe to say that Roxanya's taste in men leaves a lot to be desired," Merissa interrupted, the look she gave me letting me know that she'd seen all there was of the mistakes I'd made.

I dropped my gaze to the ground, but she moved to stand before me, lifting my chin so that I met her eyes again.

"I meant what I said before," she said softly. "You made up for your poor choices in my eyes as well as in the eyes of my daughter. Besides, I always knew you'd be the one for her. I held you as a baby when I was pregnant, and I *saw* it."

"You *saw* me and her together?" I asked, clinging to that fact, and wondering if it might give me a clue into the way this might all work out. "How old were we? Did we have a family? Did we find a way back from this mess or-"

"You know it doesn't work like that," she said softly, brushing her hand against my cheek in a maternal gesture which still felt unnatural to me after so many years of my own mother's coldness. I knew she hadn't wanted it to be that way, but it didn't change what I had grown up with, didn't make me any more used to a mother treating me this way, like she cared about more than just what I could give her. "I saw a hundred possible fates, all of which tangled the two of you up with one another. None of them mean you can thwart death itself."

I stood suddenly, knocking the stool over in my haste as I moved away from her. "If neither of you know anything that can help me then I'll seek it out myself," I growled, stalking away from them.

The Veil fluttered around me as I walked, the corridors I'd grown up in appearing in place of that golden, ever-changing palace. Roxy was walking ahead of me, fire blazing all around her as she moved from room to room, burning every last piece of it to the ground.

My heart swelled at the sight of it, watching her as she struck out against my father, stealing something from him which he would mourn far more than the life of any Fae. This manor had been a symbol of his wealth and power. To see it destroyed by his enemies would destroy a piece of him in turn.

The thundering boom of the roof cracking overhead had me moving faster, closing in on her as she fell still, her eyes closing like she was drinking in this moment.

A sharp stab of pain lanced through my chest which I knew had come directly from her, the tears rolling down her cheeks clear as I made it to her. She was hurting. Because of me. Despite all the promises I'd made to her, I'd done it again, hurting her worse than I ever had before by leaving her when I'd promised to stay.

I moved up behind her, coiling my arms around her waist, leaning in to press my lips to her neck, goosebumps rising across her flesh at my touch like she really could feel me.

"I'm here," I promised her again. "And I'm not giving up. We'll rip The Veil to shreds if that's what's required for us to be together again. I'm yours Roxy. There is only you," I swore, holding her tighter while the world fell to ruin in her flames surrounding us.

"I'll burn it all if that's what it takes," she breathed and I could have sworn her words were for me, that she'd felt me there, knew I wasn't giving up.

"Then burn it all, beautiful. Every fucking piece of it," I growled, because whatever the price of our reunion cost, I'd pay it. Anything it took to return to her. Everything it might cost me.

I watched as the flames rose up around her, her wings flaring either side of her as she walked away from me, Acrux Manor crumbling to ruins beneath the might of her power and I knew that I would keep that vow or let my soul be cast to ash in the effort it took to attempt it.

She was lost to me again and I found myself facing Hail and Merissa once more, my stool righted before them, Merissa now perched in Hail's lap while he lazily stroked her thigh. It seemed as though they'd been waiting for me, and Hail's scowl deepened as I met his gaze without so much as dipping my head in deference.

"If you'd stop storming off like a petulant child it would make this conversation pass more swiftly," Hail ground out.

I folded my arms, meeting his scowl dead on, not flinching at what I assumed was an attempt to intimidate me with that whole old, dead asshole glare thing he had going on.

"Spit it out then," I urged.

"Azriel is hunting for the missing Guild Stones," Hail said, eyeing me like I was something distasteful as I stood before him. "We believe they are the key to helping the twins now. They need to reform the Zodiac Guild and use the power of the stones to restore balance within Solaria. With the Guild at their backs, Solaria can rise once more, they will have the strength they need to take on Lionel and crush the power he has built up around himself before finally ending his reign once and for all."

"How does that help me with crossing back over?" I asked and he sighed.

"You won't let that go, will you?" Hail muttered.

"Do you really want me to?" I demanded in turn. "You'd rather I give in to this fate, leave Roxy a widow before she's even been crowned?"

"Of course we would wish to see you return if we thought it was possible," Merissa said, raising a hand to slow my anger. "But if there is a way to do such a thing then we don't know it. Perhaps some of the ancient souls who linger here would have an idea, those who were versed in the ways of old and didn't solely rely on the power of the stars for their answers in life. If you wish to defy the will of the stars, it would make sense to find a path unlit by their light after all."

I considered all they'd told me and nodded.

"Fine. I'll do what I can to help in the search for those Guild Stones, but my priority lies with my return to the Fae realm," I said.

"Then I'll see who I can find to speak with you on the subject," Merissa promised.

My brain was pounding with so much information, The Veil tugging at me as I felt the Heirs and Xavier grieving over me too, drawing me closer to them with their pain and need. I gave in to the tug, letting Hail and Merissa fade away and finding myself kneeling at my own grave alongside the other Heirs.

I took my place beside them as their grief filled the small clearing where a tree shaped like a Dragon grew over a coffin made of ice, and as I looked upon the face of my corpse and felt how much damage my death had caused, I swore to do everything I could to make all of this right again.

HAIL

CHAPTER SIX

"You don't have to be so harsh with him," Merissa said, cupping my jaw and making me look at her.

With nothing but a thought, I transported us back to our rooms, securing us privacy as I took a seat and drew her into my lap.

My fingers curled around her thigh, and I tucked her closer to me upon my throne, a thing she had created for me in this space we had claimed as our own.

This palace of death held infinite rooms, spaces that were forged by their creators. No one room was the same, all a reflection of the souls who were housed within them, trying to paint a mirage of the living world around them. But all of this was a sandcastle, waiting for the tide to wash it away, a blank slate for more lost souls to build another false kingdom upon.

"I can count his graces on one hand, but his faults are innumerable," I muttered. "I know he has done good. I have laid witness to it, but now he is here, I cannot find anything in my heart for him but contempt."

"There is more than that," Merissa clipped, her nails biting into my skin. I coveted any physical pain she caused me as deeply as her mouth against my skin. So long as we could feel each other, we were still here, still latched to a branch of existence, and in truth, I feared anything beyond this half-life we had found together within The Veil. I didn't want to move on through the Destined Door, leaving my children behind, and walking into the after where I might not be myself any longer. My biggest terror of all was forgetting those I loved, and the mystery of the after stoked the flames of that terror in a way I didn't like to put a voice to.

"There is nothing more," I insisted, tasting the lie I was weaving. Lies weren't things I usually offered my wife, but this one was caged in stubbornness. "He has wronged our daughter too many times, and now he has abandoned her in her most urgent time of need. And all of this could have been avoided had he only defied his father sooner."

"He was raised by a monster," Merissa said, her brows pulling together. "Surely you of all people know what it's like to be under Lionel's control."

"That was different," I snarled, my fingers curling harder into the smooth flesh of her thigh, riding her silver dress up higher. "Darius had a choice in many of the decisions he made. And meanwhile, my daughters were left in the fucking wastelands of the mortal realm, abandoned by every family who even bothered to take them in. And with them stuck there, Solaria fell prey to that monster all the more easily."

Merissa withdrew from me, but I didn't let her leave my lap. "That's my fault," she whispered, echoing the pain of the past. "I thought they would be safe there. I thought…"

She shook her head, and I took her hand, drawing her fingers to my lips and kissing the tips of them to soothe her.

"The root of it all is Lionel Acrux," I said darkly. "You saved them from him. You couldn't have known what would come after."

"I had The Sight," she said bitterly. "I should have known. But there were so many paths, so much fire, and blood, and torment. And worst of all… shadow. Paths I couldn't see, shrouded by darkness."

"We never could have predicted Lionel's allegiance with the Shadow Princess. A Nymph who was cast into nothingness by Queen Avalon so very long ago. However could you have known she would return as what she is today? How could you have foreseen the power she would offer Lionel, to strengthen and bolster him when he could never have been strong enough to claim the throne alone."

She nodded sadly. "I *saw* enough of the threat. And the mortal realm was the only place where I could *see* them living to adulthood with the least risk." She pressed the heel of her palm to her forehead, and I captured it, holding both her wrists in one hand, forcing her to look at me.

"You protected them, my love," I vowed, and she softened, slowly nodding, and fighting through her pain. "They would be dead if it were not for you."

"I want to go to them," she said, her voice hardening and her eyes flashing with power.

"Come then," I growled, leaning in, and pressing my lips to hers. "I feel

58

them calling."

She shivered and suddenly The Veil drew back, or perhaps we were forcing our way through it, seeking out the deepest loves of our heart.

We found Gabriel first and pain cracked across my chest at the sight of him strapped to the Royal Seer's chair in the Royal Seer's chamber, his head tipped back and a roar of agony leaving his throat.

Vard stood at his side, cupping a jar of lightning to the centre of Gabriel's chest and unleashing the power of the storm within upon our son.

Merissa ran to Gabriel, cupping his cheek and calling his name. His eyes darted left and right, visions spilling into him as The Sight tormented him alongside the torture of the lightning. The visions swirled around us in the air, as clear to us as they were to him, flashes of futures untold.

Gwendalina lost to a fearful darkness while Roxanya cried for vengeance with blood soaking her hands. Terror threaded through the air as Gabriel cried out once more and the visions swirled, a river of blood pouring from those he loved, his wife, his child, his family destroyed by this war in battles that stretched on for an age. Gabriel *saw* the world falling, and I hurried to him, placing my hand on his shoulder and promising him that if it fell, I would be there. He would not be alone, whether he knew it or not.

"Gabriel," Merissa sobbed, and he blinked, his grey eyes focusing on her like he could truly see her there. If that were true then he was closer to death than I wanted to believe, dancing the line of The Veil, threatening to cross through it.

"Mom?" the word barely passed his lips as Vard yanked the jar from his chest and panted from the exertion it had taken to hold it there. The lightning was gone, a smoking welt on Gabriel's chest the lasting sign of it, but as Gabriel's eyes became hooded and the blood drained from his face, the vile Seer moved forward to heal him.

"Stay strong, son," I growled, lending him all the power I could summon to keep him awake.

Gabriel blinked groggily at me, confusion crossing his features.

"I'm here," I vowed. "I am always here."

But The Veil was dragging me back as Gabriel lost consciousness and Merissa cried my name, reaching for me as the light stuttered out. Her hand found mine in the dark. Always and forever, we found each other this way. No matter if all light was lost, our souls would unite across the boundaries of the universe, never to part.

"I've got you," I called to her, pulling her in against my chest and feeling our souls almost merge as we twisted through the cloying dark.

"Don't let go," she called, fear wrapped around her words.

"Never, my love."

The dark retreated and we found ourselves standing at the bottom of a lake, the shimmering light ahead like rhinestones glowing in the gloom, and within it was an imposing creature built of rock and ruin. A fallen star.

Merissa's hand remained in mine as we moved as one towards the woman standing naked before this most powerful of beings, the shadows receding from her skin. Gwendalina Vega stood at the bottom of a fucking lake with a fallen star, and once again I was confounded at the trouble my children were capable of meeting with the moment I took my eyes off of them.

"By the stars, Merissa." I strode forward, but she pulled me back firmly.

Gwendalina ever-enthralled me, her wild spirit and open mind having guided her so well in this world of power and adversity. She sought trouble and adventure as keenly as it seemed to seek her, so perhaps I should have been less surprised to find her in these dangerous, yet extraordinary circumstances.

"This is important beyond all bounds," Merissa breathed, a touch of prophecy to her voice that spoke of the gifts she had once possessed in their fullest. Even now, she could sense fate changing, could pull on the right strings and find paths that were not meant for us. For the dead held no paths.

"You are shadow cursed, a mortal you shall soon be," the star spoke in a way that pulsed through my soul and made the shattered remnants of who I was pull back together, and for a moment it was almost as though I could breathe the air in this world. Though I knew it was an illusion.

The words fell over me in a dark cloud, fury echoing through my chest and Merissa and I shared a look of terror.

"She cannot become mortal," I rasped, and Merissa's fingers tightened on mine.

"Never," she growled.

"Is there a way to stop it?" Gwendalina asked, her own fear tangible, making me want to reach for her, calm her, assure her all would be well. But would that be a pretty lie painted by a desperate father?

"The fates are still being woven, thread by thread."

"Then stop weaving them," Gwendalina demanded of the star, the authority in her voice bringing a smile to my lips. I moved closer behind her, but the star's power pushed me back as if it knew I shouldn't be here. "Aren't you in control of fate? Don't *you* decide all of this? Why are you so cruel?"

The power of the star crackled through my head, and I was forced back another step as I reached for my daughter.

"We can't, Hail," Merissa said sadly.

"Cruelty is a construct of Fae, not us. When we are perched within the sky, we are neither good nor bad. We see all, we offer answers, we guide and

gift, but we may take and destroy if the choices made below us invoke it."

"So what have me and my sister done to deserve the fates you've offered us? What paths have we chosen that have made you curse us and the people we love?" Gwendalina hissed in anger.

"It isn't them," I said before the star answered in kind.

"Fate is unbalanced. The wrath of Clydinius wove your woes."

"Who is Clydinius?" Gwendalina pressed.

Hope thrashed within me at the mention of that accursed star's name. It was this truth which I had found beyond The Veil, the answer to the broken promise, the way to break the curse that I had suffered in life, and that my daughters had inherited.

"Clydinius wants you to keep the broken promise, warrior of the Vega line."

"What is the promise?" Gwendalina gasped, moving forward in desperation. "I'll keep it. Just tell me what it is. How can I fix what I have no knowledge of?"

"Tell her!" I roared, and the star's power pushed at me, shoving me back and pulling Merissa with me. "She needs the truth!"

"It is time for my end. My death is the gift of Fae, a gift all stars offer in their demise. It is why magic lives in your world, for my magic is your magic."

The light grew brighter and brighter, and the power was so keen it spilled into the pieces of my soul, trying to tear me apart bit by bit.

"Hail," Merissa gasped in fright. "We have to go. It's going to destroy us!"

The earth trembled, the lake shuddered, and the whole world awaited this new magic, ready to embrace it into the rocks, the water, the air. But it had to be cast away first and Merissa was right, we were hovering in between the here and there, vulnerable to the power that was about to blast our way.

The star shone brighter still, and Merissa tugged on my hand, even as I looked back toward my little darling in desperation, hating to leave her. But the powerful wave was rushing towards us, the burn of it blazing along the edges of my skin, my soul, trying to cleave me apart.

The Veil kept us back, the stars stowing us away within their clutches, and I could almost feel their disapproval of how deeply we had pushed out to view the living world.

Merissa gripped my arm, our eyes locking as we checked each other over, assured we were both still whole. Still together.

The brush with oblivion left me feeling unsteady in this half world of ours and I paced away from Merissa, carving a hand through my hair as I passed by the Phoenix throne here in the Eternal Palace.

"She was so close to finding the truth," I said in anger. "So fucking close."

"There'll be another chance," Merissa said, but sadness coated her words, her own disappointment clear.

"If I could write it on the walls, send her a message somehow-" I stopped walking, coming to a halt in front of a mirror with a wrought iron frame, the thing almost a foot taller than me. It was our private window into the realm of the living, letting us either view our loved ones in the privacy of our own space or revisit memories of our past, and sometimes the memories of those we loved too. We could access our hearts' desires here if we wanted it enough, but sometimes it was like sifting through silt, seeking gold in the mud. Focus was key, but the longer I remained here in the afterlife, the harder it became to control. There were some memories no passage of time, nor fragmenting of my soul could steal away from me though, and I pulled on them now, reliving a moment from my Fae life.

I held baby Roxanya in my arms, my sweet daughter cooing softly and blinking up at me with the biggest, brightest green eyes I had ever seen. Matched only by her twin who Merissa was bouncing on her knee.

Little Gabriel was waving a white bunny toy in front of her, and Gwendalina giggled at the sight until he hid it behind her back, and she cracked a sob like she believed it was gone forever. Gabriel brought it back again and Gwendalina's face immediately lit up while Merissa laughed.

"You will like bunnies always, I think," my wife murmured, kissing Gwendalina's smooth black hair.

I stroked my finger down Roxanya's nose as she curled into me. "You are always so content, my little love," I said. "Except when you are cold or sleepy or hungry."

"The same as you then," Merissa jibed, and Gabriel laughed as a smirk pulled at my mouth.

Roxanya's beautiful little face wrinkled, and I could sense a sob coming so I moved closer to the fire. "Which is it then? Are you cold?"

The fire's warmth rolled over us and Roxanya looked almost smug as I held her there, rocking her close to the flames.

I felt a hand press to my shoulder in the world of the afterlife, the memory falling from my grasp as I turned, expecting to find Merissa there to share in the longing of the past, but Marcel was smiling sadly at me instead.

I shrugged him off with a tut. "How did you get in here?"

"Merissa let me in of course," he said. "Enjoying the past?" He gazed into the mirror, seeing what I had seen because of his connection to Gabriel. "He looks just like me. And he was happy too. Look at that…" He smiled sadly. "If only I had gotten to meet him. I have so many visions of what our father-son time would have been like, but it is hard to know which might have been closest to the truth."

"He is *my* son," I growled, pushing past him, and giving Merissa a look that questioned why she had let the stray Fae into our rooms.

"Yes, and mine," Marcel said, looking back at me morosely. "Can't I watch a little longer?"

"You have your own viewing space in your rooms, do you not?" I muttered.

"Hail," Merissa warned me of my tone, but Marcel got on my nerves at the best of times.

Maybe I was just a protective asshole, but he acted as though he was as much a father to Gabriel as I was. But he had never even met the boy, let alone had a hand in raising him. He was a single, forgettable moment in Merissa's life which was only of note at all because it had resulted in the birth of my boy.

"I struggle to see him sometimes," Marcel said quietly.

I glanced back at the sad soul staring at my mirror as my memory replayed, his head cocking to one side as he tried to see more, but it wasn't his past to control.

Merissa arched a brow at me and mouthed, "Stop being an asshole."

I sighed. Though that request was rather late in the game of existence.

"Fine," I exhaled, returning to Marcel's side and he gave me a hopeful look.

"Maybe a birthday? Or, wait, maybe a Christmas. Or, hang on, what about the first time he held a Pitball?" he asked, anxiously bouncing on his toes and fuck I had to pity the man.

"Alright," I said then let the memory change, picking out the time Merissa and I had taught Gabriel the rules of Pitball. We were out on the lawn of The Palace of Souls and Hamish Grus was running about creating a mini Pitball field for Gabriel to play on. My boy was wearing my Zodiac Academy Pitball shirt, the thing so long on him that Merissa had stuffed it into the top of his shorts.

I left Marcel to watch it, my mind too full of the present and what my children were facing to spend more time distracting myself with the past.

Merissa watched the memory over my shoulder, eyes twinkling before she stood up straighter and swallowed away the pain.

"He struggles to see Gabriel," she said heavily. "Our son never knew him. He has little longing for a man he never met."

"Perhaps Marcel should move on then. Maybe that would be best," I said, and Merissa pursed her lips at me.

"His connection to Gabriel is true or he wouldn't be able to see him at all. There must be something pulling him toward him," Merissa said.

"I don't believe Marcel can visit him as we can."

"No... perhaps we should tell him what we saw," Merissa said with a deep frown.

"The man is tortured enough already, let him be. He can stay here while we work on finding the Guild Stones. I need to find Azriel."

"Azriel, you say?" Marcel called, walking over to us as the memory came to an end. "What's the news?"

Dammit.

"No news," I said dismissively, and Merissa shot me a glare.

"Gabriel is in trouble, Marcel," she revealed. "Since Lionel captured him, he is now torturing him, forcing him to produce visions and using Vard to steal those visions from his mind."

"By the stars," Marcel gasped in horror. "What can I do?"

"Nothing. We have it in hand," I said.

"In hand?" he said in disbelief. "In what way?"

"We're going to focus on finding the final Guild Stones like we planned," Merissa said. "Azriel has some leads he's been working on, seeking out old memories."

"Ah, okay," Marcel said. "You'll be needing me then, as I foresaw much about the stones while I was alive."

"Like where they are?" I demanded.

"Not exactly. More clues...and things," Marcel said mysteriously, and Merissa nodded like she understood.

"Things," I deadpanned. "Right, well you focus on those *things*, and I'm going to speak with Azriel."

"Merissa, you and I could use our higher connection with the stars to try and coax new clues into the light," Marcel suggested.

"Merissa was going to come with me," I cut in, but Merissa never was one to simply go along with what I commanded.

"No, Marcel's right. We can work together to try and amplify our old gifts. We might be able to *see* something if we tread carefully," she said.

"Here, let's see how strong we are together. Between us, we created the finest Seer in the kingdom, so this should be simple," Marcel said with a grin, offering Merissa his hand and I glowered as she placed her palm in his.

"How about you try it without touching?" I growled.

"How about you get on your way to Azriel?" Merissa insisted. "We know what we're doing."

"Hm," I grunted. "I won't be long."

I swept towards the door, but before I exited Marcel called, "Watch your step," and my foot slipped over the threshold, making me stumble.

I shot him a glare then continued on, leaving them to their mystical fucking connection that they shared without me. Not that I gave a damn.

I wound down a spiral stairway, moonbeams spilling through the glassless windows, though no wind rushed around me. This place was nothing and nowhere, the rules of the living realm almost entirely absent here.

At the bottom of the stairs, I bumped into Darius, his body clad in fine, princely clothes and gold draped around his neck. I tried to step past him, but he sidestepped into my way, so I weaved the other way, but he did the same and I halted, folding my arms.

"Have you been sent into death to torment me?" I drawled, noticing Radcliff drifting along in his wake. When he saw me, he gave me a little wave and I nodded to him in kind. We were close once; we attended Zodiac Academy together and he should have been the Fire Lord in my Celestial Council. So many could have beens hung between us now. But my fondness for him remained, and I had enjoyed our reunion here in death despite his appearance reminding me of his detestable brother.

"I have better things to do than torment an old relic who lost his crown long ago," Darius said, irking me more.

"You know, most men find it in their interest to win the favour of their father in laws," I said icily.

"Was I meant to hold a seance every night to try and contact you? To sing you songs and offer you little trinkets?" Darius asked dryly. "And by the way, how's your relationship going with Merissa's father? I hear you had to bribe him and his entire kingdom to let you keep his daughter after you stole her."

"Her father was an arrogant piece of shit who had no time for me whatsoever," I snapped.

"Wow. Sounds familiar," Darius drawled, and I pressed my lips into a tight line.

We were suddenly in a stand-off, staring at each other, waiting for the other to let them pass, but I would stand here until time ceased to exist.

"Not to interrupt this…whatever this is, but I believe we are on somewhat of a time crunch with the world falling to ruin under my brother's absolute dominion, and all," Radcliff said, shifting closer to peer around Darius's head. "And I suspect we are all looking for the same person too. Azriel Orion. Have you seen him?"

"No," I said, not breaking eye contact with Darius.

"But that's who you're looking for," Darius stated. "So we'll just tag along."

"Then you will need to move aside, so that I might lead the way," I said, raising my chin.

"I believe he is up there somewhere," Darius said, jutting his chin at the stairway. "So just move out of my way and we can get going."

"He is often in The Room of Knowledge," I said.

"We were just there, and he wasn't," Darius said. "So…"

"I would prefer to check myself."

Radcliff cleared his throat. "Maybe if we all split up and look for him then none of us will have to remain subject to this juvenile bickering? There are many rooms here, more than there are stars in the sky most likely, so it could take some time if we remain here at the foot of this stairwell. Plus I-" He gasped, swiping his hand by his ear and looking left and right in a panic. "Did you hear that? A buzzing sound. Like a bzzz bzzz. A wasp perhaps?" His throat bobbed and he took a step away from the nearest open window.

"There are no wasps in death," I said tiredly. This was not the first time Radcliff had jumped at nothing, but he was also not the only soul in the afterlife who was afraid of the reason they were here. I, myself, sometimes swore I spied a Nymph approaching from the corner of my eye, probes raised, teeth bared in a victorious grin.

"Right, yes. Of course there isn't." Radcliff swallowed, swiping a hand over his dark blonde hair. "So…Azriel?"

"Azriel," Darius and I said at the same time.

"Just waiting for the dead king to move and I'll be on my way," Darius said.

"Just waiting for my daughter's poor choice to move aside, and I'll be on *my* way," I gritted out.

Radcliff looked between us with an eyebrow raised.

"Hail?!" Azriel's voice boomed through the walls of the Eternal Palace, sending a violent shudder down my spine.

I turned, knowing at once where he was, feeling his summons resounding through to my bones. I ran up the stairs two at a time, sensing two Dragon Shifters at my back as I turned down a corridor towards Azriel's rooms. The corridor glittered gold and silver, dark and light, the floor appearing as an endless carpet of stairs only to become solid again, a black carpet stretching away into an eternal hallway lined with endless doors.

I found Azriel's room, feeling him there – which was pretty much the only way to stop yourself from getting lost in this place. Rumour had it there were remnants adrift in the recesses of the furthest rooms, their names forgotten, but a single, aching purpose keeping them rooted between here and true death, clinging to something perhaps they couldn't even truly recall.

I knocked on Azriel's door and it flew open at my touch, my mind rattling as I stepped into a place which was so familiar to me that it left an imprint on my soul. This room had been his at Zodiac Academy, the Captain's room in

Aer House, and he had recreated it here down to every single detail, from the wooden flooring to the large trunk at the end of the four-poster bed. Even the view had been remade, the rows of tall windows looking out upon the blustery fields of Air Territory, the golden glow of this place dancing between the grass the only hint that we weren't in the Fae realm. The room even held pictures on the walls of all of us as teenagers, reminding me of some of the best times of my life.

I spotted Azriel standing in the middle of the space with his unkempt black hair and inky eyes, his form barely visible as he pushed against The Veil to see the present world. I made it to him, touching his arm and his eyes snapped onto me, seeing me here and pulling me with him into the land of the living. I felt Darius tumbling after me, drawing Radcliff along in his wake until the four of us stood at the edge of a cage of night iron, my daughter Gwendalina inside it, clutched in the arms of Lance Orion on the floor.

"What has happened?" I barked in terror, but the first answer that came was a Dragon's roar blasting through the air.

I shuddered, the walls of the palace shuddering along with me, my connection to this place stronger than any other location on earth. My own magic lived here, alongside Merissa's and the power of the Vega line. It was all around me, and I could feel myself standing in this place more solidly than I could anywhere else. It knew me and I knew it, something truly alive about it as if it held a soul of its own.

"Lionel," Radcliff growled, recognising the sound of his own brother's roar.

"Gwendalina was summoned here by the Shadow Princess," Azriel explained darkly, remorse twisting his features. "She is well, at least for now."

I nodded, distraught as I moved to the edge of the cage, passing through the bars, and staring down at my daughter as she slept.

Grief lined Gwendalina's face and as Darius fell to his knees beside her and Lance, I knew whose pain it was that had reduced them to this. I feared how much time had passed since Gwendalina had been brought here, how the few moments beyond The Veil had seemed like no time at all, yet here she was, moved from the depths of a lake into the capture of the false king.

"I'm sorry, my little darling," I breathed. "I should never have stopped watching."

Darius lay his hand on Lance's shoulder, and it was almost as though Lance searched for the man at his side, like he could sense him there.

"They don't have much time," Azriel said frantically, clutching something in his hand that looked suspiciously like a crystal. He should have access to no such thing beyond The Veil, but Azriel had often broken rules and found ways to defy the stars that I had always admired. His gift for dark magic had clearly followed him into death, and I was more than happy to wield whatever trinket he had secured himself if it could help my family.

"What is that?"

"A Druid's Tear crystal," he whispered dramatically, like I knew what the fuck that was. "It lets me move more fluidly through the living realm. I can watch those who do not belong to me, not for long, but I saw Lionel at his manor, the place turned to ash at Roxanya's hands. He is coming here to punish Gwendalina."

"We must warn them," I growled in fear.

"Typical asshole," Radcliff grumbled. "If I'd been on the Council none of this would have happened."

"Great story, now can we do something?" Darius rose to his feet anxiously, looking to Azriel who turned to me.

"Your connection to The Palace of Souls is still as strong as ever," he said. "You can wield the magic here like you have before."

"And do what?" I said frantically as Gwendalina stirred and began speaking with Lance in low tones.

"Maybe *I* can do something." Radcliff walked over to the Hydra throne, climbing up on it and tugging at one of the heads.

"Stop that," I growled, but Azriel caught my arm to regain my attention.

"Help them," he insisted, his eyes pulsing with protectiveness for his son and my daughter, and I felt the very same. Azriel and I were united by them in a way I could never have predicted, though Merissa had made comments on Azriel's son in life that made all too much sense now. What she had *seen* of their love, I didn't exactly know, but witnessing it myself had been enough to tell me why the stars themselves had offered her glimpses of it. A love that was as profound and remarkable as I ever could have hoped my little darling to find. And I would protect it with all I had to give and more.

"Alright," I said, unsure what I could do, but I would try.

I moved closer to them, examining the wall and recognising the place where a secret door used to open. I pressed my hand against it, feeling it solidly there as I focused, holding the reality of it so very close as I pushed against The Veil and forced my power into existence. I tried to open that door, my teeth gritting as I begged it to give way, but the palace's magic danced along my palm with thoughts of its own, drawing on my power and guiding it towards another avenue.

"Come on," I growled, then my mind slid into the grasp of all that power, a thousand years of my ancestors placing magic in these very walls swallowing me into it.

With a growl of effort, I bound that power to the stones and let it build and build, before it sprang away from me like an elastic band pinging from my fingers and latching onto the exact place where I could feel Lionel standing in this palace. He and Lavinia were like a cold presence in the middle of a warm, beating heart. They didn't belong here, and the palace felt it too.

I formed a connection between where Lionel was prowling through the halls and the throne room, but suddenly staggered away, The Veil tugging me back with a sharp yank.

"No," I gasped but Azriel grabbed hold of me before I could be snatched away, grounding me back in the throne room where Lionel's booming voice now sounded through the walls, carried here by Vega magic.

"Do you realise how much treasure I have lost, Lavinia?! Rare coins and gemstones that are now in the filthy hands of disgusting lesser Fae. And now I have been stuck at the Court of Solaria all day and half the night to try and prepare a final attack on those fucking rebels who have vanished off the face of the earth."

"That's it?" Darius barked. "You made a little fucking speakerphone?"

"I lost control," I muttered.

"By the fucking stars," Lance cursed, realising the sound was coming from the wall, and Gwendalina shifted closer to the bricks to listen.

"I must make a stand," Lionel went on. "With the Heirs and Councillors free, and presumably gone to join with that orphaned whore, that puts the rebels in a stronger position again."

"Ergh, he sounds like a pompous ass," Radcliff said, jumping down from the throne to kick his foot against it.

"You control the press, Daddy, you can have them write a story about your greatness. They can tell the world what wicked, vile creatures those Vegas are," Lavinia's crooning voice carried to us.

I sneered, moving to the spot where the wall touched with the bars and trying to force the bricks to shatter, to give them passage beyond this cage. If there was one creature in this world I despised as keenly as Lionel Acrux, it was Lavinia and her unnatural ways. The revenge she was hellbent on seeking from my family line had spanned a thousand years, and she was more merciless than she had ever been. Now she had Gwendalina in her grasp, what would she do? How would she punish my child? What horrors was my daughter going to have to endure because of the deeds of our ancestor Queen Avalon?

"It is not good enough," Lionel spat. "Don't you understand? The Phoenixes are stronger than I ever imagined, and now the rebels' strength is bolstered once more by the most powerful bloodline in Solaria. I must make a statement in blood and death. I must show them what I am capable of."

"Of course, my King. What will you do?" Lavinia asked excitedly.

"You know what I must do," he snarled. "I will show the world what the Dragon King can do to Phoenixes. Has Gwendalina Vega arrived?"

I froze, looking to my daughter with fear carving down the centre of me, while she met the gaze of her Elysian Mate with resilience in her eyes.

"We have to free them," Darius said urgently and Azriel hurried forward too, all of us trying to pour magic into the wall to make it shatter.

"Yes, but-" Lavinia started but Lionel cut over her.

"Finally," he breathed. "I have one of my greatest enemies right here in the palace. I will have the world watch while I behead her alongside her Elysian Mate. I will prove I am far superior to the Vega line in a show of power and brutality. And I will make her bow before she bleeds."

If there was a crueller fate than being parted from her in death, it was standing here now sensing her own death on the air. And it bound my soul in terror.

"My King," Lavinia said gently. "They are under my control. I am afraid I cannot allow it."

"Allow it?" Lionel hissed venomously. "It is not your place to *allow* me anything! I am the power here. I am the ruler of Solaria."

"And I am owed a debt from the Vega and her mate because Queen Avalon banished me to the Shadow Realm all those years ago."

"You've had your fun. I will make sure they both suffer intensely before the end, and Roxanya Vega can watch her sister die on television; what better vengeance is there than that?"

"Daddy, wait," Lavinia gasped, and all fell quiet as they passed away from the magical connection I'd created.

"Useless," I growled at myself, pacing forward in desperation. There had to be more I could do, had to be a way I could protect her. I could not fail her.

"Just focus," Azriel said, looking to me intently, his fear bright in his eyes.

Lance grabbed two bars of the cage, trying to bend them apart with the strength of his Vampire Order, and Darius moved to try and help.

"Is there magic in this palace or not, Hail?" Darius barked at me.

"This cage is not of the palace," I snarled as I worked to wrangle the magic in the walls and shape it into something of use. But it was frantic, chaotic and ever-changing, not listening to my desperate demands.

Gwendalina caught Lance's arm, looking up at him with rage in her expression. "I'll fight."

Those words left me both proud and terrified as the beastly king stalked closer to claim another member of my family.

Not her. Not my little darling.

The Veil dragged me away as I reached for her and Azriel cried his son's name as we were thrown back into the beyond. I battled to get back with every drop of power I possessed, tumbling through the dark as flashes of Lionel entering the throne room darted before my eyes and terror for my daughter sliced into me.

"Gwendalina!" I cried, frantic as I fought my way to her.

"Is she quite under your control, Lavinia?" Lionel asked, and I cursed his name, tearing through the dark and reaching for him with swinging fists and merciless hate.

"Stay away from her!" I roared, my fist slamming into the centre of his face and passing through as if he was nothing. But it was me who was nothing, all because of this heinous Fae.

"Fully, my king," Lavinia said. "Her magic is being devoured by the Shadow Beast, there is little of it left at all and my creature has already stolen her Order form away from her. She's basically a mortal."

"Good," Lionel purred. "Mortals can burn."

Those words were my undoing, my soul scattering into a million fragments of terrified pieces as I tried to tear through The Veil itself to protect her.

Gwendalina stood powerlessly before this coward, her magic locked down by the shadows, and there was nothing I could do.

"Have your false queen order the Shadow Beast to return my magic so I can fight you one on one. Face me like Fae and find out which of us really deserves my father's throne," Gwendalina demanded, and I moved to her side, trying to lend her my power to break through the darkness that weighed down her magic.

"I'm here, my little darling. You can fight this," I spoke to her, though she couldn't hear me at all. Maybe she could feel me.

"You don't know the meaning of being Fae," Lionel said coldly, and rage spiked through me. "Your mother hid you in the mortal world and you were raised with the weakness of their kind burrowing into your soul. You reek of their powerlessness, their pathetic, pointless existence, and the only claim you have is the watery blood of the Vega line in your veins. But your father's power does not run true in you, his merger with a half-breed whore is clear proof of that."

"You piece of shit," I snarled.

"Don't you *dare* speak about my mother like that," Gwendalina snapped, and I rested a hand on her back, feeling that darkness in her, how it clung to every fibre of her being, but there was light in the heart of it.

"I will speak of trash as it deserves to be spoken of. Your father's failings allowed fate to collude in *my* favour. Me. A man of true worth. The dominion of purity and real power is clear for all to see now, and the world will watch you fall, the shroud finally falling from their eyes as you are revealed to them for the pathetic creature you are in your final moments."

A roar left my lungs at Lionel's words, and I charged toward him, drawing on every last scrap of power left in me to try and land a blow to the conniving asshole who had stolen my throne, but the stars pulled me away once more and I was tossed into a sea of black.

I kicked and tore and raked my nails through the nothingness, desperate to get back to her, the other souls I'd travelled here with long lost to the depths of The Veil once more. I saw Gwendalina fighting, saw Lionel struck and hurt by her attacks, her magic somehow returned, only to fail her once more as the Shadow Beast took over.

Lionel suddenly had her in his grip, a knife in his fist that had long ago belonged to Merissa. Then all was dark again and I screamed my daughter's name into the nothing, begging for her to be spared.

And when I finally made it back to her, pushing against the weight of The Veil with all I had, I found Gwendalina on the floor, bloody and broken, her soul hovering at the very verges of her skin.

The Veil was humming, the stars calling for another soul to join them and I called out in defiance of them.

"She will live!" I demanded.

The blackness tried to steal me away once more, but I wouldn't go. Not for anything. Not when she needed me, my baby girl bleeding on the floor. And I wasn't there.

"I'm here, little darling, I'm here." And there, without warning, I found myself above her while Lance Orion worked to heal her with what modicum of power he still possessed. She was lifeless in his arms, and I brushed her hand, her fingers winding around mine as the essence of her tried to escape this life and head into the beyond.

"No, it's not your time," I whispered to her. "Stay here in your mate's arms, stay here where the world will one day be kind to you again."

I pulled my hand away, pressing it to Lance's shoulder and offering him all the power I possessed, even if it was nothing but the wasted dregs of a lost king.

"Save her, bring her back. Don't let her go," I demanded of him. His face pinched in terror at the thought of losing his mate, the silver rings in his eyes glowing with their bond. "Protect her like you swore you would!"

"Please, Blue. Please stay with me. I've got you." Lance closed his eyes, pushing his magic into her body while I fuelled him with whatever I could give in this wretched form.

"Hurry up!" Lavinia cried, and I glanced back at her, finding her in the clutches of the Death Bond, her life hinging on my daughter's. Her soul shimmered at the edges of her skin and I felt the deep rumble of Crucia in the depths of the fields of chaos, hungering to claim another victim into his land of agony. But her death would only come once Gwendalina had faced hers, and no matter how savagely I wanted to see Lavinia claimed by the punisher of the underworld, my daughter would not pay the price of her passage.

"Take everything," Lance commanded while I fuelled his power with all the energy I could conjure. "Take it all, Darcy Vega."

Slowly, she began to heal, the burns on her legs fading first before the soft snap of bones fusing came and I released a sigh of utter relief.

She was alive. Coming back to the living, her soul resting soundly in her body at last.

The stars stole me away before I could spend another precious moment with my little darling, taking me back to the void beyond life. And with a violent tug that felt like my death happening all over again...I was gone.

DARIUS

CHAPTER SEVEN

T he rooms Hail and Merissa had created for themselves in the ever-changing Eternal Palace materialised around me and I scowled at the golden walls, the serene music which was playing just beyond the window, the perfectly balanced temperature.

"This place is bullshit," I muttered, though my mind was really on Gwen and Lance and all they were suffering through. Azriel and I had glimpsed the end of my father's attack, seeing Gwen well after she had teetered on the brink of death. It had been so difficult to keep my grip on the Fae world that I had only snatched that view of her for a moment before I had been shoved firmly back here again.

Azriel looked at me with a frown marking his brow. "It's meant to reflect your perfect idea of peace. In your own rooms you'll probably find it more-"

"I don't have or want my own rooms here," I replied flatly, but at the mention of them, the world drifted around me once more, Azriel coming along for the ride, leaving Radcliff and Hail behind.

Hail started yelling about something or other, but his voice faded too, and I found myself standing in an enormous, empty room, a vaulted ceiling arcing overhead and stone pillars leading out to a balcony where an equally empty sky awaited me.

"This is...cosy," Azriel said, turning slowly to take in the blank walls and blanker floor. "Your taste is very...minimal."

"My taste is fire and ruin tempered by the kiss of a woman who has always and will always be out of my league," I growled, and the room promptly provided an enormous fireplace with a roaring fire, my battle axe hanging on the mantle above it. No Roxy though.

"Lovely," Azriel said, stepping closer to the fire and holding his hands out like he was warming them, though I got the impression he was just looking for something to do with himself. His brow was heavily furrowed, and I had to think his mind was firmly on his son and the predicament he was in. Lance had landed his ass in worse situations though, and I had faith in him. Alright, maybe not many worse situations, but still.

"Look, about Lance-" I started, but Azriel cut over me quickly like he couldn't bear to talk about him right now.

"This wall will provide you a private view into the world of the living whenever you wish for it – you can form it into a mirror if you like. Many like to do that. I think it makes it feel more personal, like peering through a window," he said, and I glanced at the wall, finding exactly what he had described appearing there. "You can revisit memories or simply watch those you love as they continue to navigate life."

I grunted in acknowledgment of that, not wanting to waste time watching things I couldn't be a part of any longer, though I imagined I'd spend plenty of time staring at that wall all the same, my desperation to be with those I loved drawing me to it even now.

I eyed the man who had once been a familiar presence in my childhood. I used to hate him. Not because he was a bad man, but because he was a good one. There was a tree on the boundary between the Acrux Manor estate and the Orion lands which I used to climb as a small boy and I'd watch them; him, Lance and Clara, running about, laughing, playing.

My father's idea of a game was to lock me in a box for hours at a time to help rid me of any claustrophobia I might have. And if he was especially pleased with the way I handled myself, I could look forward to the joy of avoiding a beating, or at the very least, he would heal me directly afterward instead of leaving me to suffer with my injuries.

So in my petty, jealous way, I'd hated this man. Hated the proof he offered me that the world didn't always work the way it did within the walls of my home. Hated the way I had to watch him dote over his children when they thrived, or console them when they failed. Never once had I seen him raise a hand to them. I'd tried to catch him out occasionally, thinking he just hid his violence the way my father did from prying eyes, but I'd never caught him, and I'd come to realise I never would. It had been impossible to forgive him for that at the time. Now...well, now I supposed I just pitied him for the time he'd had stolen.

"Spit it out," I muttered, my muscles tight with the need to move. But I didn't know where to go or how to even begin seeking what I required, so there I stood, the reality of all I'd witnessed in the living realm pressing down on me so heavily that I couldn't breathe.

"Hmm?" Azriel looked to me, his expression marred with confusion, and I growled low in the back of my throat.

"Don't try to pretend that death has made you this forgiving. I'm the reason your son never got to follow his dreams. I was there the night your daughter was sacrificed to the shadows. So say it. Or hit me. Whatever the fuck you want, just don't linger in this silence where the words can fester."

"You think I blame you for any of that?" Azriel asked softly, moving from the flames and stepping closer to me, reaching out for me before thinking better of it and lowering his hand with a shake of his head. "Darius, I don't blame you for the actions of your father. Hell, Lance only had any light in his life at all because of you for a very long time. For a while, I even hoped the two of you might become something more-"

"Me and Lance?" I scoffed. "He fucking wishes."

"The two of you did have all of those sleepovers. He drew me to him in a nightmare once and I was filled with excitement when I found you in bed with him, your arms wrapped tight around him, offering comfort, the two of you in a state of undress and-"

"Those were platonic sleepovers," I said, rolling my eyes. "And I was never fucking naked for them-"

"I believe you'd been out flying together," Azriel pressed. "You'd had a particularly difficult encounter with your father, and you had ended up drinking. Lance dared you to drink several kegs worth of beer in your Dragon form..."

"Oh yeah." I snorted in amusement. "I got totally shitfaced and burned half of that distillery down. I paid for the damage though – I'm not a total asshole."

"Yes...well, I'm sure the owners of the business felt the same way... once they'd finally made all the repairs and replenished their stocks and got themselves back up and running again. Anyway, it turned out you'd simply shifted and passed out and Lance had stayed with you to make sure you didn't choke on your own vomit or whatnot. It was rather disappointing when I realised the two of you hadn't actually done the deed."

"By the stars." I turned away from him, swiping a hand down my face.

"Anyway, now I see that he was always meant to be with Gwendalina, er, I mean, Darcy. I think the two of you would have been a little too...well, never mind all that." Azriel cleared his throat, and I shook my head, wondering how the fuck I'd even ended up having this conversation with him.

"I need to speak with Merissa," I said firmly. "How do I get back to-"

The palace walls melted then reformed, leaving me standing before a large door with a Hydra branded into the wood, a Harpy flying above it.

Azriel smiled while I frowned at it. "In this place, the wanting is the doing," he explained like that even made sense. "Go ahead – knock."

I raised my fist and pounded it against the door, potentially using a little too much force as the sound echoed down the serene corridors.

"Turn him away," Hail's voice came from beyond the door.

"I came to see your wife, not you," I called in reply.

"He is the king you know-" Azriel said in a low tone. "He might warm to you more if you showed a little respect."

"He's not the king anymore. And I'm the one who married one of the true queens – so maybe he should be the one bowing to me," I replied, not bothering to lower my voice as the door swung open and I found Hail scowling at me from his throne, Merissa pressing a hand to his chest to keep him there.

"You forget that you're as dead as me, boy," Hail ground out and I shrugged.

"You're a relic. I'm a martyr. Besides, I don't intend to remain dead for long."

Hail shoved to his feet, a deep, rattling growl spilling from him as his body shook with rage before an enormous serpent leapt from his spine, the nine-headed black Hydra appearing behind the throne, every mouth baring its teeth at me threateningly.

In reply my Dragon tore its way free of my flesh too, the tiles rattling as it landed behind me, its bulk even larger than the creature it faced.

"Stop," Merissa snapped, flicking Hail between the eyes and making him curse as he batted her hand away from him. "This is getting us nowhere. Hail, I told you, go with Marcel, he can help you with the stones-"

"I need some time to meditate on it," Marcel added, his tone ambivalent as he peered at my Dragon with interest, though I noted he held no fear in his expression.

"Surely, I can make progress with this task without the need for his assistance," Hail gritted out and the corner of my lips lifted in amusement. Seemed like Hail had some jealousy issues when it came to Gabriel's bio daddy.

"Without my assistance, all shall perish," Marcel said mildly, turning towards the door and clipping Hail with his wing as he went.

"I have some documents on this subject too, your highness," Azriel added. "Perhaps we can head to my rooms to look them over?"

Hail huffed out a breath then turned and strode from the room without another word to me. His Hydra spilled back into his body as he went, and I watched it with more interest than I really wanted to admit to.

"Why do your wings remain a part of your body while my Dragon separates from mine here?" I asked Merissa before the door had even closed behind them.

"It's complicated but it's also a choice. Your Dragon isn't a separate entity to you but the magic binding you to your Order form is freer here, meaning you can fully unleash it as you have now. That said, if you want to shift in the way you are more used to then you can, you simply have to focus on the act - which is more difficult than it sounds after doing it instinctually throughout your entire life. It's a little simpler for me because Harpies are a Divisus Order, so I always kept a lot of my Fae form even when shifting. You'll get the hang of it in time."

"Big Dragon," Radcliff commented around a mouthful of food, and I flinched as I turned to find him lingering in the corner of the room, stuffing his face from a buffet I hadn't even noticed before. "Almost as big as mine."

"Where the fuck did you come from?" I demanded.

"I think I faded for a moment there," he admitted like I was supposed to know what that meant. "I was trying to go see some of my people but...well, no one really grieves for me enough these days and then that got me feeling all kinds of shitty and the Destined Door to the beyond appeared like the sneaky son-of-a-bitch we all know it to be and-"

"Okay, got it," I interrupted him, not really caring because time was slipping by and in this place that wasn't a direct measure of anything. I could have been dead for hours, days or weeks at this point in the living realm and I had no idea which it was. "You said you'd help me find what I need to get back," I said to Merissa.

Roxy's mother looked me over, her eyes roaming across my face like she could see so much more than I was offering to show her. It was disconcerting. This whole thing was disconcerting. I was surrounded by people who I never should have even met, given the chance to speak to them and know them in a way that many of the living would give all they had for the chance, but I didn't want it. The greatest yearning of my heart was simply to return to what I'd lost. I needed to get back, to keep the promises I'd made and find my way through death to the woman I loved once more.

"There is a remnant who lingers in the depths of the old forest," she said softly, almost hesitantly. "She shunned the rooms offered to her here in the Eternal Palace and created her own residence out there where she clings to death like a barnacle on the hull of a sinking ship. She has been here longer than any even know, refusing to pass on despite the years that slip by. She is said to know all there is about this place. If anyone can help you then it will be her."

"Where do I find her?" I asked, already turning for the door but Merissa caught my arm.

"There will be a cost," she breathed, glancing at the walls like they might be listening. "I don't know what, but you must consider it carefully before you agree to anything. I want my daughter to be happy more than anything in all the world but a lifetime without you would pale to insignificance in the face of some things."

I wanted to dismiss her warning, but something about the fear in her eyes held my tongue and I nodded instead.

"I won't agree to anything unless I'm certain of it," I swore to her and she visibly relaxed.

"Come then. I'll take you to her," she said.

"I'll just stay here then, shall I?" Radcliff called as we left the room without him, and I exchanged a look with Merissa whose lips twitched with amusement as neither of us asked him to join us.

"So," Merissa began as we stepped out of the heavy door emblazoned with the Hydra and the Harpy, finding ourselves outside beneath the golden sky instead of within the Eternal Palace this time. "I thought the bike was a nice gift," she said, and it took me a moment to realise she meant the bike I'd bought Roxy for winning the race against me all those months ago.

"Yeah? She sure took her time in coming to look at it."

"Well, it was good of you to admit that you were wrong and accept that she'd won something. But you could hardly expect her to forgive you without making you work your ass off for it."

"Some days I'm still not convinced she has forgiven me, or more like I'm not convinced I deserved her forgiveness at all," I muttered, looking at the path which spilled out before our feet, dropping away though a serene valley before twisting towards a darkened woodland area beyond. The trees closest to us were bright and green, but there was something about the way the light didn't quite touch the trees deeper into the forest which made a shiver run down my spine.

"I take it we're headed there?" I asked, pointing to the patch of shadows.

"How did you know?" Merissa asked, leading the way down the path, her silver gown floating around her on the light breeze.

"Take any given situation, look for the worst possible outcome and I'll generally find myself in the thick of it. So, if I'm looking at a perfect view coated in dappled sunlight and there's one creepy patch of shadowy doom, then I can bet with pretty decent accuracy that that's where I'll end up."

"That's a rather morose view on yourself," Merissa noted.

"My luck in life has been decidedly shitty. At least it was before her."

I could feel Merissa's eyes on me, but I didn't return the look, striding down the hill and heading for the trees at a fast pace.

"I take it the scumbags don't come here?" I asked. "The murderers and the like?"

"They pass through the Harrowed Gate," she confirmed, and the sky darkened at the mention of it. "The place we're heading to is the closest you can get to the fields of chaos without actually entering them."

"Any guesses on why I ended up here and not there then?" I asked because honestly, I'd done plenty of bad things in my life, taken lives, lied, followed the path my father laid out for me all too often.

"I think it's a balance of your actions and the truth in your heart. The world isn't good or evil, everyone is a mix of both, but intent, the harm caused by your actions and the way you feel about that are what tip the scales. Some Fae serve a sentence of years there for their crimes, others an eternity. It is all decided by the stars ultimately, when we are weighed and measured in the moments of our deaths. Hail has often wondered why he found himself here instead of there, but I know his heart and I know why."

"He seems like a real sweet fella," I said flatly, and she laughed.

"There was a time when he likely would have hurled you straight through the Destined Door upon meeting you here. The blatant contempt and utter rudeness he's offering you is actually a good sign."

"Feels like it," I deadpanned.

"Truly. He just needs a little longer to see in you what Roxanya does. He knows you make her happy, he sees what you've given for her."

"Honestly, I don't care," I said. "My own father never liked me so why should I wish to have hers feel differently? I've only ever held value to men like that through the worth they put on me. My father wanted me to be powerful to bolster his own name, Hail wants me to be powerful to bolster his daughter's. Who I am has little to do with it. What I am even less so. I know the only reason he tolerates me at all is because she chose me in the end, and he won't go against her. But I get it, I'm not good enough. The thing is, the only person I'm ever going to care about proving myself to in that regard is her. So Hail can hate me all he likes, my focus won't shift from what she needs, and right now that means I need to find a way back to her."

Merissa smirked at me, her elbow knocking against my arm. "See, I knew she picked well."

I tried not to care what she thought of me either, but I couldn't help the twitch of my lips. I hadn't ever expected to gain her approval and it wouldn't have mattered to me if I hadn't, but I could quietly admit that having it felt good. It helped me feel at least a little more deserving of Roxy's love if she wasn't the only person who thought I might be worthy of it.

The shadows beneath the trees were dappled and beautiful, the path winding jovially through the wide trunks, butterflies fluttering lazily between beautiful blossoms which seemed to bloom from every branch in every colour imaginable.

The sound of hooves drew my attention to the path on our right and I looked around just as a completely naked dude riding on the back of a huge black Pegasus appeared through the trees. A group of six women followed a few paces behind him, all equally nude and all riding on what I assumed were their own Order forms which ranged from a Cerberus to a Manticore with four brightly coloured Pegasuses bringing up the rear.

"I know you," the dude said, but if that was true then it was only because I was famous, because I had no idea who he was.

"Good for you. We're busy," I said, making to walk past him, but his Pegasus trotted forward to block the path.

The naked man leaned down to offer me his hand which I assumed he expected me to shake. But seeing as that hand had been resting in his lap alongside his bare cock five seconds ago that was going to be a hard pass.

"I'm Reth," he said brightly, not seeming to mind one bit that I didn't take his hand and using it to indicate the group of girls instead. "This is my herd. Kaitlynn Ragan, Chelsea King, Justice Sharpe, Savannah Peters, Ashlee James and Natasha Yatsallie. We come out here so that the noises we all make during our alone time don't interrupt anyone's peace in the Eternal Palace. If you catch my drift? You've probably heard of me…"

"No," I replied flatly, and Merissa stifled a laugh.

"I'm kind of a big deal around here," he pushed.

"I've got a whole merchandise range," I deadpanned. "I know about being a big deal and I subsequently couldn't give a fuck about it or whoever you were before you died."

"Oh, no, I wasn't a big deal when I was *alive*," Reth corrected, not seeming to get the hint, that friendly smile still on his face like my rudeness didn't even bother him. "I mean I'm a big deal here. As in beyond The Veil. Because I'm the man who almost lived…"

"Reth's situation won't help you with what you're seeking," Merissa interrupted as that got my attention.

"Almost lived as in almost passed back through?" I demanded, suddenly more interested in this naked nice guy, wondering if he might hold the key to what I needed. Although the almost part was hardly reassuring.

"Kinda," Reth replied, his herd all cooing like the fangirls I hated so much back in the living realm. "I peered through a hole in The Veil when it was torn open. But in the end, I had to make the hard choice and-"

"How was it torn open?" I demanded, moving closer, his cock disconcertingly close to my face as I looked up at him on that damn Pegasus.

"It's a long story, maybe we can catch a beer and chill while I tell it?" Reth suggested.

"I don't chill," I growled.

Reth's eyes roamed over me and he nodded. "I see that. Well, it was this whole cataclysmic collection of stolen power that was used in a single blast instead of released into the world as the stars intended. I wasn't actually involved in the doing of it, but don't worry – that can never be done again. The power doesn't exist anymore."

"I told you," Merissa said, nodding towards the path beyond Reth. "That was an anomaly which almost ended in disaster. Every soul beyond The Veil could have torn their way through and shattered the balance between life and death for good if Reth had tried to follow that path. It can't be repeated either. We need to seek your answer elsewhere."

I huffed in irritation and sidestepped the Pegasus. Reth waved jovially from its back as we strode away from him, asking me to come chill with him later if I changed my mind and I offered no reaction to his words whatsoever as I kept walking.

"A lot of the people here are fucking weird," I muttered, and Merissa nodded.

"Yes, it's not meant to be forever. This is a place where Fae can wait for those they love, watch them grow and live and reunite with them before passing on if they so wish. But remaining in the in-between for too long can cause certain personality quirks to say the least. If your tie to the living is strong enough then you can keep hold of yourself, but if it fades or those you love pass over too, then the unchanging nature of this place can have a strange effect. Almost all souls pass on eventually."

A door grew in the centre of the path at her words, vines crawling from the earth to create an arch surrounding it, the door cracking open, bright light beckoning from within.

Merissa paused, staring at that slice of light for a heartbeat too long and I caught her arm, tugging her attention back to me.

"Your children still need you," I reminded her. She blinked and the door vanished as if it had never been there before.

"Thank you," she breathed, patting my hand. "The door's call gets louder as time passes, sometimes its song can capture my attention for longer than it used to. But don't worry. I have no plans to pass on any time soon."

We walked on, the air cooler where the door had been, whispers brushing against my ears as I passed that space, but they retreated as we moved deeper into the trees.

The darkness grew, the natural woodland sounds falling away until nothing but our footsteps sounded in the gloom.

A rocky outcrop appeared between the barren branches of the trees, and I paused as I looked at it. The grey stone was cloaked in shadow, but at the heart of it, those shadows thickened impossibly. It took me several seconds to realise that it wasn't shadow at all, but an entrance to a cave filled with purest darkness.

"See?" I said. "I'm forever drawn to the dark."

"Some would say that makes it more impressive when you continue to find the light."

I shook my head, wondering if Merissa might be hoping to find more good in me than I truly held for the sake of her daughter. Then again, she had been watching, she'd seen more than I could know, so maybe I shouldn't doubt her judgement.

I stalked toward the cave, tension spilling through me though I knew I had no reason to fear anything within the confines of death. But there was something off about this place. Something that set my hackles raising and made me ache for the feeling of my axe in my grip and my fire in my veins.

The cavern was pitch black, the darkness enveloping me the moment I stepped into it, the light outside not able to penetrate the depths of it at all. I drew in a deep breath, the scent of damp and moss clinging to old walls pouring past my senses.

I could hear Merissa following as I moved deeper into the darkness, my pace slow in case I collided with something, but my objective set.

A chill brushed against my cheeks as I moved deeper into the dark, the temperature falling as we moved, nothing of the balmy warmth that filled every other part of The Veil left to surround us.

My outstretched hand met with a damp, rock wall and I hesitated, feeling my way along it, and using it to guide me as the path I walked began to twist, turning first right then left before revealing a pale blue light up ahead.

It looked like a hole had been punched in the roof of the cave, the grey rock climbing up and away above my head towards the source of the pale light.

A large misshapen boulder sat in the centre of the open space before us, a flicker in the light drawing my attention to a figure I hadn't noticed there initially.

I stilled, glancing at Merissa who had paused at the edge of the pale light.

"That's her. Some call her Mordra, but I don't know if that's her true name," she breathed, folding her arms across her chest as she looked towards the remnant who was little more than a shiver in the light.

I nodded, leaving Merissa where she stood, just within the darkness, not seeming to want to cross into that glow.

I had no such reservations.

I strode towards the rock which adorned the centre of the space, my eyes trailing up the circular walls that spiralled away above my head. Moss grew in thick patches, clinging to the grey stone, and plants with trailing vines jutted out from any small outcrop they could find, their pale blue and orange leaves shifting in a breeze I couldn't feel. At the very top of the cave, I didn't find the hole I expected. Instead, the undulating motion of rushing water capped the top of the cavern as though I were looking up at the river from beneath.

I frowned, wondering what magic had been used to create such a place where no Elemental power seemed to exist beyond The Veil.

I looked more closely at the walls, noting the grooves scored into the rocks, the thin lines marking them in countless places, always in groups of five, almost as though someone had torn into the rocks themselves with nothing but their own fingernails-

A distant scream pierced through my soul like a dagger striking my chest, a rush of movement above making me snap my head up to look at the river once more just as a dark figure rushed along, propelled by the current. It was there and gone again in the blink of an eye, making it hard to decipher. There was a flash of dread-filled eyes, dark hair billowing in the rushing water and lips parted in a scream of pure terror which burned its way into the backs of my eyes.

"They rush to their doom, do they not?" a hiss breathed from behind me, and I whirled around, my fist closing on nothing as the magic I'd once owned ignored my call.

I caught sight of long fangs but as I tried to focus on them, they disappeared.

The misshapen boulder which lay in the centre of the space was twice as tall as me, flattened spots halfway up it and one near the top marking what might have been perches for this wretched creature to rest on. The spaces between those spots were littered with small objects which glimmered in the pale blue light, buttons, pins, hair clips, cufflinks, jewels, small scraps of cloth in every colour and fabric, each of them stuffed into a crack in the rock, peeking out just a little.

"Tokens," Mordra breathed, seeing where my attention had fallen, her words a breath on my neck which had me fighting the urge to flinch away. "Small pieces of the clothing worn in the final moments of those who pass through. There's a blink, a pulse, a flash, and sometimes, I snatch something from the other side in that space between their final heartbeat and The Veil, collecting them. Payment for the ferryman." She broke a laugh, and I stepped closer to the rock, my eyes drawn to the perch at the very top of it which appeared empty, yet somehow I knew she was there.

"You cross back through?" I asked, catching the most important part of what she'd just said.

A sigh. "Yes and no, here and there, a blink as I said, a space between breaths, nothing more. Can't catch anything so big as that." A hand appeared, the fingernails yellowed and cracked, a single finger pointing upward, making me look a beat before another soul rushed past in the river above, this one thrashing and kicking against the current, screaming for the life they'd just lost, fighting a losing battle to try and return to it.

"Do you want to?" I asked, frowning.

"Capture a doomed soul? Pah. No." The space at the top of the boulder shimmered, dark hair floating around a face without features before slipping away.

"What dooms them?" I asked, unable to stop my curiosity as another soul screamed their way down the river overhead.

"What indeed. Perhaps the stars will deign to tell you if you ask them. Not here though, their eyes can't spy us here." A flash of teeth and eyes without irises, the pupils black holes which devoured the pale blue light surrounding us.

I looked up again, paying more attention to the cavern, noting what it was, or at least what it mimicked.

"You hide in an amplification chamber," I noted. "I tried that once too."

"Did it work?" she purred, bare feet pressing into the stone, legs forming above them like grains of sand building her up bit by bit.

"At the time, yes. We hid what we were doing from them, but they figured it out once we were back beneath their gaze and made it impossible for us to hide from them that way again," I admitted, remembering the heat of Roxy's skin against mine in the dark, the blindfold covering her eyes, the way she moaned as she was pressed between my flesh and Caleb's.

Smoke rolled up the back of my throat, jealousy mixing with the allure of that memory. I wasn't a creature born to share.

Mordra huffed, her legs forming entirely, her body following on, greying skin clinging to bones which looked brittle even beneath the layer of flesh.

"You should have stayed hidden," she chided.

"In that chamber?" I asked. "Forever?"

"Forever is a time far longer than any concept you might construct," she scoffed, a hand waving my words aside like batting at a fly.

"I don't need forever," I said, taking a step closer to the rock, eyeing the so-called tokens she'd stolen from the bodies of the dying while she continued to find form before me, her body almost complete, a head taking shape on her shoulders, a scrap of white lace, dog-eared and dirty, clinging to her frame. "I just need the time I should have had."

Those soulless eyes reappeared, roaming over me, drinking in the sight as fangs bit down on a cracked lip. She was a horror to look upon, a corpse animated into motion, her skin clinging to rotting bones, sagging in the hollows of her cheeks, with that dark hair clumped in patches and missing in others across her scalp.

I didn't flinch away from her though. She was my only hope.

"You wish to pass back through?" She smiled, a hollow, heartless grin.

"I need to fulfil my destiny," I replied darkly. "I need to return to my wife and see my father dead at my feet."

"Such pretty words for such a tainted soul," she sighed.

Twin screams drew my attention to the rushing river above as a pair of bodies ripped past.

"They head to the Harrowed Gate," she hissed, her hands landing on my shoulders, her ripe breath in my ear.

I flinched back but stopped myself, looking into the emptiness of her eyes as I found her right before me, perching on the lowest of the platforms the boulder provided.

"Their souls will be tortured, their death a horror worthy of the atrocities they committed in life. Why did you pass to this place? Why don't you find yourself in that river?"

"I don't know," I replied, a tightness forming in my gut because I knew that I likely deserved that fate. I'd hurt people, killed Fae and Nymphs alike, though never out of petty cruelty or a desire for violence. But I had done bad things in the name of what I thought was right.

"Nobility," she chuckled. "Humility. Regret. Remorse. Honour. These are the attributes which buy you a pass with the stars, which allow you to bypass the river and the torment it leads to. But some of us are capable of both remorse and contempt. I may regret the death I caused in life on principle, but my hatred for those I killed doesn't waver. So, do I deserve to escape the river, sweet Dragon prince?"

"Hatred isn't a sin," I replied. "And there are those who deserve it more than any other emotion."

Mordra tilted her head to the side until the motion became unnatural, her head looking likely to fall clean off. Then she was gone, nothing, a twist in the air, a scent in the room.

"If one were to cross then the price would be high indeed. What might it take to bribe the ferryman?" she mused, her voice without a body to give it life.

"Give me that answer and I'll offer it willingly," I swore.

"So certain. So, so, certain," she sighed. "They watch, you know? Always watching, always steering, toying with us all like pieces on a board."

"The stars?" I assumed.

A pulse of cold air which might have been affirmation.

"Not me though. Never me."

"Tell me what to do," I begged.

"A long, long time ago, there was a way to steer fate without the interference of the stars," she mused. "A magic which they can't control. One which they can't even take from us in death. This is a prison, you know? A void of their creation, a place they use to harvest the power they once gifted so freely."

"What is that supposed to mean?" I asked.

"You tell me. Where are your flames? What happened to your ice?"

My blood tingled as I tried to draw on the Elemental magic which had once been so intrinsically a piece of me. I could almost feel that power stirring there, but none of it rose to the surface of my skin the way it once had so easily.

A bloody smile appeared to my right, where a platform was surrounded by a ring of small jewels.

"Ether doesn't bow to the stars," Mordra whispered. "But you need someone on the other side to figure that out for you. There is a place within the Library of the Lost where such knowledge is hidden, deep beneath the earth, rock and water secreting it away from the greedy eyes of the stars, guarded by those who cherish that knowledge above all else. Seek it, claim it, use it."

I opened my mouth to ask her more questions but a gnarled hand with yellowing fingernails appeared before me, palm up, a ghoulish face leering at me beyond it before Mordra blew a waft of rancid breath straight into my face and I was hurled from her domain.

The cave fractured and fell away around me, the pale blue light fading to darkness before brightening to gold once more. I could feel Merissa with me, her hand closing on my wrist as we were hurled from the chamber and thrown back out into the balmy heat of the trees beyond.

My back hit the forest floor hard, but pain was a construct which didn't appear here unless I willed it, so I simply let my head fall back into the blanket of leaves, my mind racing as I stared up at the gently shifting canopy overhead and the silent stars beyond.

The Veil slipped around me, the forest falling away until I found myself laying on soft grass instead, a tree in the shape of a Dragon rearing over me, the girl I loved more than life itself laying there with reddened eyes and a shattered heart beside the icy coffin that had been created for my body.

"Where is she?" Roxy breathed and I knew her soul was aching for more than just grief for me. She was in desperate need of her twin, not knowing where she was or what cruel twist of fate had befallen her.

I reached for her, but even I could feel the distance this time, my hand falling against hers without feeling it, unable to press through and take so much as a memory of her touch in that moment.

"God, I wish I could hate you the way I used to," she hissed, her words for me though she didn't know I could hear them.

Her hand curled into a fist instead of taking mine, thumping against the side of the coffin, the weight of her power causing a spiderweb of cracks to form all over the side of the casket before they solidified once more at her touch.

Roxy shoved herself to her feet while my heart tore itself apart in my chest and I was left as nothing but a witness to her grief as she stood at the edge of the cliff and screamed her pain for the world to feel, her agony trapped within a silencing bubble so that her suffering would stay contained to her own personal hell.

She was so alone. And though I was here, I wasn't, not really, not in any way that counted against the sharpness of her pain.

Roxy turned from the mountainside and stalked away, passing right through me without ever even knowing I was there, something breaking within me as I was forced to watch her leave.

I faded then, hopelessness stealing me away and leaving me trailing in the void for more time than I could be certain of, but as I drifted, lost in my own failures and fear for the woman I loved, I felt her again. It was like a yank on my leash, a tightening around my throat and a tether on my damn soul.

I found myself standing within a stone chamber behind Roxy while the other Heirs, my brother, Geraldine and the ex-Councillors all exchanged heated words which she didn't seem to be listening to, her pulse thundering in my ears as panic rose within her and she closed her eyes against the noise.

They were discussing our wedding, the Councillors gasping and questioning, Geraldine proclaiming it the most beautiful occasion that ever there was.

I reached for Roxy as I felt her need for me swelling, her pain turning to panic, her Order form rising within her flesh.

She didn't react to the touch of my hand on her skin, nor the feeling of my arms as they wound around her small frame from behind, but as my fingers met with the ruby pendant which still hung from her neck, I felt an echo of my old magic awakening within it.

I threw everything I had at that flicker of power, heat building within it, the flames licking against the red stone and burning its way to her skin. I needed her to know I hadn't left her, I needed her to believe that I was fighting to return to her too.

Roxy curled her fingers around the ruby pendant as she felt that heat, a shiver rolling through her flesh as finally, she felt me there, surrounding her, holding her, refusing to let go. She inhaled deeply, leaning back into me and stealing whatever strength she needed. I knew she felt it and the relief that spilled through me had a laugh breaking from my lips as the door banged open, and Roxy's eyes snapped open with it.

Her connection to me shattered but as The Veil tightened its hold on me, drawing me away, I knew she'd taken that strength from me, I knew she'd felt my presence even if only for a moment, and that truth gave me the strength I needed to go on too.

CATALINA

CHAPTER EIGHT

"Flans for fingers, I've done it again!" Hamish cursed and I turned to him, looking away from the view beyond our window in the Eternal Palace. Today it was a serene landscape of barren ice and lonely wilderness. Yesterday it had been a sandy beach with waves crashing against the shore.

"What have you done, my love?" I asked him, the ache in my chest building as I tried to focus on the here and now.

My boys, my only purpose in the world we had been so cruelly ripped from were both in agony and I couldn't help either of them. Xavier was drowning in the pain of his grief, trying to find his way to see any light in the world at all after having his brother and mother stolen from him so brutally, and Darius was chasing myths through The Veil in hopes of reuniting with his heart's greatest desire.

"Lost the thread of the nobble-gobble right when the picking is nigh," Hamish gasped, reaching towards an empty wall as if it might hold some answer for him.

My brow furrowed and I hurried to him, the silken gown I wore in this place flowing across my flesh like liquid metal, the silver colour of it catching in the light.

"The children?" I gasped, reaching him, and clasping his hand in mine.

"Nymphs approach at speed and I can only fear that that hoppity poppet Lionel can't be far behind," he said, his eyes wild with concern as he wrapped a hand around mine and looked into my eyes. "They prepare for a quarrel of darkest designs."

"Flans with jam, I can feel it!" Florence Grus cried as she spilled into the room, her arms flying wildly above her head as she sprinted for us, countless layers of multi-coloured silk wafting around her small frame as she ran.

"What's with the flan references?" I demanded, knowing this had to be one of Hamish's endearing oddities but needing further explanation to understand it.

"The whole world is on a baking scale, my dear," Hamish replied. "Bagels on the hoppity morn, scones in a crisis, jam tarts to alert the masses, and flans for a flap of flantastic design."

"So…flans are bad?" I surmised just as Florence reached us, taking hold of our clasped hands and holding them tight within her own, not letting go when I pulled back.

"Flans are the work of devils and maybugs," she whispered like she thought she might be overheard. "And I feel a whole pallet of them baking in my wobbling waters."

"Florry, I keep losing hold of our Gerry-pop whenever the wind turns wally-ways and tumbling back on my noggin in this place, but I feel her there, in greatest need-"

"Hold on to your fannies," Florence growled, her nails biting into the back of my hand as she tightened her grip on us. "Into the yonder we dive."

The Veil pulsed around us, a tug in my chest bringing Xavier and Geraldine to the forefront of my mind, my need to protect them becoming the only thing that existed to me as the living realm materialised around us in a clash of Nymphs and flaring fire.

I gasped as I took in the scene, a battle unfolding at the foot of the rebels' camp, our children fighting for their lives against those monsters once again, but this time I wasn't there to help.

I tried to reach for them in the carnage, but the world flashed with lightning strikes, time jumping from one place to the next, Phoenix fire giving way to thorny vines racing across the ground, a tidal wave careering downhill, Geraldine screaming a battle cry-

"Wait-please!" a voice I recognised called out among the lingering dregs of the carnage and I turned on the spot, the world falling still as I looked at the man Lionel had brought into our home time and again in the lead up to him seizing the crown. Miguel Polaris. "I wish to speak to the Vega queens. I am not your enemy."

"Kitty?" Hamish asked curiously as I led them closer to the Nymph who knelt naked on the ground in his Fae-like form, Antonia Capella standing over him with a snarl on her lips.

Seth and Max moved to stop her from ending the wretched creature's life and I stilled, uncertain what I was seeing, only knowing it was important.

"Look at the will-o'-the-wisps," Florence whispered so close to my damn ear that I flinched aside.

"The what?" I hissed.

"The glowing tendrils of fate. You can see them if you squint just so." She scrunched her face up into a tight ball, her eyes little more than slits as she looked at the man I had known only as Miguel. I hadn't been privy to the meetings Lionel took with him or his wife and brother-in-law, but I had been trotted out to entertain them when they had arrived at our house a few times. I'd figured out what they were after they departed one evening and Lionel threw a fit of rage over the audacity of the Nymphs who he was offering such a great alliance to.

Despite my better judgement, I followed Florence's lead, squinting at the man who knelt trembling in the dirt, my heart skipping a beat as I saw what she meant, tiny wisps of starlight dancing around him, darting away like miniature shooting stars, leading towards Tory who was stalking across the battlefield further up the hill.

There was a disagreement between the ex-Councillors and their sons and Caleb suddenly grabbed Miguel, shooting away with him, and dropping him at Tory's feet.

"Look to the dampening sky, my dears," Hamish breathed, drawing our attention to the forest where the Nymphs had come from, a dark shadow building across the sky which only we could see.

"They're going to have to flee," Florence breathed. "Before the stars show the great dunga-Dragoon where they are. Oh look how savage our Geraldine looks, Hamster." She nudged Hamish then waved wildly at Geraldine as if that might draw her attention. "Gerry-jammmm! Gerry-jam we are watching from the never-more! Love you, my beauteous sock puppet!"

I swallowed thickly, seeing the danger looming on the horizon, knowing she spoke the truth even if the only evidence we had of it was a shadow crossing the sun. But I knew Lionel. He had the rebels on the run and the scent of blood in his nose. He was coming.

I shoved back into The Veil, releasing my hold on Hamish and Florence before turning and sprinting away through the Eternal Palace.

Our rooms faded to corridors, Hamish and Florence's footsteps hounding after me as I ran.

I wasn't sure where I was going but the palace understood my need and Hail and Merissa's room appeared before me as I turned the next corner. I

95

hammered on the door marked with a Hydra and a Harpy, my chest tight with panic, time slipping away from me too fast.

"Is it Lionel?" Merissa gasped as she wrenched the door open for me and I nodded.

"The rebels are going on the run, I don't know where, but Lionel is hunting them. We need to help, to do something-"

Merissa turned to look at someone behind her and I leaned into the room, expecting Hail, but finding Azriel instead.

Lance's father had once been my dearest friend. He'd been just as trapped in the corrupt politics and dark desires of my husband as I had, his own wife undermining him at every turn. He'd seen what Lionel was doing to me, even if he hadn't fully understood. He'd tried to help where he could. And I trusted him completely.

"If enough of us flock to them we can shield their movements from the stars," he said, striding towards us, his brow furrowed as he thought on it. "Lionel is relying on the prophecies he can steal from Gabriel. If we can shield them, then maybe he won't be able to *see* them at all. At least for a little while. Perhaps long enough for them to escape."

"Who do we need?" I demanded, heavy footsteps sounding at my back, recognition tumbling through me as I turned to find Darius there.

"What is it?" he growled, the weight of his grief laying heavy on his shoulders, the need in him to return to the living making his figure appear more solid than most of the others in this place. My heart broke to look at him, my beautiful boy, his life stolen from him just as he had managed to rip it away from that monster who had fathered him.

"The rebels will all have souls watching them from this side of The Veil," Azriel said, taking a pulsing blue crystal shard from his pocket.

"What is that?" I asked.

"A piece of the orb from The Room of Knowledge," he replied, placing his hand over the top of it and closing his eyes. "I can send a message to the dead with it. I can rally them, get all who have a tie to the rebels to push into The Veil at once."

"Then do it," I commanded, the assertiveness surprising those around me, but this was my child's life on the line. Xavier had already lost too much and fought too hard. I wouldn't see him fall to the vindictive desires of his father while there was anything I could do to help.

Darius placed a hand on my shoulder as the crystal shard glowed brighter in Azriel's grasp, the blue light pulsing as an echo rolled throughout The Veil, a call going out to all those who needed to hear it.

"What now?" I demanded.

"Now, we fly," Azriel replied, a dark glint in his eyes.

The ground bucked beneath our feet and Darius tightened his hold on me, keeping me upright as the world flexed around us, light from the living realm spilling over us.

I blinked as I found the rebels gathering across the hill, many of them shifting into their Order forms, cries going out for them to keep their movements wild and follow without thought.

Behind me more of the dead pushed against The Veil, appearing between the crush of the rebel army, moving close to their loved ones, swelling the numbers surrounding us beyond measure. If only we could have done more than simply watch over them, if only these numbers could join forces with theirs and truly join in the fight against my ex-husband. But I would take the weight of our power shielding them if it was enough to get our loved ones to safety.

"What are they doing?" Darius asked, his focus on the rebels, his head turning to follow the passage of a Manticore as it flew overhead.

"They're dodging fate," I breathed, watching as the chaos unfurled around us. "Not making any firm decisions, keeping the stars guessing so that Lionel can't find them."

"Then let's make sure it works."

Darius's form began to tremble as he called on his Dragon, the roar that burst from him as he shifted making my hair billow across my face.

He leapt into the sky, a host of the dead racing upwards with him, those who could fly in their Order forms heading for the heavens, moving to act as a shield above the heads of the fleeing rebels below.

Hamish howled as he watched the rebels go, pointing out a lilac stallion as he galloped between the masses, making my heart swell with pride even as the pain of seeing the stumps where Xavier's wings should have been cut into me.

My beautiful boy galloped on, his friends whooping, howling, and laughing as they ran with him, my heart aching as I felt the pain which he couldn't shake even as he galloped.

"To the skies, my dearest dandelion?" Hamish offered and I nodded, the Dragon within me growling in delight as I called it forth.

Shifting wasn't like it had been before my death, the beast in me almost tearing from my skin entirely as the change took me, but I grasped hold of it and refused that impulse, staying one with that most intrinsic part of me as scales coated my skin and a roar escaped my lips.

Hamish leapt onto my back as I spread my wings and I took off into the sky with a triumphant bellow, The Veil fluttering against my flesh with every moment that passed. A thrill danced through me at the thought of Lionel seeing me now, offering a ride to my love, defying his nonsensical laws about Dragon supremacy and simply enjoying flexing my wings and showing the man I loved what I could do.

The dead rallied around me, roaring, howling, baying, and hollering in support of the rebels who fled for their lives below.

I could feel the stars turning their gaze towards them but as the army of the dead created a blanket of motion above their heads, the ethereal beings found their eyes blinded from the choices being made below.

I raced after Xavier, Darius roaring deafeningly as he swept in to fly at my side, our wingtips brushing against one another, the love I felt for him transcending my soul and reaching out to caress him as we found ourselves racing along with Xavier beneath us.

Hail bellowed from the heavens in his many-headed Hydra form and the rebels upped their pace as if they could feel the strength of the dead wrapping around them, protecting them, and shielding them on their journey across the land, towards the distant sea.

The world was alive with motion, the rebels a stampede which never faltered as the coast rose in the distance and they charged for it as one.

The golden glow of The Veil grew around us as we all pushed beyond the limits of what was allowed, our souls brushing against that impenetrable barrier, refusing its call as it tried to draw us back.

We held on, defiant in the face of protecting the ones we loved, determined to see them safe, whatever the cost.

The rebels finally made it to the coast, and I watched with victory soaring through my chest as they carved a lump of land clean away from the edge of the continent and set out to sea where the wind, the rain and chance could choose their path and no Seer could predict it.

They were safe.

And with that all-encompassing knowledge, the army of the dead were summoned back into the embrace of The Veil, the glow brightening until all sight of the living realm was lost to us. But it didn't matter. Because it had worked. And the rebels were safe once more.

HAIL

CHAPTER NINE

I roared to the sky in my Hydra form, almost feeling the rush of the wind in the living realm before The Veil tugged me deeper into its grip.

Merissa came flying towards me, wings of silver spread wide and a look of fear in her eyes. Her fingers found mine as my Order retreated and she tugged me along before The Veil could snatch me away again.

I felt the call of my son before his name passed her lips.

"Gabriel," she gasped.

The world swirled around me, furious stars shimmering in my periphery before we arrived in the Royal Seer's chamber. We wore the fine clothes we'd been in before, both of us forged of ethereal magic now that we had no true bodies anymore, no longer left naked by the shift.

Gabriel gazed unseeingly into this place which amplified the messages of the stars. I could hear them whispering, a rush of words spoken in a language so old that it had no name I knew of.

We ran to Gabriel, resting our hands on his arms and his visions burst out around us, flashes of untold futures, coming and going in bursts of light that left me frantic. Death, chaos, and war carried to us on the wings of fate, promises of so much pain yet to come. I could hardly stand to watch as my daughters fell to ruin before my eyes alongside Gabriel's dear family, including my grandson.

"This can't be their fate," I growled, my hand tightening on his arm and he blinked up at me as if seeing me for a moment. "There must be a path that does not end like this."

His eyes shuttered, wincing as he fought to bear the weight of it all.

"We're here, Gabriel," Merissa called to him, but he showed no sign that he heard either of us.

"My love, what can we do?" I begged of her, feeling so desperately useless to my boy in his time of need.

Another fate flashed into existence; Gabriel throwing his head back against the throne he was lashed to, attempting to crack his own skull and kill himself before Lionel could seize the fates from his mind.

"No!" Merissa screamed, and relief only found me when that fate played out, showing it would fail regardless.

I heaved a sigh, though no true breath parted my lips.

The visions slowed around me, and I gazed at one of an island floating in a calm sea, the very piece of land the rebels had carved from the earth and taken as a place of refuge.

My throat thickened as Gabriel tried to turn his mind from it, the fate flickering darkly before coming back into full focus. His shoulders relaxed as he realised he couldn't predict its movements, the island floating at random, this way and that into the far-flung regions of the ocean, avoiding the power of The Sight in doing so.

The Veil tugged us back, trying to pull us from our son and we were washed away into a pitch-black tide, tossed this way and that as we tried to hold on.

"Hail!" Merissa cried, her fingers finding mine as always, and together our power was undeniable in the face of the stars. "We cannot leave him."

Our souls tangled as one, and we became nothing more than a pinprick of light in an endless chasm of darkness. But then we were back, finding our way to him across the realms, even if we weren't truly there at all.

Time had passed, and Gabriel was in the hands of Vard as Lionel watched on with impatience. Vard's eyes had slid into one bulbous orb and his hand lay flat to Gabriel's forehead, forcing him to hand over his visions.

Gabriel thrashed and fought with all he had, but Vard got his way, descending on my son's visions and snaring them for himself with a greedy grunt of satisfaction.

"You rat," I snarled in Vard's face. "You're nothing. You don't hold a speck of the power in your veins that my son possesses. His mother is the greatest Seer who ever lived, and he will match her in every way."

"He will surpass me," she said powerfully. "I *saw* it in life, and I *see* it now. His gifts can transcend all that has ever been known in this world."

Gabriel murmured a plea for the disgusting Cyclops to stop, but he did no such thing, taking all he could with a hungry delight.

"Finally," Lionel said in relief, and I turned to him with a sneer, placing myself between him and Gabriel even though I was nothing to him now. "Take everything, Vard. Leave no vision behind."

"But it could kill him, sire. He is already waning," Vard said just as a seizure took over my boy and a bellow of agony left him.

"Fight it, I know you can," Merissa half sobbed, wrapping her arms around Gabriel.

I turned to them with terror in my soul, The Veil thinning, offering a passage for a coming soul.

"You cannot have him!" I bellowed at the stars and my Hydra roared somewhere deep within The Veil, wings spread wide as it tried to hold off Gabriel's passing.

"I said take it all," Lionel snapped. "If you kill him, I will tear out your liver and feed it to you. Is that motivation enough?"

"Y-yes, sire," Vard stammered in fear, his power pouring into our son and making him shudder.

The stars were whispering in a rush of words, the glimmer of their touch hovering at the periphery of my vision but I shut them out, holding them back with whatever power my soul still possessed.

Those whispers changed from inaudible to loud, and words rang out among them all.

Take heart, son of fate.

My gaze locked with Merissa's, hope dancing between us at the strength the celestial beings were offering Gabriel. They weren't tearing him into their arms, they were offering him a chance.

I turned from them, throwing my power into Gabriel instead while Merissa's silhouette began to shine with her own offering of strength.

Gabriel dragged in a breath as Vard withdrew from him, assuring me he would survive. The Veil tugged us back once more, stealing us into the place where we truly belonged now.

Merissa collided with me, hands winding around my neck, and I gripped her tight, placing a kiss upon her brow.

"He's alright," I said heavily.

"We have to go back to be sure he is well, then we must seek out Gwendalina. I fear so terribly for her Hail. Since Lionel almost killed her..." Her voice cracked with terror and I held her even tighter, the two of us united in our fear.

"Let's go," I whispered and together we pushed against The Veil, seeking out Gabriel once more.

Time had fallen away again, mere moments to us equalling hours here where Gabriel was being dragged towards a cage of night iron in the palace amphitheatre, two brutish Dragon Shifters unlocking it and pushing him inside. Gabriel fell to the ground in exhaustion as the door banged shut behind him, and the two Fae left him there alone.

Gabriel's fingers fisted in the sand, his eyes closed and fatigue pulling him into sleep. Slumber was the easiest way to reach a living Fae, their mind in a state of in between where the dead could visit. And if our connection was strong enough, if they pined for us deeply, sometimes we were able to gift them memories, or forge realities that never were for them to view as dreams.

Merissa knelt beside Gabriel, her wings unfurling from her back and coiling around him as she embraced him, encasing him in a cocoon of soft silver feathers.

"I love you, Gabriel," she whispered. "You're my little star, my guiding light."

I pulled on a memory of Merissa cuddling Gabriel as a little boy, offering it to him like luring a star down from the heavens and laying it in his hands. If it found him in the darkness of his sleep, it might just bring him peace for a while, but in this place of torture and imprisonment, I didn't know if it would be strong enough to soothe him.

Time fell away in the blink of an eye, and reality changed before me. One moment, Gabriel was laying on the floor in the arms of his mother and the next he was standing in front of Lance Orion in the sand outside the night iron cage.

This amphitheatre set a feeling of all-too-familiar horrors crawling down my spine. Murders commanded at my hand, bloody, brutal shows of death to the chorus of a bloodthirsty crowd. The guilt of it would never leave me, even now I understood whose orders had really been passing my lips. Nothing could rid me of the atrocities I had dealt out under Lionel Acrux's Dark Coercion, not even death.

"You will sift through his fates, Gabriel," Lionel instructed, gesturing to Lance. "And Vard will syphon your visions from you while you do so. You will leave no stone unturned; I wish to see every fate in his future."

"I'm sorry, Orio," Gabriel murmured, and Lance let his head hang forward, accepting what had to be done. Vard hurried to him, slicking his tongue across his lips, a sickening excitement on his face. The ugly scar crossing his missing eye held only a little satisfaction to me, though now I wished I'd aimed truer when I'd given him that scar, and the sun steel blade had driven deep into his skull instead.

The Cyclops touched the back of Gabriel's head, and I whispered a prayer to the stars to protect my daughter's Elysian Mate.

The world flickered and time danced like dust in the wind, scattered away across the universe. I stood closer to Gabriel when I re-emerged and Merissa frowned as she drew near, taking my hand and tugging on the threads of her old gifts, working to show us the visions that Gabriel was seeking in Orion's future. Suddenly they sparked around us in the fabric of the atmosphere, like burning parchment turning to embers before our eyes.

There was nothing but a blur of torment, Orion on his knees in a bloody chamber, his arms chained above his head, and I felt a torment of my own at seeing his suffering, gritting my teeth as I weathered out the nasty visions of this man paying the price of my daughter's curse. It was impossible to deny the gratitude I felt in the face of it too, his torture buying her a chance at salvation. His love for her was bound in blood, his body a sacrifice on an altar to save her from damnation, and there was no denying the profoundness in that.

Among the cruelty and the darkness coating his fate, a glint of possibility twisted between the cords of destiny. Gabriel's jaw pulsed as he *saw* it and I felt powerful magic forming in his mind as he worked to secure that single glimmer of hope and shield it from Vard's eyes. Merissa guided him, securing that piece of information from Vard, she and my son working as one to weave a shield around it. She knew the ways of The Sight far too intimately for me to dare to interfere.

When Gabriel had that vision secured, kept well away from Vard's prying intrusion, Merissa helped me *see* it, the future playing out brighter than all the others like sunlight was woven into it.

Lance found a way into the walls of The Palace of Souls through the door I had detected in the back wall of his and Gwendalina's cage. He wound down the passageway I'd long ago walked the path of myself, knowing exactly where it headed.

Finally, he arrived before the bright silver door with a huge coat of arms at its centre, the Vega crest glittering there, ancient and brimming with the power that held that door shut.

The vision shifted to show Lance walking through the heart of the Vega treasury, a place of wonder that held priceless heirlooms, all of it waiting for my children to claim. The Vega trove was a collection which had been gathered and added to for centuries, and soon, it would damn well be theirs.

The fleeting final moments in the visions showed Lance with a book in his hands, the cover woven from bronze feathers, and the look in his eyes gave me more hope than I'd had in weeks.

"Wait," I gasped as the vision began to fade. "Merissa, hold the vision."

Her forehead creased as she concentrated, desperately trying to tug on the strings of fate to keep it open to me.

"Hail, I can't," she cried, her voice an echo as The Veil dragged us back and the living realm faded rapidly.

But as we were snatched away into the grasp of our true location, I *saw* it. A shimmering silver music box with diamonds studded onto its sides and an intricate engraving of the Libra weighing scales on the lid.

In all my years as king, I had never noticed it there among the masses of beautiful items. In truth, it was not a thing that easily caught the eye in the face of all the gleaming gemstones and artefacts in that place, sitting unassuming on a shelf full of glittering trinkets. I didn't know its importance yet, but by the moon, I felt the weight of its significance in that vision. The stars were purring in my ears, urging me towards it, and for the first time in a very, very long time, I had a path handed to me which was guided by their divine hands. A path fit for a living Fae, yet a long dead soul had been given it all the same.

Merissa's hand found mine - like always - and a smile curled my lips.

I had not been handed it. *We* had. Of course. She and I were one, and this fortune was ours to share. A gilded road paved for two lost souls, so perhaps we could be of true use to our loved ones at long last.

"Did you *see* it?" I cupped her face in my palm and she nodded, possibilities dancing in her eyes.

"Gabriel did not," she said in awe. "The stars offered it to us and us alone."

"Then they must know we can do something with it," I said fiercely, leaning down and capturing her lips with mine.

We were back in our rooms now, and I stole a desperate, aching moment with her against me. Her mouth moved with mine as perfectly as if it was designed for me – which of course it was. My mate, my creature.

My palm scored a line up her spine as I drew her closer, the temptation of her as keen as ever. Even in death we were infatuated with one another, her taste as sweet as it had been in life. She could never truly die in my eyes, her soul would shine on no matter where we went, and mine would follow ever on, the two of us dancing away into the darkness of the universe if that was the only place left to go.

Her fingers scored lines down the rigid muscles of my arms, and I tugged her hair in my fist, exposing her neck to my teeth. I bit her with savagery, and she moaned, the sound like a dark caress against my soul.

Someone cleared their throat, and I snapped my head up, finding Marcel there loitering by our window to the living realm. "Is this a good time to let you know I'm here?"

"What are you doing in our chambers?" I barked.

"I...um..." He blinked heavily and the fringes of his soul shuddered. Then he was gone.

"Finally," I sighed, tugging my wife against me more firmly, but she untangled herself from my arms and gave me a worried look.

"I'd better go to him," she said. "He keeps scattering lately."

"Then let him scatter," I said, striding after her.

A knock came at the door, and I growled as Merissa slipped away from me again, walking across the room to answer it.

Darius stood there with a frown on his face and darkness emanating him so deeply it seemed to taint the air around him.

"Yes?" I clipped.

"I'm here for Merissa," he said, looking to her.

"What did you find?" she asked keenly, and I glanced between the two of them, sensing some secret in the air.

"About what?" I asked.

"Nothing that involves you, relic," Darius said, striding into my chambers as if he owned them.

"Hail, I need to talk to him," Merissa said, giving me a pointed look. "Go to Azriel and tell him what we *saw*."

"What did you *see*?" Darius asked, intrigued.

"Nothing that involves you, poor choice," I said in the exact same tone he'd used on me.

I walked past him and exited the room, my mood souring by the minute, but it lightened a little when I focused on my task. My path.

I made my way to Azriel's rooms, but a half visible soul fluttered into my path before I could get there.

"Lost…lost the boy. Doesn't remember. The unforgettable has forgotten the forgettable," Marcel muttered to himself, flickering in and out of existence then looking to me in confusion.

I made to step past him, but he floated into my way, head cocking to one side. "He remembers you."

"Marcel, I am busy," I snipped.

"Must have been nice," he said, smiling sadly. "I shared a life with him in visions and impossible futures, but you…you touched him skin to skin. Fates bound. Paths interwoven."

The Destined Door to the beyond crawled into existence from the shadows at his back, the Eternal Palace sighing and groaning as it offered a soul passage beyond this place of in between, to the final resting place…wherever that may be.

Marcel's form flickered again, and he turned to look at the door, his feet not walking now, just drifting, toes scraping against the fine carpet. His lips parted and his soul began to fragment, pieces of him turning dark, cold, and lifeless, like chips of bark falling from a fire.

"It is so rare for him to think of me at all," Marcel whispered, the lights overhead flashing on and off as the darkness of that door crept deeper into the corridor.

I recoiled from it as it called to me too, anchored here by the love my family felt for me beyond this realm. There had been a time when my children never thought of me, years of them not knowing of mine and Merissa's existence, but we'd held on whenever the door had come for us. And once they had started wondering about us, learning of their heritage, seeing the visions and memories Merissa had left behind for them, we became rooted here once more, and now I felt almost as solid as I had when I was Fae. I hadn't exactly been overjoyed when my son found a father figure in a private investigator who had a fondness for hookers, but at least Bill Fortune had been there for him.

Marcel had never met Gabriel, and our boy hadn't spared much thought for his biological father so far as I was aware. And now that he was in the midst of a war, he had far bigger concerns to occupy him.

"If I could tell him I love him, just once, before I have to go..." Marcel pleaded with the door, the yawning chasm within beckoning him closer.

"By the stars," Azriel gasped as he stepped out of his room across the hall, hurrying forward to help. "Are you moving on?"

"I do not wish to," Marcel croaked. "But if I stay, I shall be lost in the nevermore. Forgotten, cracking, shattering."

"He'll become a remnant," I muttered. "Probably time to go then, Marcel. You had a good run." I clapped him on the shoulder, steering him towards the door.

"Yes...time to go, I suppose," Marcel said, hanging his head and looking about as heartbroken as one could get. He'd probably feel better when he was beyond that door.

Azriel cut me a look that said I was being an ass, and he was one of the few people in this world who I allowed to declare me as such.

I huffed a breath.

"Gabriel will think of you again," I said, and Marcel looked to me, a desperate longing written into his features. Features which were an echo of my son's. Everything about him reminded me of him, from his height to the deep bronze colouring of his skin, to the breadth of his shoulders, his features a clear foretelling of Gabriel's.

"How can he think of me when I am nothing to think of?" he whispered, and the door inched closer.

"We shall make you something to think of," Azriel said, his tone far kinder than mine as he stepped closer to the scattering soul. "Gabriel needs you. He just doesn't know it yet. But we will find a way to help him know you."

The door snapped shut and vanished as simply as that. Marcel's feet touched the floor again and he swept forward to embrace Azriel, his black wings fluttering into existence and slapping me in the face.

I spat a snarl, batting the feathers away and shooting Azriel a look that told him I was already regretting keeping Marcel here. But then I remembered why I had come this way at all.

"Azriel, the stars offered Merissa and I a vision. A true vision, just for us."

"It cannot be," he said in disbelief, releasing Marcel and hounding toward me.

"It can. I *saw* something of great significance in the living realm. A music box."

"A music box?" he gasped, then turned on his heel, running for his door.

I shared a tense look with Marcel then pushed past him, feeling him sweeping after me on silent wings.

Inside, I found Azriel rifling through a wooden chest, tossing artefacts left and right, shimmering things that glowed or sparked or hummed with the darkest kind of power. I looked around the familiar House Captain's room in Aer Tower, a sense of nostalgia creeping over me.

"Will you ever tell me the secrets of how you came to possess these things, Azriel?" I asked with a hint of humour.

Azriel grinned up at me from his knees, his black hair wild and unkempt as always. "Deals with the dead, mostly. Far more items have made it beyond The Veil in pockets of magic and through mishaps of the stars than you can imagine."

"What did you have to bargain with?" I scoffed.

"I did not come empty handed beyond The Veil," he said with a dark grin. "I was well prepared for my death."

"In my kingdom, there are people like you who we call the Shaded," Marcel said, moving closer to examine Azriel's trove. "Fae who deal in all things dark, knowing how to wield artefacts that perhaps should never be wielded."

"There are no light or dark objects. All are neutral," Azriel said. "It's a common misconception, brought in by fear mongering from the royal family. They outlawed the use of so-called dark magic, condemning it alongside the Nymphs. Our enemies were far more adept at its use than most Fae could claim to be. But in time, the knowledge that was burned or destroyed resurfaced on the black market, and wielders like me studied it in secret."

"In Voldrakia, the Shaded have their hands cut off and are banished to the wastes for using such magic if they are caught," Marcel said grimly.

"Yes, well Emperor Adhara always was something of a barbarian and his heir is no better," I muttered coldly. He and Merissa's mother still existed here and I was forced to endure their company from time to time, though I avoided it whenever I could.

"Says the Savage King," Marcel taunted.

"You know exactly why I was given that name," I hissed, pointing at him.

"No, do remind me," Marcel said, innocently. "Or will you be holding another seminar in The Room of Knowledge like last time?"

"I have a right to clear my name."

"To every soul who walks through The Veil?" Marcel taunted. "Seems a little overkill."

I opened my mouth to retort, but Azriel grabbed something from the depths of his chest, holding it up with a look of triumph.

"Here we are," he said, rising to his feet and holding out his hand, showing us a tattered notebook with a faded red cover. "My hunt for the Guild Stones was an arduous one, but it did not come without reward. I discovered six of the stones in my lifetime, well seven actually if you include the one which I know to be in the hands of the FIB. But I didn't manage to recover that one before my death. However, the six I did manage to claim now reside with my son thankfully, and I found one of them inside *this*."

He thumbed through the pages and paused on a sketched picture of a music box that was very similar to the one I had *seen*. Although this one held the symbol of a scorpion on its lid, for Scorpio.

I snatched the book from his hand, examining the thing and reading the annotations around it. The description of a haunting game held within its depths that Azriel had taken on involving a metal tank that had filled with water while he worked to solve a difficult puzzle and a monstrous half-scorpion-half fish had tried to eat him.

"Why didn't you ever tell me about this? I could have faced this with you." I looked up at him.

"Well, you were dead," he said simply.

"Right, that," I said with a note of dark amusement colouring my voice.

"Deader than a doornail," Marcel sung, moving between the two of us and looking down at the book. His black wings curled around us and one of the feathers tickled my ear, making me jerk my head away.

"This doesn't really concern you." I elbowed him away, but he didn't budge.

"Oh, I am not so sure about that," he said.

"Did you manage to glean any clues from the stars about the whereabouts of anymore Guild Stones?" I asked, knowing full well he hadn't as Merissa had informed me of their failings.

"No, but-"

"And have any of the glimpses you had of them in the past led to one of us discovering a Guild Stone?" I pressed.

"No but-"

"I rest my case," I cut over Marcel again and he scowled at me.

"You'll never guess where I found this music box," Azriel said, a mischievous look crossing his features and drawing our attention back to him.

"Where?" I prompted.

"King's Hollow, hidden in a secret chamber in the depths of the tree bough," he said. "I knew there were other music boxes, but I never had any luck finding them. The trail went cold after I discovered the truth of the Hollow."

"The truth?" I asked keenly.

His eyes glittered with knowledge. "I'll show you."

"And me?" Marcel asked hopefully. "Is Gabriel in your story?"

"Er, no," Azriel said, and Marcel's face dropped.

"It's a very old story and it took me some time to piece it together," Azriel said. "But it has holes…" He trailed off, getting that look on his face that said he was about to have an epiphany. Ever the damn scientist. "Wait a minute! By the stars, I never realised…dammit, why did I never realise it?"

He glanced around his room, then grabbed something shiny from his wooden chest and shoved it into his pocket before marching from the room with intention. Marcel whipped me in the fucking face again with his wing as he ran after him, and I hurried to keep up.

"Marcel," I snapped.

"Yes?" he called innocently.

"Do that again and I'll rip your wings off and shove them up your ass."

"Touchy little king today, aren't you?" he said as I made it to his side and we followed Azriel down the long corridor at a fierce pace, his shoulder bashing mine as we each worked to get ahead. "You never did get over my divine connection with Merissa."

"Get her name off of your tongue," I hissed. "Whatever connection you think you had with my wife was extremely short lived, mine is ever enduring and indestructible."

"Whatever you say, mighty king. But you'll never understand what it is to share a connection that could never truly be."

"I experience that frequently," I said. "I simply walk past a random Fae and forget their existence in an instant. And there you have it, a connection that never was."

"Oh, Hail," he said like I was so naïve. "Seers know so many lives. I may not have shared time with Merissa in the living realm beyond our single night of burning passion and desperate want but-"

"Enough," I snapped.

He cast me a sideways look. "There is no need to envy me."

"That is the last thing I feel towards you."

"Mmmhmm," he hummed, clearly not believing me.

Azriel turned onto the stairway at the end of the hall then headed up the spiralling steps with Marcel and I in his shadow. He climbed three floors before turning down another corridor of endless doors. Deep green walls reached high towards a dark ceiling where a gold mist swirled like a living creature, writhing and shifting as if it had noticed our passage beneath it.

Azriel walked tirelessly on down the corridor, murmuring numbers under his breath as if he was counting the doors he passed. Finally, he stopped in front of a door that was just like all the others, moving forward and hammering his fist against it.

After a beat, the door swung open and a beautiful woman came into view with tumbling blonde curls that ran all the way to her waist, looking to be in her mid to late twenties – though that didn't mean much around here. Once you stepped beyond The Veil you could choose whatever age to appear as. Some stayed as they been upon their deaths, others grew younger, while others aged, all finding a natural place they felt at peace with.

The woman's skin was a rich brown, her eyes as bright as two golden coins, and she wore a shimmering bronze dress that cascaded down to her bare feet. Her movements were fluid and graceful, a confidence about her that was obvious at once.

"Azriel," she said warmly, a purr rumbling through her chest.

"It's good to see you again, Felisia," Azriel said with equal warmth. "This is-"

"Shit a potato, it's the Savage King." She inclined her head to one side, her lips tilting in a grin. "And this stranger is?"

"Marcel," he said, holding out his hand and she snatched it, shaking it vigorously, then tossing it away like it was a mouldy tissue.

I stifled a snort as Marcel's eyebrows rose in surprise.

"Come inside, come on, don't wait out there for a fart to come swallow you up," she urged, wafting us past her and we were forced to brush past her into her rooms.

My lips parted as my feet hit the solid boards of a pirate ship that was laden with treasure, the huge vessel rocking gently on a calm sea that stretched away in every direction. The night sky twinkled above, and the sails fluttered in a wind that felt impossibly real.

"This is…" I had no words.

"Home," she said brightly, then stuck two fingers in her mouth and whistled sharply.

Two women and one man came running up from a stairway that led beneath deck, all of them beautiful with the most incredible hair. The man reached us first and I took in his dark gleaming skin and eyes as bright as the moon, his black hair tumbling over his chest which was carved from muscle.

"I'm Purrsy," he said, fucking smouldering at me as he offered me his hand, then took Marcel and Azriel's in turn.

"Furnanda," the closest woman said, her hair as white as dove feathers, fluttering around her in a sheet of silky strands that looked almost liquid beneath the starlight. Her pale body was inked in places, each mark a constellation that held a sleeping lion or lioness within it.

"Kitsy," the final woman introduced herself, her hair a river of chocolate falling down her back, and her eyes that same deep hue. She wore black leather armour, her rich bronze skin adorned in places with little scrawled tattoos, words written in a language I didn't know.

"This is my pride," Felisia announced, practically glowing as she looked between the three of them with love brimming in her eyes. "Well…technically everyone in life thought Purrsy was our king, but I was always head cat, right Purrsy?"

"Always," he smirked.

"She's our queen," Furnanda breathed, a want in her eyes that blazed as she looked upon the Lioness Shifter who had claimed her.

"Our everything," Kitsy added.

"And you're mine," Felisia said, then whipped around to face us, tossing something up and down in her hand. I realised it was the piece of the orb Azriel had been carrying around lately. "Is this a gift or did you come unprepared for my light fingers?"

"A gift I knew you would claim whether I offered it up or not," he said.

"And this," she said, twirling a black feather between her fingers as her golden eyes turned on Marcel. "This is mine now."

He glanced at his wings in surprise. "How did you pull it out without me feeling it?"

"She is Felisia Night," Azriel laughed.

"Night," I said, suddenly realising who she was. "The famous thief who managed to steal from The Palace of Souls?"

"In the flesh." She beamed, white teeth glinting at me. "Well, not quite.

I kind of left the flesh behind when I died and all. Happens to the best of us, does it not, old king?"

"And the worst of us," I agreed.

"If only the worst of us would die a little sooner." She smiled, tossing the piece of the orb up and down in her palm. "I've been watching the war. My favourite descendants have gotten themselves in such trouble. One in the rebel army, another locked in Darkmore. I love the chaos my family creates."

"They still think of you?" Marcel asked forlornly.

"Yes, they do. I'm a legend, see? Over a hundred years dead and they still think of me."

"As they should," Kitsy said, stepping closer to her and gently combing her fingers through Felisia's hair.

She nuzzled her, the two of them sharing a light kiss before Felisia rounded on Azriel. "What is it then? You want something. Spit it out before you choke on it, Azzy."

"I have just connected some dots that were right in front of me this whole time," he said, and I was surprised he didn't object to the nickname.

Furnanda suddenly pounced on Marcel, knocking him to the ground and snaring a mouthful of feathers between her teeth.

"Argh, what in the hundred realms are you doing?" Marcel batted the Lioness Shifter off, kicking her away and Furnanda leapt to her feet, spitting out some feathers with a laugh.

"Caught ya, little bird," she growled. "Can't escape me."

"I wasn't running," Marcel hissed as Felisia and her pride laughed riotously, and I sniggered at him on the floor.

"Then run next time, I'll still catch you." Furnanda gnashed her teeth at Marcel and the Harpy bristled, shoving to his feet and squaring his shoulders in preparation of a fight.

"Nice catch, baby." Felisia tiptoed over to Furnanda, twirling her finger under her chin and kissing her deeply. Furnanda pulled Felisia against her possessively and Purrsy nuzzled into them, laying a hand on Felisia too.

"Before an orgy descends, can you get the information we came for," I muttered to Azriel as Kitsy went hurrying over to join their heated embrace.

"Fucking cats," Marcel growled, straightening out his wings.

Azriel cleared his throat. "Felisia, I have a question or two, if you don't mind?"

Felisia untangled herself from the three sets of hands pawing at her and came padding back to us with curiosity in her eyes. "What is it? I can sense something crazy exciting about all of this."

"Hail has been handed a fate. A true one," Azriel revealed, and Felisia looked to her pride in delight then back to us.

"And what has it got to do with me?" she asked, eyes whipping between us. I realised the piece of the orb was now in Purrsy's hands and he was examining it with interest.

"You are one of the four who founded King's Hollow," Azriel announced.

Felisia grinned from ear to ear. "How did you figure that out?"

"I'm hunting the Guild Stones. I found one hidden there. I had discovered pieces of your story, and it has just now occurred to me that for the stones to have been claimed in the ways they were so long ago, an incredible thief would have been necessary. And the timeline it all occurred in well…that places you at Zodiac Academy right when it all happened," Azriel said, a hint of smugness to his words. "You were famed for the crime of stealing a set of priceless jewels from The Palace of Souls, so…perhaps those jewels were stones, and perhaps those stones were Guild Stones."

Azriel had always been an intelligent asshole, and Felisia's growing smile said he was right on the mark.

"So what do you want from me, Azzy?" she asked, tossing her hair over one shoulder.

"I am hoping the gift I presented you with might be worth your tale from beginning to end, to fill in the gaps I could never fill," Azriel asked hopefully.

"What use is an old story in a treasure hunt you can no longer chase the tail of?" she asked, considering him.

"My son is chasing it," he said. "He is on the path of reforming the Zodiac Guild once and for all, to restore balance in the Fae realm."

"Lance Orion," she said with a light laugh. "My decendant Leon likes him. He licked him once, you know?"

"That makes him his," Kitsy said, and Felisia nodded her agreement with a serious look.

"Right, well, okay," Azriel said, clearly unsure how to respond to that. "So, you'll help?"

"A story for a trinket and a feather," Felisia pushed her lips out as she thought on it. "Alright. But I want something from him too." She pointed at me.

"I don't have anything," I scoffed. "This is death, I don't possess items here like Azriel has managed. My trove remains with the living."

"Oh, big bad king, you have so much, silly bean," Felisia said, laughing openly at me. "Memories and regrets and loves and losses."

I gave her a dry look. "And how will I give you one of those?"

Felisia and her pride laughed again, all of them mocking us like they were in on some joke I didn't get.

"She'll steal it, dead man," Purrsy said.

"Don't worry about the whens and the hows." Felisia moved forward to clap my cheek like she was a far bigger threat than she appeared. "I'll deal with all that."

"Fine," I huffed, just wanting to get on with this, sure she couldn't steal any such thing from me anyway. "Tell us then."

"I'll do you one better." She danced away from us and Purrsy and Furnanda whipped her into the air, placing her on their shoulders between them and gripping her legs as Kitsy sprang ahead of them, landing lithely on the stairs leading below deck.

"I guess that's our cue to follow," Marcel murmured and Azriel took the lead as we moved below deck on the rocking ship.

More treasures awaited us there, piles of gold and shining gemstones, though I wasn't sure how much of it was real and how much was just an illusion for their living space.

A mirror rested against one wall, the frame encrusted with sapphires and an intricate design of seashells threaded between them in the silver metal, presumably their window to the living realm.

Felisia beckoned us closer as the members of her pride placed her down before it and memories stirred within it like a pool of mysteries.

As I closed in on her, she slid something cool into my palm and I frowned down at the shining purple crystal she'd placed there before she handed one each to Azriel and Marcel.

"What is this?"

"A piece of amethyst crystal," Azriel said, turning it over in his palm with his thumb.

"It will let you live it, not just see it, new friends." Felisia stepped back, allowing us to close in on the mirror.

A vision of Zodiac Academy whirled into existence, and the amethyst grew colder in my palm. Before I could decide whether I truly wanted to go through with this, I lurched forward, crashing into the memory and landing right in the mind of Felisia Night herself.

DARIUS

CHAPTER TEN

"I need to know the limitations," I said firmly; folding my arms as I remained standing over Merissa who had taken a seat on the throne she sometimes shared with Hail.

"It's not that simple." She pressed a hand to her face, closing her eyes and leaning back into the throne. "The limitations are all based on your connection to the person you're trying to affect. If someone is in the depths of their grief, begging the stars to return you to them then it is possible to do far more than if someone simply gives you a passing, wistful thought."

"The first one. Roxy is grieving. She wants me back. So tell me the limitations of what I can do with that level of need. She has to hunt for the ether that Mordra told me about. I need her to go looking for it, so I have to be able to send her after it."

"You can maybe flip the page of a book or stir the wind. Perhaps pull a particular tarot card from a deck she's-"

"Not good enough," I growled.

"I once heard of a Fae who claimed to have been able to draw a heart in the steam left on a mirror for his wife. There were a lot of doubts over the truth of that claim though."

"A single heart won't be enough. Roxy needs the path laid before her feet. She needs to seek out this missing knowledge and do whatever it is that Mordra believes might be possible to create a trade with the ferryman and send me back across."

"Darius…" Merissa got to her feet, that pitying look in her dark eyes once more, but I shook my head, turning from her and waving off the embrace she looked so close to offering.

"I don't need your pity any more than your doubt. I just need to know how to send a message to my wife," I insisted.

"I've told you all I know," she said softly, reaching for me despite my rejection, her hand landing on my arm while I kept my back to her. "Try reaching out when you feel the pull at its sharpest. You'll have the most power then. Her grief is so violent and her power so great that perhaps you'll be able to manage more than those who came before you."

I nodded, taking in her words and thanking her before stalking from the room once more, leaving her there.

I hated this place. The way the corridors melted and reformed around me, no room ever remaining the same as my own needs and wants were anticipated, any and all desires offered up to me. Memories billowed through the golden haze around me, moments I'd stolen with the woman I loved or with my dearest friends, each of them playing out like they had when I'd lived them. Whenever I found myself in the near barren room which belonged to me here, I simply stood staring at the window to the living realm, watching them, wanting them, needing to return more than anything.

But I didn't want to sit in a pool of the past, rehashing those times, revisiting those feelings. I wanted the life that had been stolen from me, not the one I had already experienced.

Time shimmered around me, shifting, stalling, speeding up again. I had no sense of what day, week or even month it was in the living realm, my reality too skewed by this place to grasp the concept of time which had once seemed so linear to me.

But then it struck me. Like a hammer to the chest, the weight of her grief collided with me, and I was hurled through the mass of golden nothingness, thrown against the cloying barrier of The Veil and somehow standing in an unfamiliar room in a building I had never seen in life.

Black and red roses bloomed across the wall and ceiling, a copper bathtub sitting beneath a window formed from ice, a huge bed perfectly made up in the centre of the space.

But all of that paled to irrelevance as I looked to her, the girl who had captured my soul so completely that it would only ever be hers.

Roxy crumpled where she sat on the edge of the bed, a silencing bubble bursting from her a beat before she screamed with a raw and brutal energy that was so filled with pain that it rocked the centre of me, making me quake where I stood, the world tilting around us.

She slipped from the bed, falling to the floor and I followed, reaching for her and pushing against The Veil with all I had, needing her to feel me here in this time of such sharp need.

She screamed louder, the power of her Phoenix erupting from her flesh, wings of brightest fire burning from her spine and flames hotter than the depths of a volcanic pit exploding around her body, incinerating her clothes as the bed was sent flying back away from her.

I dropped down, reaching for her, the flames unable to touch me in the place between places, my fist closing around the ruby pendant which hung from her neck, my own energy coursing into it as I willed her to feel it, to feel me there with her.

"You can bear this," I growled, urging her to feel those words even if she couldn't hear them. "You can shoulder this pain for now and I swear to you it will pass. I will return to you."

Her soul seemed to shimmer through the light of the flames, eyes of thunderous rage and power lifting and looking straight into mine, as if she could see me or at least feel me there with her.

I threw all the knowledge I'd learned from Mordra into the ruby which still hung from her neck, willing her to tread that path, to seek the ether and figure out a way on for the two of us. I pushed all of myself into that stone and I could feel the power of my soul thumping inside it like a pulse, the beat heavy against her chest until I was certain she could feel it too, the stone heating even more than her flames as the might of my Dragon poured through it.

I wound my arms around her, feeling her thrashing heart against my chest even though I knew she couldn't feel me there, even though she didn't soften into my embrace the way she always had before. But I willed her to feel me all the same, to understand that I was fighting this fate too, that I would always fight for her, no matter what it took to do so.

She was still cracking open, but I felt her pull in a heavy breath, that strength I had always admired in her raising its head once more, the power of her drawing in as she let herself break while still clinging to what mattered most.

The door banged open and the pieces of me which she had been so desperately holding onto shattered as her grief was interrupted by Caleb's sudden arrival.

I looked to him, noting the chests he carried into the room, filled with my treasure, feeling his own stab of grief as it tugged at me too. But the moment was gone, The Veil fluttering softly yet firmly and I lost my grip on what had been keeping me there, falling back into its embrace.

I fell to my knees in my room within the Eternal Palace.

Had she understood any of the message I'd been trying to send her? Did she even recognise the fact that I'd been there?

"I need to go back!" I roared at nothing and everything, my fist colliding with the hard stone of the floor, no physical pain finding me in this form without form.

My own grief burst through me like a wave cresting a dam, my chest throbbing with a pain beyond all comprehension as I thought on all I'd left behind in the living realm. All I'd lost.

"It gets easier," Radcliff's voice sounded behind me. "Once you accept what you are now. Once you come to accept that you are here, and they are there and-"

"Never," I snarled, shoving to my feet, and pushing past him, time and place swirling all around me as I stalked toward the orb in The Room of Knowledge where I had first taken a look back at the realm of the living.

If The Veil wouldn't allow me closer from here, then I would go there to look upon her. I would see if she had felt my direction and if not, I'd try again and again and again until she did.

The glimmering building which held the orb appeared at the end of a twisting path ahead of me and I stalked towards it, ignoring the souls who were travelling around me, slamming my shoulders into them if they didn't move aside quickly enough and shoving my way to the front of the line.

There were seats raised up all around the glimmering orb, gilded and inviting, meant for reclining while watching the lives of those who had been left behind play out.

I ignored them, moving straight up to the metal barrier ringing the glowing orb and reaching out to press my hand against the swirling magic within.

There was a pulse of power which echoed across the entire orb as I pressed my will into it, rippling away from my hand and passing over every other memory or present moment that was being viewed by all the other lingering souls in the room.

There were cries of outrage and protest as the great orb flickered beneath my power, but I ground my teeth, ignoring all of them and demanding it bend to my will.

Roxy's face appeared then, her eyes wide and full of wonder as she moved through a darkened chamber within the Library of the Lost with Caleb at her side.

I sucked in a sharp breath. Had she felt any of the urging I'd tried to send her? Or had fate been listening instead, whispering her name, and guiding her to this place where our destinies might be changed.

I didn't care. All that mattered was what lurked in the darkness of that chamber, the weight of the unknown magic making my skin prickle as I sensed it close by. The thing Mordra had spoken of, the power which might be capable of changing my fate.

The stars shifted all around me, but I growled, knowing this wasn't for them, not wanting them to see it and whether through force of my will or some divine turn of fate, they slipped away again, their focus drawn elsewhere.

Angry souls were storming from The Room of Knowledge, hurling insults at me and cursing me for spoiling their time with their lost ones, but I ignored them, utterly enraptured as I watched Roxy and Caleb heading deeper into the darkness.

She was moving through a gap in the wall, the whispers of dead souls growing all around her, drawing a frown to my face.

Those souls weren't here. I could hear them clearly, knew they were beyond the realm of the living and yet they weren't ones which had passed into this place either.

What did that mean? Were there other places where the dead could reach out more freely to the living? Could they have been those who had passed through the door? But then if that was the case why was everyone here so certain that passing on would be the end of all there was here? Surely that kind of finality would put you further from life not closer to it.

My focus was stolen by the room Roxy found herself in as she pulled her way free of the crack in the wall. The five pedestals which stood around the space each contained a book which hummed with power so vibrant that I could feel it through the eternal space that parted us.

Caleb manipulated the stone to create his own way into the chamber, but I kept my gaze focused on the walls surrounding it, the runes carved into it, the scent of moisture on the air like there was water just out of sight. It reminded me all too readily of Mordra's cavern and I wondered if it might have been created like an amplification chamber too, the eyes of the stars unable to look upon it for years beyond measure.

A shiver tracked through me as Roxy moved to stand before a red book, its cover marked with the zodiac signs and symbols linked with fire, the power from the thing making a buzz of energy roll through me which I had never known in either life or death.

Caleb inspected another of the books, this one marked for earth magic, the low hum of its power filling this place too.

Trepidation rolled through me as I pushed my sense of self into the orb and finally fell through the divide, The Veil bending to allow me closer until I was standing in that chamber with them, looking at the lost tomes too.

"Should we open them?" Roxy breathed, her hesitation drawing my attention, though it was obvious why. This chamber was thick with unknown magic and something about the way these books had been placed so reverently had me hesitating too.

But this had to have been what Mordra had wanted us to find. I felt the truth of that right down to my core. Why then did it feel so wrong?

I stepped around Roxy and Cal, looking first to the book for water then air, the deepest power in the room resonating from the fifth podium, a low growl seeming to spill from it as I moved closer.

"Why are there five?" Caleb asked, his attention clearly following mine.

"Shadows?" Roxy questioned, but I could feel the wrongness of that as an answer.

She made to move closer, but Caleb shot in front of her, making me look to them again as he pointed to the floor and the pentagram which had been painted there with darkness itself.

"Look at the marks on the floor," he murmured.

"A pentagram," Roxy observed. "With a book at each corner. But why?"

Their words faded as they kept talking, the heavy weight of power in the room lulling me closer, drawing my lost soul towards that final book, luring me in.

My body became weightless, drifting, spilling apart as I closed in on it, a blink becoming another, my eyes falling closed entirely as The Veil tightened its hold on me again and I fought to remember why I didn't want that, why I needed to stay.

No.

She needed me.

I had to make sure she found what she sought.

I felt her as she called for me, the power of her grief spiking, her hand locking tight around the ruby necklace, anchoring me to it like she'd known I needed her to pull me back.

With a surge of determination, I reformed in the chamber, now behind Roxy as she stood over the book marked with a single word.

Ether.

Her fist tightened on the ruby, that touch seeming to give me more power as I pushed my energy into the stone, heating it from within and winding my arms around her waist.

I breathed in the exquisite scent of her, feeling her more closely than ever, before I exhaled again, goosebumps rising along her neck as if she'd felt my breath.

I growled at the idea of her truly feeling me, dropping my mouth to her neck and kissing her skin, feeling the warmth of her there, so close, so perfectly real. More goosebumps trailed the path my mouth took, and she leaned into my hold just enough to make me think she might be able to feel me there, at least a little.

A sigh slipped from her lips, longing and heartache merging as The Veil closed in and I roared my defiance, fighting it while it tore me away, drew me back from her despite how desperately I fought to stay.

My gaze caught on the Book of Ether as I fought the pull of that unstoppable force and fear spilled through me, the weight of its power seeming to loom in the darkness of that chamber.

I had so wanted her to find this place, so needed her to discover whatever magic it was that Mordra had hinted at, but in that moment, I saw the fullness of the danger that book contained and a bellow escaped me that had nothing to do with grief and everything to do with my need for her to hear me.

I wanted to warn her, tell her to step away from this path as the fear of it drove deeper into me, but The Veil lashed around me too tightly, its hooks digging in as it ripped me away until finally, I was thrown into a chair before the great orb which had fallen utterly dark.

Her words were the only thing to follow me from that darkness, nothing of where she was or what she was doing appearing on its empty face.

"Do you think he knew he'd die on that battlefield?" Roxy asked and I knew she was talking about me, the raw pain in her voice worse than the strike of that blade as it had pierced my heart.

"I don't think he would have willingly left any of us unless it was the only choice remaining to him. And the one that would save those he loved," Caleb said slowly, his own grief clear.

"This doesn't feel like he saved me," Roxy replied, her words cutting into me with a brutality that only she had ever managed to wield against me. "It feels like he destroyed me one final time. Like this was all some big joke, leading up to the annihilation of everything I was and ever could have been."

"You're still you, Tory," Caleb said, my own tongue a solid weight in my mouth as the truth she'd spoken and the pain I'd once again caused her cut me to ribbons.

"No. I'm not. I'm just an echo left behind, a malignant spirit set on revenge, and I'm far beyond the point of salvation. Which means there isn't anything in this book I won't use if that's what it takes to right the wrongs which have been done against me and mine. Do you understand?" Roxy growled, her voice a cold, dark thing. I'd done that to her. I'd broken the light in her and left her with nothing more than what she spoke of. That fitful need for vengeance.

I knew then that no matter my doubts, she was already set on this path.

There would be no turning her from it.

I dropped my face into my hands, my grief consuming all that was left of me, my own rotten soul left here to linger, shredded by the pain of losing her and all the others who I had loved so fiercely.

Horror and self-pity consumed me as I began to fade there in that place of darkness, Roxy's condemnation enough to break what little was left of me. I'd abandoned her when she needed me most and now I'd watched as she stepped onto a path so steeped in darkness that it was hard to fathom any hope blossoming along the way. Worse. I may well have been the driving factor that pushed her to find this darkness through nothing more than my own selfish desire to reclaim a life which I had long ago forfeited any right to.

The truth of it all was too much to face, and I could feel my soul splintering, cracking, fading away, my words the last thing to drift as the pit of nothing within that cursed door yawned wide and called my name.

"What have I done?"

HAIL

CHAPTER ELEVEN

"*R*un like the fires of frangle hill are burning up your Harriot hole, Felisia!" Wilbur Grus called to me, throwing a wayward blast of fire over his shoulder.

I squeaked in alarm, feigning left and hearing a crackle as the fire bloomed and singed a couple of golden hairs on my head.

"Wilbur!" I roared, patting my beautiful hair as he poured a stream of apologies my way. But I had bigger problems to deal with as the rush of paws sounded behind me. One glance back showed Cyrus La Ghast chasing us into the trees of The Wailing Wood with his Lion Shifter pride at his back, all of them golden and beautiful, their huge claws tearing through the mud. Cyrus had an enormous cobalt blue snake wrapped around his neck, and I recognised Isla Draconis with a sickening feeling in my stomach.

My friends were ahead of me as I focused on casting blocks in the path of the Lions pursuing us with my earth magic, and my heart hammered up into my throat.

"Felisia!" Birdie Cain yelled, throwing out a shield of earth at my back and my breathing hitched as I heard a Lion slam into it.

I raced on, my flowing mane fluttering out behind me and glinting in the sunlight that cut through the trees above, my sneakers pounding against the mud. I put on a burst of speed as I rounded a turn in the path, but came crashing into the solid, muscular back of Ren Imai.

He twisted around, his deep brown eyes full of worry as he caught my hand, keeping me from crashing into the mud.

"I got you, Fee." He pulled me against him, and I took in the line of Lions who must have carved a path through the woods to cut us off. The rest of the pride drew in at our back and I glanced between my four friends, the Fae I'd bonded with time and again in this situation. Always the target of the assholes who ruled Zodiac Academy.

My friends drew closer, Marigold Kipling closing in on my left while Wilbur and Birdie kept close to Ren's other side.

Cyrus La Ghast shifted among the Lions, the biggest of them all even in his Fae form. He toyed with the beautiful gold signet ring on his thumb which held his family crest, the sunlight bouncing off of it and capturing my attention. He was tall, tanned, and athletic in a way that said he spent all his free time working out. He was sickeningly good looking, with too-bright teeth and green eyes that glittered like jade.

He pushed his hand through his flowing chestnut mane, then stroked the giant snake that was draped around his body, concealing his cock until the creature dropped to the ground. She shifted into her Fae form, revealing a girl with jet black hair and sharp features which were twisted with cruelty. She was venomous in her Basilisk form, but even more so like this. Isla Draconis was a nightmare made to haunt me, and sometimes I didn't know if I'd ever escape her.

A couple more of the Lion pride shifted and someone passed a pair of uniform pants to Cyrus which he tugged on, taking his time as the Lions closed in around us. Isla pulled on an oversized shirt and strode toward us on bare feet, a smirk pulling at her mouth.

"So? No one's going to fight?" she asked. "Have you all finally learned where you belong? Because if that's so, you should get right down on your knees in the dirt this second."

None of us moved, but Ren's hand curled around mine, squeezing in reassurance.

"How about you, Wee Willy Wilbur?" Cyrus strode towards the dark-haired Grus, shoving my friend in the chest.

Wilbur staggered back. "I, er, er, beg your pudding, but I do not appreciate that n-n-nilly nickname." He thrust up his chin and Cyrus laughed coldly, the sound echoed by his pride in grunts and roars.

"D'ya hear that?" Cyrus crowed. "He doesn't like my n-n-n-n-nilly nickname for him," he mocked.

Anger rose in my chest, and I stepped forward, making Ren curse under his breath as my hand left his.

"What do you want?" I demanded of them, but as Cyrus and Isla's eyes flashed onto me, I suddenly didn't feel so brave.

"Don't do it," Birdie whispered frantically, fisting a hand in her short brown hair.

"Oh look, it's the Lioness who's got shift fright." Cyrus sneered at me, and Isla wetted her lips, watching Cyrus as he drew closer to me.

"Hurt her, Cyrus," she urged him. "Let me feel it."

The bitch recharged her power by feeling other's pain, and she never let us go before some blood had been spilled. She was a psycho, and she gave me the heebiest of jeebies on the best days.

Cyrus angled his head down at me, glaring in a way that told me to submit. A powerful Lion demanding a cub to bow. But I didn't respect this asshole, and I wasn't going to let him see me cower.

"Come on, shift for me, little cub," he commanded, reaching out and grabbing a fistful of my hair, his signet ring digging hard into my scalp.

I growled in fury, swiping a hand at him with my nails set to draw blood. No one touched a Lion Shifter's hair except those they allowed; people they deemed worthy. And it was the biggest insult Cyrus could offer me by acting as if he could touch me like that.

My nails struck home, swiping down the golden skin of his cheek and tearing it open.

Isla hummed her approval at the first taint of pain in the air, even if it was her ally's.

"Make her pay for that," she encouraged. "Or step aside and I will."

"This can be resolved reasonably," Marigold Kipling said professionally, like we were at a meeting instead of a brawl. "We can write out a formal agreement. You stay in one territory, and we'll stay in another. I can have it formatted by eight o'clock this evening."

Cyrus yanked my hair tighter in his fist, dragging me by it to Marigold and keeping me close. "What did you say to me, freak?" he spat at her.

Marigold cleared her throat, back straightening and face neutral as if she was entirely unaware of the danger surrounding her. "I said, we can write out a formal agreement. You stay in one territory, and we'll stay-"

Cyrus sent a blast of air at her so fast that it both knocked her to the ground and sealed her lips tightly shut, binding her limbs to her side at once.

"This doesn't need t-t-to descend into a donder jig," Wilbur tried. "We can go on our merry way and head to the bambercrooks of the academy, far out of sight, as invisible as gnarly wobs on a dinghy. What say you, fine fellow?"

"Yeah, what say you, fine fellow?" Isla taunted, looking to Cyrus with excitement flashing through her expression.

"I say, let's find out how wee Wee Willy' Wilbur's willy is," Cyrus said, *nodding to someone over Wilbur's shoulder and I gasped a warning before one of his lackies yanked Wilbur's pants and boxers down around his ankles.*

"Holy shit," Isla gasped, and Cyrus gaped down at Wilbur's very not small dick which hung out in plain sight for all to see, practically hitting his damn knee.

"Why do you always shift in private then, freak?" Cyrus asked in dismay, his fingers knotting tighter in my hair.

"Bless my bottom berry," Wilbur murmured. "I get a case of the ginger goblins sometimes, the Harry happenings, the hobbly wobbles-"

"In a language we can all understand, freak?" Cyrus demanded.

"Oh my, I-I-I simply don't know how to say it any clearer," Wilbur stammered.

"He gets nervous," Ren supplied for him in a dark voice, drawing everyone's attention to him. He was the biggest of our group, muscles stacked on muscles, a Senior who had once been top of his game in the academy Speed Flying team and House Captain for Terra. But then he'd fallen from grace after his father had been Power Shamed for forging his FIB suitability test results and the whole school had turned on him too. His confidence had been knocked to shit, and he'd ended up with us sorry lot who had been targeted the second we arrived at Zodiac Academy.

"Shift fright, just like my pathetic excuse for a cub here has." Cyrus yanked on my hair and made me mewl in pain while Isla stepped closer to feed on it.

"Shift, little cub," Cyrus urged, getting his face close to mine.

"Get off of me," I snarled.

"Leave her alone," Birdie said in a high-pitched voice and Cyrus whipped towards her.

"Birdie Cain," he said with a snigger. "The Vampire who has to suck the cocks and clits of her friends to get a blood donation."

"I do not," Birdie hissed, fangs flashing at Cyrus. "They give it willingly."

Cyrus hollered a laugh and his pride joined in again, all of them stepping nearer, their sharp teeth aimed our way.

"You're meant to claim power, not ask nicely for it," Cyrus spat, then rounded on me again. "You could be a good little cub for me. I'll let you rise from this pit of losers and maybe even join my pride one day. But you've got to do what I say. Anything I say." He smiled viciously and I swiped at him again, but he caught my wrist this time in an iron grip that made me wince.

"I'll never be your bitch," I said in disgust and my Lioness roared inside my chest.

"Make her bleed," Isla demanded. "Come on, Cyrus. Hurt her and I'll pick another one."

"Fight me as a true Lioness would," he demanded. "Shift."

He shoved me into the dirt, and I called on my Lioness, willing her to come to me, burst from my flesh and tear this bastard to pieces. But it wouldn't come, a barrier seeming to form between my skin and the Order part of me that was so crucial, yet so impossible to reach sometimes.

Please, please, please come to me.

"I want the big one," Isla purred, closing in on Ren, weaving a path towards him like she was still slithering along in her Basilisk form. "I want him screaming."

She captured Ren's gaze and locked him in a vision which he clearly didn't fight because his knees hit the ground in an instant, his lips parting with the horrors of what Isla was showing him inside his head.

Birdie trembled as a huge Lion closed in at her back while Marigold continued to thrash against her air binds on the ground, and Wilbur just stood there with his cock out, his hands raised and shaking as if he was trying to get his magic to work.

Cyrus kicked me in the side, and I coughed out a breath. "Shift!" he barked.

I shut my eyes, trying to focus, to force my Lioness from my skin and fight this asshole Fae on Fae. My fingers clawed into the dirt, and I gritted my teeth, begging my Order to listen.

Cyrus stamped his heel down on my fingers and magic shot from my palms, rocking the ground violently at his feet.

He stumbled back with a curse and my eyes whipped open, my head ducking as he blasted air at me. The power of it snared my limbs, throwing me onto my back and pinning me there as Cyrus leered over me.

"Shift, you piece of trash. Or are you not Fae enough?" His foot pressed to my knee, his weight shoving down and making me scream. "Shift!"

"Shit, Professor Major is coming," someone called, and Cyrus growled, tossing his mane over one shoulder as he looked over at Isla.

"One more second," she breathed, in obvious bliss as she fed on Ren's pain inside his mind.

"Come on," Cyrus said. "We can find them later."

Isla sighed, pulling away from Ren and leaving him sagging forward, panting and resting his hands on the ground. The air magic released Marigold as Cyrus and Isla went running off into the trees with the Lion pride racing after them.

Birdie was nursing a bite mark on her arm and Ren got to his feet, wordlessly moving forward to heal her. The rest of us were freshmen, and we hadn't even learned how to do that kind of magic yet, but Ren always looked out for us on that front.

Marigold wordlessly pulled up Wilbur's pants for him and Wilbur finally snapped out of the shock he had been frozen in.

"Shameful shoals," he muttered. "I didn't know whether to hither or to blither and I ended up in a dither."

"It's alright, Wilbur," Marigold said. "Next time, we will have a ten-stage plan, and a contract written up for them to sign."

"They're not going to sign some fucking contract, Marigold," Birdie huffed, shoving past Ren as he finished healing her.

I pushed myself up to sit in the mud, my head falling forward and golden hair spilling around me to shield the world from view.

"Good day," Professor Major said and we all muttered our acknowledgement of him as he passed by.

"Perhaps if we provide a presentation first and lay out all the positives in coming to a treaty," Marigold suggested practically, not even seeming fazed by having been tied up in the mud and forced into silence.

"Golly grouts," Wilbur muttered. "A treaty is a fig of an idea. They'll never agree."

"Fee," Ren said as he crouched down before me and I looked up at him, taking in his familiar face, the masculine line of his jaw, his straight, strong nose and his wavy brown hair that was always just a little wild. "Are you hurt?"

"Just my pride," I muttered, and he reached out to push my hair away from my face, one of the few people in this world I allowed to do that. Ren was my best friend in many ways; me and him had this wordless connection, both of us on the same wavelength in life. Marigold kept stating he was my Nebula Ally like it was a fact, and I wondered if she had a point about that.

Ren took my hand, pulling me from the mud and placing me on my feet. I looked up at him, giant that he was, and he knocked his knuckles against my cheek. "Forget them. I've seen you shifted, your Lioness is huge and damn powerful too."

"But why can't I shift when I need my Lioness most?" I whispered, emotion burning the back of my throat. "I can never get it to happen when I need it, so what kind of Fae does that make me?"

I turned from him, striding off down the path and Birdie shot to my side with a flash of her Vampire speed. "I wish we were stronger. I wish we could fight. I'd make them bleed, make them pay."

"Mm," I grumbled.

"It is not our strength that is the problem," Marigold said, striding along to walk on my other side while Wilbur and Ren followed at our backs. "I have carefully analysed all of our powers, our Elemental gradings, our Order sizes,

and compared them with the opposition. Cyrus La Ghast and Isla Draconis are superior to us in some ways, but not all. Most of us are quite above average, in fact. Though one of us is very weak by comparison."

"Which one?" Birdie clipped.

"You, Birdie Cain," Marigold said simply, no tact at all. But she never did have any of that.

"What?" she hissed, rounding on Marigold, her grey eyes flaring with murder and fangs bared. "That's bullshit."

"It is fact," Marigold shrugged. "As the sky is blue and the grass is green."

Birdie spat a snarl then shot away from us into the woodland, disappearing out of sight.

"Now you've gone and dallied with her dinger," Wilbur said, moving swiftly into Birdie's place while Ren stepped closer to me. "Did you really have to deliver the blow like a filliper's axe, dear Marigold?"

"How else am I to speak the truth? It comes plainly from my mouth. If Birdie does not like the truth, should I seek to lie to her?" Marigold frowned, not understanding.

"Lies can be daisies balanced upon a crown of thorns," Wilbur said.

"When you looked into Cyrus and Isla, did you find anything that could help us deal with them?" I asked Marigold, knowing Wilbur was never going to convince her to understand white lies, especially with his way of explaining things. He and Marigold were at odds with each other, but they cared for each other all the same.

"Yes, I have analysed the data thoroughly," Marigold said. "Cyrus La Ghast and Isla Draconis have few weaknesses, but upon accessing their private files in the academy system, I discovered two things of note. Cyrus La Ghast is deathly allergic to whittle grass and Isla Draconis has ties to a rather terrible street gang in Alestria that could sully her name, should it happen to come out."

"So what? No one would believe us about Isla, and we're not exactly going to kill Cyrus," I said, pressing my lips together.

"Of course," Marigold said. "I forecast the outcome of each path, and neither reap ideal rewards. But I believe I have found another answer all the same."

"You have?" Ren asked in surprise.

"The Guild Stones," Marigold said.

Ren groaned, pressing his fingers into his eyes. "Not this shit again."

"Shh," I hushed him, my ears pricking up. "I love this shit."

"I do so love to ponder upon the randy rocks of the lost circle," Wilbur said excitedly.

135

"I believe I have pinpointed the location of four stones," Marigold said.

"What?" I blurted, running around to grab hold of her by the lapels of her uniform blazer. "Why didn't you say this sooner?"

"She hasn't found four Guild Stones, don't you see how ridiculous this is?" Ren said in frustration. "The best thing you lot could do would be to work on honing your power, study more, build your confidence-"

"Says the guy who stopped fighting back after his fall from grace," I shot at him and hurt coloured his features, making me almost regret the comment, but it was the truth.

"What have I got to fight for? The only thing waiting for me upon graduation is a bunch of doors slamming in my face. My father's shame will follow me everywhere now."

"So prove you're different," I said fiercely. "Make a splash. Seize some Guild Stones with us and make a new name for yourself."

"That's crazy and you know it. I just need a fresh start," Ren murmured. "Solaria is never going to accept me, and my father has gone into hiding. He won't answer any of my letters, our house is becoming a ruin. The rest of my family has turned their backs on me, so there's nothing left for me beyond this academy."

"You have us," I said passionately, hating the words falling from his lips.

Ren frowned at me. "Not forever, Fee."

"Yes, forever," I insisted. "I don't care how anyone treats you, we've got your back. Just like you've always had ours. That's what holds us all together."

"We still need to decide on a group name," Wilbur said keenly. "Perhaps the Dashing Outcast Nerds Group."

"The Dong?" I deadpanned and Ren snorted.

"Pull my walloper," Wilbur gasped, clapping a hand to his mouth. "Minds of filth, the lot of you." He laughed and the tension fell away between us, though my heart twisted as Birdie reappeared, stalking back to us through the boughs.

"Hey," she muttered.

"I did not mean to hurt your feelings," Marigold said with the least emotion imaginable.

"Yeah, it's fine." Birdie kicked the ground.

"Marigold has found four Guild Stones," I told her and her eyes immediately brightened.

"Seriously?" she gasped. "Where?"

"I have not found them. I have located them," Marigold corrected.

"So where are they?" I pushed.

"This is ridiculous," Ren said.

"Oh, do stop being such a whelk on the bump of a barnacle," Wilbur pleaded. "If we were to claim the stones of power, we could ascend to greatness. We could flap those uncomely blunderbins with a whomp and a flomp of our own. Then they would see." His shoulders pressed back and Birdie bit her lip, her eyes shining with the idea.

"Come on then, Marigold, tell us what you found out," I urged.

"The old Guild was made up of the twelve power families, as you know," Marigold said. "The balance was set, each of them made equally as powerful as the others. Alphard, Vega, Acrux, Capella, Altair, Pollux, Rigel, Andromeda, Denebola, Castor, Betelgeuse, and Pleiades."

"Yeah, then one of them stole a stone from the other and upset the power. The story says it was Alphard from Altair, but some versions of it say it was Acrux from Vega," I said, caught up in the story.

"And that set out an unending chain of destruction," Ren added. "Powerful assholes fighting powerful assholes for their stones, each seeking to become the one ruling power."

"The stones were hidden," Marigold said with a nod. "Far and wide, each family fighting to keep the power from their enemies. And just yesterday Queen Leondra Vega made a comment in an interview that alluded to her still possessing four of the stones." Marigold whipped out a folded piece of newspaper from her pocket and unfolded it, showing us the article.

I took it from her, and Ren leaned over my shoulder to see while Wilbur leaned over my other to read the passage Marigold had highlighted.

"-still four priceless artefacts in my keeping which ensures the Vega line will thrive on regardless of any challenge that ever comes to our door-"

"That doesn't prove anything," Ren said. "She could be referring to all kinds of artefacts."

"Of course, it is a guess, but to make such a statement is quite telling. I could list them all, but I assure you I would be wasting breath when we could simply plan how to seize the stones," Marigold said.

"This is insanity," Ren said, and my chest deflated. "You're freshman, for one. You're talking about stealing from the most highly guarded place in the entire kingdom for two, not to mention the layers of magic that are protecting that place, or the fact that you couldn't pinpoint those Guild Stones inside it even if you did somehow find your way in. Which you wouldn't. There is no chance of it happening."

"On the contrary, I believe we have a chance. Not a great one, but a chance all the same," Marigold said.

"It's not only stupid, it's a death sentence. And for what?" Ren scoffed.

"Power," I said darkly, and Ren stepped forward, his eyes darkening as he assessed me.

"Don't be an idiot, Fee. This shit won't last forever. You will rise up. You're more powerful than you think, or you wouldn't even have made it into this academy."

"I can't even shift when I need to, Ren," I said in anger. "My family are embarrassed by me. They think I don't have the Night spirit. They think I'm a dud. And you know what Lion prides do with the cubs that don't make the cut? They cast them out."

"Then don't let that happen, prove them wrong," Ren said forcefully.

I nodded, a frown creasing my brow as I thought on all the times I'd been pushed in the dirt by Cyrus, the times he had broken into my room in Terra House to torture me in front of an audience. Then I thought of my parents shaking their heads at me, shame colouring their faces and their backs turning on me. "Maybe I will."

My hand slipped into the pockets of the students swarming around me as I walked into Venus Library, seizing little tokens, quills, crystals, auras. It wasn't about the prize; it was about the game. And the more I practised, the better I got.

I'd taken Ren's advice and worked my ass off for months now. Sophomore year was looming, and my grades were rising. I barely slept, forgot to eat. Every morning, I raced the sun and won, following the dark paths from Terra House to Venus Library or to the hills in Earth Territory to study. And I wasn't alone. My friends and I rose together, met at the entranceway to Terra House to slip away into the dark.

And then, we practised. Ren taught us skills he had perfected, and I always demanded to know about the concealment spells and anything that could make my new hobby thrive. I was getting damn good at thieving, but Ren insisted I stopped focusing on thievery and worked to hone other skills.

"You still can't shift whenever Cyrus or Isla corners you," he growled at me while we stood under the light of the moon on our favoured hilltop. "What good is picking pockets if you can't defend yourself?"

His chest was bare, muscles on show and there was a grit about him that said he was hungering for the shift. He was a Manticore, so he understood the Lioness part of me more than the others. Though his Order wasn't nearly as pride orientated as mine. He didn't need all these people around him, but I did. I needed them more than I'd ever admit. Him most of all.

Birdie raised her head from Wilbur's wrist, her fangs glinting wetly with his blood before she swallowed. "Ren's right, you should practise attack spells like I am. I want to be strong enough to rip Isla's head from her scaly body the next time she comes for me."

She said it with such hatred that I could have sworn she meant it.

"Wilbur gets it, don't you?" I pushed.

"Does a pygmy gumble know the ways of its snout?" he laughed, and I frowned in confusion. "Yes indeed! My knees knock and my heart flambles. Shifting in front of those blasted barracudas is a challenge indeed."

"See," I said pointedly to Ren, and he folded his arms across his chest, staring at me in concern.

"You're going to get hurt again and again. I'm not going to be here soon to teach you. I graduate next month. And then...well you know what I'm planning."

My heart clenched and I turned away from him, unable to bear it. "Don't remind me."

"The Waning Lands," Marigold said bluntly, sitting cross legged on the ground in orange dungarees. "You're less likely to get into that place than we are to get into The Palace of Souls."

"You cannot seriously still be planning that," Ren sighed.

"So you don't believe we can steal the Guild Stones, but you can take a boat to The Waning Lands and find a way into a kingdom that's war torn and full of death? Why would you even want to go there anyway, Ren?" I demanded.

"Because no one will know me there, and I can actually make something of myself," he barked.

I growled deep in my throat. "It's crazy."

"Oh, I'm crazy?" he laughed. "At least I have a plan. You talk of those four Guild Stones as if they're already yours. You think picking pockets and breaking concealment spells is enough to get you in there? You'll be dead before you reach the front door."

"Actually, taking the front door would be wildly foolish," Marigold said unhelpfully.

"All thieves have to start somewhere," I said firmly.

"You're not a thief, Fee," Ren said furiously. "You're a freshman Lioness who can't even shift when danger calls."

"Ouch, Ren," Birdie hissed as my heart crumpled in my chest, my confidence shattering just like that.

"Wandering stars, that was a little harsh," Wilbur muttered, tugging his pants a bit higher.

"Of all the people who don't have faith in me, I never thought you would be one of them," I said, pain coating my words as I turned my back on him and moved to sit beside Marigold on the ground.

"Fee," he said sadly, and I felt his eyes on me, but I ignored him, hurt still blossoming in my chest.

I'd prove him wrong. I'd prove all of them fucking wrong.

"Any luck on locating the stones more precisely?" I murmured to Marigold.

"Nothing yet, but I am scouring articles old and new on the Vegas. Perhaps a snippet of truth will find its way to us soon."

Birdie cursed as she tried to break a concealment spell that Wilbur had cast and failed. "I just can't get it, what am I doing wrong?"

"Nothing, I believe," Marigold said. "You are simply the weakest of our group. There is no way you can break a spell cast by Wilbur for he is greater in power, and skill for that matter."

Birdie turned to her with blazing cheeks. "I'm not weaker."

"Oh but you are, by quite a stretch," she said. "You will likely need to stay behind when the time comes for the heist."

"What?" Birdie gasped, fury tearing across her face. "I'm not staying behind. I'm a part of this."

"She is," I said firmly. "We all are. Except Ren apparently."

"I'm just trying to protect you," he said in frustration, but I still didn't look at him.

I slid my hand into my pocket, taking out a crystal I'd stolen from Professor Quartex's pocket yesterday. I was good. Better than good. But I needed a real challenge to test out how good I truly was, something that would push me to my limits and prove I could achieve things no one would ever believe I could do.

So I made a decision that set fear burning in my veins, but that was what made me certain I had to do it. Because if I could pull it off, maybe I could pull off a real heist. And then Ren would see what I was capable of. They all would.

I was going to break into Cyrus's room and steal his family ring.

My hands grasped the gaps between the bricks, the cold air fluttering at my back, tugging the black cloak I wore and reminding me of the immense drop which lay below me. But I wasn't letting go of Aer Tower.

I grew a vine from the wall, wrapping it around my hand, securing me in place before I reached up and grew another, pulling myself higher and creating a stone foothold for my boot to land on. This was easier than I'd *imagined. I'd been practising my climbing skills all across campus, but Aer Tower was the highest building at Zodiac Academy, and I'd been saving it for this very moment. Because almost at the very top of this tower was an asshole sleeping soundly in his cosy House Captain's room with a ring on his finger that was mine for the taking.*

I heaved myself higher, my black hood not shifting from my head thanks to the sticking spell I'd cast to keep it there, hiding my golden hair. It was the middle of the night, but that didn't mean students wouldn't be out in the grounds, and as that thought crossed my mind, a Werewolf pack howled to the moon. It was a dusky crescent tonight, veiled by grey clouds, so the light wasn't bright enough to pick me out on the side of the tower. I had plenty of concealment spells hugging me too, shadows drawn closer by my power and losing me among them. I was capable of spells even seniors struggled with, the amount of time I'd practised them amassing a number of hours that didn't even bear thinking about. But my dedication would pay off if I could just secure myself that ring.

Finally, I made it to one of the tall windows that lined Cyrus's curved bedroom wall and tucked myself into one side of the sill, squinting in at the dark room. There was a gap in the curtains that let me see the shadowy shape of a bed, but I could make out little else in the gloom.

I pushed the glass, my hand not leaving a single print on the pane thanks to the slithening juice I'd dipped my hands in earlier. Professor Gonder made us use it in Potions class sometimes as it worked as a barrier against particularly dangerous chemicals. It effectively created a second skin, and I'd realised it left no mark at all after touching something, no fingerprints. Nothing. It made me a ghost so long as no one ever saw me, and it didn't even affect the use of magic; it let my power slide on through it like it was permeable on the side that touched my palm.

The window was locked, but it had been worth a shot. Undeterred, I ran my hand over the place the lock sat and focused on creating a soft piece of metal between my fingers, willing it to grow and extend into the keyhole. I closed my eyes, letting the metal expand and feeling all the parts of the mechanism inside. Foreign magic fluttered against the edges of my own and I acted fast, sending a bubble of power out around it and crushing it away with a growl of effort. The magical lock dissolved, and I smiled as I let the silver form into a key that perfectly fit that hole, twisting it with a light click.

And then...I was in.

The pane swung outwards on a hinge, the thing designed to let the flying Orders dive out of their windows anytime they liked. And it made it especially easy for me to walk quietly into the room, my movements muffled by a silencing bubble that I cast against the edges of my body.

I gently shut the window behind me, not wanting the wind to stir Cyrus from sleep. As I stepped down off the sill, my eyes adjusted to the dark and my heart stalled.

Fuck.

Lions. Everywhere. All in their shifted forms, lazing on the floor, stretched out, legs in the air, huge jaws wide and teeth pointing at me from every angle. In the middle of them was a giant bed where Cyrus lay in his Fae form, naked with a sheet twisted around his muscular body. The king of his domain.

I took a quiet breath and started forward, weaving my way between giant paws and beasts that growled in their sleep, setting my pulse racing in my ears.

Keep moving.

Don't stop.

You've got this.

The simplest route to the bed was blocked by two Lionesses who were curled up together, one of their tails swishing like she wasn't as deeply asleep as I would have preferred.

I swallowed the lump in my throat, pushing away thoughts of what would happen if the pride woke up. I'd be ripped to pieces most likely. And no one would ever remember my name.

My fingers tightened into a fist in anger at that thought, and I found my resolve within it.

I was Felisia Night, and one day, everyone was going to know my name.

I cast my eyes to the ceiling, letting four vines grow down towards me, reaching for my body then wrapping under my arms, around my waist and hips. With a surge of magic, I willed those vines to lift me higher and carry me silently over the two giant beasts at the side of Cyrus's bed, moving me to hover right over the sinful creature below.

Cyrus La Ghast. A Fae who had been the reason for my suffering right alongside Isla Draconis, the two of them having made me an act in their horror show one too many times.

I steeled myself as the vines lowered me down and my fingers rubbed together in preparation of the act I was about to commit. I'd practised a thousand times on a skeleton hand in the library, the thing enchanted to grab me any time my fingers touched it. So if I could slide a ring off the finger of that creepy thing without disturbing it, then I could do it for real now.

I made the vines hold me half a foot above Cyrus then reached for his hand which was resting on his broad chest, slowly rising and falling with his even breaths. His dark mane spilled out around him on the bed, practically glistening even in the dim light of the room, and his roguishly handsome face was almost boyish in sleep.

I slid my hand down my hoody, taking out the heliotrope crystal stashed in my bra which could give some numbing effects and held it close to the intended finger, the kiss of its magic rolling over him.

Then I stashed the crystal again and took hold of the ring, biting my lip hard as I twisted it up to his knuckle, sliding it along, then-

My magic faltered, all of it abandoning me at once and I came crashing down as my vines vanished. I trapped a scream in my throat before I hit the bed on top of him, landing softly like a cat as my knees and hands took the brunt of the fall either side of him on the mattress, but my body brushed his and he groaned, his hand sliding around me and grasping my ass.

His right hand brushed my arm, and I felt the power of the signet ring on his finger affecting my magic, keeping it at bay.

"Isla?" he purred, his mouth finding my jaw and grazing along it.

A hiss sounded somewhere near my feet, and I glanced back in horror to find the bedsheets writhing between his legs. There was something under there. Something that hissed and slithered, and there was only one fucking person it could be.

Cyrus's hand clamped harder on my ass, drawing me flush against him and rutting the hard length of his cock against my thigh.

Holy fucking fuck.

I did the only thing I could think of and grabbed his right hand, and ground down on his cock, making him groan. And while my fingers threaded between his, I worked that damn ring right off into my fist and felt my power wash back into me as the anti-magic spell shattered in my grip. I knew there was only one thing left for me to do as Isla wriggled out of the sheet, and I found myself one second from being a dead bitch. I swung my leg over Cyrus, launching myself off the bed and casting a vine from the ceiling.

A roar came from behind me that made my heart leap into my throat.

"Hey!" Cyrus yelled and every Lion Shifter in the room woke up.

I caught the vine in my grip, swinging like a wild monkey over the heads of the beasts below as they stirred. One swiped at my legs and another snapped their jaws at me, but it was the big motherfucker who was pouncing from my left that was the real problem.

I let go of the vine, hitting the floor hard to avoid the collision and the Lion sailed overhead.

A blast of air magic slammed into me, but I was already on my feet again close to the window. The air sent me flying but I was ready, riding the wave of it and kicking the pane so it swung outward and let me escape.

Suddenly I was falling, the campus stretching away ahead of me and Aer Tower whipping past me as the ground rose to meet me. I threw out my palms, softening the earth with moss and mud before slamming into it, rolling and rolling over the slope as pain tore up my left arm and knee.

Blasts of air magic came from above, tearing the earth to pieces around me. It was carnage, and one step forward had me slamming into an air shield, proving me trapped.

Or so they thought.

I turned my gaze to the ground and carved it apart, tearing a hole into the earth and tumbling down into it. I scored a tunnel through the rock and rubble around me, forcing it back as I gained my feet and ran into the pitch blackness with a whoop tearing from my throat.

I was pretty sure I'd done some decent damage to my left arm, and I was limping between steps, but I didn't slow down, casting a Faelight ahead of me as I worked on my tunnel, filling it in at my back and sprinting away towards the safety of Terra House.

Cyrus and his pride would be hunting for me long into the night, but they hadn't seen my face, I was sure. And I was banking on the fact that they'd never suspect one of their daily torture victims as the culprit.

When I made it back to Terra House, I hurried through the winding tunnels, seeking out Ren's room and bashing my fist on it. After the tenth knock, he answered, shirtless and bleary eyed, his hands raised defensively as if he expected me to be an enemy, but I quickly dropped the concealment spells and let him see my face.

"Fee?" he gasped, looking me over, covered in mud and moss.

I smiled from ear to ear, holding up my hand and unfurling it to reveal the golden signet ring within.

"Is that Cyrus La Ghast's ring?" he asked in shock.

"The one and only," I said, then squealed and threw myself at him.

He crushed me in his powerful arms automatically, reminding me that I was injured as hell and I crumpled against him with a mewl of pain.

"Shit, come inside."

Ren carried me into his room, kicking the door shut and placing me down on his bed, carefully pulling off my muddy cloak and tossing it on the floor, leaving me in a thin shirt beneath. He eyed the swelling that was blooming around my elbow with a taut frown and his fingers brushed my skin, healing away the damage and making me sigh in relief.

"Anywhere else?" he asked.

"My left knee," I admitted and without a word, he peeled off my dirty pants to reveal my undergarments. I'd stitched a little red paw into the silk and

144

Ren's eyes immediately fell to it.

"Cute," he remarked with a snort then knelt down, drawing my leg into his lap and skating his thumb over my reddened knee.

I shivered a little at his touch and he glanced up at me while he healed the wound away.

"Did he see you? Is he coming?" he asked.

"No and no. He'll be running all across campus looking for the thief, but he'll never suspect me. Are you impressed?"

He sat back a little, assessing me for a moment then smiling. "I'm impressed."

"Good," I said with a smirk, thumbing the ring in my hand with a thrill dancing in my chest. "If you look this shocked now, I can't wait to see what you look like when I steal the Guild Stones."

"Fee," he warned.

"Ren," I tossed back, prodding his stomach with my toes. He caught hold of my ankle, his large hand wrapping around it tight.

"I graduate next week," he said, sullying my mood just like that.

"And then?" I pushed, thinking of his constant declarations of leaving Solaria for a new life.

"You know what then," he said.

"Stay," I said, the word coming out huskily.

He met my eyes and I knew he felt the depths of that request, the unspoken reason for why I couldn't bear for him to leave which neither of us voiced or dared act upon.

"I can't stay forever," he said finally.

"Stay a while longer at least," I pleaded. "Don't just take the first boat to anywhere."

"The longer I stay, the harder it'll be to leave in the end," he said darkly, his brows drawing low as his gaze tracked the length of my leg.

"Then don't go at all," I said, a smile quirking up the corner of my lips.

"There's no fate in which I don't go, Fee," he said seriously. "I will always be no one here."

"Not to me," I said passionately, my victory bolstering my confidence, making me speak the words which had been waiting on my tongue for too long. "You're the best kind of someone to me."

His thumb circled my ankle bone and a wicked heat burned between my thighs, telling me what perhaps I'd known for a while now about us I. But if we went there, it didn't change anything. Ren would still go, and I wasn't sure I could bear the heartbreak of following that path to its bitter end.

I slid my foot from his grip and rose to my feet, picking up my muddy clothes from the floor. "Night, Ren."

"I'll stay until the end of fall," he said, and I glanced back at him, smiling sadly as I nodded.

"Better," I said, and he smiled back, this heavy goodbye hanging between us that I knew was going to rip my heart out and destroy it.

Fall. Of course it was fall. Because when Ren left, it would feel like the first bite of winter, the leaves of our friendship turning gold then brown, only to fall and turn to dust.

Ren graduated. But it only started hurting when I returned to Zodiac as a sophomore and Ren didn't return with us.

The summer had been long, hot and spent with my friends as much as possible. We spent the last couple of weeks in Sunshine Bay and my hair was a brighter gold than ever by the time we came back to the cooler air of Tucana. Though it was by no means cold yet, even if the leaves on the trees were threatening to change and steal Ren away with them when they fell.

Cyrus had been on a rampage the last time I'd seen him before the academy broke up for the summer, days and days of him questioning students, beating down anyone he suspected. But he never found his ring. Because it belonged to me now, and while he and his vile friends were busy hunting for a perpetrator they deemed capable of pulling off the theft, they had left us alone for once.

My gut told me that wasn't going to last, but I'd also been working hard on both defensive spells and shifting under pressure over the summer.

Marigold and Birdie had tried blasting magic at Wilbur and I, threatening to crack and crumble the ground beneath our feet while I was on a time limit to shift.

Ren had gone for the more aggressive approach of carrying me or Wilbur into the air while in his Manticore form then dropping us from a decent height. The idea was that we'd shift and land on all four paws, and it worked like a charm. Time and again, no matter what my friends threw at me, I managed to shift even when my mind scrambled, and Wilbur got the hang of it too, shifting into his Cerberus form and barking excitedly at the achievement.

So I was at least returning to the academy with some newfound confidence, and Wilbur had a skip in his step that said he was ready to take on the whole world. But our little group didn't feel whole without Ren in it as we walked into The Orb together to get breakfast on the first day of term.

My eyes immediately locked on Cyrus where he sat up on a table in the middle of the room, speaking loudly to a gathered crowd around him while Isla sat beside him looking like a dark princess, the only one of their group who wasn't fawning all over Cyrus.

"Turns out, no one stole my ring after all," he said.

"But I was there, and I saw-" one of his pride started but Cyrus's foot shot out, his shiny shoe slamming into the boy's face and silencing him.

"Anyway, seems it had gotten lost down the back of my bed. The cleaners found it over the summer." He held up his hand, twisting the gleaming golden ring on his finger to prove his story.

My upper lip peeled back, and a growl rumbled up my throat. I was stepping forward before I could stop myself and Birdie gasped, grabbing my arm, trying to pull me back.

"Don't," she begged, but my hand was already sliding into my pocket, taking hold of the ring I'd been carrying everywhere with me ever since I'd pulled off the theft.

I slid it onto my middle finger and lifted it into the air, aiming it right at Cyrus. "I call bullshit, Cyrus La Ass-ed," I shouted loud enough to draw the attention of everyone in the Orb, the insult not my best, and kind of spoiling the drama of my moment. But still.

"Galloping grapes," Wilbur cursed, sweeping closer to my side as Cyrus's gaze locked on me and Isla cocked her head with interest.

"I scaled Aer Tower, broke the magical lock on your window and crept through a hoard of sleeping Lions to claim this, and you never once suspected me." I twirled a lock of my golden hair around my finger, smiling like it had been so very easy, playing up to the onlooking crowd. I found I quite liked attention when it wasn't because I was being used as a Fae punching bag.

Mutters and gasps broke out, and Cyrus's tanned cheeks turned red as he glared at me, a look of disbelief in his eyes.

"By the stars, did you really let that little shift fright freak get one over on you, Cy?" one of his pride laughed, and Cyrus roared in anger, leaping to his feet on the table while Isla spat a hiss.

"Make her hurt," Isla whispered, her eyes glinting.

"Oh, I'm planning on it," Cyrus snarled, pouncing off the table, the crowd of Fae parting for him as he came charging my way.

My heart stumbled, but I didn't back down. Call me vain, but I was not going to let Cyrus sweep my victory under the rug, even if it cost me a beating now. At least everyone would know what I'd achieved, and if he wanted his ring back, I wasn't going to let him take it without a fight.

"Now you've done it," Birdie snapped.

"I want the trembling royalist," Isla decided as she hurried along at

Cyrus's side, her gaze pinned on Wilbur.

"Wallabies on a waterslide," Wilbur gasped, raising his hands in alarm.

"I do believe we are about to be humiliated," Marigold stated. "But perhaps it is time to make a stand, even if we end up on our backsides." She raised her hands, expression blank as a couple of Cyrus's lackies joined him, ready to take her and Birdie on.

"My cousin married an Acrux you know!" Birdie cried as if that would save her, but one of the Lionesses descended on her regardless.

Cyrus threw a fist my way, a blast of air bursting from it and I cast a rough metal shield on my arm, lifting it just in time to deflect the blow.

Cyrus roared, tearing his shirt clean off and leaping forward as he shifted, sending Fae running for their lives, breakfast trays and food flying everywhere as his huge Lion form landed right in front of us.

He towered over me, one huge paw already wheeling my way with glinting claws ready to rip the flesh from my bones.

I tugged the shield from my arm, throwing it at his face and he mewled as it smacked him dead between the eyes, his swipe missing me narrowly as a result.

I darted away, pulling off my blazer and tossing it aside, trying to focus on everything I'd practised over the summer. A battle cry to my right made my eyes wheel towards Wilbur and I found him wielding a chair, swinging it hard into the side of Isla's head.

She shivered while her own pain fed her power, then her face twisted viciously, and her uniform slumped to the floor as her body vanished, replaced instead by a large blue snake twisting within her clothes. Before she could make it out of the pile, Wilbur bundled it up in his arms, running across the room still crying out like he was charging into battle. He stuffed Isla in the trash can and slammed the lid shut, carving a hole in the ground beneath it with his power and sending her tumbling away into the dark chasm. A riot of laughter sounded out from the onlooking crowd, and my heart lifted at his victory.

But I was forced to focus on Cyrus again as he leapt at me, jaws wide and deadly. I dropped to the floor, skidding under the nearest table as more students made a dash for safety. I scrambled along on my hands and knees, trying to get my head together as a huge paw swiped under the table. Cyrus's claws caught in my shirt, tearing it off of me and leaving me in my thin camisole and skirt as I hurried along on my knees.

"Shift fright, shift fright, shift fright," Cyrus's pride started chanting, and more and more students joined them until my whole head was ringing with it.

Birdie was screaming as she went rolling along the floor, wrapped up in *streams of toilet paper while someone tossed jelly covered toast at her.*

Chaos was reigning and my heart was hammering wildly, my thoughts scattering as fear took root. Another swipe of Cyrus's giant paws sent the table flying into the air, revealing me beneath him.

I cried out, trying to get up, raising a hand to defend myself but his paw slammed against my chest, pinning me down and making my ribs scream under the pressure.

I grasped his golden fur as his other paw slammed down on my arm, pinning it there, his jaws closing around my hand which held his ring, and terror took hold of me as I realised he intended to bite it off.

"No!" I cried, thinking of all the times this bastard had forced me beneath him, how he'd belittled and abused me. How this entire school had outcast me because he was the king of this place, and they did everything he said. But I was done. So fucking done, and the ring I'd taken from him was mine. *Proof of my power over him.*

A roar spilled form my lips and the shift rippled through me, my Lioness bursting free of my skin. I slammed my paw into Cyrus's face, claws tearing into his skin and making him rear back in pain.

I was on my paws in the next second, not quite as large as him in size, but I was big enough and full of fury right down to the pit of me. I leapt at him with claws and teeth ready to do their worst and I came down on him so hard that he collapsed beneath me.

In the next second, my teeth were in his neck, ripping in hard as I shoved my paws down on his shoulders and kept him there. I growled a warning, demanding he submit to me. But he rolled, throwing me with him and kicking me with his back feet as he went, his claws tearing along my belly. I barely felt the pain as adrenaline took over, and I forced us to keep rolling before he could get me beneath him once more.

I took no prisoners this time, catching his neck between my jaws again and biting hard enough to taste blood until a noise left him like an injured kitten. He went limp beneath me, submitting to my power and when he went fully still, I released him, standing up on top of him and raising my head as I released an almighty roar.

Cheers collided around me, students calling my name – some getting it wrong altogether, but dammit they were trying. It felt like I'd just changed the course of fate, like the stars were peering my way just for a moment, long enough to acknowledge what I'd done. What I had made of myself.

I dropped my head, baring bloody teeth in a cat's smile as I hunted for my friends, and the members of Cyrus's pride backed away from Birdie who was in a nest of toilet paper on the floor.

Marigold stood victoriously over a girl trapped in a net of vines and Wilbur was playing whack-a-mole with Isla's serpentine head as she tried to get out of the muddy earth at his feet, using his damn shoe as he tried to beat her back underground.

It was carnage. But we'd won. We'd shown them what we were made of. Or at least, Wilbur, Marigold and I had, and for now that seemed to be enough.

Cyrus backed off, but Isla went from a level ten psychopath to a level one hundred. We were getting far better at defending ourselves, but Isla's attacks were cunning and vicious, and she fast proved herself more powerful than Cyrus. So it wasn't long before the shine of our victory wore off.

If Isla wasn't cornering us and forcing us into one of her violent hypnoses where she dismembered us in slow, torturous detail, she was slipping Griffin shit in our food or laying traps for us all across campus.

Wherever we went, there could be hidden pitfalls with star damned spikes at the bottom, or flesh eating lugger worms, or a pissed off nest of norian wasps.

If there was one thing that was positive about it, it was like being trained for war. I got really good at catching myself the moment the ground gave out beneath me, my mental shields grew tenfold with constant training, and Isla's hypnosis traps took longer and longer to break into my head. I'd learned to heal myself from all kinds of maladies as well as my friends, and though Isla was a determined bitch of a serpent with the unholy wrath of a scorned goddess, I had to be grateful for the way my grades were rising and my gifts were being crafted in ways that I shouldn't have even known about until senior year. And with that, my thievery skills got better too.

It was Night tradition to cut your cubs off from their inheritance until they proved themselves a worthy member of the family pride. I was, to put it bluntly, the horrifying failure of my family. News of my constant bullying didn't make my parents sympathise with me, no, they saw it as weakness. A runt of the litter who was never going to bring glory to the family name.

Since I'd started at the academy, I was denied everything until I earned it. Birthday presents, Christmas presents, family vacations. My father had promised to buy me this beautiful music box made by my favourite jewellery designer Amber Tulandia for my first Christmas at Zodiac Academy, to celebrate how proud he was of me. But I hadn't made him proud. So instead, he had let me watch while he melted it before my eyes, my entire family staring on as we gathered around the Christmas tree, and the cruellest of words left his lips. *"Nights make their pride proud. Failure is not family."*

Meanwhile my three brothers and two sisters had all graduated Zodiac Academy with gleaming grades, Pitball trophies, and the kind of reputation that made me look even worse by association. Even when I'd written home about my recent victory over Cyrus, I'd only received a response that said, 'That's nice, darling. Do let us know when you achieve something worth wasting parchment for.'

So I had to do something bigger, better, greater. Something my parents and siblings could choke on over their morning hog roast.

The weekend was my favourite part of the week, because I packed a bag, took the bus to Tucana and walked to Ren's new apartment. And there I'd stay until early Monday morning. The others joined us sometimes, and this was one of those times, which I was extra pleased about because I had a plan stacked on a dream today, and I was ready to pull it off.

"Fee." Ren's face lit up as he opened the door in a casual pair of pants and a grey shirt, and I lunged at him, nearly knocking him off his feet as I hugged him.

A laugh rumbled through his chest as I nuzzled him, breathing in his familiar scent of freshly cut grass. He looped an arm around my shoulders, drawing me up the narrow stairway that creaked beneath my feet. We passed by a scowling neighbour who shrank from Ren and muttered something about shame under his breath, making my heart clench in my chest.

"Aren't you going to say something?" I prodded Ren.

"No point," he muttered. "Come on."

He led me into his apartment which was more of a glorified box really. A single bed shared a room with a carved coffee table and a tiny kitchen. Ren had made it nice though, casting ivy up the walls and a little jungle canopy on the ceiling, huge green leaves masking the worn paint.

Wilbur, Marigold, and Birdie were already there on the couch, having taken Wilbur's car earlier on. But I'd had to finalise my plans in the library, ready to present to them once and for all.

"I have a proposition," I announced, whipping the folded plans from inside my long brown coat and waving them at my friends.

"I do love a proposition," Marigold sat up straighter, ironing out a crease in the bright red trousers she wore.

"Ding my dongler, I do as well," Wilbur said brightly. He was working on growing one hell of a moustache lately, and it was really something. It suited him to be fair, especially with the way he kept twisting up the ends and making them all curly like his hair.

"If it's not a plan to rid the world of Isla Draconis forever, I don't want to *hear it," Birdie said, pursing her lips. "Maybe I can get my cousin's wife to eat her. She's a Dragon, you know? An Acrux."*

"Yeah, we know," Ren said. She'd only told us a thousand times.

Birdie had cut her short brown hair even shorter over the summer, giving her a quirky kind of look that really suited her.

"We are going to destroy Isla though, right?" she pushed.

"Well...not quite. But this could help us with her long term," I said keenly, and Birdie perked up at that.

"This best not be what I think it is," Ren growled low in my ear, making me jump as he leaned over my shoulder to try and look at my plans.

I slapped him in the face with them and wafted him over to the couch. "Go sit down. And prepare to be wowed."

"This is rather the dalliance of the day, isn't it?" Wilbur said with a smile, clasping his hands together and waiting for me to go on. "Let's hear it then! And when it is done, I have a spiffing pot of news to share."

"Well now you've got me all curious, Wilbur," I said, folding my arms. "What is it?"

His chest puffed up and everyone looked to him as he plucked the lapels of his brown jacket. "The Queen's Jubilee is coming up like a goose upon a gander stool, as I am sure you are well aware, and as is tradition, she has offered one family the glorious honour of serving her at The Palace of Souls for the ceremony. Furthermore, if that family pleases her, she will offer them quarters of residence and an official position serving beneath the royal Vegas." He was practically gushing as he went on. "And that family is my family, can you believe it? The Gruses. I am as exulted as a slug in a soaking sack." His eyes watered. "The honour! The prestige! The veneration! And as you know well, my family has fallen upon hard times of late, so this could truly not come at a better time. It is a pecan in the beak of a skeletal jaybird." He broke down sobbing and Birdie patted his back while Marigold stared at him in mild surprise.

"That's perfect," I gasped, throwing my plans down on the coffee table. "Wilbur, that means you'll be there on the day of the Jubilee. It's the only hole in my plan. I need an in, and you're it. This must be fate!" I squealed, turning to Ren but finding him cocking a brow at me, arms folded.

"You can't be thinking what I know you're thinking," he said in frustration.

"I found the Guild Stones," I said, grinning wide.

"You did?" Marigold asked, intrigued.

"Holy halibut," Wilbur gasped.

"Where are they?" Birdie demanded.

I unfolded my plans and took out a newspaper cutting from within it about the Jubilee. *"Queen Leondra wears this crown for special occasions only,"* I said. *"It comes out of the treasury so rarely because it's damn precious. And I figured out why."* I pointed to the four beautiful gemstones that sat in the clasps at the front of it. An opal, topaz, a ruby and a turquoise stone. *"They have to be Guild Stones."*

I passed the photo to Ren and when he gave it a flat look, I snatched it away again and passed it to Wilbur.

"By the rising moon over the land of our great fortune," Wilbur breathed. *"These indeed match the descriptions of the lost stones."*

"What do you think, Marigold?" Birdie took the newspaper cutting and handed it to her, looking hopeful.

Marigold had done more research than all of us, she'd even made twelve binders, each one detailing a Guild Stone and all the history she could find while poring over ancient texts. She never had much emotion about her, but as she looked at that image, I swear her face lit up. *"How could I have missed this? They were there in plain sight all along."*

"So it's them?" I pressed, everything riding on my guess being true.

"I believe so. Opal for Libra, topaz for Scorpio, ruby for Cancer, and turquoise for Sagittarius," Marigold said. *"Unless these are simply beautiful gemstones of superior quality, and not, in fact, Guild Stones-"*

"Which they could be. Easily," Ren said. *"The Vegas love to brag about their wealth. And it would be simple for them to pretend they possess four Guild Stones. But if anyone looked close enough at their fancy fucking crown, I bet they would find they are not the real deal."*

"Why are you getting so angry?" I clipped.

"Because I know what you're thinking, Fee. And if you attempt to get anywhere near that crown, you'll be arrested and sent to Darkmore in the best-case scenario. Worst? They'll kill you during your wildly stupid attempt to steal from the queen of Solaria."

"The best-case scenario is me walking out of that palace with four fat Guild Stones in my pocket, actually," I said haughtily, and Ren gave me a cool look.

"This is insanity," he muttered.

"It isn't. Look." I rolled out my plans to show a blueprint of the palace. It wasn't complete by any means, but I'd managed to get a lot of detail down by studying. *"That crown isn't going to be worn for the entire day. It'll be held here after the morning celebrations because it is only worn for the ceremony – she said so to the press when she wore it for her uncle's funeral two years ago."* I tapped on the room where the crown would be held. *"Not only that, but it will be on display in a glass box because chosen members of the public*

153

are going to be given access to the palace for a walkthrough tour. Between two and four pm, the crown will be right here-"

"Protected by the fiercest kind of magic and surrounded by guards, no doubt," Ren cut in.

"Ren's got a point," Birdie frowned.

"The crown itself won't be protected," I said excitedly. "The glass box will have a magical lock, admittedly a powerful one, but there are no traps on the crown because of this." I folded out another newspaper clipping, this one from twenty five years ago. "There was a fire in The Palace of Souls during Queen Leondra's coronation. This crown was on display along with many of the Vega jewels and the guards had to disable the locks on the cabinets and take the treasures to safety. But there were such powerful defensive spells on the jewels, that a guard ended up dying trying to move them to safety. So, since then, I'll bet my ass the only spells protecting them while they're on display are on the cabinets, and the guards have to be able to open them. Which means they need a touch signature. So-"

"That's a lot of guesswork, Fee," Ren growled, and I shot him a dark look.

"It stands to reason," Marigold cut in before I could go to bat for myself. "That a death in the palace would change the policies on such things. I would also, as you say, bet my ass on a touch signature activation of the cabinets being introduced. They will be alarmed though."

"Of course," I said. "Which is why my plan is so genius, because-"

"Fee."

"Ren," I snapped. "Stop cutting over me."

"Stop saying insane things then."

I growled and he growled back at me, the two beasts in us rising to the surface.

"What do you want the stones for anyway?" he demanded. "You beat Cyrus. You can beat Isla in time too, you just need to train harder."

"It's not enough," I said passionately. "I'm never going to be enough unless I prove I'm worthy of my family name. If I seized the Guild Stones from the Vegas, how could they ever question my power again?"

"You don't need to prove your worth to them," he said in a low tone. "You're worth everything to us. To me."

My throat thickened at his words, and I looked to the others, finding them nodding. All but Birdie who was still staring at the crown in that photograph.

"I think you can do it," she said slowly. "I've seen how good you've gotten at stealing, Fee. We all have." She looked to Wilbur and Marigold for backup and my heart lifted.

"You have the light fingers of a fancy fairy, dear Felisia," Wilbur agreed.

"But...I..." He pushed his hand into his thick curls. "Oh my dandelions, I fear now that my family has been bestowed this great honour to serve the royals, I am caught between a canary and a cantaloupe."

"You're in the perfect position to help us get those stones, Wilbur," I pressed, hurrying forward to perch on the coffee table in front of him. "All I need is one ticket, and a couple of other teeny tiny favours. And that's it! I'll do the rest."

"Blast my blubber," Wilbur said, tugging at his collar as if he was getting hot.

"Pretty please?" I asked. "I swear I won't get you or your family into trouble. Double, triple swear."

Marigold thumbed through my plans, looking to us and Wilbur caught her eye.

"Is it a flan of a plan? Or is it a clotted cream of a pipe dream?"

"It is, as you would say Wilbur, a chocolate dot of a clever plot," Marigold said frankly. "Infallible, if all goes well."

"If all goes well," Ren echoed with a humourless laugh. "This is insanity."

"I think she can do it. How can I help, Felisia?" Birdie asked excitedly, wetting her lips. "Give me a role. I'll do whatever I can to help us get those stones."

"She does not need you," Marigold said. "You are not factored into the plan."

"Why not? I can help," Birdie insisted, hurt crossing her face.

"It's not personal, I just don't want to get any of you in trouble," I said seriously. "If Wilbur can get me in, and do a couple of completely minor tasks, then I can do the rest. And I'll bring us home the reward."

"Who says you won't just keep the stones for yourself?" Birdie accused and my heart twisted.

"Because we're friends," I said. "And I'm doing this for us, not just me. We've all tasted enough shit at the bottom of the barrel already. These stones... they could change everything."

I glanced back at Ren, hoping beyond hope that they could help him prove himself in society once more too. Then he wouldn't have to leave. They were the answer to all of our problems, and I was more than happy to put my neck on the line for a chance at a better future for us all.

"Wilbur?" I asked hopefully. "Can you get me the ticket?"

He swallowed visibly, then nodded and took my hand in his, shaking it firmly. "We are but flowers that bloomed in the shade together, dear Felisia. All of us are. We formed the Dashing Outcast Nerds Group. And I shall never, upon my nelly, forget the bond we have forged in the dark valley of the

D.O.N.G."

"Yeah, we really need to talk about that name again," Birdie said irritably, and I laughed.

"I'll bring them home," I promised, looking to Ren. "I'll change our fates, I swear it."

My mind was yanked out of the memory and I found myself standing before the mirror in Felisia's ship once more where she gave me a smirk.

"That's all for today. Half now, half when you've paid your share, old king," she said.

"Is this even going anywhere?" I demanded. "So far, all you have shared is some bullshit origin story."

"Oh, it's going somewhere alright. A big bad everywhere in fact," Felisia purred. "Now be on your way. I'll come fetch my price when I'm ready."

I scowled, looking to Azriel who gave me a nod, assuring me force wasn't the best course of action here. Felisia's pride herded us upstairs, and it was only when I stepped out into the corridor with the door swinging shut at my back that I realised Marcel wasn't with us. And neither was the piece of amethyst crystal that had been clasped in my fist.

Oh well. C'est la vie.

I headed towards the stairwell, talking in low voices with Azriel about what we'd seen, but he had gone into analyst mode, a notebook propped against his forearm as he scribbled down whole paragraphs in between speaking with me.

"Do you really think this is going to help?" I sighed, still reliving the rough shove of Cyrus's hands and the way the dirt had felt beneath me. I had never been at the bottom of the food chain, and not once had I felt so powerless in the face of opponents at Zodiac Academy. I had always come out on top, but Felisia and her friends had been crushed into the mud time and again, and it left me feeling uncomfortable.

"I know so. The Guild Stones are vital to the twins being able to win the war. If we can track them down, then somehow help our children find the stones in the living realm, it could tip fate in their favour at last." Azriel looked up at me, a half grin on his face as we moved downstairs side by side. "I'm going to write everything down before it fades. I'll come find you soon."

I nodded to him, and he split away into the hall that led to his rooms while I continued on towards the ground floor, wanting to check on my family in The Room of Knowledge. I didn't know how much real time had passed while I'd been captured by those memories, and I feared how long my mind had been turned from my loved ones.

"Lost…is it this way or that? Where can I find him?" Marcel's voice carried up the stairs and I slowed as I found him nearly drifting out an open window towards the night sky.

I almost let him float off like a lost balloon, but at the last moment, I caught his arm and tugged him down to stand in front of me.

He blinked slowly, hardly seeming to perceive me at all.

"Where did you go? You were in Felisia's memory with us," I said.

"I was, and then I wasn't. I remembered somewhere I had to be…" he trailed away towards the window again and the frame twisted as the silent chasm of the door to the beyond crawled into existence, beckoning Marcel closer.

My fingers were still locked around his arm, but I considered letting go and denying all knowledge of ever witnessing this. Merissa would eventually notice he was missing and realise he had moved on, then that would be that.

"Gabriel?" Marcel croaked, looking to that door as if it held a way to his son, and by the stars, it was hard not to feel *something* in the face of his desperation. "Perhaps he is there, waiting just beyond the dark…"

I ground my teeth then turned my mind towards Gabriel, feeling out his presence in the living realm and that longing he felt for me, however faint. It was enough of a connection to find my way to him, and I dragged Marcel along with me, guiding him there to stand before my boy.

Gabriel was sleeping, his head resting back against the Seer's chair and his chest rising then falling slowly. He was still restrained, and he didn't look much at peace while he slept, but he was still breathing, fighting for another day.

I released Marcel and he staggered forward, brushing his fingers against Gabriel's cheek with a look of adoration on his face.

"I know you," he whispered. "Even if you will never know me. And I am so very proud, my darling boy. I have loved you from beyond The Veil for so many years, watching you whenever I was deemed lucky enough by the stars. I am sorry I could not be there, that I am not here now. Death is wicked like that. A partition of souls that yearn for one another, how cruel. But please know that I do yearn for you, Gabriel. My son, my wonder. And I will never stop." He laid a kiss upon his brow and Gabriel's features relaxed a little, his fingers flexing against the arm rest as if reaching for Marcel. I watched as my son's biological father grew a little clearer, his edges sharpening, features brightening, unsure what to feel on the matter. Though perhaps I felt a touch relieved.

Marcel turned to me, tears wet on his cheeks and no arrogance or superiority about him as he closed in on me. He held out a hand as The Veil drew us back into its embrace and we lost sight of the boy we both loved, and for once I didn't question whether his love was truly founded.

I let him take my hand, shaking it before we shared tight lipped smiles and our palms parted.

"Thank you," he exhaled. "You have bought me a little more time with him, and though I feel it waning already, it is more than the stars would have offered me."

I nodded stiffly and he moved past me up the stairs, leaving me with a strange pull in my gut that felt all too close to empathy for my liking.

I continued downstairs then out into the golden light beyond the Eternal Palace, wishing to check on my daughters in turn.

When I stepped into The Room of Knowledge, I hurried to the great orb, knocking past some disgruntled souls who were grumbling about someone as they exited.

The place was suspiciously quiet, the final souls drifting out of the room, while a couple of remnants remained way up in their seats, glimmering a little then fading once more, their features barely intact, some reduced to just vague globes of light.

My gaze fell on one sorry soul who sat alone with his head in his hands, elbows rested on his knees and a look of utter woe about him.

My lips twitched and I closed in on the great orb, ignoring him as I rested my hands on the rail and sought out Roxanya and Gwendalina, my heart aching for them. Each were safe for now, if not in the best of circumstances, and their fates weighed heavily on me as I moved around the room to find a place to perch. I continued walking, finding myself taking a seat two along from Darius.

"Did something happen that I should be aware of?" I asked sternly and he lifted his head from his hands, his eyes finding mine with no bravado or malice, just purest pain.

"Oh," I breathed, knowing that feeling to the root of me and beyond.

"Just fuck off if you're going to sit there judging me," he muttered.

He sat back in his seat, destitute and forlorn, and I bit back the retort that came to my lips.

"Look, I cannot imagine what it's like to come here alone, to leave behind the one person you…love."

He frowned at me as if waiting for my words to turn sour.

"I am only so harsh on you because I love her too, and when someone hurts my family, I tend to get murderous. The fact that I have not dragged you to the cursed river and tossed you in for the demons to claim beyond the Harrowed Gate is a testament to how much I do think of you."

"Trust me, if I could go back to the moment I trapped Roxy in that swimming pool, I'd bring down a world of wrath on the man I was that day. There are so many things I'd change. But how am I to destroy a monster who is me?" he asked bitterly, hatred glossing his eyes.

I sighed heavily, knowing that feeling too. "Your father Dark Coerced you in many ways, perhaps not so many as I, but I assure you I know the bitter taste of regret for the things I did under his influence. And I believe I have seen enough of your love for Roxanya to know that you are a changed man. You are free of your father's taint, and I believe, had you stayed in the realm of the living, you would have made an…adequate husband to her."

"Had to cut me down at the last moment there, didn't you, relic?" he smirked.

"I cannot have you growing a bigger head than you already have, poor choice," I said, my lips hooking up at the corner. "So, what happened?"

"Roxy's going down a dangerous path. I'm just…worried," he said tightly, though I suspected there was more to it than that.

"My daughters seem to like dangerous paths." I frowned. "They tread them far too often. But perhaps that makes them experts in the matter."

"Hm," he breathed a laugh. "You might be right there."

"I'm not often wrong, but when I am…I do attempt to admit it." I didn't say anything more, but perhaps he knew what I meant, even if I didn't quite have the words to voice it.

Darius Acrux was not all bad, I supposed. And if there was one thing we had in common that neither of us could deny, it was that we were both pining for more time with a girl who had been lost to us. My little love, who was not so little anymore.

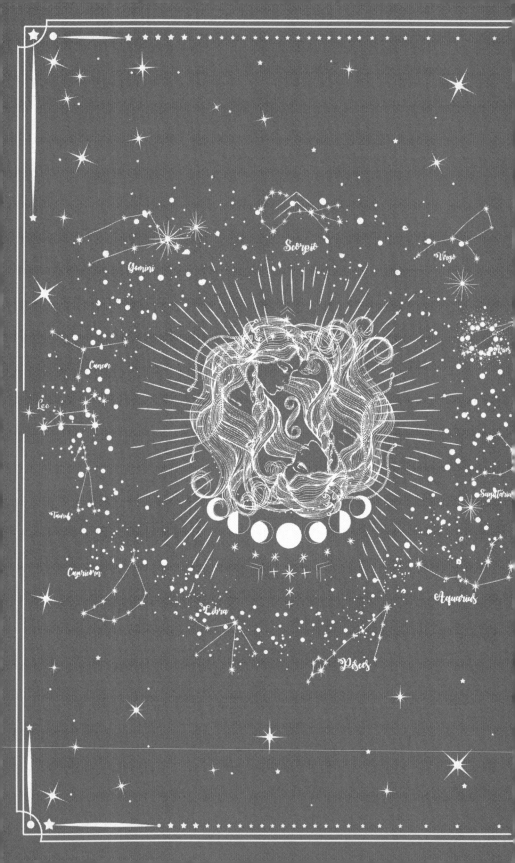

MERISSA

CHAPTER TWELVE

"Don't think I didn't see you earlier," I said softly as Hail moved across the room towards the old oak drink cabinet that he'd had in The Palace of Souls, the thing just the same as it had been in the living realm, chipped corner and all.

"See what?" he growled, pouring himself a measure of tequila which I promptly took from his hand as he raised it to his mouth.

His lips twitched, irritation, amusement, the desire to both punish and praise me. He never had quite figured out which he preferred.

I smiled at him over the rim of the glass, sinking the entire drink in one hit and he took the glass back to refill it for himself. We didn't need food or drink here, but we could partake when the mood suited us, and old habits died hard.

I looked beyond my brute of a husband, my eyes trailing Darius's broad frame. He stood silhouetted by the golden light streaming in through the window, his posture rigid, but that hopelessness was gone now that the two of them had returned to the Eternal Palace, determined to continue down the paths we had begun walking, for better or worse. In its place was a fierce resolution which made me both proud and a little wary.

"You know I see everything," I teased, causing Hail to growl beneath his breath. "You offered an olive branch – you went soft on him."

"The boy has his faults, but I cannot deny the love he feels for her," Hail grunted, the words seeming to cause him some pain. "Much as I might have wished for her to find a gentle, kind soul to match with, I suppose a ferocious, passionate one will have to do."

"Is that so?" I stepped closer to him as he took a sip from his drink, placing a finger on the base of his glass and encouraging him to finish it in one hit as I had.

Hail complied, just as he had all those years ago.

"This path frightens me, Hail," I breathed, keeping our words between us. "But I fear there's no turning from it now."

"No choice has ever been made easy for my bloodline," he growled in reply. "The curse hounds us so doggedly."

I sighed, wishing it wasn't so, wondering what might have been if the curse had been lifted in a time before ours. Then again, Hail likely wouldn't have ever ventured to Voldrakia if his life had been different. We wouldn't have met. And there wasn't any fate that I could ponder where the fire between us didn't ignite.

"Do you think he might find a way back?" I breathed, my voice even lower as I made utterly certain that Darius wouldn't overhear. Not that he appeared to be paying any attention to us; his gaze was fixed on the horizon, his thoughts clearly elsewhere. Getting to grips with the reality of your own death was never easy. To have been ripped from the arms of all you loved while in your prime…it had taken me years to accept the fate of missing out on seeing my children grow. I watched from afar while every knee was scraped, every lesson learned, every tear fell, and I could never help with any of it.

But perhaps I could help now.

"If anyone is determined enough to do so, then it would likely be him," Hail grunted, setting his glass down.

"What happened with the Guild Stones?" I asked, turning my attention from the issue of Darius to the other task which nipped at us.

"I have seen…things," Hail said, his brow furrowing as he seemed to suppress a shudder. "Azriel led me to Felisia Night who apparently knows where more of the stones are and-"

The floor of the room quaked beneath our feet and I gasped, grabbing Hail's arm on instinct, my wings flaring to help keep my balance.

"What is that?" Darius demanded, turning to us, but I had no answer for him.

"I've never felt anything like-" I gasped as a force rippled through me, a line coiling tight around my core before yanking me away, The Veil snapping around me, my grip on Hail's arm tightening to the point of pain as he was dragged along with me.

The realm of the living appeared around me, my knees hitting grass as I was tossed at the edge of a group of Fae who stood at the summit of a small hill.

I blinked against the brightness of the light, turning to look at the floating island the rebels had created as a safe haven from Lionel, and I smiled as Hail stepped closer to me.

"What is this?" Darius muttered, moving towards the other Heirs, my daughter and Geraldine Grus who were gathered at the peak of the hill.

"Something important," Hail replied, and I followed him as he moved closer to the group.

"Are you really sure about messing with this stuff, Tory?" Max asked, eyeing her cautiously as she flicked her fingers at the ground and burned a perfect pentagram through the grass right at the apex of the hill. "I don't think Darius would have wanted you to risk-"

"That's the thing about dying," Roxanya hissed venomously. "You give up the chance to want anything at all."

"What are they doing?" I asked, worry itching at me as I felt the taint of dark magic colouring the air.

"This is my fault," Darius said, his face paling as he moved closer to Roxanya though none of them noticed us at all.

"We could just stop you from doing this," Seth said firmly, moving to join Max and I could feel the tension growing between the group, the building storm as each of them rallied their power.

"Do you really think so?" Roxanya challenged, a slight shimmer igniting in the air between them, making it clear that she'd placed a shield there with lightning speed.

"I'd like to see them try," Hail chuckled darkly, but worry built in my gut as I stepped right up to the edge of the pentagram where Roxanya stood. I tried to move into it, but my foot couldn't pass that barrier, even from beyond The Veil. It wasn't her shield that was keeping us back, but something in the magic she was casting which crossed the lines between realms.

"I don't like this," I breathed.

"Yeah," Seth growled, rising to the challenge, and taking a step closer to my daughter. "I think we can. And for another thing-"

"Leave it," Caleb growled, shooting around to place himself between the other Heirs and Roxanya, his fangs flashing in the light as he bared them.

Darius sucked in a sharp breath, his eyes widening as he watched his brothers lining themselves up on opposite sides of a fight for what had to be the first time, one of them picking a side against the others.

"Caleb, what the fuck?" Max growled, but he didn't back down.

"She needs to figure out this magic. And I swore an oath to help her do it."

I believe she can, and I agree with her on the Darius point. If he'd wanted a say in what she did, he should have stuck around to voice his own opinion," Caleb spat, and I glanced at Darius who looked like he'd just taken a knife to the chest at hearing those words.

Geraldine casually swung her flail in one hand, moving to stand at Caleb's side, an eyebrow cocked in challenge as she made it clear that she stood with her queen as always.

"I don't like this, Hail," I repeated, wishing I could do more than simply lay witness to whatever was happening while that potent power built around us, a dark cloud closing in at our backs.

"I know," he replied, his eyes on Roxanya who was ignoring the argument entirely now, dropping down to sit cross-legged on the floor, various herbs sprouting from the ground around her under the guidance of her earth magic.

The others continued to argue, but I ignored them too, moving as close as I could get to my daughter, crouching down and looking at the herbs while she gathered them, trying to figure out what she was doing.

She muttered beneath her breath, her brow furrowing in concentration as she began to twist the herbs together, tying them into place as she formed a roughly fashioned corn doll, something in my heart telling me what it was supposed to look like – or rather who.

"She's trying to find Gwendalina," I breathed, looking up at Hail who had come to stand over me. "She's hunting for her sister."

"Then let's see if we can help her find her," he replied.

We watched as Roxanya carefully picked a sprig of vervain and pushed it into the doll. Next, she added chamomile and then some sweet marjoram before picking up a dagger and cutting off a small lock of her own hair to press into its chest.

The argument between the others came to an end, presumably because it was clear that there was no stopping this now it had begun anyway.

"Vervain for aiding astral workings," Geraldine breathed as she began to walk in a slow circle around the edge of the pentagram where Roxanya worked, her steps guiding her straight through us as if we weren't even there. Which I supposed we weren't. "And to induce the psychic ability to part one's soul from their flesh. Chamomile to capture the gifts of the sun and borrow its almighty power when it is at its highest peak. Sweet marjoram to call on her one true love – for what greater love is there than that of two sisters?"

"You're making this whole thing sound very romantic," Max muttered.

My throat thickened as the power grew all around us, the weight of it cloying, pressing down on my shoulders while The Veil whipped against my spine, but it didn't try to draw me away.

Next, Roxanya took a lapis lazuli crystal from her bag, the deep blue stone filled with pure golden swirls.

"That's mine," Darius hissed as he looked at the priceless stone, smoke spilling between his lips.

"The dead don't get to keep possession of any treasures, fool," Hail muttered, and Darius growled like a feral beast.

"Bullshit. That crystal is mine and the rest of my treasure is mine too and I'll be back to claim it before any other fucker can lay their hands on it," Darius snapped.

"The lapis lazuli is the epitome of wisdom, intuition and clarity, it will help keep her wandering soul on track to find the answer she seeks," Geraldine said, her voice eerie as she continued to tread a path around the pentagram like she was guarding the girl who sat within it.

"Stop making this weird, Geraldine," Seth complained. "I already don't like it, and you're making it all kinds of freaky."

Roxanya took her dagger and lifted it over the stone, her brow furrowing in concentration as she etched two runes into the flawless face of it.

That unholy power pulsed as she worked, lashing at my spine and causing Hail to grip my shoulder.

"We should stop this," Hail said but Darius shook his head.

"There's no stopping Roxy when she gets that look in her eyes," he said, a note of pride mixed with hopelessness of his warning.

"Fehu for luck and Dagaz for awareness," Geraldine cooed, and Roxanya pushed the lapis lazuli into the corn doll's chest then pinched the opening closed, sealing everything inside it as she positioned herself in the centre of the pentagram.

The power pulsed faster now, thunder crackling through the air around us, though the sunlight surrounding Roxanya didn't so much as flicker. Did she feel it too? Did she understand the weight of the magic she was toying with?

I sucked in a sharp breath as Roxanya turned the blade around and slit her finger open on it, her blood spilling onto the doll and sizzling as the magic that had been building all around us rushed toward it, a blazing path of light spilling between our realm and theirs, pouring into that doll before arcing out of it in five blazing ribbons. Each of them struck a corner of the pentagram and the whole thing began to burn, the ground glowing with a ferocity which defied the stars themselves.

Roxanya tipped her head back to the sky and spoke a set of words so thick with power that a flare of it tore from the world of the living and blasted itself across The Veil, slamming into the three of us and hurling us from our feet in an explosion which only seemed to have taken place on our side of the divide.

The corn doll Roxanya held burst into flames, a scream of agony escaping it as everything it contained was consumed by the fire in a flash of heat.

I pushed up onto my elbows to watch in horror, that dark power throbbing all around us, fear for what it might cause consuming me.

A wave of power bloomed from the doll as it fell to nothing but ash, and Roxanya gasped as it hit her, her body lifting from the floor, spine arching backwards unnaturally.

"Tory!" Max yelled while Darius roared in terror, scrambling back to his feet and racing towards her like he might cross back over here and now if that was what it took to get to her.

"It's working!" Geraldine gasped as Roxanya's eyes flew open and her unseeing gaze stared up at the sky.

The Veil dragged me back, the world shattering as Roxanya's body fell limp to the ground at the top of that hill, but her soul lifted straight from the heart of it, rising to balance on the edge of The Veil, teetering between life and death.

The panicked faces of the Heirs and Geraldine faded away as time flashed and twisted in vortex around us, and Roxanya blinked at the shadowy line beneath her feet. Bright sunlight lay on her far side, the realm of the living beckoning her home, while the golden glow of the after pulsed with heady urgency where Hail, Darius and I stared at her in awe.

"Holy shit, it actually worked," Roxanya muttered, her gaze fixed on the path before her, her posture rigid as she seemed to be fighting the draw of what lay beyond The Veil.

"She mustn't look this way," I barked, something in the pull of The Veil telling me that was the truth even if I had no idea how I knew it. "She can't be tempted into death. Don't let her see you," I added, looking to Darius who seemed on the brink of cracking and running for her.

But he stilled. His huge body locked with tension as he held himself in check and nodded.

"Darcy," he said firmly. "You came looking for Darcy."

Roxanya lifted her head at those words, either hearing them or feeling the truth of them as determination filled her shadowy posture. She was more solid than those of us who had truly crossed into death, but the edges of her form flickered like candlelight, each second that passed drawing her closer to our side of the divide.

"Follow my lead," I commanded, reaching out to first take Hail's hand then Darius's before closing my eyes and letting my form dissolve, guiding them along with me until the three of us appeared as nothing more than golden orbs which hung in the air.

I could feel their presence close to me as I shot forward, racing up to Roxanya and spinning around her, the hazy glow of my form brushing against her skin and pressing through her hair.

My soul lurched with pain as I felt that contact between us, the closest I had come to truly holding her in my arms in so many years.

Roxanya gasped as the three of us spun around her, greeting her, letting her sense that we were here to help before I focused on the pull of my heart which led to her sister.

I shot away from her, a blazing, golden path spinning out behind me as I led the way between time and space, life and death, shadow, and light, making sure she never wavered from the thin path which divided our realm from hers.

Darius and Hail danced with me as we led her on, the world blurring, fading, then finally brightening again so she could peer back into life and see what it was she'd come here for.

Gwendalina and Lance sat in the night iron cage in The Palace of Souls, the two of them huddled together, looking so close to breaking that it fractured my heart to see it.

Roxanya cursed as she spotted them, understanding filling her, giving her the knowledge she needed.

I lingered there, twisting around her as nothing more than a ball of golden light, willing her to feel my love as Hail and Darius did the same, the essence of our souls caressing hers, offering whatever she might need to take from us and more.

A tear slipped from Roxanya's eye, and she wiped it from her cheek before setting her jaw with determination.

"I'm coming for you, Darcy," she swore. "Look for me, because I'm coming."

The cloying weight of that power pressed closer, and I could feel The Veil tugging on me too. It felt her here, where no living soul should step, and it hungered for her.

I flew at her, pressing into her spine and Hail and Darius joined me, pushing her back, forcing her to turn. Roxanya must have felt it too because she didn't resist, turning away from her sister and breaking into a run as she raced down that shadowy path, a glowing light in the distance marking the way back to her body.

The air trembled around us, that rolling thunder making fear shoot through me as we chased her back towards life, the seconds dragging out, then stalling, time shifting unnaturally.

"Don't look back!" I cried, but if she heard me, I didn't know.

The Veil yawned wide behind us, but Roxanya didn't once turn to look at it, her focus fixed on that distant glow, her pace increasing as she sprinted for it. She had too much to live for to let death tempt her away, and as she dove into the bright light of the living, a clap of pure power rang out across all the realms.

We were blasted away, our glimmering forms tumbling across the boundary of The Veil, each of us fighting its call just long enough to see her suck in a shuddering breath as she returned to her body.

Geraldine and the Heirs rushed to her, and I smiled as I left her to their care. I might have been lost to the ocean of death, but so long as she and my other children bathed up there in the balmy glow of life, I was at peace.

AZRIEL

CHAPTER THIRTEEN

"Twelve stones," I murmured, flicking a page in my notebook, and reading through my hypothesis. "The Guild restored…ah." I tapped my finger on the symbol of a rising sun I had scrawled in the corner. "Thought that was obvious, should have made it clearer. Oh Lancelot, if only I could speak to you…"

My heart tugged at the thought of my son and all he was going through, but that pain was gilded in pride. If he could only hold on, he could break Lavinia's heartless curse on Darcy, and they might be free once more. Although, I could not help but foresee the countless dilemmas with that plan…

The word of a monster draped in shadow was hardly one to trust, but there was little Lavinia could do about the curse breaking if the terms she set upon it were upheld. The Death Bond was my greatest concern, so I was not letting it lie. I sought answers from the oldest souls who remained here, seeking magic lost and spells long forgotten. So far, I had found the most value in speaking with a Vampire from the blood ages. A man called Kaige Winter who had been a part of the most fearsome coven in history.

He spoke of magic that could only be found between coven mates, blood magic that was both outlawed and dangerous beyond bounds. But perhaps an answer lay in it, which was why I finally visited the woman I had long avoided. A woman I still despised to my core and who would find no loving arms to walk into when she one day stepped into death.

My wife.

She was always thinking of me lately, though it was not grief that tugged on me so much as regret. With a simple turn of my mind, I let that pull draw me to her, finding her in a dark bed chamber in The Palace of Souls.

Stacks of old tomes were lying open everywhere on the floor and between them all was a broken woman with shuddering shoulders.

I drifted through the room, noting the slimness of her frame, the pallor of her skin. She was suffering, and I felt no pity for her. In fact, I revelled in it, seeing her pay the price of all her poor choices at last. Though it would never be enough to undo what she had done.

"Stella," I sighed, stepping past her, and looking down at the book clasped in her hand. "You are looking in all the wrong places."

She cracked a little sob, true tears rolling down her cheeks and falling to her knees. It was rare to see her like this these days, real pain bleeding into her expression. She was so very good at wearing masks.

I had seen less and less of the truth of her after we were married. We'd had some good years, which turned to good months, then good days, then only good moments, until eventually, all the good was gone.

Her love for Lionel had never really left her, and deep down, I'd known her devotion lay with him. For a time, I'd fooled myself into believing I'd won her heart, but it was not to be. And truly, I wasn't sure I had ever really loved her either.

Regardless, what we had shared had birthed two creatures I loved deeper and more unshakably than anyone or anything I had known before their existence. My children were my meaning, my reason for a life well lived, even if it had not been a perfect one. Perfection was an impossibility, as I knew well from my research. There was only polarity. You could not have good without bad. You could not have light without dark. And it went far deeper than that too, the inner workings of the universe were built on this system of balance, of a scale tipping one way only to tip back, until eventually the scales levelled out. It was why I was so very unsurprised that my son was a Libra, the man who would reunite the Guild born under the star sign of the balancing scales, how fitting. If only he could pull it off.

A glow caught my eye, and I looked over to find my daughter Clara appearing, perching on the edge of a carved wooden desk. She held far more sympathy for the waif in this room than I did, but I never tried to poison her against Stella. She was her mother after all, and Clara had been through things I would never truly understand, so perhaps she saw something in Stella to empathise with. For she knew what it was to wander down the wrong path in life, but from my point of view, it had been her mother who had led her down it.

"At least she's trying," Clara said sadly. "I think she's really starting to see what she's done; she's trying to make it right."

"Trying is not doing," I said icily, seeking out the book Stella needed and finding it on a shelf. An ancient tome on coven law and the teachings of some old blood magics. The answer may not lie here, but it was the right start.

I pushed all my power into my hand, trying to force that book to fall from the shelf, willing it to move. I cursed at the way such effort sapped my energy, but pressed harder against The Veil, reaching for that book, and demanding it move, the importance of this too great to see me fail. A zap of energy sparked away from my hand, crossing the boundary, and knocking it onto the floor with a heavy thump.

Stella gasped, sitting upright, and looking around the room in fear. Magic crackled at her fingertips as she rose to her feet, hunting the shadows in the corners as she crept closer to that book.

"Is someone there?" she called, and Clara slipped from the desk, moving closer to her and laying a hand on her arm.

"I'm here, Mom," she said gently, and Stella shivered as if she could feel she wasn't alone.

"Azriel?" she whispered, voice dropping with fear and hope. "Is that you?"

"Just read the book, Stella," I growled as she crept closer to it and leaned down, scooping it into her hands.

"Coven law." She frowned. "Does an answer lay here?"

She looked around the room, wide eyed and lost, then shook her head and muttered to herself, "I'm going crazy in this old place."

She moved onto the bed, opening the book and I let The Veil pull me away again, returning to my chambers in the Eternal Palace, my room a familiar haven that reminded me of my time at Zodiac Academy.

Occasionally this room appeared as Lance's nursery, or Clara's. Other times their bedrooms as they grew older, or the garden where we often played together. But sometimes the reminder of holding them in my arms and swinging them up into the air, or kissing their little rosy cheeks on a winter's day was all too much to bear.

Zodiac Academy was a neutral space where I could focus and study, just as I had when I'd attended it. Of course, it had looked a little more chaotic than this back then, my room always full of open books which had little colour coordinated tabs sticking out of them. There had been crystals too, tarot cards tossed everywhere and every manner of trinkets I could get my hands on. But it was the hidden things that had caused me most intrigue. The dark magic books and shadow bound artefacts stashed in a carefully hidden compartments in the wall, concealment spells keeping the truth of my deepest fascination a secret.

I slipped out of my room, intending to find Hail but a familiar woman was standing there, her hand raised to knock on my door. She had ebony hair which hung to her shoulders in tight curls, dark skin and large brown eyes which were full of hope.

"Serenity," I said in surprise.

I'd been helping her for some time now with a confounding situation she had discovered herself in once she had stepped through death's door. If anyone had unfinished business, it was her. She had searched The Room of Knowledge for answers to her death, discovering the poison Tiberius's wife, Linda, had slipped to her, stealing her from the world out of jealousy of Tiberius's true love. This woman before me who had been forced to watch her son be named as Linda's after she had fallen pregnant with Max, whilst Linda had faked a pregnancy of her own to claim Max from her when he was born.

But beyond that dark secret that had culminated in murder, Serenity had discovered another, perhaps even more wicked a deed that Linda had committed against her in life.

"Did you have any luck with the scrying bowl technique?" she asked frantically.

I placed a hand on her arm. "I could not reach anyone that way any better than usual. I tried many times, I assure you."

"I must speak with Tiberius, Azriel, he needs to know, he has to go to him," she said in desperation. "Please. There must be something you haven't tried."

"I promise I will keep trying. Darius Acrux is here, and he has been exploring some new...avenues. I will talk with him and see what he has gleaned from his research," I promised.

She nodded quickly. "Okay, yes, I will speak to him too if I see him."

"Of course," I said then her eyes glazed with tears and her form began to drift, her soul called away to someone in the living realm. And from the look of love in her eyes, I had the feeling it might be her son.

I headed off down the hall, making my way to Hail's rooms but pausing when I found the door ajar. I knocked it wide, stepping into the place which was dark except for the two burning blue and red wings of the throne that took up the heart of this room.

"Hail?" I called. "Merissa?"

I spotted the soft glow of golden light beyond the next door, and I slipped that way, pushing into the couple's bedchamber, finding two souls by the arched window, hovering as singular orbs beside one another.

I moved around the giant, fourposter bed which had Hydras, Harpies and Phoenixes carved into the wood, making it to my friends and reaching for their shapeless light in confusion.

"Come back to me." I pressed my power into them, letting them feel my good intentions, the familiar touch of my soul against theirs. And with a pulse of light, they stood before me once more, their hands coming together at once and locking tight.

Merissa exhaled a shuddering breath, focusing on me and rushing forward in the next moment.

Her arms looped around my neck, and I held her as Hail moved to clap a hand to my shoulder.

"It was so very hard to come back until I felt you there," Merissa said, stepping away and looking to her husband.

"What happened?" I asked in concern and Merissa explained how her daughter had soul walked to seek out her twin.

My brows arched and the scientist in me took note of the intensely dangerous dark magic, a thrill dancing through me over its well-executed use.

"Wonderful," I breathed.

"Terrifying," Hail corrected sharply.

"Yes, and that," I agreed with a wry smile. "The two reasons I am fascinated with such magic. A corn doll, you say? And did she use chamomile or lavender to ground herself? Or perhaps both?"

A violent yank in my chest told me my son needed me and I went to him in an instant, my questions forgotten as I reached for him across the void of nothing that parted us.

Lance sat with his back to the wall in his and Darcy's cage in The Palace of Souls, his eyes hollow, his expression empty, the wounds on his chest half-healed and speaking of another torture session with the monster who was keeping him prisoner. The darkness clouding his soul was almost visible here between realms and I raced to him, falling to his side in terror.

"Lance?" Darcy tried to draw his attention to her, but he didn't look her way, like he couldn't even see her.

"Talk to me," she urged, shifting closer and taking his hand, but still, he didn't respond.

"Lancelot," I growled, resting a hand on his shoulder, and trying to make him see me. "It's time to wake up."

Darcy's face was torn with grief, her fear for her mate colouring the air and spreading into the atmosphere. My gratitude toward this woman was as vast as the sky, for she had saved my son from so many dark fates. Depression, solitude, even death itself, but this…without her power available to her, there was little she could do.

"Lance?" she croaked, crawling into his lap, and cupping his cheek in her palm.

He blinked slowly, a storm of darkness twisting through his gaze as he finally focused on her, but he still didn't speak.

"Please come back to me," she whispered in desperation, tears rolling down her cheeks, her face a picture of torment. "I'm so sorry that this is our fate. It's all my fault. I should have stayed away from the rebels. I should have realised sooner what was happening to me. You shouldn't have to be paying the price of this curse. It isn't fair." She pressed her lips to his, but he didn't move, or blink. He was fading and I had to keep him there, because I could see the way the shadows were eating at him, deep in his bones now, and there were few ways to call him from the brink of oblivion.

When he had chosen this path and handed himself over to Lavinia as payment for his mate's curse, I had been both horrified to witness it, and so deeply honoured to be the father of this man who had learned to love another Fae with such ardour that he would bathe in torment for her. I had never found a love like he possessed, and I would have made any sacrifice to ensure their bond endured. It was precious beyond all bounds, and protecting it was vital.

I was gone at once, seeking out the only person in this world who could help Lance now and was surprised to find myself walking back into the throne room at her side.

Stella had already come to him.

"I can help," she said firmly.

"Stay away from us," Darcy warned, rising to her feet, and hastily swiping the tears from her cheeks.

Stella ignored her, drifting closer, trying to look past her to Lance, and I urged her on, knowing exactly why Darcy would fear her presence, but Stella was the only one gifted enough with dark magic to save him. I pressed a hand to her spine, trying to force her to move faster as time blurred a little and The Veil tried to pull me away. I fought to remain, and Darcy's voice echoed powerfully through the Savage King's palace.

"Why would you help him?" she demanded. "You disowned him."

"He will always be my son. It doesn't matter what words have passed between us," Stella said in earnest. "Perhaps you will understand one day, if you have a child of your own." A sad smile lifted her lips as she closed in on the cage and I couldn't help but see the honesty in her remorseful gaze. "You know…I thought his relationship with you was some pathetic little rebellion against me."

"Hurry up, you waif," I snarled, but of course she didn't hear me.

"Not everything is about you, Stella," Darcy said frostily, and I damn well agreed. "I love your son more than you can even comprehend."

"I see that now. I've seen his silver rings."

"The rings don't change what we felt for each other before the stars offered them to us," Darcy hissed. "The world decided to validate our love the second we were mated, but we loved each other long before that. The people who really care for us accepted that well before the stars had their say. *You* are not one of those people."

Time flickered again, like a heavy breath against a candleflame, and I roared into the abyss, defying it as I stayed with my flesh and blood, the child I loved with the ferocity of the stars themselves. He had a life to live, and I would deliver it to him even if I had to die all over again to secure it, even if my soul was cast to ash and scattered to the farthest reaches of the universe, never to be restored. I would do it for him, as I would do *anything* for my children.

"Your son is the most incredible Fae I have ever had the privilege to know," Darcy called to me as I struggled my way back to him, her voice Polaris in the night sky, drawing me north. "And he deserves happiness and peace. I vow on all I am that I *will* give him those things, and I will destroy anyone who takes them away from him. That includes you, Stella. I have a long list of enemies now, and your name sits close to the top of it."

"Forgive me," Stella sobbed, true pain coating her words. "I should have stuck by him when Lionel bound him to Darius. I should have been there more when Clara was taken from us. I should never have let things come this far. And I should have been a mother he could bring you home to."

"You have forfeited that privilege, but you can lay on the altar of it now and offer him what good you have to give!" I bellowed.

"There's nothing you can do that will ever earn my forgiveness," Darcy said bitterly, and my heart went out to her, because I knew that hurt, that betrayal. It belonged to my son, but she bore it too. His burden was her burden. There wasn't a Fae in any realm, in any time, that I would have chosen for Lance over Darcy Vega. "To hurt him is to incite my wrath. You turned your back on him and left him alone in the world when he needed you the most. There is nothing that can undo that."

I looked to Stella with longing, knowing she was his only chance now.

"Save him," I commanded.

"I can help him. Please. Bring him closer. Let me help him. I'll bring him back to you," Stella vowed, and it was as if she were saying those words to me as well as Darcy.

Darcy stepped aside, seeing this hope laid out before her but she was clearly grappling with trusting this heathen who had caused her so much suffering.

"Baby boy, come to me," Stella tried, reaching as far as she could and grasping his leg.

He didn't stir and I could see the indecision in Darcy's green eyes as she looked from Lance to Stella, her throat bobbing.

"Swear you won't hurt him," she hissed, looking straight at Stella as she made her choice, and relief rattled through me.

Stella would not have come at all if she did not wish to help, and I knew my wife's masks better than anyone. For once, she wasn't wearing one, and so the words she spoke were as true as could be.

"I swear."

Time blurred again and when I managed to regain my grip on it, Lance was close to the bars and Stella's fingers were pressed to his wrist, the words of the incantation of the tenebris convocation passing her lips, the dark power building within her.

Darcy knelt at Lance's side, and I moved to kneel with her, placing my hand on top of Stella's and chanting those same words in time with her. A yank in my chest told me my power had connected to the spell and Stella winced marginally like she felt the change in the magic, the increase in power that now rolled into our son and tugged on the darkness he was trapped in.

"The stars and I will lay a trail of light for you, Lancelot," I whispered. "I am working to change your fate, but you must come back and be ready to place your feet upon your new path."

Lance groaned, reaching for Stella like she held some answer to his suffering. She brushed her fingers over his temple as he leaned against the bars, her brow knitted in concentration, and I wondered if he had any idea who it was that was helping him.

Darkness pooled against the edges of his skin, and she sapped it away into her own, her words intensifying and mine growing louder and faster to match the pace of hers.

Slowly, Lance opened his eyes revealing the glimmer of his silver rings and Darcy lunged at him with a squeak of delight, knocking him sideways so they fell to the floor in a tangle of limbs while she kissed him.

"You're back," she whispered in relief, and I sagged against the floor, my own relief washing through me.

"I'll always come back to you, Blue," he promised, and I knew he meant that. Nothing in life or in death would easily part them now.

"The dark is deep," Stella panted, sitting back on her heels in exhaustion over that spell, and I knew she still had a long night ahead of her. She would have to bleed to let it out, siphon that darkness from her own veins and capture in it a vessel before it could be truly destroyed. "But I can keep it at bay. At least for a while."

"If you're waiting for a thank you, you will only get one from me," Darcy said as Stella peered in at them, looking like she wanted to stay. "Thank you for bringing this man into the world. He is the best thing you have ever done."

The Veil tugged me away with such force that I knew I had to go, but those words wrapped around me, the pure love in them warming me through. She was right, of course, Lance and Clara were the best things Stella had ever offered this world. And I prayed there was still time for her to do right by at least one of them.

DARIUS

CHAPTER FOURTEEN

Time turned fluid where I lingered in the dark. Whatever form I'd held when coming here had faded, all I was now reduced to that small, golden glimmer, my soul contained within it, pining for the things I'd lost.

What have I done?

I floated in twisting circles, the darkness before me alive, yawning, whispering words of true peace and eternal rest.

Some part of me understood that I was hovering close to the Destined Door. Some part of me wondered if I should just slip through it now and stop the harm I always caused for good.

Even from death, I was hurting her.

I'd watched in awe and horror as Roxy took that step into death, her soul parting from her body, walking a line that was all too thin, risking everything because of that damned book which I had so wanted her to find.

I'd pushed her towards it. Whether she'd felt me urging her towards that fate or not didn't matter. Regardless of my influence from this side of The Veil, she had ended up in that cavern, claiming those cursed books because of me. My death had pushed her from impulsive to reckless in her hunt for vengeance.

Any small inclination she'd had towards self-preservation had fallen away when she lost me, and now I was staring that reality in the face. She would risk anything, gamble everything and pay any consequence to rescue Darcy,

Gabriel and Orion. Any cost to herself had become irrelevant to her in the face of what she'd already lost, and she was playing games with her own life, her star damned *soul*.

It was my fault. Whichever way I spun it, it all came back to me.

She would be better if I slipped through that door and left her to find a path which wasn't tainted by my presence, but wasn't it already too late for that?

"You lied to me." Her words jarred through me, echoing around the empty space I found myself in, making the golden glow of all that I was flicker and falter as the pain in her words cut me deep. "You promised you'd stay," she spat.

I could feel her grief, sharp as knives, all of them slicing through me, calling me to her. But how could I go to her now? How could I face her after watching her balance her own soul on the precipice of death because of that fucking book. Because of the magic I'd wanted her to seek.

There was danger in ether which went beyond my understanding, but I could feel it in everything from the weight of that book to each and every spell, potion or word which she took from it.

Her grief was like a sucker punch to my gut, urging me to her, reeling me in. But I couldn't bear to look into those green eyes and face the nothingness in her gaze as she failed to see me in return.

A pause. Doubt, pain, hurt.

She was aching for me and for once I wasn't racing to answer her call. I was letting her down again. But which was worse? My presence or my absence?

"You also swore you'd never see me as your queen," Roxy spoke from the realm of the living again, the words so clearly meant for me that I could hear them as if she were stood at my side. "So, I'm willing to bet this will make you all kinds of pissed off."

I couldn't help it, I fell towards her, the darkness of that door tumbling away as The Veil shifted, revealing her in that room with the red and black roses, a gown of pure midnight hugging her frame.

I gasped as I took in the crown of silver and blue which she'd taken from my treasure hoard and placed upon her head, the obnoxious smirk on her sinful lips which had never once failed to get a rise out of me.

She knew.

She knew I was watching and even now she taunted me, played with me, riled the beast within.

In that smile I found the strength which had been fading.

"Mine," I growled, moving closer to her. But the word was no claim on the trinket she'd stolen to place upon her brow. My claim was for her. The true treasure in that room. The only thing I ever needed to claim anymore.

I reached for her, my form suddenly returning as I moved to stand at her back, looking at her reflection in the long mirror which stood before her just as she studied it too. I met that fiery gaze of hers, my fingers tracing the curve of her spine as I inhaled the perfect scent of her.

"I'm so sorry, Roxy," I breathed.

For dying. For leaving her. For everything that had come before this moment and for all the moments which should have come after. And for setting her on this path laced with darkness.

She closed her eyes, and I drew my hand away, my chest tightening with the reality of what I knew she was capable of now. I was luring her closer to death every time I reached for her like this, and the fear I felt over that was all consuming.

I sank back beyond The Veil, whether by choice or not, I wasn't even certain, leaving my queen there alone once more.

My chamber in the Eternal Palace materialised around me, my weight falling heavily into a throne backed with Hydra heads, the thing which I had once fought for so reverently now nothing but an uncomfortable seat which didn't seem to fit me at all.

I could feel a darkness to the energy in the room, something telling me that Roxy was currently moving further into the shadows, taking a path which she wouldn't be drawn from.

I frowned at the bare wall before me, wondering how I might turn her from this trail, how I might protect her from herself.

But I knew in the depths of my soul that there was no doing that.

Anger rose in me, fury at her for her own recklessness. She was needed there. Darcy needed her, my brother, the Heirs, Gabriel, hell, the whole of Solaria needed her.

I was just a thorn in her side who was drawing far too much of her attention.

I growled, the Dragon in me writhing with unspent energy, but I didn't move. Something was building in the air around me. Something drawing closer which I couldn't keep fighting forever.

A dark circle appeared on the wall before me, a shimmering light reflected in the centre of it, and my spine prickled.

There was something about that circular object which felt…wrong. It didn't belong here. It had slipped through the cracks in The Veil somehow and was looking for me.

I didn't rise from my position on the throne, my gaze fixed on the rippling liquid within that circle of midnight as a face appeared beyond it.

A face I knew too well.

Roxy's eyes shone with the ferocity of her grief as she gazed at me and I stilled as I found her truly looking, truly *seeing* me.

"Darius?" she breathed, a plea in my name like she was begging for this vision of me to be real.

And it was.

I had no idea how, but it was. She was looking straight at me, the thick, cloying energy which spilled into the room reminding me of that damn book she'd stolen.

She drew in a shuddering breath, tears breaking free of her restraint, a sob catching in her chest. Her tears fell against the liquid barrier which stood between us, making it shimmer and ripple, her pain splashing against my skin wherever they struck.

"You promised you'd stay," she accused and the rage which had been set to consume me flashed through me like thunder. I had never wanted to leave, and she knew it. I'd given everything fighting for her, fighting for an end to the man who had tried to forge me in his image.

"You promised you'd find me," I replied, a hateful smile twisting my lips, that anger building beyond anything I'd felt since coming here, something in the darkness of the power which was allowing us to speak like this stirring only the most hateful of my feelings into words. Some small part of me just wanted to tell her to be safe, to keep fighting, to know that I loved her. But the petty, aching, desperate piece of me which wanted nothing more than to return to her arms by any means possible was what had hold of my tongue now.

"Tick tock, Roxy," I growled.

Pain flashed across her features, the liquid rippling then racing away, the cloying darkness chasing after it, a feeling akin to a bucket of ice-cold water dropping over me.

I sagged back into the throne, panting, aching, flickering in and out of substance.

What the fuck had that been?

I made to stand up, but the energy in my chamber rumbled uncertainly, the walls themselves closing in, the golden light fading as memories arose in the space. Me and her, a thousand moments, a million kisses, endless desire, lust, love.

I couldn't breathe for the scent of her, couldn't see for the sight of her, couldn't feel for the touch of her skin against mine.

She was everywhere and nowhere, the room rocking and shaking around me as some magic took hold of it which I could neither understand nor fight against. Not while I felt her like that. Not while my need for her grew so potent that I could do little more than wallow in it.

184

I could feel her lips against mine, her hands on my skin, in my hair, fisting there, pulling me closer, no part of me wanting to refuse.

She was it. And if some piece of her had found its way to me here then I would gladly be a slave to that magic. Aching for her was becoming too much to bear and this taste of near reality was too tempting to refuse.

I needed her so desperately that it devoured me.

The darkness fell to ruin like a slap to the face and suddenly I wasn't in her arms anymore, I was standing above my dead body on a battlefield, watching as she cursed the stars themselves, swearing her vengeance on each and every one.

There were others here now though. Souls which hadn't been present when I watched this play out before.

I turned away from the sight of Roxy standing over my dead body and a flash of horror rolled through me as I spotted the three women who stood there watching us too. They were stunning to behold, utterly naked and painted in blood, but all three of them were disfigured by the darkness of the magic which had guided them here. One had sewn her eyes shut, the other her lips, while the third had cut off her ears.

They grinned at me. Not at my corpse, or the girl blazing with power as she cursed the stars themselves, but at *me*. Summoned here in death to witness whatever was happening now.

"You don't hurt her," I snarled, time twisting around us, Roxy here but not, her memories playing out while her consciousness remained outside of this moment. She couldn't hear me, but they could. "Do you understand me?"

"Hurt her?" the one whose eyes were sewn shut gasped, touching a hand to her heart as if the idea repulsed her. She bled freely from a wound to her arm, blood splattering her pale skin. "We wish only to offer her the truest desire of her heart."

"And that's me?" I surmised, their growing smiles the answer I needed.

I looked around, the weight of this memory pressing close, my own corpse a morbid reminder of what I was now.

"Can you bring me back?" I demanded, the ache for that a burn in my soul.

The one whose lips were sewn shut shook her head.

"She might though," the one without ears cooed. "We can set her on the right path…for a price."

"What price?" I stalked towards them but no matter how many steps I took, I didn't end up any closer to them at all.

"We wish to burn in your passion," the one without ears said, biting down on her lip, her hand trailing over her breast. "One night. You can relive the love which burned between you for a single night and it will feel as real as it did when you lived it. You will be able to touch her, kiss her, taste her, fuck her, you will feel it all and so will she. You can even pick the memories, relive whichever you want as many times as you wish between now and sunrise and we will get to taste the heat of that passion while it roars."

The memory we hung in shifted, replaced by endless heated moments where my flesh had claimed Roxy's, where the fire between us had blazed the hottest. My cock hardened at the sight of it, her body bending to mine, claiming mine, owning mine, and some part of me knew they were offering her this same deal.

"There's nothing else to this?" I asked, suspicion lacing my tone.

"The power of a joining such as yours is compelling indeed, but none of us can partake in any such act in full. Virgin blood works best for our work, so we remain as such. We can steal a taste though. That is all we want. You have our word," the one whose eyes were sewn shut swore, painting a bloody cross over her heart.

I knew I should have been refusing, but even as I thought of it, the memories around me faded. I found myself standing just outside a clearing in the woods, ancient trees forming a perfect pentagram around us and Roxy standing at its centre beside a stone altar.

I knew this was no vision, but the truth of where my wife now stood within the living realm.

She was surrounded by the three women, each of them tracing their hands over her flesh, making the Dragon in me growl with a possessive claim that I refused to relinquish even in death.

I knew they'd offered her the same deal as they'd just given me, and I knew my answer was the selfish choice which I shouldn't have been making. But when it came down to it, there was only her.

"Done," Roxy said firmly, and her word was like a leash winding around my throat, tightening, drawing me to her, but I had no desire to refuse.

I stepped to the edge of the trees and the magic there buzzed powerfully as I made to pass over it, the words of those creatures pressing into my mind before I could continue on.

"*Memories only,*" they breathed. "*Nothing new can pass between you once you enter that clearing.*"

I swallowed the lump in my throat, knowing there were so many things I needed to tell my wife, so many words that needed to be spoken. I couldn't utter them if I agreed to this bargain.

But she stood there, vulnerable, hurting, needing me. And if the only way she could feel my presence was by reliving the memories we'd already shared then I would pick the best of them all and make sure she felt every second of pleasure just as deeply as the first time it had occurred between us.

I took another step, falling into the first memory which came to me. We'd been in the burrows, fucking all night and yet it was never enough. My shirt had already been off, my hunger for her consuming every thought as I stalked towards her.

"Roxy," I growled, and she looked to me, that memory forming around us, the room appearing as it had that morning, the reality of the clearing, of her dress and the sword at her waist tangling with it as she hesitated to give in entirely. "You're wearing far too many clothes," I spoke the words from the past, almost seeing my t-shirt on her body as well as the dress.

One of the oracles started tugging her dress free and Roxy unbuckled her own sword belt, her eyes never leaving me as I prowled closer. The sight of her body made my cock throb with need, and she moaned softly as the dress slipped from her form.

The corner of her lips lifted, her hand moving between her thighs just as it had that day, putting on a show for me as she began to toy with her pussy, pushing her panties aside and biting that sinful bottom lip of hers.

I pushed into the memory, the naked Nymphs fading away as I gave myself to it, not wanting to see them at all, only wanting to look upon the perfection of my bride.

I let Roxy have her way with that memory, fucking her the way we had that morning, worshipping her flesh until the sound of her moans faded and I found myself beyond the line of the trees once more, blinking in confusion.

Then she drew me back to her, the night I had found her outside the burrows beginning to play out, the first night we had spent together after breaking the Star-Crossed bond.

I gave myself to that memory too, loving the feeling of her skin against mine, the tightness of her pussy around my cock, the utter bliss I secured when she came for me, until that faded away too and I was beyond the edge of the trees once more.

This time, I pushed my own will into the memories, picking one which I had fucked my own hand to more times than I could count because it had been that perfect.

Roxy's head fell back against the memory of her pillow, her eyes shut as I stepped into our room at the burrows, chest rising and falling in sleep, the beauty of her as captivating as always.

I pushed the door closed at my back and leaned against it, my hand twisting at my side, magic forming as I cast an illusion into place. Though I didn't move, the feeling of my hand brushed against her ankle, tracing its way up her leg while I remained where I was by the door, watching, waiting.

Roxy moaned softly as those phantom fingers rolled up her thigh where she lay on her side before tracing the curve of her ass, caressing the rounded flesh there and moving higher still.

I fed the feeling back to my own hand, the illusion conveying the softness of her skin to me while I remained out of reach, watching, waiting.

The sheet slipped from her shoulder as my illusion passed over it then dipped to tug at the firmness of her nipple.

"You're ravenous, dude," she mumbled, her spine arching like a cat while that word built a growl in the back of my throat.

"What have I told you about that word?" I asked and her eyes flickered open in surprise as she realised I wasn't beside her at all, a flash of confusion passing over her features as she spotted me by the door.

"What word?" she asked innocently, refusing to so much as blink at the illusion I was using on her.

"I'm not your dude."

She smiled tauntingly, rolling onto her back and leaning on her elbows as she looked at me.

"Sure you are. We hang out, go running together, grab food in the same places and-"

I cut off her words with a shove of my will into the illusion, the phantom hand fisting around her panties and ripping them clean off of her, leaving her there in nothing but my shirt, the oversized material swamping her smaller frame.

Roxy bit down on her lip then had the nerve to continue. "We have the same friends, we like to party, we even-"

The phantom hand took hold of her chin, the shadow of my thumb pushing between those wicked lips, stopping her words, making her suck on it while I held her in place with the magic.

Roxy moaned as she took it into her mouth, her body always so willing to seek pleasure in mine, her rough voice turned to much sweeter sounds as she sucked.

"If I were simply one of your dudes, you wouldn't purr for me so prettily," I pointed out, my magic weaving its way into the illusion, more of it taking form, an arm building then a chest, head, legs, until there was another version of me standing over her, driving his thumb deep into her mouth, taking control of her.

Roxy looked from the illusion to me, her gaze heating before she sank her teeth into the false thumb in her mouth. The pain translated to my own hand as an echo of sensation, and I smiled at her as I curled it into a fist and the illusion released her.

"So, what's this then?" Roxy asked, her attention shifting from me to the false version. "Are we playing something new?"

"Don't go accusing me of playing, Roxy, or I'll have to remind you how serious I am again."

"Don't go making promises unless you plan on keeping them, big man," she replied, her attention shifting from me to the fake me again.

"You think I won't?" I challenged, the idea of this more appealing with every moment.

"I think your jealousy runs so deep that you won't be able to stand it," she replied. "Remember when we were in that amplification chamber with Caleb and-"

"No," I snarled, heat tearing through my core as I took a step closer to her, the illusion reaching down to unbuckle his belt. "I only remember you. Only ever you."

"Jesus," she muttered, looking from me to the illusion again, that one word the answer I needed because she only ever said it when she wanted something so badly all other words fled her.

I smiled darkly stalking towards the bed. "Take the shirt off," I commanded.

As expected, she gave me a flat look of refusal, but while her attention was on me, my illusion grasped the hem of it and tugged it over her head for me.

Roxy cursed as it fell to the floor by the bed, her nipples diamond pointed, her breaths coming shallowly, pupils dilating.

"You were bossy enough when there was only one of you," she commented.

"And you're mouthy enough for two even while you sit there alone."

She lifted her chin. "Illusions take a lot of concentration," she said, her voice taking on a tone which sounded all too like an attempt at my own.

"You remembered your lesson," I praised, laying it on a little thickly and enjoying the way her eyes flashed at the patronising tone.

"You really think you can concentrate on keeping it up once I'm riding you?" she asked, the doubt in her voice clear. "You usually forget your own name when I remind you who owns you, baby. I just don't believe-"

"Is all this talk because you don't think you can handle two of me, Roxy?" I teased, dropping my pants and kicking them off, my cock solid since the moment I'd stepped through the door.

Her eyes fell to it ravenously and the illusion dropped his pants too, drawing her gaze to him as he slowly walked around the bed.

"On your knees," I growled, moving to stand before her on the bed, my fingers winding around her slender throat as she thought to refuse that command. I tugged her up so that she was kneeling there, her mouth close enough to claim with my own.

I dragged her to me, kissing her hard, my tongue sinking into her mouth, the taste of her so sweet that I never wanted to stop. It was hard to think about the illusion while I had her in my clutches like that, but I forced my will into it, his hands trailing down her spine, cupping her round ass.

She moaned as I tightened my grip on her throat, locking her there, devouring her mouth. My free hand teased her nipple, the illusion reaching around her to toy with the other one, her moans growing louder.

I loved the sounds she made when I fucked her. She never held back, didn't even seem capable of it, moaning and screaming as she took my cock, always wanting more, never done with me.

I could feel how turned on she was in the hardness of her nipples, the eagerness of her kiss, but I wanted more proof than that.

I dropped my hand, scoring a line down her stomach, the illusion following my lead and trailing his fingers down her spine. I could feel both sensations, the echo of his touch on her flesh translating into my own skin, and a growl built in my chest as I fought to keep control of the magic.

The illusion slipped his fingers around her ass as I rolled mine over her clit, the two of us meeting at her soaking core, her wetness practically dripping as I pushed into it, unable to resist.

Two of my fingers sank into her, making her cry out into my mouth where I swallowed the sound and urged the illusion to join me.

He pushed two more fingers into her from behind, her pussy stretching as we worked it, the rhythm all too easy to find with my own mind controlling both bodies.

Roxy gasped, breaking our kiss, her pussy pulsing around our fingers, her nails biting into my biceps as she clung to me for support.

I looked into those green eyes, smiling darkly as my thumb rotated against her clit and as simply as that, she broke for me.

My cock throbbed with need as she cried out, her head falling back against the shoulder of the illusion, my jaw gritting as I fought to keep it in place while watching the perfection of her orgasm play out.

"I want to fuck this dirty mouth of yours while watching you take my cock in your pussy too," I growled, my grip firming on her throat, the demand in my tone unyielding.

This was the one time when I could get her to bend to my will. The one time she would ever give in to me, even if she won that battle of wills just as often as she lost it.

But if ever Roxanya Vega would take a command from me then it was when she was high from coming for me and her greedy body demanded me, allowing me to claim it in whatever way I saw fit.

She nodded, still moaning and I took my fingers from her slick cunt, sucking them into my mouth before shifting my hold on her throat to fist in her hair.

Roxy dropped onto all fours between me and the illusion which I had to force myself to concentrate on, her tongue rolling around the tip of my cock before I'd even moved to claim her mouth.

I sucked in a sharp breath and the illusion flickered, my hold on it almost cracking before I forced myself to focus on it again.

"I fucking love you," I told her as I looked down at the beautiful creature positioned on the corner of the bed, her mouth lined up to take me while her ass rose in anticipation of the illusion claiming her too.

"Prove it then, asshole," she taunted, leaning in to lick the tip of my cock again and I groaned.

I frowned in concentration as Roxy took my dick into her mouth, sucking hungrily, swallowing me straight to the back of her throat and making my grip on her hair tighten. Of course she would take control of me even in this position. But I couldn't find it in me to care.

I grunted as I focused on the illusion, feeling her skin echoed into my own hands as he took hold of her hip and fisted his cock in his other hand.

I watched, a growl of jealousy building in my chest even though I knew it was all me, but I wanted every piece of this woman at all times, and if that meant I got jealous over myself having her then so be it.

He slicked his cock against her pussy, rolling the head of it down to her clit, making her arch and swallow my dick deeper. I grunted, able to feel her pussy and her tongue on my cock at once as the magic fed his feelings back to me, the sensation too perfect, the desire to come already rising in me.

I bit down on the inside of my cheek, commanding the illusion to rub his cock from her clit all the way back to her ass, pressing against the tightness of that hole.

"If you come on his cock, I'm going to break the illusion and fuck that perfect ass of yours," I warned her in a low tone.

Roxy's eyes snapped up to mine, surprise and more than a little excitement in her gaze as she nodded in understanding of those words, accepting the deal.

My pulse thumped harder, my eyes moving to her ass, desire rising in me headily. I'd fucked her in more ways than I could count but I hadn't claimed that yet, and the idea had been building and building in me, the need to take ownership of every part of her filling me with a desire so endless that I could barely contain it.

I smiled at her, using my hold on her hair to drive her down onto my dick as I thrust my hips forward, fucking her mouth the way I knew she loved it, hard and without mercy. Then I pushed my will into the illusion, and he thrust his dick into her drenched pussy too.

Roxy cried out around my cock, and I gasped, the illusion flickering in and out of existence as I was overwhelmed by the twin sensation of fucking her in both places at once, my dick jerking, cum almost spilling from me already.

But I held back. Through some miracle, I managed to gain control of myself, panting through my teeth as I fought to return the illusion to its full form, Roxy crying out as his cock reappeared inside her again.

I couldn't help but stare at the way my dick thrust in and out of her while simultaneously sinking down her throat.

My whole body was shaking from the combined pleasure of it, her moans and frantic movements making it clear just how much she was loving it too.

Her spine curved beautifully as she was pinned between us, the wetness of her mouth and tightness of her pussy pushing me towards the edge far faster than I wanted, but I knew I couldn't hold off for long. It was too much. Too perfect.

But just as I felt oblivion calling for me, Roxy came all over my illusion's cock with a cry of pleasure that vibrated right through my real dick where it was lodged at the back of her throat.

I almost came with her, the illusion shattering as her pussy squeezed tight, the sensation flooding into me while her lips tightened too, and I knew she wanted me to join her in bliss.

But there was something I desired more than this release and as I dragged my cock out from between her lips, I knew she knew it too.

"Do it," she panted, rolling over on the bed, her ass raised as she leaned on her forearms, her face pressing into the pillows.

"By the stars, I don't think any man has ever wanted anything more than I want you, Roxy," I told her, reaching for the drawer beside our bed and grabbing a bottle of lube from it. The thing was brand new, her pussy always so wet for me that we'd never needed it before, but my dick throbbed with need as I slicked the satin liquid over it now.

I moved over her, the illusion forgotten as I climbed onto the bed, a deep sigh escaping me as I slipped my cock between the cheeks of her ass.

Roxy moaned softly, arching her spine, driving her ass upward, allowing me enough room to slip my hand under her and find her clit.

"You ready, baby?" I asked her, my dick pressing against her ass, the need in my flesh so frantic that my entire body felt like it was buzzing with it.

I wouldn't last much longer, but I wanted this so badly that I couldn't stop now. I wanted to claim her in every way possible.

"Yes," she panted. "Please."

"Fuck."

Roxy only begged when she was too turned on to care, the sound of that word on her lips making my dick jerk with need and I growled as I pressed my hips forward, pushing inside her at last.

I massaged her clit as I eased into her ass, my breath catching at the tightness I found there, her moans encouraging me deeper, my cock throbbing with pleasure.

She was trembling beneath me, the wetness of her pussy sliding over my fingers as I rubbed her clit harder, my dick settling deep within her.

I gave her a moment but as she pushed her ass up, I knew she was done with holding back.

A Dragon's snarl parted my lips as I began thrusting, my cock gripped tight in her ass, her moans of pleasure echoing my own.

She was so tight, so fucking tight and I wanted to come so badly that it took all I had to hold off. But I wanted to destroy her like this, wanted her pleasure even more than my own, my fingers grinding against her clit as my weight flattened her against the bed.

She gripped the sheets and I threaded my fingers through hers as I leaned over her, the tightness of her hold and throaty moans breaking from her filling me with ecstasy as I ran my mouth up the back of her neck.

She writhed beneath me, panting, screaming and finally coming so hard that fire spilled from her palms and burned holes into the mattress.

I came with her, roaring like the beast I was, thrusting deep into her tight ass, filling her with my cum and marking her as my own. Like I'd done time and again. Like I'd continue to do as often as I could for the rest of our lives.

I fell over her, my weight pressing down on her for several seconds as we panted our way through that bliss, her head turning so that she could capture my lips in a kiss that stole the last of my breath and had me drowning in the depths of my feelings for her.

I pulled out of her, rolling off of her and drawing her against my chest, placing a kiss against her hair.

"Mine," she growled, sounding just like a Dragon as she claimed me, and I smirked like a lucky motherfucker.

The memory fractured, the Nymphs appearing for a moment, their greedy hands trailing our flesh before I found myself standing at the edge of the treeline once more, unable to deviate from the memories at all. I had so much I needed to tell her, but I was lost to the power of this magic, and I gave in to it willingly.

I went to her again, the shimmering springs appearing around us this time, the anger I'd felt that day rising in my chest alongside the undeniable lust which had been about to find an outlet at last.

And so the night turned into day then night again, the two of us reliving all of the most passionate memories we owned, the magic guiding us until the distance caused by The Veil finally drew me away again and I was left with the reality of being without her once more.

But before it could cast me aside entirely, I caught sight of Roxy waking alone on that stone altar, unaware of me as I lingered close by, the taste of her kisses staining my lips.

A note lay beside her with the Book of Ether, the deal she'd made with those creatures complete.

The words written on it set my senses on edge, but there was something far more dangerous about them too. Because within the perilous instructions they provided, it seemed there might be one thing which I was probably a fool for still harbouring. Hope.

In the heart of the Damned Forest, beyond the Waters of Depth and Purity, lies the Ever-Changing Winds of Sky and Spirit. The Endless Drop will take you through the Fires of the Abyss and beyond them, where the ether lies thickest, your answers await.

HAIL

CHAPTER FIFTEEN

The great orb in The Room of Knowledge was the object of my attention, my gaze fixed on my children while anxiety plucked a miserable tune from the chords of my heart.

Merissa stood by the railing, head tilted to one side, the space between her blinks growing longer as if she couldn't bear to miss a mere flash of the reality painted before her. She was a mother watching on, torn away from her duty to love and care for her babies. I mourned the time I had missed with my family, but it was somehow worse to witness my wife's suffering.

When I'd wed her, I had promised her a full life that would overflow with love, and I had sworn to offer her the deepest desires of her heart long into old age. Instead, that life had been fleeting. Our union was too brief, our family born and blooming for only a moment in the sun before darkness fell upon us all. I doubted I would ever rid myself of the guilt.

Darius might have been walking a fool's path, but it was one I had walked myself once, seeking an alternative. But when the gates of death sealed at your back, there was no returning. Now…I had made peace around my own demise, acceptance the only path to follow after so many years. But in all this time, I had not made peace with Merissa's death.

I rose, moving up behind her and shifting the hair away from her neck, placing a kiss there.

"Husband," she sighed, a shiver of delight passing through her.

"I miss the sun in your hair," I said, curling a lock of it around my index finger. "And the way it turned your skin to molten bronze." I kissed her neck again. "I miss our summers swimming in the sea, our falls walking through frosted woodlands, our winters curled up with books in the glow of warming fires, and our springs watching blossoms fall and life flourish all over again."

She looked back at me with a tear sliding down her cheek. "Oh Hail," she whispered. "I miss it too."

"If I had known how fleeting each moment was…" I shook my head, sorrowful and full of memories I could never truly touch again.

"It would not have made it last longer," she said, smiling sadly and turning to me, pressing her mouth to mine.

I pulled her closer, grounding myself with the presence of her. "Had you not chosen me as your husband, you could still have it all now. Is there a part of you, no matter how small, that dreams of a life where I was not your bane?"

"Not for a moment, nor a breath, nor a fraction between seconds have I ever doubted my path. And you are not my bane, Hail Vega, you are my fate. I would not forgo you nor my children even if I were offered another entire lifetime in the sun in exchange for you all." She fisted her hand in the gold cloak that hung from my shoulders and I released a breath of relief, my forehead touching hers.

At a thought, I stole her away back to our rooms and turned her to face the mirror that would show us memories of the past. I chose one specially for her, turning her in my arms to watch our wedding day. Merissa cooed and laughed, and I smiled at the perfection of that event, basking in its glow once again, but just as it was getting to our wedding night, something brushed my arm.

I wheeled around with a snarl, finding Felisia Night standing there. "Thanks for the show. How many people have the memory of that wedding? It was pretty small. That makes me special, I think." She smiled at Merissa and my wife gave her an assessing look.

"So this is the cat queen you told me about," Merissa said.

"That's her. How did you get in our rooms?" I growled.

"Simple. You gave me an open invite, silly." She nudged my arm playfully and my scowl deepened.

"I did no such thing."

"You did, I'm afraid. When you made that little old deal with me which said I could have one of your memories or the like in exchange for my story. I couldn't have come to see it unless I was allowed in your rooms. I guess the deal we made gave me a ticket." She smirked, proving she had known it would do just that.

"Fine," I muttered as Merissa laughed.

"Did you get outwitted, Hail?" she teased.

"He did," Felisia answered before I could.

"I was not outwitted," I grumbled. "Like you say, I gave you the invite.'

"Don't go backtracking now, dead king," Felisia said, stepping closer to Merissa with over familiarity. "Hello Savage Queen, I believe you are almost as legendary as I am."

"Is that so?" Merissa hooked up an eyebrow. "Well I believe two legendary women would enjoy quite the evening together talking of all things legendary."

"You and I?" Felisia asked excitedly. "Yes, I'd like that very much."

"We don't need more friends," I drawled.

"She wasn't inviting you," Felisia said. "She was inviting me, and she and I clearly need one more friend at least."

"At least," Merissa agreed, and I huffed out a breath.

Felisia danced away towards the exit. "I shall be waiting in my rooms whenever you wish to continue with my story, dead king."

"Will it be more to the point this time?" I questioned, but her only answer came in the form of a laugh as she went on her way.

"I'm not so fond of that woman," I said.

"Really? I rather liked her." Merissa moved closer to adjust my cloak which had been skewed crooked over my shoulders. "Go to her. I wish to speak with Marcel. He's not himself of late."

"He's scattering. The Destined Door will take him soon. I bought him a little more time by taking him to see Gabriel, but-"

"You did that for him?" Merissa blurted.

"I wouldn't say I did it *for* him. I simply…did it."

Merissa gave me a knowing look and I pressed my lips together.

"I didn't do it from the kindness of my heart," I hissed, her expression accusing me of just that.

"I know," she said airily. "Your heart is crammed full of dark deeds and wicked sins."

"Are you mocking me?"

"Of course not." She beamed, then kissed my cheek. "Love you, darling. Now go seek the rest of that story, it may be of use."

She walked away, but I caught her hand, yanking her back to me and kissing her with wild abandon. Her mouth parted for mine and I sank my tongue between her soft lips, my hand splayed across the base of her spine as I crushed her against me.

"Was that a reminder of who possesses my heart?" she purred against my lips, her nails digging into my spine and making me reconsider whether I would be letting her go at all.

"Perhaps."

"And I suppose it has nothing to do with the fact that I am going to see Marcel," she said questioningly.

"Marcel is of no consequence to me," I said.

"Well, he may not possess my heart or soul, but he is special to me, Hail," she said.

"Mm," I grunted. *Fucking Marcel.*

"As a friend," she impressed. "And he is in need. So I must go to him."

She pushed at my arms, but my body was rigid, and I found myself unable to let go.

She frowned. "What's going on?"

"I miss you, that's all. I've been…dwelling on the past. The future. The present."

"The present?" She picked up on the extra emphasis I had put on that word and I sighed, giving her the real truth.

"Seeing Darius parted from our daughter, it makes me think of how terrible a fate it would be to be parted from you." My brow furrowed. "I would shatter without you, Merissa."

"And I you," she said, sadness tainting her expression. "Which is why I must believe there is a path for Darius to get back to Roxanya, no matter how unlikely it seems."

I weighed that possibility in my mind. "I just don't see a way."

"Sometimes our truest path lays hidden beneath a layer of impossibilities, but if we can find a way to believe it is there, then we can finally place our feet upon it."

"You know more of fate and destiny than I, so I will place my faith in your hope," I said, releasing her at last and she waved goodbye before exiting our rooms.

I carved a hand through my hair, glancing back at the mirror and urging a memory into the glass with nothing but a thought.

I held Gwendalina by the waist as she balanced on a little rocking horse, blinking up at me with those big green eyes. She trusted me not to let her fall, knowing that I would keep her safe no matter what, and I intended to keep that promise to her and my other children.

"I'll find the Guild Stones," I promised her in the here and now. "I will find a path that keeps you safe."

I headed from my chambers with the intention of finding Azriel, but he was already waiting for me in the corridor, as so often happened in this place. We could feel the intentions of other souls we loved, drawing near to one another, especially when our need was dire.

He had his notebook in his hand and an eager look about him, but perhaps there was some darkness there too. "I bumped into Felisia. She says she has claimed what she needed from you to continue with her tale. Are you ready?"

"Indeed," I said, and we started walking side by side. "Are you well, old friend?"

"Well? Ha," he said humourlessly. "No, I am not so well, Hail. Lance is going through a gruelling torture and the shadows are binding to his soul. I believe he would have succumbed to them entirely, only Stella saved him."

"Stella?" I balked. "She has shown little care for him before now."

"It seems she has had a strike of conscience. Or perhaps guilt. I do not know. But I fear how very reliant Lance will be on her now. If she turns her back on him again, it could be the end for him." He said it as if laying out simple facts, but there was a tightness to his voice which spoke of his desperation. "I am so frightened for him."

"I have seen few Fae endure what he has, Azriel. He is stronger than we can ever know. I do believe he is capable of anything in the name of my daughter."

"Yes.' Azriel turned to me, clasping my shoulder with love in his eyes. "They protect each other with the ferocity of starlight. I think often of their Elysian Mating, the purity in it. To find such love is a rarity indeed, and for my son to find it with the daughter of my best friend. Well, I…" Azriel smiled at me, and I couldn't help but return it.

"Yes, in all this darkness, we must not forget to cherish the light," I said. "Truly, I am honoured to have our families joined in this way."

"As am I, Hail. I have not forgotten what you told me the night of their Elysian celebrations."

I recalled the night, the raucous party we had all descended into here beyond The Veil, while our children partied in kind.

"It had slipped my mind," I said, recalling how I had kissed him on both cheeks, declared him my brother then climbed up to the roof of the Eternal Palace and hand painted the Orion constellation and the Vega star there myself.

"That night is never far from my mind," Azriel said with a laugh. "Do you remember when Florence Grus did a naked handstand and commanded Radcliff to shoot an apple off her foot?"

"How could I forget?" I laughed as we rounded into the stairwell, finding our way barred by a naked man leaning through the window where he was perched on a large flying Pegasus, his mouth locked in a kiss with none other than Clara Orion.

"Clara?" Azriel gasped and his daughter whirled around to face him.

"Oh, shit. Hi, Dad." She shot a sideways glance at the man who was now bracing his hand on the window frame, a smoulder on his face that I would have knocked right off of it had I found him kissing one of my daughters.

"Who's this?" Azriel asked keenly, stepping forward to offer his hand to the naked man.

"Reth," he said, taking Azriel's hand. "I guess you've heard of me?"

"I'm afraid not," Azriel said.

"He was just leaving," Clara said quickly.

Reth looked a little crestfallen as she shut him down and he guided his Pegasus away from the window. "Oh I…thought I could take you for a ride, C?"

"You did?" Clara blinked up at him hopefully.

"Well don't let us keep you," Azriel said, taking Clara's hand and helping her up onto the windowsill. "Up, up and away, I say."

Clara shot him the widest smile I'd ever seen on her before Reth helped her climb onto the back of his Pegasus, tipped Azriel a salute then flew away with Clara whooping in delight.

Azriel chuckled, watching them go for a moment longer before turning back to me.

"You're just going to let her go off with a stranger?" I asked in surprise.

"He's not a stranger, his name is Reth." Azriel continued striding up the stairs and I fell into pace with him. "Besides, she is long past the time when she needs my approval for anything. She can do as she pleases, and it seems that this new fellow pleases her. So long as that remains the case, I will delight in her happiness. The stars only know she deserves it."

"And if he turns out to be a cretin?" I growled, and Azriel gave me a dark look that reminded me of the times we had gotten into so much trouble back in our Zodiac Academy days.

"Then I may be less inclined to be so accommodating," he said, a promise of violence in his eyes that got my heart thumping, or at least, it almost felt that way. I ached to dive into one of our past memories, the two of us tangled in the fray of a fight. "Besides, he can hardly be a worse choice than Lionel Acrux." Azriel shuddered at the thought and I held my tongue. Roxanya's taste in men was poor enough, but I couldn't imagine what I would have done if one of my girls had ended up in a relationship with *Lame Lionel*.

We made it to Felisia's rooms and Purrsy let us inside, leading us across the creaking ship. I admired the glittering moonlit water stretching out around us, the illusion feeling so beautifully real.

Purrsy led us down to the lower deck where Felisia sat on a wooden throne while Furnanda massaged her feet and Kitsy braided her hair.

"Good to see you again, Azzy," she said brightly, then nodded to me. "And here's the dead king who never smiles."

"I smiled mere moments ago. You missed it, cat queen. I suppose you will try to steal one from me soon," I said flatly.

"Oh he has a sense of humour today," she said to her pride, cupping her hand around her mouth yet taking loudly so I could hear. "Purssy, give them the pieces of amethyst."

He nodded, handing out the slivers of crystal and guiding us to the mirror. I shared a hopeful glance with Azriel before I was dragged away into Felisia's memories once more, drowning in them so deep that I became her in the past, witnessing it all as if it existed right now.

No pressure, Felisia. You only promised to steal the Guild Stones from the Crown of Starfall right under the nose of Queen Leondra Vega in The Palace of Souls.

My nerves meant I'd had no appetite for breakfast at all this morning, only eating a bowl of oatmeal, two apples and a questionable nectarine. Oh and those wild strawberries I'd picked outside Terra House. I was practically running on empty.

Wilbur had come through on the ticket for the Jubilee and the whole of Zodiac Academy was already well under way with their celebrations when I left just before midday, praising Queen Leondra for her twenty fifth year in power. She was a pretty good queen, I guessed. I wasn't much interested in politics or boring people who died a hundred years ago, so I usually took a nap in Professor Taffety's history classes. Then he'd get mad, and shout, and it would seriously mess up my sleep patterns, and if I cast a silencing spell to block him out, boy did that make him go crazy. One time, he took my pillow, hurled it out the window and blasted it to hell in an inferno of fire. Instead of making his classes more interesting, he took it out on me and the cosy things I brought to help me get the best kind of snooze time. Completely unfair.

Safe to say, I wasn't entirely caught up on the current events of the world, but I did know that the Vega Queen was pretty well liked around the kingdom. She was also the richest bitch in Solaria, so I didn't feel bad about taking a couple of priceless artefacts off her hands.

If I pulled it off.

Which I would. Definitely.

I had to take two busses to The Palace of Souls, and they were crammed full of people wearing fancy dresses and shiny shoes, all of them headed to the celebrations. There were street parties going on everywhere I looked, little tables of liquor set up along the cobbled alleys of Tucana, and a market with Jubilee souvenirs running along the river in Asterella. It was getting really wild in the bustling roads of Celestia, Pegasuses flying overhead sprinkling glitter across the crowd, stalls everywhere selling Vega merchandise, from giant hats to gleaming faux Sphinx tails to celebrate the Queen's Order. Everyone was wearing them, the tails enchanted to swish left and right.

Bells tolled somewhere off in the city towards the parliament buildings, but after a few more stops, my bus headed away from the excited crowd, moving out of Celestia towards my final destination.

The Palace of Souls loomed on the horizon and my heart beat harder as we passed through the lush countryside and tall trees that bordered the city. The palace had a sprawling estate that must have had hundreds of acres of lands, with a whole forest, a stream and no doubt all kinds of secrets nestled within. There weren't many photographs in the newspapers, but the old blueprints I'd found had detailed some of the geography of the place, and the high fence that ringed it all in a giant oval shape. The palace had been built hundreds and hundreds of years ago, and it was still the biggest dwelling in the whole kingdom.

Take that, Professor Taffety. *I might have been bored to death and beyond during his lesson, but I'd taken plenty of interest in the palace history during my planning sessions.*

The bus finally met with another crowd that was gathered at the gates of the palace and I was forced to disembark and walk the rest of the way. My dress was baby pink and encrusted with little diamonds in the huge netting of the skirt, the bodice strapless and laced in at the back. I'd cast an illusion over my hair to make it appear brown so as not to draw too much attention. My beautiful golden locks were too damn recognisable. No one's hair gleamed like that except mine. And though I had shuddered to hide my mane, it was only for a day. I certainly didn't need people admiring the glossy golden hue of my true hair and committing it to memory. Brushing it five times a day and soaking it in lilla tree milk twice a week was the trick. I'd have to give it extra TLC to make up for hiding it. But it was a small, if a little painful, price to pay for this opportunity. My Momma would faint if she saw me like this, concealing my true Lionesshood, but then again, she might just have the energy restored to her by discovering the depths of my cunning plan.

My family may have appeared to be upstanding citizens, but they were particularly adept at trickery, deception and coercion. My father was a debt collector, and that just happened to be one of the most dangerous professions you could get into, considering the Fae he went after were willing to fight to keep their possessions. It was Fae nature, I guessed. Especially the Dragons. Father had taken one on last year and come home with burns on his arms, but a damn glint in his eyes too. He collected that debt, and he got one hell of a raise for it.

Father got his pick of the month's takings. Literally. Twenty percent of anything that was seized for debt collection went right in the back of Father's truck, and Mom and Momma took everything he claimed and sold it for the best price they could get.

They were savage with their sales pitches, and I swear to the stars, my mom could sell a family of fleas to a Werewolf. My siblings were following in their footsteps oh so perfectly, but me? I was yet to bring home the bacon. But today, I planned on bringing the whole pig with a little hat on and a name tag declaring him as Glory.

My hands trembled just a tiny little bit as I moved through the crowd, my ticket clutched in my fist like a weapon.

I slinked my way through the thronging bodies, slipping past members of the press who were taking photographs of some famous Fae in front of the fence. The woman looked vaguely familiar, sharp features, sleek black hair. Pretty sure she was one of those Vampire racers. Birdie had been to watch the finals last year out on the salt flats in Evanda, though apparently she hadn't seen much at all because the Vampires moved so fast. Sounded kind of dull to me, but each to their own.

"Miss Orion!" one of the press cried, trying to get her attention and I took the opportunity to dart for the gate while their focus was elsewhere. The last thing I needed was being caught in the back of a photograph when the lawmen showed up and started looking for the stones. Though I didn't plan on them figuring out what I'd done for a long, long time if I could help it. The fake Guild Stones stuffed into my corset were devised just for that. Marigold had helped me craft them, her attention to detail ensuring they were a perfect match to the real Guild Stones.

I handed my ticket over to a man in a suit and he smiled and waved me through the gate just like that. I headed up the long drive with my heart in my throat, unable to believe the beauty of this place. The palace was stunning, the gardens were full of fruit-laden trees and white rabbits were hopping between them, nibbling the grass. My lips parted as I realised they were Shifters, and they must have been pruning with their little Rabbit mouths.

I hurried to join the group ahead of me, walking a couple of steps behind a dark-haired man and woman who were arm in arm and a blonde man and woman holding hands at their side.

As we made it to the giant doorway, another suited man greeted us, his eyes lighting up at the group I'd made myself seem a part of.

"Ah, Lady Acrux," the man beamed, shaking the blonde woman's hand and smiling to who I guessed was her partner. "So good to have you back. And Lord Capella, it is so good to see you and your wife again." His eyes trailed

my way, but Lord Capella started making a joke about the Rabbits on duty in the gardens, calling them the queen's fur-vants, and getting a confused look from the suited man.

I took the opportunity to slip past them into the palace, and quickened my stride while the lord's wife laughed wildly and kept all attention from me.

Inside, was the most opulent stairway I had ever seen, swirling away towards another level above, and perhaps another after that. The ceiling was painted with a littering of stars with the sun at the heart of it and an incredible painting hung at the top of the stairs of the queen in her shifted form. She was regal in her Sphinx Order, front paws crossed on top of one another, and her female face lifted towards the sky with chestnut hair falling around her shoulders. Stacks of books were painted around her, some lying open at her feet like she had just been reading the texts within. Sphinxes loved a good book, and I guessed if reading was how I charged my magic, I would have loved them just as much. Would I have enjoyed Professor Taffety's dull reading list though? I highly doubted it. I'd be asleep in under a minute. Curse of being a Lioness. Dreamland was never too far away, and it didn't take much to send me into it. Especially when the sun was shining, and I found a perfect grassy patch out by Aqua Lake on campus. That right there, was bliss. Except when Isla found me unawares and slipped skiller spiders in my hair...

"This way for the private tour, beautiful ladybug. They start upon the hour so don't dilly or dally," a woman called to me from an open doorway to my right, her dress bright yellow and made up of ruffles upon ruffles. "We are setting off this very moment."

I hurried to join her, the way she spoke telling me she just had to be related to Wilbur. A large group was already waiting to go on tour around the palace, all of them dressed in such finery that the glitter and gleam of their dresses kept catching my eye.

"I'm Doris Grus," the tour guide announced, patting her hair which was brown and swept into an extravagant do that just kept spiralling up and up, ending in a sort of waterfall of hair at the top. "My nephew Wilbur is here learning the ways of the wackadoodle today, because my family have been bestowed the great and wondrous honour of serving the Vega crown. I cannot even begin to count my blessings, I would get lost upon a cockle and wander right on out to sea." She fanned her hands under her eyes and a few people clapped while one man simply cleared his throat then silence rang out. I craned my neck, spotting Wilbur standing a couple of steps behind her in a bright purple suit, his curly hair slicked back, and his moustache twirled within an inch of its life.

"So!" Doris cried. "Let us embark upon our voyage around the ancient *rooms of this most prestigious of palaces." She led us into an opulent lounge where chandeliers sparkled and even the ashtrays were made of solid silver. My fingers itched to take things as we passed by priceless ornaments and shiny, shiny things that called my name. But there were only four things I was here for today, and I could not get distracted.*

The tour went on for over an hour and my eyes kept trailing to the clocks in every room, one of them whistling and singing a whole song from the mouth of a spinning partridge when it chimed two o'clock, and Wilbur caught my eye so many times that I wanted to berate him for it. He was working up a real sweat on his forehead and kept patting it with a handkerchief, until the thing looked sodden.

Finally, after another half an hour of walking through endless rooms that looked like wealth had vomited more wealth all over the place, we arrived in a long chamber that was simple in decoration, but held the most incredible jewels and artefacts in cabinets and on stands around the room.

"Please feel free to browse some of the most prized possessions of the Vega family themselves," Doris gushed.

I glanced at the guards manning the doors and the ones positioned towards the middle of the room, dressed in royal blue robes with bright silver chest plates and swords at their hips. They likely didn't even need those weapons, trained to kill with their magic alone, and the way their eyes roamed over the crowd set my pulse racing.

Fuck.

This is it. This is my chance.

The group split apart, and I drifted between the glass cabinets, eyeing the beautiful trinkets within. Tiaras, necklaces, bracelets, and breath-taking rings were among the hoard, but there were weapons too. Curved daggers with gemstones glittering on the hilts, ceremonial swords and staffs, and a whole host of divination objects, from a giant crystal ball that looked like rain was falling inside it, to a deck of tarot cards that were carved into gold plates. There was a scrying bowl that was famed for predicting a long-ago battle called the Night of Shattering Fates, and a pendulum that had famously decided the marriage of an ancient princess to an enemy prince, reuniting the once divided kingdom of Solaria. It was all sort of interesting, and yet... where was the star damned crown?

I did two circuits of the room before I gave Wilbur a desperate stare, my gut clenching with anxiety.

"Where is it?" I whispered as I joined him, painting on a smile that would disguise the tension I was feeling inside.

"Jolly jam sandwiches," he breathed, dabbing at his forehead with his

handkerchief again. "I do not know."

"Relax," I growled. "You need to get it together, Wilbur."

He swallowed visibly, nodding and glancing over at a giant silver clock on the wall. "Time is fluttering away like a bag of feathers shaken to the wind."

"Make way!" a male voice bellowed, making me straighten like a rod had been shoved up my ass.

A huge man walked through the door with the Crown of Starfall perched on a red velvet pillow, the thing so shiny it made me let out a possessive growl.

The guard was a little older than me, attractive as hell with all those muscles, his dark skin and sinful eyes looking like the kind of trouble I wanted to get wrapped up in. But it was his hair that did it for me most. A tumble of glossy black locks that were so well kept, so perfectly styled that he simply had to be a Lion.

He moved to an empty cabinet near the wall, touching his hand to it so it opened, and he placed the crown inside on its cushion before shutting it tight.

I caught Wilbur's arm, towing him over to the guard as he took up position beside the cabinet and the crowd shuffled closer to get a look at it.

"You know what to do," I whispered to Wilbur.

"Oh f-f-flapjacks," Wilbur stammered.

"You've got this," I encouraged, then tossed Wilbur towards the burly guard and slipped around the back of the cabinet where no one else was standing.

"The Crown of Starfall has an extremely ancient history, hailing all the way back to the blood ages when the Barbarian Queen reigned across Solaria," Wilbur called out, gaining everyone's attention. "A bloodthirsty Vampire at the head of the largest coven ever to roam the kingdom, the self-proclaimed queen lived in this very spot long before The Palace of Souls was even built. For this land is sacred, does anyone want to have a gander at why?" Wilbur asked and I shifted closer to the cabinet. "Legend goes, that the first star to ever fall from the heavens landed in these here holy grounds, and from there the first Elemental magic was born, bursting out into the earth like shimmering rivers of light."

Wilbur painted the story well, gesturing wildly with his arms as he went on and I waited for my moment, sure it was coming. If only Wilbur could pull it off.

As he re-enacted the star falling from the sky and slamming into the earth, he slipped backwards intentionally – though it looked like an accident with how well he faked it – flying into the guard so hard that he sent him stumbling into the cabinet containing the crown. As Wilbur went down, he took hold of the guard's sword as if to catch himself, drawing it from its sheath and making the crowd leap back in fright as he swung it around then dropped it with a clatter.

The guard's hand landed on the cabinet, his signature unlocking it but simultaneously setting off the alarms from how hard he collided with it. I flicked my fingers, casting a vine across the ceiling and making it rip through the candelabra hanging above us. It came crashing down towards the crowd and screams rang out as burning candles fell from the thing.

Someone blasted water magic at it as it hit the ground, the light in the room snuffing out at once.

Wilbur grabbed hold of the guard's leg with a pitchy scream that sounded almost feminine and I moved fast, my hand sliding into the cabinet while the alarm was still ringing and darkness had fallen. I took hold of the crown and yanked the four fat stones out of their clasps. I shoved them down my corset, taking out the fakes, my focus honing in on this task as the seconds ticked by, chaos descending around me.

Breathe.

You've practised this a thousand times.

A Fae light went up into the air, then another and another, my heart in my throat as I shoved the fake stones into the clasps and tossed the crown into the cabinet just as the guard looked my way. But I was already slipping into the crowd, crying out in fright along with them. I threw one small glance back to find the guard locking the cabinet once more then working to silence the alarm as a rush of air fell from my lungs in relief.

Wilbur was sobbing apologies on his knees, still tugging at the man's trousers and keeping him half distracted from the task while I helped to restore order.

"Gracious, Wilbur!" Doris grabbed his arm, hauling him to his feet and giving him a stern look. "What hullabaloo and honky dang doo is this?"

"Apologies, dear Doris," he said, bowing his head shamefully as the guard gave him a cool look, folding his arms tightly against his chest. "I am but a crud-footed cretin with a wobbling carriage."

"That you are," Doris said, shaking her head and apologising profusely to the guard.

The crowd muttered as Doris led Wilbur out of the room and I kept in the middle of the throng, glancing at the guard who gave me a piercing look that made my bones shiver.

I offered him a little smile, flirtatious maybe, and he frowned, his lips quirking up at the corner like he liked that. But a law-abider and me weren't mean to be.

I headed off to the next part of the tour, the power of the four Guild Stones *humming against my flesh and making my skin buzz with magic. I couldn't believe I'd done it. That I was walking away from the scene of the crime with the stones tucked tight between my breasts.*

A hand locked tight around my arm and panic bolted through my chest.

"Wait," a harsh voice growled, and I nearly blew my own cover, ready to fight and run and run and run, but as the guard spun me around, he had a grin on his face that made my cheeks heat.

"I shouldn't do this but…there's something about you." He slid a piece of parchment into my palm. "My name is Purrsy, you can contact me via this crystal."

"And why would I do that?" I asked, all mysterious and sexy and stuff.

"So I might court you," he said in a gruff tone that set my heart racing.

"I see. Well, Purssy, maybe I'll be in touch."

"Maybe?" he asked with a frown as I pulled away.

"Did I stutter?" I grinned then hurried to catch the crowd, glancing down at the silvery crystal in my palm before sliding it into my cleavage along with my other prizes.

I waited until the tour returned to the entrance hall, gave Wilbur a little wink, then I was gone. Off across the grounds as if taking in the sights before slipping out the gate and heading straight for the bus, Guild Stones seized and glory calling my name.

Felisia Night, you're going to go down in star damned history for this.

"So where are they?" I blurted as Felisia's memories spat me out, and she gave me a twisted smile.

"You'll find out if you keep watching, dead king," she said, sitting on her wooden throne while Kitsy, Purrsy and Furnanda brushed her hair and preened her.

"Nice morals by the way, Purssy," I said with an arched brow.

"Is the Savage King judging me?" he laughed. "My life was dull until this one walked into it. I gave up the law for love."

"Eventually," Felisia said with a laugh. "I think I recall you trying to arrest my ass a bunch of times."

"Well you were a wanted criminal," he said with a smirk. "And besides, I recall we had a lot of fun fighting each other."

"Mm." Felisia bit her lip. "Can't deny that."

"What happened to Ren?" Azriel asked. "He seemed to object rather strongly to your dangerous antics."

"Keep watching," Felisia sang.

"This is an extremely roundabout way of telling us where those stones are," I growled. "You could summarise the final parts of the story and we'll get out of your hair."

"I would never let you in my hair in the first place, dead king," Felisia said, shutting her eyes and moaning as Kitsy began massaging her head. "Besides, the story needs to be told. It is legendary after all. Do you know how privileged you are to see it like this? Only my descendants were gifted the truth of it, and even they didn't get the story direct from the cat's mouth. You are rather lucky for a dead person."

"Where do the music boxes come into the story?" Azriel asked in fascination. "Are the stones contained within them for protection?"

"Azzy, you know I like to tell stories all at once or not at all," Felisia said with a little pout.

"Ah indeed," Azriel conceded. "I shall be patient."

"Well I shan't. This is ridiculous. We are on a merry-go-round and she has no inclination to let us off it," I said in frustration.

"Hm," she smiled. "You sounded a little like Wilbur then."

"Perhaps I shall seek him out instead and ask his version of the story," I said.

"Wilbur moved on a long time ago, and anyway do you really think a Grus is capable of saying anything succinctly?" Felisia laughed. "Nights tell their stories well, weaving all their magic into the details, and I am nothing if not a Night."

"I have seen a fair bit of your decendants' antics, and I cannot say I see the appeal in making everything into a parade with whistles and balloons, songs and dances. Just cut to the point," I pushed.

"How boring, dead king," Felisia said sadly. "Even in death you do not have time for life. We are stuck here with nothing but time to spare, and yet you act as if yours is running out."

"Not mine, but my children's. They are in grave danger, my son and daughter are imprisoned while my other daughter seeks a man who is long beyond the grave, and all the while Lionel Acrux gets his claws deeper into my kingdom."

"There's your problem, see? You haven't let go," Felisia said. "It is not your kingdom anymore."

"No," I admitted heavily. "But it will soon belong to my family again if I can help them."

"Poor little ghost," she cooed. "I know what that's like, watching them. Our cubs, living on as we fade into the past. And how we love them so, but the past cannot catch up to the present. We're not meant to interfere with the now."

"This time I am. I'm sure of it," I said fiercely and Azriel nodded.

"He's right, Felisia," my friend confirmed. "I believe we can help them, and your story may offer us the knowledge we need to do so."

"Then continue," she said, frowning a little like she empathised, pointing to her mirror. "I'm not withholding the truth, you just have no patience."

"Alright," I muttered. "But I swear to the stars, this best be coming to a conclusion soon."

"It is," she said, sadness weighing down her features and horrors sparking in her gaze that seemed rather ominous. "I promise you that."

The stunned silence that filled the room wasn't quite what I had expected. A round of applause maybe? A standing ovation. The popping of a champagne bottle. No?

I waved my hands above the four fat gemstones on Ren's coffee table, wiggling them a little for dramatic effect.

"Wow," Bridie exhaled, shifting closer and reaching out to touch them.

Marigold was slowly nodding her head, a look of mystery and analysis on her face, but one of her eyebrows was drifting towards her hairline, and I guessed that was pretty profound when it came to her steady emotions.

Ren was behind me, as silent as a duck holding in a fart, and I didn't want to turn to look at him, because maybe, just maybe, I cared what he thought most of all. Wilbur was still at the palace, and I was sure he would have been gushing with a stream of 'oh my gobbles' and 'would you take a gander at that' if he had been here now.

"Well come on, say something," I pleaded, hearing Ren step closer behind me.

He took hold of my wrist and a roaring fire built in my core, the burn so deep I had to close my eyes for a moment to centre myself. The thrashing of my pulse was all I could hear as he turned me around with a sharp tug that made me feel like I was twirling on top of a cloud, precariously balancing on the edge of nothing.

My hand came out to steady myself and it landed on his chest. I didn't want to look up, to see the anger in his eyes, see his lips twist before he hurled a string of profanities at me for doing something so unbelievably reckless. But then his rough palm gripped my face and I blinked, glancing up at him, daring to look and finding an ocean of pride, admiration and perhaps I was crazy, but I swear I saw love there too. More than the friend kind, the kind we had been dancing around for months now.

"You are more remarkable than I ever imagined, Fee. And I'm so fucking

212

sorry for doubting you." The words were full of grit, but I felt them surround my heart like the softest of feathers. And in the next second, his mouth was on mine and my head was in a rush like no other, my fingers grasping at his shirt and pulling him closer. It was hard and warm and full of promise, ending far earlier than I wanted it to and leaving me aching for more.

His mouth quirked up at the corner and I stepped away, glancing back at the others to see their reaction. Marigold did little more than blink, her focus still on the stones, but Birdie's face was twisted, and her eyes were sharp.

"What in the stars was that?" she barked, and my spine straightened at the challenge in her voice.

"A kiss," I said simply. "Have you got a problem with that?"

"We are meant to be a team," she said coldly. "If you two get together, it unbalances us."

"Don't be ridiculous, Birdie," Ren scolded. "We aren't getting together."

I looked to him in surprise, the scold burning me too. "No," I agreed, throat thick as Ren's walls went up and his eyes didn't slip my way. "We were just caught up in the excitement. A friend's kiss, right Ren?"

"Right," he said with such conviction that the burn sizzled a little deeper.

The door sounded and all of us stiffened, thoughts of the FIB and royal guards flitting through my head and making magic crackle at my fingertips. I grabbed the stones, shoving them in my pocket and when I turned back to face whatever was coming our way, I found Ren had placed himself between me and the hallway.

"Well pick a daisy and call it a rose," Wilbur's voice filled the air, and the tension ran out of my body. "You did it, dear Felisia!"

He ran around Ren and suddenly I was swept into his arms, a tickly moustache brushing my cheek as he placed a kiss there and started singing some crazy old war song about an army of fifty winning a battle against a thousand. By the second chorus, I'd picked up the words and was singing along, arms raised in the air while Wilbur leapt onto the table, kicked off his shoes, rolled up his trouser legs and did some wild, bare-footed dance that made me laugh so hard, I forgot the tension in the room and soaked in my glory at long last.

"So four of us keep one Guild Stone for a day, then we rotate?" I suggested as we sat on our hilltop in Earth Territory. Ren had come to visit, and though alumni were allowed to use the library on campus, the principal was starting to make comments about how much time he spent at the academy since

213

graduating.

"No, we should take it in turns to have all of them," Birdie said. "And as you've been holding onto them for three days now, it's someone else's turn." She shifted closer on the grass, the sun just cresting the hills of Earth Territory and painting them in gold.

"I haven't used them," I said. "I've been looking after them."

The first couple of days had been stressful to say the least as we waited to see if news would spread of the missing gemstones, but no announcement was made. The crown would be returned to the treasury until the next ceremony called for its use, and that could be years down the line. But one day, someone might realise the stones in it were fakes, and that the greatest heist ever had been pulled off long, long ago. By me. Felisia Night. Not that I ever planned on them finding that out. But maybe I'd make a point of having it etched onto my gravestone so my name would finally be known across the land and get the recognition it deserved.

Birdie pouted, but before she could pipe up again, Marigold spoke. "I have been researching the usage of such stones and how they were wielded by the Zodiac Guild. Unfortunately, it seems we cannot unlock their full potential without possessing all twelve and forming a-"

"Cut to the cusp of the cookie! How do we jabber their jellies as they are?" Wilbur cut in. "Do we flay ourselves beneath a blood moon? Or perhaps a Sandellion salsa when the tide is high, stripped down to our bare bottoms and-"

"Why do all your suggestions involve us being naked?" Birdie laughed and I snorted, sharing a look with her that ensured me the previous anger between us was long gone.

"There is much magic in being a nude Jude," Wilbur said, matter of fact.

"Are we sure wielding them is the best idea?" Ren questioned and I shoved his arm.

"You're such a bore, Ren Imai," I teased, and he shoved me back playfully, his hand falling to my knee and staying there. The heat I felt through my uniform skirt was like the kiss of the sun and made me want to lay my hand right on top of his. But then my gaze caught Birdie's and I remembered the way Ren had dismissed our kiss as purely platonic. I subtly pushed his hand off of me, and felt him withdraw.

"What did you find out, Mari?" I looked to Marigold who produced a book from her tartan bag and took out a long, white piece of wood that was knotted and gnarled. As she placed it on the grass, the blades withered a little, leaning away from it as if the thing were cursed.

"What is that?" I breathed, the thrum of power it emitted like a warning

214

beating through the atmosphere.

"Bark from a damned tree, fashioned into a wand by my hand," she said.

"Call me Wendy and hammer me in the cockles," Wilbur whispered.

"A damned tree?" Ren gasped. "Impossible."

"How impossible can it be if it lays right here at your feet?" Marigold asked and Ren fell quiet.

"Can I touch it?" I reached for it, but Ren caught my arm.

"Is it safe?" he demanded of Marigold.

"Quite safe, if it is used correctly," she said, then added. "I would prefer if someone else was its keeper for now. I find its texture rather arousing."

Birdie burst out laughing as my lips parted and my eyes flicked sideways to meet Ren's. Wilbur didn't seem particularly phased. But as long as I'd known Marigold she had never shown sexual interest in any Fae, so this was a little surprising to say the least.

"Is it the dark magic?" I guessed.

"No, not at all," Marigold said blandly. "I am a dendrophile."

"And what's that when it's at home?" Ren questioned.

Wilbur laughed, flicking the ends of his moustache up with his finger and thumbs. "Oh Ren, I thought perhaps you had swung your Long Sherman to the tune of the Mulberry bush enough times to know of such things! Perhaps my experience of the sensual world is a canary more than yours though, eh chap?"

"If you're swinging your Long Sherman anywhere, I think you're doing it wrong," Ren said through a grin.

"Ah-ha, see. You are but a fig missing a pickle, dear friend," Wilbur said with a smug expression. "The sauce is in the pickle." He tapped his nose like he held some secret.

"So the drendo-thing?" Birdie pushed. "What does that even mean?"

"It means I am sexually aroused by trees," Marigold said, and my lips parted.

"All trees?" I blurted, as if that was the most pressing question. But I had far bigger questions, mountains of questions. Like, what were the logistics of that? Did she have sex with them? Had I passed by trees in The Wailing Wood that she'd...what? Dated?

"Not saplings, of course," Marigold said. "And I have a general aversion to pines because of their arrogance. Evergreen trees in general have a rather haughty demeanour, but the deciduous trees...oh yes, they are far more inviting. I am currently in an open relationship with a gentle sycamore and a titillating oak. They have such rough bark..."

She breathed a little heavier then pushed the wand towards me. The object should have been the centre of my attention, but the news that my friend was not only into trees, but was in a serious relationship with two of them was the sort of news that needed a minute to be digested.

"Do they have names?" I asked, fascinated.

"Of course not. They are trees, Felisia," Marigold said, shaking her head at me.

"Oh, right," I breathed. "So how does it all...work?"

"Lots of grinding," she said. "And my oak has a particular notch at just the right height for penetra-"

"I think we should all respect Marigold's privacy," Ren said quickly. "But er, I'm happy for you."

"Are you?" Marigold frowned. "It must be difficult to learn of your friend having such robust sexual conquests when you are going through a particularly long dry spell, Ren."

"I'm not going through a dry spell," Ren scoffed, though one glance at him told me he was flustered. How dry was this spell exactly? Not that I cared. Although maybe I did. A little.

"My cousin Glorinda told me that if you do not walk the nobbled path to blissville regularly, your garden bloom or Long Sherman can wither and crumble," Wilbur said ominously.

"Let's get back to the wand," Ren said firmly, and all of our attention turned on it again.

"Felisia, if you place the stones inside the holes I have carved into the bark..." Marigold shivered a little at the memory then pushed the wand towards me with the toe of her boot. "It should act as a conduit and channel the power of the stones to you. It cannot access their full strength, but it will certainly give you a boost – though how much so is yet to be determined."

Wilbur rubbed his hands together excitedly as I picked up the wand, the dark energy rumbling through it making the hairs rise on the back of my hand. I slid the stones from my pocket and placed them one after the other into the grooves Marigold had made for them, each slotting in perfectly.

"Now what?" I looked to her.

"Now you simply make the wand an offering and the power should last as long as you keep feeding it."

"Feeding it?" I grimaced, not liking the sound of where this was going.

"Blood, of course," Marigold said. "Yours, or someone else's. Either will do."

"I don't think we should be messing around with this kind of thing," Ren said. "There's no need for this. Fee proved she could beat Cyrus. And Wilbur, you stuffed Isla Draconis in a trash can and buried it."

"But Isla has been a nightmare since then," Birdie snapped, pain flashing in her eyes. "She gets in my head and makes me watch my little sister die over and over again." She winced and my heart tugged for her. Her sister had died of a rare disease when Birdie had been eight, and the loss had never left her. Isla was sick to use that against her.

"So challenge her," Ren encouraged. "Fight back."

"I've tried," Birdie growled. "She is more powerful than I will ever be. And it's not just the stuff she does in my head, she has tortured me so many times – and Cyrus too. He might have backed off on you, Felisia, but him and his pride are more than happy to play with me like a weak little mouse."

"Birdie has hit the halibut on the noggin," Wilbur said solemnly. "I may have come out victorious once, but nary a time again."

"And you?" Ren rounded on me, making my heartbeat falter a little at the ferocity of his stare.

"I want to taste true power," I admitted. "I want to know what it's like to never fear finding myself in the dirt again, made nothing in front of everyone."

"You will never be nothing," he gritted out. "You have no idea, Fee. Look what you have achieved." He pointed to the stones. "Isn't that enough?"

My throat thickened and I glanced at Wilbur, Marigold and Birdie, then back to Ren, thinking of all the times I'd seen them on their knees, forced to submit, to suffer in the shadow of our enemies.

"No," I said darkly, my fingers curling tightly around the wand.

"Please," Ren said quietly, just for me. "If you're found with this..." He shook his head at the dark contraption in my hand, and the four glittering gemstones that could land me in Darkmore for the rest of my days if they were ever found in my possession. But I'd known the taste of dirt too many times, and I craved a taste of the sky.

"I won't be found," I said firmly, then cast a little silver blade in my free hand and cut a line along my finger. The blood seeped out and I pressed it onto a series of runes that were etched into the handle of the wand. The wind picked up around me and I swear I felt the stars curse as they watched on.

Birdie shifted closer, her tongue whipping out to wet her lips as she watched with rapt attention.

The power flooded me all at once, a merciless wave of strength burrowing deep into my core and latching on tight to my own magic, fuelling it. It felt unnatural, ungodly, but as that power coursed through my blood, a head rush followed that was like nothing I had ever felt before.

A moan passed my lips and a shiver tracked down my spine, my head tipping back as I let it all take over, trying to grow used to the ecstasy of the strength washing through me.

"We'll take it in turns," I said breathlessly. "It's mine today, tomorrow it's Wilbur's, then Marigold, Ren then Birdie. We'll cycle it."

"Why am I last?" Birdie growled, but I couldn't hear her anymore, a deep laugh falling from my chest as I rose to my feet and raised my free hand to cast magic. It poured out of me like a hurricane, and I wielded the earth at my feet growing a circle of silver spikes around our group, the sharp tips glinting in the morning sunlight. And I got the feeling we were untouchable now.

We made a pact to be subtle. To use the magic to better our grades and fend off anyone who targeted us, but we had to be careful not to draw attention to our newfound power, or the wand which we kept tucked up our sleeves. I felt invincible on the days it was in my possession, and I soon found myself counting the days until the wand would be mine again.

Ren was reluctant to try it at first, but he planned on using it to try and gain some respect back in society. I hated that the world had turned their back on him, especially when it wasn't even him who had been Power Shamed. The stars only knew what abuse his father was facing by comparison. I shuddered to think of it. There was nothing worse in our world than losing your position as a Fae. It was a star-given right to claim power, to rise through the ranks and prove yourself worthy in our world. Ren's father had been stripped of that right, and by association Ren had lost his footing too. It simply wasn't fair.

Birdie was my biggest concern of late. Every turn she took, she went a little further than before, wielding her magic secretly to lay traps for Isla and Cyrus so as not to draw suspicion on herself. I'd heard Cyrus's screams when he'd fallen into a pool of quicksand that had not only sucked him down, but had seared the skin from his legs. Birdie had been so damn proud of how she had grown malum weed into the sand, the toxic leaves having poisoned Cyrus's skin so badly that he had been in the Uranus Infirmary for a week. The same day she had poisoned him, Isla had gone missing on campus, and no one had seen her since. It was unsettling, and no matter what I thought of Isla and Cyrus, this wasn't sitting right with me.

Today was Birdie's day once more, and I hurried to catch her at The Orb before lessons started. She had denied any knowledge of Isla's whereabouts, but she had also been avoiding me like Fae flu, so I knew she was lying to me.

"Birdie." I hurried over to her by the breakfast buffet and cast a silencing bubble around us. "We need to talk."

"About what?" she asked lightly, filling a bowl with oatmeal.

"Isla Draconis," I hissed seriously. "Where is she?"

She shrugged innocently.

"Don't lie to me," I growled, a warning coating those words. "This is going too far."

"Was it going too far when Isla made me eat grugga worms out the back of the Pitball stadium? Or was it too far when Cyrus and his pride tied me onto the roof of Jupiter Halls covered in seeds so the crows came to peck me for four hours? When did it get too far, Felisia? Tell me, because I am so interested to hear your answer."

I swallowed the lump in my throat. "Birdie, I know what they did to us. I was there. I've faced it too. But we're better than them."

Birdie scoffed. "Maybe you are, Felisia. But me? I don't plan on being better than them. I plan on being worse. And if you're not with me on that, then you're against me. So which is it?"

The power brimming in her eyes told me she was in possession of the wand, hidden away up her sleeve, and my heart stammered at the threat she suddenly posed to me.

"I'm just trying to protect you," I changed tact.

"No, you're not," she said. "You're trying to protect yourself. You don't want the wand getting found."

"Obviously not."

"And it won't be," she said. "So just play with it how you like on your days, and don't interfere with my days. Got it?" She walked away and I was left with a pit in my stomach, wondering if I'd made a terrible mistake by stealing those stones.

Things took a nasty turn when Isla was found. For three weeks she had been locked in an underground chamber built of metal, and she had gone through some unknown hell in there that had left her shaken, half-starved and just a shadow of her former self. She didn't know the name of her captor or anything about the way they looked, their identity concealed with powerful spells the entire time she had been held and tortured in their company. But I knew. I knew and it haunted me every time I closed my eyes.

I'd seen the emergency unit arrive from the hospital, seen the healers surround Isla's withered body, seen the principal drop all the wards so she could be stardusted to the nearest hospital immediately. Isla had been covered in blood from wounds long healed, her clothes shredded, her right eye swollen and bulging from a more recent attack. And the worst part of it all, was that Birdie had stood there watching with an evil fucking smile lifting the corner of her lips, satisfaction sparking in her eyes.

I sat on our usual hilltop in Earth Territory just before midnight, waiting for Birdie to appear and make the swap. But the moment I had that wand in my hand, I was going to ensure it was never passed back to her. Wilbur and Marigold had accompanied me here and Ren was on his way. It was an intervention of sorts. If she resisted, we had all made the agreement to subdue her together, even if it was sort of unFae. But the risk she posed with that wand could see us all ruined for the rest of our lives.

Anxiety buzzed through me as I waited for Birdie to appear, but the only figure who emerged from the dark was Ren, wearing a frown that deepened with every stride.

He said nothing as he joined us, but silently took my hand, his fingers curling around mine in the dark. And then we waited. And waited. And waited.

But Birdie never showed.

The FIB ran a full investigation into Isla's capture and torture, but no trace of Birdie's involvement was found. Birdie avoided us day after day, casting strong repellent spells to keep us at bay whenever we got close, and I was at a loss for what to do. We couldn't report her to the FIB or she would bring us down with her, and trying to capture her ourselves was a risk none of us were sure we wanted to take.

Marigold warned us of the wand's dark power, how if Birdie had been feeding it blood regularly, then it could twist the magic of the Guild Stones into something fierce. Not only that, but if Birdie had been offering it the blood of another, a victim laid out as a sacrifice such as Isla, then the wand could turn malignant, even leave a dark mark on Birdie's soul that she would never be rid of.

Couldn't have mentioned that sooner, Marigold??

The fact was, we were in the situation we were in now, and we had to figure out a way to stop Birdie before she got caught and took us all down with her. So we had a plan. A crazy, reckless kind of plan, but those tended to be my forte. And being a fully-fledged thief now, I was at the heart of it.

I met Ren outside the Pitball stadium, the evening light tinting everything in amber. Ren's eyes were dark, hollow and the set of his shoulders told me something was deeply wrong.

"What's happened?" I rushed to him, hand outstretched, but he retreated from me with a single step that told me to stay back.

"Forget it. We need to deal with Birdie." He turned to walk into the

stadium, but I caught his elbow, making him look back at me.

"Ren," I growled. "What's going on?"

He warred with answering, jaw ticking before he finally relented. "Someone broke into my apartment."

"What?" I gasped.

"Yeah," he muttered, eyes slipping from mine. "They ransacked the place. Broke most of my stuff then..."

"Then?" I pushed, my heart racing with fury.

"They wrote 'get out' on the wall."

"Who would do that?" I demanded.

"One of the neighbours. Or all of them maybe. They hate me staying there, they say it...affects the place."

"Affects it how?" I snarled, pacing now as the urge to shift ran through me. I wanted to hunt, to find who had done this and make them pay for it.

"My societal standing makes them uncomfortable, I suppose. I know at least one of them has mentioned to the landlord that no one will wish to rent out her apartment when she leaves."

"But it isn't even you who's power shamed, it's your father. How can you be punished like this?" My hands curled into fists and Ren caught my shoulders, forcing me to stop moving and look up at him.

"It's a ripple effect, Fee. And the stars only know what Father's facing if this is what I endure." A frown drew his brows together. He rarely spoke about his father or what he'd done, how he felt about him since.

"Have you spoken to him?" I asked.

He shook his head. "Can't."

"Why not?"

"He cut me off. Said it was for my own good, to give me a chance at finding a place in society. He thinks people will forget who I am after a while. Especially if I move away from here...change my name perhaps, though I hate the idea of that."

It was the first time I could really see why he had to go. Tucana was never going to accept him, but that didn't mean he had to run to the other side of the world. "How about Sunshine Bay? We loved it there. And I could move there too once I graduate. Maybe Wilbur and Mar-"

"No," he cut me off so sharply that I felt that word like a thump to my heart.

"Why not?" I snarled.

"Because I will never be able to truly rise in society. My family are well known in Solaria, and I might outrun my name for a while, but honestly, I don't want to outrun it. I'm an Imai, and I'm damn proud of that Fee. What my

221

father did shouldn't mean our name has to fall with him. What I truly want is to redeem it. To make everyone respect it again. But I can't do that here. Not in Solaria."

I gritted my teeth, his words so painful they tore my heart in two. "So you're really leaving?"

"How many times do I have to confirm that to you?"

"At least once more. But this time, tell me if there's anything you'll regret when you go."

His eyes raked over my face, falling to my lips then rising to my eyes once again, and all the while I held my breath, feeling like I was being weighed and measured.

"I will have no regrets by the time I leave," he said, and ice coated my veins.

I nodded, looking him up and down before turning my back on him in an insult, pushing through the door to the stadium.

"Fee," he called after me, but I didn't look back, done with him and done with the wild beatings of my heart whenever I got near him. He wanted to go? Fine. Fuck him. Let him sail off to The Waning Lands and become one of the barbarians who lived there. Let him follow his dream of becoming someone in another world, while I made myself into a queen right here in my homeland.

I made it to the large oval field of grass that sat at the heart of the stadium, spotting Wilbur and Marigold standing by the circular pit in the middle. Wilbur waved and I strode over to meet them with my mind setting firmly on this evening's task.

"Are you ready for the Battle of the Banded Cocks?" Wilbur asked excitedly.

"Is that really the name we're going with?" I sighed.

"Oh yes indeed!" he whooped. "The Banded Cocks were four fine warriors who wore a gleaming crest upon their chests featuring a proud cock with a shining red crown that held a white pearl at its very tip – and we shall be Banded Cocks this day!"

"When you say cock, you mean rooster right?" I frowned and Wilbur threw his head back and laughed, but didn't give me any more of an answer than that.

Ren appeared and I pointedly didn't look at him as he joined the group.

"The bait is set, now we await the prey," Marigold stated.

"Come on then," Ren muttered, moving towards the pit and forging a set of steps from the mud with his magic. I made a point of not using them, climbing down into the pit using a vine of my own creation, feeling Ren's eyes on me as my boots hit the dirt at the bottom.

I drew in the shadows around us with a concealment spell as we all fell quiet and waited for Birdie to appear. Marigold had forged an impressive letter to her from the principal, stating that she was to be given an award for excelling in her classes, rising from the bottom and proving herself worthy as Fae. And a small ceremony was to be held at the Pitball Stadium this evening to offer her an award.

Birdie had always been chasing accolades, so it was the best kind of bait we could come up with. I just hoped she'd fallen for it.

We worked together to form the illusion, melding our magic and casting an image of Principal Snowfleur standing in front of a table holding a glittering golden trophy. We created illusions of other teachers and students gathered around it; Ren even added some chatter between them that was so realistic I almost commended him for it. But then I remembered he was a friend-abandoning asshole with no regrets about leaving us forever and I bit my tongue.

We had plotted out every part of this plan, practised it a hundred times and I knew every step of it like it was etched into my skin. Nothing could go wrong so long as we stuck to the strategy.

"Principal Snowfleur?" Birdie's voice set my pulse thundering and magic crackling at my fingertips.

Wilbur touched his fingers to his throat, calling out to her in reply, his voice changed to sound just like the principal's while Marigold worked to puppeteer the illusion of the principal's mouth moving in time with the words.

"Good evening, Birdie Cain!" he called. "Come collect your award!"

The soft padding of Birdie's footfalls drew nearer, and I moved into position while Ren stepped up behind me. We'd practised this so many times yet as he placed his hands on my hips, it felt far more intimate than when we'd done it before in his apartment. His fingers lifted the edge of my shirt, the tips of them grazing my skin and sending a wave of heat rippling down my spine.

I gritted my teeth to focus, but as his magic flooded into my body, a gasp hitched in my throat. The heady rush of his power joining with mine was like no other, and as I drew it to the edges of my hands, a smile curled my lips. This was where I thrived, on the brink of war, ready to dive into the fray.

"Ready?" Ren breathed against my ear, the heat of him close. Too close.

I nodded, sensing Marigold and Wilbur moving into position on my right, Marigold's hands pressed to Wilbur's back beneath his shirt feeding him magic, yet their stance seemed far less intimate compared to Ren and I.

I wielded a disguise from the deep, rumbling magic in my veins, weaving grass over my body and his, covering every inch of ourselves.

"We have a surprise for you, Birdie," Wilbur spoke in the principal's voice *once more. "You won't believe who we found."*

This part of the plan was cruel yet necessary. There was only one thing we could think of that would get Birdie to drop her guard long enough for us to make our move. And as twisted as it was, this might give us the best chance of getting that wand from her.

Marigold made the ground rise beneath Wilbur's feet and his form changed, morphing into that of a young girl who was just five years old. The illusion was perfect, Wilbur's skill with such magic a magnificent thing to behold. Most Fae cast protections over their identity so they could never be impersonated, but unless family members decided to protect the dead from being mimicked, there was nothing to stop Wilbur casting himself as Birdie's sister now.

As he stepped into the illusion of the crowd and moved through it, a tug of remorse in my gut made me hurt for Birdie. I never wanted it to come to this, but we had no choice.

The moment Birdie saw her little sister emerging from the crowd, a noise left her that was half pain, half disbelief.

"No, it can't be," she gasped.

"It is," Marigold took over forging the principal's voice, puppeteering the crowd too as Ren and I focused on the next task.

I placed my hand against the mud wall in front of me and wielded it with my gifts, the mud drawing me into it, parting and moulding around the two of us, pulling us into its depths. We held our breath the moment the earth enveloped us and drew us skywards, the grass against my skin growing thicker as I willed the ground to push us out the top of it.

We were one with the field, laying prone upon it, Ren pressed close to my left as we moved within the grass and the earth, circling around Birdie to position ourselves behind her. At a glance we looked nothing more than the wind shifting the grass at her feet, the cast so perfect it had me brimming with pride. But I had to keep my head, couldn't get carried away thinking about how amazing I was right now.

Birdie dropped to her knees, opening her arms for her little sister and embracing her tight, a sob racking through her throat. "Impossible. It can't be real," Birdie croaked.

Wilbur held her and magic slid subtly from him, vines creeping up from the grass, preparing to tether Birdie in place. I lunged from the depths of the earth at the exact same moment Ren did, and while his power exploded from him, forging bars of iron that grew from the ground like bamboo, I dove towards Birdie.

My hand was up her sleeve before she even knew what was happening, finding no barrier of magic to stop me while her guard was down. She cried out as Wilbur's vines latched around her and in the next moment, I had the wand in my grasp and was turning, running as fast as I possibly could in the opposite direction, leaving the others to cage her.

The moment I reached the edge of the field, I turned back, finding Wilbur, Marigold and Ren surrounding Birdie in the cage. Birdie threw herself at the bars with a shriek of purest hate, snapping some of the vines binding her arms to her sides and spitting curses at Wilbur for appearing as her sister.

"It was the most simple way to ensure you let your guard down," Marigold said.

Birdie shook her head. "I thought I was being overly cautious making the forgery, but of course you couldn't let me have my moment of glory. You were always happy to let me be the bottom of our pile of dirt, and now you've proved it."

The vines snapped off of her body one by one and a chill ran down my spine as I looked at the fake wand in my hand, realising what she meant. It crumbled into a white powder and I gasped, trying to shake it off of my palm but it clung there like wet sand. It crawled over my hand like a living creature and suddenly it was burning, sizzling against my skin and making me scream bloody murder.

Ren ran my way just as the cage around Birdie exploded and deadly shrapnel from the shattered metal shot in every direction.

Ren slammed into me, knocking me to the ground and sending us deep into the earth, letting it swallow us up as metal collided with the mud. His body went rigid and his arms tightened on me even further, then he went slack, the weight of him crushing me and the press of mud to my face making my lungs roar in a demand for air.

The earth trembled violently and I knew whatever awaited us above was danger embodied, but we couldn't stay down here to suffocate in the dirt.

I held tight to Ren and forced the earth to shove us up and out onto the field once more, launching us into a calamitous battle above. Marigold was feeding Wilbur magic while he held off Birdie's ferocious attacks with walls of earth and shields of metal, desperately trying to keep safe.

Ren was unmoving as he tumbled off of me, a huge spike of metal stuck in his side and blood soaking out across his white shirt. I screamed in horror, lunging at him and pulling the metal free from his side. I covered the wound with shaking hands, my magic latching onto his as I worked to heal him with everything I had to give.

Birdie's attention swung our way and our eyes locked over Ren's body. I refused to remove my hands from the wound, healing him more important than

225

anything else in this world.

"Stay back!" I roared, my Lioness aching to come out and make her hurt for this. The wand had to be concealed somewhere on her body, pressing skin to skin to allow her to draw on its power. But where?

There was no obvious bulge beneath her clothes as she raised her hands at me, her upper lip curling back, and a demon in her eyes that spoke of the wand's corruption. "With you all gone, no one else will know I have it. This power. This gift the stars offered me."

"You will never get away with it, you crumpus crumpet!" Wilbur cried, diving out from behind one of his earth walls and raising his hands defensively. A boulder burst from his hands, growing in size and gaining momentum before it collided with Birdie, knocking her to the ground with a crack that said her leg had broken.

She scrambled to get up and Ren sucked in a breath beneath me, his eyes finding mine, full of fear, like it was me who was the one laying in a pool of blood on the ground. I leapt to my feet before any words could pass between us, springing over him and running for Birdie on the ground, her gaze still fixed on Wilbur.

Birdie dragged herself along, her hand reaching for her mangled leg to heal it, a snarl leaving her that revealed her fangs.

"You nincompoop! I shall cast you into the never more!" Wilbur bellowed, casting a swirling storm of vines at Birdie just as I collided with her on the ground. The vines bound my body to hers and she snarled, twisting around to try and ger her fangs in me. But my head swung forward, slamming into hers and dazing her as stars sparked before my eyes.

Her hand reached feebly for her twisted leg again and I spotted a glint of white peeking out from her trouser leg. I cast a small blade in my hand and sliced through the vines, scrabbling over her and snatching the wand from where it was bound to her calf. Magic poured from her, a blast of rubble slamming into me and sending me flying backwards.

She screamed for the wand, but it was tight in my grip, buzzing with power and I wasn't letting go.

I tumbled over the grass, then found Ren there righting me, pulling me along. "Go!" he urged, and we ran, sprinting away across the field, deep into the stadium then out the other side with the footsteps of Marigold and Wilbur on our heels.

Ren tore his bloodied shirt off as we made it through the doors, wiping the red from his side and keeping it balled in his fist as we moved.

Birdie was no match for us now I had the wand, but that didn't mean I would slow my pace. We were going to get it as far away from her as possible and hide it somewhere she could never reach it. I kept throwing glances over my shoulder, expecting to find Birdie taking chase with her Vampire speed, but perhaps she had given up, because she didn't appear.

Either way, none of us stopped running as we ran through The Wailing Wood, only slowing our pace to a walk as we passed other students, stitching on smiles and trying to act casual. My breaths came heavily as Marigold took the lead, guiding us off the path into the trees with the last stage of our plan in mind. I kept the wand out of sight, and I could have sworn the dark power of it was seeping into my skin, tempting me to use it. With a jolt, I realised some of Ren's blood must have gotten on it from my hands.

The wand's pull was undeniable, a call in the centre of my chest that begged to be answered. It had to be wielded. It wanted to be. And it could make me so very, very powerful if only I gave in. It would be so simple to do so, to let that intoxicating magic take over and find a home in the crevices of my soul. I had stolen the Guild Stones after all. If anyone owned this wand, it was me. My friends would understand that. They would want that for me if they were true friends. And if they didn't. Well...they could be silenced.

I shuddered, rejecting the thought as it crossed my mind and gritting my teeth against the power. But it was so, so hard to resist. Like it was in my blood now, a part of me that would never let go. This was how Birdie must have felt in its grasp, and she would surely crave it now she was parted from it. Hunting for it to the ends of the earth until she possessed it again. But I couldn't let her have it. It was mine. I was owed it. I had earned it.

"Just here should do," Marigold said, slowing to a stop in a clearing in the woodland.

My feet came to a halt alongside my friends, and they looked to me expectantly. Waiting for me to do what we had decided. But who were they to decide what was right for this wand? Wasn't it mine to make decisions for?

They were jealous, that's what it was. They wanted to take the stones, steal them from me. But I was the greatest thief this land would ever know. I had stolen priceless jewels from the belly of The Palace of Souls. I was as much a queen as the Vega who ruled the kingdom.

No...why should I give it up when I had proved I was worthy of it? They had thought I was insane to attempt it, but here I was with the evidence of all I was capable of, and now they wanted to take it from me.

I grazed my thumb over the handle of the wand, the runes there buzzing with untold power, feasting on Ren's blood. Ren. The one who was leaving, abandoning us. Abandoning me. He held no regrets either, he had said so himself. He would walk away from me and never spare a glance over his shoulder for the Lioness he had thought so incapable of claiming this prize.

And perhaps he planned to take my wand with him...

I glanced between my so-called friends, suspicion clouding my thoughts. Marigold with her emotionless gaze and Wilbur with his too-friendly demeanour. But I could see the devils in their eyes now, the truth they were trying to disguise.

I raised the wand, aiming it at the one who had hurt me most, who made my heart rip and tear like claws were slicing right through it. *"No regrets. That's what you said, wasn't it Ren? You'll leave on the next boat to anywhere the moment you get your chance. But what are you waiting for? You could have left but here you stand. Now I know why."*

"What are you talking about?" he asked, confounded. Another lie painted on his face.

"You could have left if you wanted to leave. But you realised there was something to stay for, didn't you? You saw this wand and knew it had to be yours. So you bided your time and now-"

"The wand is corrupting her," Marigold cut me off. *"It has been fed too much blood that was won in violence."*

"Holy bluetit hole," Wilbur gasped. *"We have to help her."*

"Fee," Ren said in a low voice, drawing my attention back to him. *"I didn't stay because of the wand."*

"Liar," I snarled, raising my free hand as the power of the stones rushed into my blood and set my skin prickling with a wild energy.

"I said I will have no regrets, but I didn't say I would have no heartbreak," he growled and something in his tone made me hesitate on blasting him away from me. He took another step closer, his eyes unblinking, boring into mine. So familiar, dark, and blazing. *"I will not regret walking away from you because your path is climbing to the stars, and mine is descending into the dirt at my feet. Until I can change that and find my own way towards the sky, I will never be a good enough Fae. Maybe in your eyes, but not mine. I would grow bitter, hateful, and I would never inflict that upon you, Fee. But I will suffer in every moment we are apart for the rest of time. I know that. Yet I still choose to leave because once shame is cast, it cannot be undone. Not here anyway. Though perhaps it can be in another land, a place where I can become worthy again, a Fae I am proud to be. So yes, I stayed for you, for a while longer, because I'm weak. And walking away from you will destroy me more certainly than the moon falling from the sky and crashing into the earth. I will miss you in every breath I take when I go. But I will go, Fee. Just not...yet."*

My hand lowered and my love for him crackled under my skin, searing away the dark until I was me again. And I remembered that the wand was the true enemy.

I shook my head to clear it, his words still ringing in my ears and leaving me speechless. Then I raised the wand in the air and my three friends flinched as I drove it down into the ground at my feet with a cry of effort, wielding its power. My magic poured from me and a giant oak tree grew from the ground, higher and higher towards the sky, the bough thickening until it was wider than the four of us put together. Branches spread out above us, shading the sun as bright green leaves sprouted from them and fluttered in the breeze. The branches continued to grow and spread and thicken while a new shape took form within them. A large treehouse that was built of beautiful wood, with walkways and balconies and a roof that glinted silver.

I pulled the wand from the ground and moved toward the tree trunk, then pressed my hand to it, a door forming at my touch. I set magic into the very bark that would allow only the worthy to find refuge in this place, willing everything I had into that cast, using the power of the Guild Stones to compound and make it impossible to deny. The power of the stones themselves would allow only Fae whose hearts and souls were incorruptible to enter here, those they chose to guard them.

I stepped through the door, finding myself in a wide room before a perfectly carved stairway that glinted with Faeflies, as if the creatures themselves had been born here, or perhaps they had been lured by the magic in the wood.

I turned to find my friends stepping through the door behind me, looking around in awe. I led the way up into the treehouse, standing in a room filled with carved wooden furniture, a stone fireplace dominating the wall to my left.

"Well toss me in a side salad," Wilbur breathed. "This place is the cream in our whiskers."

"Only Fae that the Guild Stones deem worthy to protect them can access this place," I told them. "Birdie won't get in."

I looked down at the wand in my hand, then clenched my teeth. "We shouldn't use it anymore, agreed?"

I looked to the others who all nodded.

"How do we destroy it?" I asked Marigold.

"It can be burned in the lava fields of Nestrula," she said.

"Then that's where we'll go," I said. "And the stones can remain here."

"Wait," Ren stepped forward. "We should use it one last time."

"Gestating Jack Russells," Wilbur gasped. "For what purpose?"

"We're not considering the bigger picture here," Ren said. "Think of these stones getting into the wrong hands. Birdie is a small threat in comparison to a powerful Fae getting hold of them."

"No one even knows we have them," I said.

"Not yet. But any day now, someone could notice the fakes left in the

palace. And once the theft is announced, and a hunt ensues, the lawmen will not be the only Fae who come looking for them. The power of the Guild Stones is legendary, and if we could figure out how to wield them then I'll bet any number of powerful psychos could figure it out too."

A lump built in my throat. "So what more can we do?"

"It is obvious, is it not?" Marigold said with little expression.

"I am as lost as a dinky bat in a bubble bath," Wilbur said in dismay, and he had a point there.

"We lay a trap, or multiple traps. One for each stone. Yes, that would be best." Marigold nodded once. "Four containers, and a clever contraption within that is triggered whenever someone tries to take the stone out of it."

"You should make them," Ren said to me, and Wilbur nodded quickly. "You know how to wield it now."

"Alright," I said, taking the wand into my grip once more and feeling the lick of its power, like a dark beast welcoming me home. I directed my magic towards the table, focusing on forging four containers from metal and urging the power to form a trap inside each of them.

A shiver tracked down my spine and I took in a ragged breath as I felt the stars whispering in my ears and the wand in my hand began to vibrate. The power was unimaginable, building and building while fate seemed to touch my hand and guide its movements. The wand zig-zagged this way and that, and I wasn't sure if I was directing it, or perhaps the stones were, or even the stars. But it moved all the same, weaving from left to right, the magic in the air electrifying, like static sparking against my skin.

The others gasped, Wilbur and Marigold withdrawing, but Ren moved closer, looking ready to dive in and wrestle the wand from my grip if necessary.

Words slipped from my tongue that I had never spoken in my life, the power of them zapping through the air and slamming into the table, scorching a mark across it. As the containers began to form, my mind slipped back to that music box Father had denied me at Christmas and melted before my eyes because I hadn't earned it. Well here I was, wasn't I? Earning it once and for all, branding my name onto the slate of destiny and ensuring it was never forgotten. I was Felisia Night, and one day, everyone would know what I had done, one day they would speak my name with reverence. A legend. A queen.

The containers shimmered with glittering light then my arm dropped, and exhaustion swept over me, making my knees hit the floor.

Ren was there in an instant, pulling me upright and steadying me, checking me over. I let the wand slip from my fingers as my eyes found his, needing nothing more in that moment than him.

"By the light of the bare moon's behind," Wilbur breathed. "Behold, the

wonders of your creation."

I turned to look, finding four beautiful music boxes sitting on the table along the line of the scorch mark, each one engraved with a star sign linked to a Guild Stone.

Marigold picked up the wand, plucking the stones from it and moving to the boxes. *"I suppose we simply place them in, and that will be that."*

"Be careful," I warned, and she nodded, casting a vine instead to carefully move the opal stone into the Libra music box. It snapped shut, vibrating for a moment before falling still once more, and Marigold repeated the process with the final stones. *"There,"* she announced. *"Whatever traps lie within, I suspect we will be better off avoiding them."*

"Let us keep them as hidden as dandelions in a teacup," Wilbur said, moving to one of the smooth bark walls and pressing his hand to it. He created a hidden hatch in the wall, revealing a carved out space beyond it.

Marigold picked up the boxes, placing them inside and Wilbur sealed it with an intricate concealment spell.

"We are bound now, dear friends." Wilbur looked between us ominously. *"This here hollow is ours to protect. A fortress built of courage and gallantry."* He raised his hands, wielding the wood in the wall opposite and marking down four letters. *"K for Kipling, I for Imai, N for Night, and G for Grus."* Wilbur jutted up his chin. *"King's Hollow this shall be, now and forevermore."*

"That's...actually pretty good," I said in surprise.

"Of course it is, dear Felisia," Wilbur said, puffing out his chest. *"My family are renowned for their wondrous acronyms, and this is no exception!"*

"We should destroy the wand," Marigold said. *"And I suppose apologies are in order. I believed it to be an ideal tool, I have now been corrected."* She didn't look particularly guilty or anything, but that was Marigold. And from her, this meant a lot.

"Do not bother your badger about it, Mari, my dear." Wilbur rested a hand on her shoulder. *"Mistakes are found along paths with dead ends. The good thing about having feet is that we can always use them to turn back."*

"Indeed," Marigold said. *"So, I shall go with Wilbur to the lava fields, while you two guard the stones. There could be more trouble afoot otherwise."* She picked up the wand, took Wilbur's arm and guided him towards the stairway.

I was left with Ren and far too much silence passing between us.

"This place, Fee..." Ren stared around in disbelief.

"I'm sorry," I blurted, and he turned to me in surprise. *"Earlier when I had the wand. I...lost myself for a moment. I think I might have done something terrible if you hadn't talked me down."* I didn't mention what he'd said to call

me back to him, those words still buzzing through my mind and leaving me at a loss.

"It was the wand," he growled.

"Was it the wand for Birdie too?"

He contemplated that. "You didn't give in to it, she did."

"I don't know..." I sighed, moving to the window and gazing down into the trees for any sign of Birdie. I pictured Ren laying on the ground covered in blood and a growl rolled up my throat. Ren was right. She had used it to hurt us, I hadn't. That set us apart. It had to.

A week passed and Birdie didn't show up to classes, though a rumour had spread that she'd told Principal Snowfleur she had to go home for a family emergency. It was the least of the principal's concerns as she was still hunting for whoever had wrecked the Pitball pitch.

I didn't know if Birdie would come back or if perhaps she would drop out of Zodiac Academy and we would never have to face her again. But my gut told me I would be fooling myself to think she was out of our lives for good.

We all slept at King's Hollow every night, though we were probably being overly cautious in guarding the stones in a place I was sure no one could enter but us. There was something about the Hollow that I loved though. It was a space just for us, and we added more and more furniture to it, home comforts too. It had fast become my favourite place on campus.

With the wand destroyed and the Guild Stones locked away safely in a magic tree, in a secret compartment, inside music boxes that held untold dangers, I guessed we didn't really need to stay there too, but something about the power of that place just felt safe and welcoming.

Even the safety of King's Hollow couldn't protect us from the announcement that stared back at me from a newspaper in a girl's hand as I walked into The Orb though.

Four priceless gemstones stolen from The Palace of Souls.

I snatched the newspaper right from her hands with a gasp, and when she tried to take it back, I growled so fiercely that she staggered away again. My gaze dropped to the article as my pulse drummed in my ears and the air felt like glue in my lungs.

In a theft set to rock the kingdom, four priceless gemstones have been stolen from under Queen Leondra Vega's nose. The FIB have stated that an anonymous tip off came in late last night stating that they might want to check on the Crown of Starfall. A ruckus was caused at the palace when the FIB requested entry just after midnight and the royal treasury was opened to retrieve the crown.

A shock to the Queen herself, the four gemstones pictured in the crown below, were confirmed missing with four exquisite forgeries in their place. And she has since made this statement.

"These four gemstones are heirlooms with great importance to my family, and I am devastated to learn of their loss."

Anyone who has encountered the crown in recent months is now going through rigorous Cyclops Interrogation, starting with the palace staff, but it is likely this will extend to ticket-holders who attended the Queen's Jubilee-

I stopped reading, dread making my blood run cold.

I clawed a hand into my hair and searched The Orb for my friends. Wilbur sat alone at a table, his face as white as a sheet and his mouth moving as he muttered something to himself, gently rocking back and forth.

I hurried over to him, tossing the newspaper down between us and he met my gaze with terror fogging his eyes.

"Felisia," he rasped, casting a silencing bubble around us. "Whatever shall we do?"

"I don't know. Fuck. I don't know."

"This is the doing of a dastardly traitor. Birdie Cain walks a path of vengeance, and she shall not rest until we sit deep in the belly of Darkmore." He started trembling like a leaf, a noise of sorrow leaving him, and I leaned forward to rest my hand on his shoulder.

"We're not going to Darkmore. No one knows it was us."

"They will when a Cyclops rifles through our minds like a finger scrolling through a binder – woe! Woe is me!" He leapt to his feet, looking in a panic, like he might run or do something even more crazy.

"Wilbur," I snapped. "Keep it together."

He nodded, murmuring apologies as he sank back into his seat and stared at the newspaper in desolation.

"We'll think of something," I said, though as I rested my palms on the table, nothing came to mind but the thought of being dragged away to Darkmore. Made a disgrace. Felisia Night, a taint on the Night family. Spoken of only with shame and embarrassment.

I shuddered at the thought.

Marigold came rushing over to us, looking more flustered than I'd ever seen her as she joined our table. "We are in a lot of trouble."

"Do you have any ideas?" I demanded.

"We could return them to the palace, perhaps," she said.

"They're inside music boxes with traps in them that could be deadly for all we know. What if the queen tries to retrieve them and ends up killed? Even if she was injured, we'd be responsible for that," I said in despair. "They can't go back." There was a note of possession to my voice, because it wasn't just the issue of the music boxes. Those stones were my claim to glory. I wasn't giving them up. Not for anything.

"Oh, of course," Marigold whispered, her face a little ashen. "Perhaps we could retrieve them ourselves?"

"And risk our own necks?" I scoffed. "I don't want to be killed by a music box."

"No, indeed," she agreed, frowning as she thought on it.

"Wilbur," I rounded on him. "Your family work at the palace, you could get more information. Maybe work out how long we have until the interrogation falls on the ticket holders. They won't suspect why you're checking up on them after hearing this news."

"Y-yes," he stammered. "I shall go to them the moment classes are done. I won't dilly or dally."

"I have an idea," Marigold said. "I shall take the stones, hide them well in places across the kingdom then drink a memory potion so I cannot recall their locations."

"King's Hollow was designed to protect them. That's the safest place they can be," I said sharply, not to mention the fact that I wasn't going to become clueless to where those Guild Stones were. They were my legacy.

"And what about when we graduate?" Marigold said a little sternly. "We cannot leave them in the Hollow forever."

I saw her point, but we didn't even have the wand now, how we were supposed to create anywhere as secure as King's Hollow?

"We should never have taken the stones of old," Wilbur said forlornly. "What use are they to us now anyway? Locked up in trip-traps and hidden in hidey holes?"

"There must be other ways to wield them," Marigold said. "If we can keep them safe, and ensure the FIB do not interrogate you both, eventually we will be able to use them again."

"If we hadn't locked them up in lethal music boxes that is," I said.

"How lethal can they be?" she mused.

I shrugged, because to be fair I had no idea the extent of the traps inside the boxes. But I had felt the power pouring into them, the dark and potent magic the wand had conjured alongside those stones to create something truly frightening within.

"I think Marigold may have the pinprick of a plan," Wilbur said thoughtfully. "We could each take a box, hide it, then drink a memory potion to forget not only its location, but the entire heist. Everything between then and now."

"I don't want to forget it," I blurted.

"Would you rather be sent to Darkmore?" Marigold asked coolly.

I pursed my lips, feeling cornered.

"It is our only choice, dear Felisia," Wilbur said sadly.

My shoulders dropped and sadness weighed on me. "Alright," I gave in. "Find out how long we have to do this, Wilbur."

"You can count on me!"

Ren was more than pleased to get rid of the stones and wipe away all the memories that incriminated me, but when the two of us walked into King's Hollow the very same night the robbery had been splashed across the news, all I felt was anger. Wilbur had said the interrogations could start as soon as tomorrow, so there was no time to spare, but I hated that there were no other options than this.

"This is for the best," Ren said. "We can have a clean slate. These stones aren't worth a lifetime in Darkmore."

"I guess," I muttered. "It just seems extreme."

He came at me, boxing me in against the wall of the narrow stairway inside the hollow of the tree bough, and my breath hitched. "What's extreme is that the queen herself has sent units of FIB out hunting for you, Fee. You are who they're looking for, do you understand that?"

"Of course I do," I growled, trying to get past him, but his hands slammed down either side of my head to pen me there.

"Then protect yourself, dammit. And protect us too. If one of us goes down, we all go down. We're your accomplices. The four of us locked up in Darkmore, is that what you want?"

For a moment, I pictured it, locked away with my four friends. Ren never able to leave me. It was a selfish, wicked thought, but it would mean he had to stay. That we would always be together.

Then I dropped my head with a sigh, letting that wild thought die. I wasn't going to do that to the people I loved. And I wasn't going to set my name on fire either.

"Surely there's another way?" I pleaded and Ren sighed too, lowering his head so his forehead pressed to mine.

"If there was, I promise I would do it. But there's no simple way we can keep those stones now that the world is looking for them."

"You're going to forget I'm a legendary thief. You won't be in awe of me anymore," I said with a pout, and he lowered his mouth to mine, lips grazing and pressing, the heat of his powerful body flush to mine.

"I was in awe of you long before you pocketed some pretty stones, Felisia Night."

The rumble of his voice sent a quake through the core of me, heat burning between my thighs and demanding his attention. The way he said my name was the way I wanted the world to say it, and I drowned in the feeling of being revered, tipping my head back and allowing his mouth to sail lower, my hand fisting in his hair and guiding his head that way.

Queens didn't serve, they were served.

Ren nipped at my throat, his fingers fisting in the black dress I wore and a growl of want leaving him. Then he was gone, walking away as if he had never touched me at all, heading on up into the treehouse and leaving me there unfulfilled once again.

I stalked after him, lips pressed together as I watched him take the four music boxes from the compartment in the wall.

He held them out to me. "Take your pick."

I moved closer, pretending I was completely unaffected by our moment in the stairway as I selected my favoured box.

I weighed it in my hand, eyeing the intricate Scorpio star sign symbol on the top of the gleaming silver metal. It had been my grandfather's sign, and though he had been a strict asshole, he had always said he saw greatness in me. Something the rest of my family hadn't been so keen to agree on.

I was a Capricorn, obviously. And if there had been a Cappy box to claim, I would have fallen on it. Alas, it was not to be.

I slid the Scorpio music box into the purse that was hanging across my body and Ren pocketed the others.

Without another word passing between us, we headed across campus to meet Wilbur and Marigold, each of them selecting a box for themselves. Marigold took the Libra one, while Wilbur took the Cancer, leaving Ren with the Sagittarius.

We headed out the campus gate and Wilbur produced a little bag of stardust. "My aunt is given quite the stipend since working at the palace," he said smugly. "We can travel away into the wind or the water. Wherever we go, *it shall likely be deep into the yonder.* "

The wind stirred at my back and a roar cut through the air that made me look to the sky in surprise. There, descending from the dark clouds was a figure so huge for a moment I thought a star was falling. But instead, an enormous silver Dragon emerged, slamming to the ground behind Marigold and making the earth quake beneath my feet.

I stumbled back in alarm, unsure what was happening as Marigold stepped up to its side with a smile that was so wholly unlike her usual emotionless expressions that it unnerved me. "I told you my cousin married an Acrux."

That voice. It didn't belong to Marigold at all, yet it was coming from her all the same. And there was only once conclusion to draw as her features changed before our eyes, and Birdie was revealed instead.

My hands came up in defence, magic blazing at my fingertips as fury and fear collided inside me. "Where's Marigold?"

Birdie frowned, her fingers tracing lovingly over the box in her hands. "She had to go."

"Go where, you gumpus goon!?" Wilbur wailed, hands raising too as Ren pressed a hand to my shoulder, ready to offer me power in a fight. But with that Dragon spewing smoke from its nostrils at her back, I didn't feel so confident to take on this battle. And that wasn't just any Dragon. It was a fucking Acrux.

"There's only one way I could be wearing her face, Wilbur. The same reason you could wear the face of my sister," Birdie spat, and horror rolled freely through me.

"No," I begged the stars for it not to be true, but Birdie's eyes were cold and so, so dark. The wand's corruption still lay there in her gaze, and I knew she wouldn't rest until she had reclaimed its power once more.

"Hand over the others," Birdie demanded. "They belong to Luxie and I now."

The Dragon rumbled her assent of that, stepping forward, her sharp claws scraping along the ground in a promise of violence.

I glanced back at Ren, then to Wilbur, seeing this fight failing before it had even begun. We couldn't defeat an Acrux Dragon, so there was only one option left to us.

"Get to the Hollow!" I screamed, tearing the earth apart in front of us, throwing up an explosive spray of debris and rocking the ground beneath Luxie and Birdie's feet with an almighty earthquake to buy us a modicum of time.

We turned and ran through the gate, sprinting together across campus and blasting up the path behind us with earth magic. Luxie took to the air, flying after us with a roar that made my heart judder in my chest.

237

Birdie raced after us too, using the speed of her Order to catch us quickly, but I sent a rock hurtling her way that knocked her onto her ass and dazed her long enough for us make it to The Wailing Wood.

Fire bloomed overhead and the treetops crackled as the leaves and branches were singed by the heat of the fire blossoming between them. I felt the heat, the burn against my back, but I never stopped moving even when I was sure I was about to be cooked alive.

Ren never left my side and Wilbur weaved through the trees left and right with light-footed nimbleness just ahead.

Everything was so dark between the trees as the fire sizzled out at our backs, and I was disorientated, unsure which path to take until Ren grabbed my hand and drew me to the left. Then I saw it, the huge oak that would offer us salvation in the clearing up ahead.

I put on a burst of speed, head down, while Ren dragged me along so fast I nearly lost my footing.

Wilbur made it to the tree first, but a spiral of hellfire tore down from the Dragon's jaws above, cutting us off from him and the tree, forcing Ren and I to fall back. We hit the ground, scrambling away from the flames and the moment they flashed out, Ren cast a huge vine that wrapped around my waist and threw me across the clearing. I cried out, colliding hard with Wilbur, the two of us smashing into the tree trunk, and the door opening for us so we fell through into the hidden stairwell within.

I turned to look for Ren, finding him running across the clearing, arms pumping at his sides, the Sagittarius music box gripped tight in his fist. Luxie landed with the power of a building collapsing, crushing him beneath her talons and making him cry out in pain.

"No!" I screamed, leaping forward, but Wilbur caught my arm, dragging me back.

Ren punched Luxie's scaly cheek with the music box and her head swung sideways, her jaws about to close over his arm and tear it clean off, when I opened my palm and made a wild decision. I sent a net of vines at her face, latching tight around her jaws and yanking them apart so her teeth couldn't close. Then I snatched the music box from his grip with a vine and tossed it into the trees, sending a Faelight after it to distract Luxie from Ren.

Luxie immediately reared off of Ren, knocking down a maple tree in her haste to reach the music box. Ren got up and I ran to help him as he staggered my way, swinging his arm around my neck and shoving my hand under his shirt to heal him.

But we weren't moving quickly enough.

One glance back showed Luxie claiming the music box in her claws and *taking off into the sky, then Birdie appeared tearing through the trees at high speed.*

I forced the earth to buck beneath us, sending us flying forward through the doorway in a heap. I spun around as Birdie came racing towards us, slamming into an invisible barrier that stopped her from entering King's Hollow, sending her flying backwards with a bloodied nose, cursing our names.

I shoved to my feet, intending to go out there and claim the Libra music box from her, but her eyes widened as she saw me coming and she shot off into the trees.

Wilbur healed away the last of the gouges on Ren's body, and I sagged forward, falling against them, and holding them tight. Their arms came around me, and we broke as one over the loss of Marigold, grief making me ache.

I was starting to think the stones were a curse I had brought down upon all of our heads, and with two of them now lost to dangerous hands, I had the feeling the carnage had only just begun.

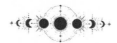

The interrogations went on for days. Hundreds of Jubilee ticket holders were summoned to the FIB in alphabetical order, and with Wilbur being a Grus and me a Night, he was the first to be called. At breakfast, he solemnly poured the exact dosage needed to erase his memories from the past couple of months into his morning orange juice. It would rouse suspicion almost certainly, but without proof of his involvement, what could the FIB really do?

Maybe some terrible investigation that involved torture.

"Wait," I gasped, slapping my hand over his juice and he looked up at me in surprise. "I can't let you do it."

"But this is the way of the nambleberry. Sometimes it does not crumble the way we wish it to crumble. But crumble it must," he said sadly.

"There's another way to crumble it, Wilbur," I sighed, getting to my feet, glancing at the chair beside him which should have been occupied by Marigold. There was still no sign of her body, but her parents had come looking for her, and a new investigation was underway to help locate her. Rumours were circling around campus about the torturer striking again and Isla went on the defensive everywhere she went, ready to fight. She had recovered from her ordeal in a way that made her suspicious of the whole world, and though I had been on the end of her cruelty more times than I could count, I couldn't help but feel awful for what she'd suffered through.

"Whatever are you thinking?" Wilbur asked.

"You'll see. Just trust me."

"I only have an hour before I have to answer my summons," he said in despair.

"Then an hour will have to be enough," I said thickly.

I walked away as he warbled out a sorrowful tune, and I quickened my pace out of The Orb, knowing I needed to act fast. I made a path for Terra House, casting magic at the symbol above the door to gain entry and heading into the deep tunnels which led under the hillside. Skylights sat in the peak of the domed roofs above, casting slanted shafts through the hallways.

I made my way to Birdie's room, took hold of the handle and blasted the thing right off its hinges with a spray of metal shrapnel.

A curse came from inside as I kicked the door open, hands raised and teeth bared, but I wasn't remotely prepared for what I found inside. Birdie's hand was on the back of a girl's neck as she forced her towards the Libra music box, the lid of it flicked open and a haunting tune carrying from the depths of it. The moment the girl's hand touched it, she disappeared, tumbling away into the box without a trace.

"What the fuck?" I gasped, casting a shield of metal against my arm in case Birdie tried to attack me.

My old friend look crazed, her eyes bloodshot like she hadn't slept in days and her face twitchy. "Can't get it out, can I? And I'm not going in. But they never come back. One after the other, in they go, bye, bye, bye. But they never come out!" She pointed at me accusingly. "You. You can get it out, can't you? Because you're the one who made it." She carefully picked up the music box by the base, holding it towards me and revealing a twirling ballerina within.

"Stay the fuck away from me," I warned.

"Or what? You'll tell on me?" she hissed. "And then what? The FIB will take us all away."

"Where's Marigold? What did you do with her?"

She said nothing, but her eyes darted to her closet and ice rolled down my spine. I side stepped that way, then again when Birdie made no move to stop me, opening the door and spotting a large wooden chest inside. My hand trembled as I opened it, finding Marigold's broken body twisted up within it, the soil spilling from her lips telling me how she had died.

"Monster," I rounded on Birdie with a crack in my voice and tears searing my eyes.

"She never thought anything of me," Birdie said in anger. "So when I got into her room while she slept, I slipped her some Medusa venom, let the paralysis take over before I killed her good and slow. By the end, she knew who the greater Fae was, and she knew how deeply she had underestimated me."

A snarl of rage left me and I sent a blast of rocks at her, forcing her to dive and take cover behind the bed. I leapt onto the mattress, glaring down at her with magic crackling at my fingertips, but she lunged at me with a syringe in her fist, trying to drive the needle into my leg.

I caught her wrist with a vine, latching it tight while my foot came out and booted her hard in the face. She shrieked in anger as she fell back and I wielded the vine, plucking the syringe from her grasp and bringing it to my hand.

"Medusa venom?" I guessed and her cold stare told me I was right.

Her eyes darted past me to the door, and she made a run for it with a burst of Vampire speed, causing a violent tremor to rock the ground and send me crashing to my knees. My hand raised and gritted my teeth as I sent the syringe after her on another vine, jamming it into the side of her neck just as she made it to the doorway. The vine forced the plunger to depress, and she made it only a few more steps before she slumped to the floor with a groan of desperation, her body growing limper by the second.

I hurried out into the corridor, looking left and right but finding no witnesses there to see what I did next.

I fisted my hand in her hair, dragging her back into her room, and kicking the door shut, standing over her just as she might have stood over Marigold before she died. Her fingers twitched but no magic came to her aid as she fell fully still beneath me and I leaned down, pinching her chin between my finger and thumb. "My name will one day pass through the ages, descendant to descendant. It'll be immortalised in history books and plays will be written to capture the glory of my life. But you? You will be forgotten. I will make sure of it."

Felisia Night, of the reputable Nemean Lion family of the same name, has been officially sentenced to sixty-five years in Darkmore Penitentiary for the theft of the four treasured gemstones belonging to Queen Leondra Vega which were stolen during her twenty fifth Jubilee. The full extent of the shocking story was uncovered in court yesterday afternoon, corroborated by Cyclops Interrogation, painting the picture of a student at Zodiac Academy who found herself at the bottom of the pecking order. In a daring bid to prove herself, she set out a plot to steal the four stones from The Palace of Souls, training day and night for the momentous task. And, upon the day of the Queen's Jubilee, she enacted her plan and walked away with four priceless artefacts in her pocket, which the kingdom have been hunting for since the anonymous tip off was received. A tip off, which has now been confirmed to have come from the source herself. Felisia Night held her chin high when she told her tale, and it was impossible to deny the sight of raised eyebrows in court, along with a few murmurs of astonishment.

Despite Miss Night's clear misdemeanour, which she will now suffer the price of for many years, it is clear she made an impression in court that will be long lasting. The first, and no doubt last Fae to ever steal from The Palace of Souls, her name will likely go down in history for the act, especially considering the fact that she had not even finished her education. A full inquiry is still underway in the palace to seek out the gaps in surveillance, and the security will be tightened up accordingly, ensuring no such theft ever occurs again.

With Miss Night refusing to give up the location of the gemstones, and the memory of their location destroyed by what Dr Eyling, of the Cyclops Order, has concluded was either a memory potion or a complex memory removal spell, there is still no trace of the artefacts.

To read the full account of Miss Night's story, turn to page 16.

I lowered the newspaper, heart thumping and a smile twisting my lips. My golden hair danced around me in a late fall breeze as I sat on the edge of the wooden pier, gazing across the open ocean towards the red gleam of the oncoming sunrise.

"How did you do it?" Ren's voice sounded at my back, though I'd heard his approach long before he spoke, his heavy footsteps impossible to miss.

"Do what?" I asked innocently, my smile widening.

"Fee," he pressed, and I glanced over my shoulder at him, eyes glittering. "How can you be here while the press are reporting that you are deep in Darkmore this morning? Do you know how terrified I was? I almost didn't come when I got your letter. I thought it was a trick."

My smile fell. "I had to let everyone believe it, to protect you. You did destroy it, right? Like I asked?"

"Of course," he said, and I pushed to my feet, drawing my brown coat tighter around me as the cold wind tried to find its way inside it. Ren moved forward, gazing at my face like he was still unsure if he could trust it was me.

"Help me understand this," he demanded.

"I caught Birdie," I said. "Dosed her with Medusa venom – only because she tried to dose me with it first. But then I had her and...well, I took her to Isla Draconis."

"Isla?" he breathed in surprise.

"Yes, I told her it was Birdie who tortured her. And considering everything

242

Isla had been through, she was pretty keen to get payback on Birdie. Although, she wasn't malicious like she usually is. She just seemed kind of...sad. She even apologised to me for everything."

Ren's eyebrows rose.

"I know, right?" I breathed. *"So, anyway, I let Isla inside my head to see what I'd done. The whole palace heist. All of it."*

"What?" Ren barked.

"I know, I know. It was a risk. But my back was against the wall, Ren. And Wilbur was going to be interrogated by the FIB. They would have seen him helping me in the palace. He would have been arrested, and Wilbur's too good for that life. His family were honoured by the Vegas, taken into the palace and their name raised in society. I couldn't take that away from him."

Ren nodded slowly. *"Alright, and then?"*

"Then...once she knew everything, I asked her to place it all in Birdie's head. It was a big ask, and I didn't even know if she could do it, but Basilisks can fuck with people's minds really well, as we know, and she didn't even have to think about it. She put it all right there in Birdie's mind, but left all of you out of it. The memories were cropped, altered, I guess, but firm enough that no one would detect the change. Then things got fucked up."

"They weren't fucked up before that?" Ren asked with a smirk.

"No, not compared to this part." I sucked on my bottom lip, wondering what he would think of me when this truth was out, but there were no secrets between us. *"Isla had to convince Birdie she was me. She gave her my memories, childhood memories, ones of me at school, with my parents. Everything she needed to secure the identity. Then I just took the protections spells off of my body so I could be impersonated and Isla bent Birdie's mind, willed her to cast the magic that would make her take my form. She forced her to forget she had ever been anyone else but me, and she sent her on her way to the FIB with one desire in mind: to confess to her crime."*

"By the stars," Ren gasped.

I nodded, kicking my foot against the ground. *"It's not forever. Isla bought me a month, then it'll all fade. Birdie will return to herself and the truth will come out. Plus, anyone who looks closely enough will see that her hair isn't even half as shiny as mine, but some things just can't be replicated with magic."*

"Why?" Ren said in horror, ignoring the hair comment which was odd because it was pretty important and my hair looked particularly good in this light so he should have complimented it really. *"Why not leave her there to rot with it forever?"*

"Because of Marigold," I said tightly. *"And not just her, there were others,*

Ren. Birdie forced them into the Libra music box to try and retrieve the Guild Stone. I've tracked down who they are, people who have gone missing from nearby towns. She preyed on the weak, Fae even weaker than her, I guess. But their families deserve to know what happened to them. I buried Marigold out on our favourite hill in Earth Territory and Isla planted that memory in Birdies head for the FIB to find. I hate to think of her family still looking for her, hoping they'll find her, but I didn't know what else to do. It won't be too much longer until they know the truth."

I slid the Libra music box from my pocket, holding it up to the crimson light of dawn which made the silver metal appear blood red. "I don't know how to help the others."

Ren closed his hands over mine around the box. "Whatever is in there, I suspect there is no coming back from it. Don't go looking for death, Felisia Night."

"When Birdie's identity comes back to her, they'll interrogate her. They'll find out about the murders, about everything. Well...nearly everything. There were some memories I made Isla pluck right out of her head. Like about you, and Wilbur and Marigold's involvement in the heist. Everything else is on me. I made sure of it, and Isla covered her tracks well. Any Cyclops or Basilisk could have been responsible. There'll be no proof it was her."

"You could have just made Birdie admit to it as herself. Why have her be you?" he said in distress. "Once her identity is revealed, the FIB will hunt the kingdom for you. They'll never stop."

I smiled, placing my hand on his arm and stepping into the arc of his body. "Oh Ren, you really don't know me at all if you think I would let Birdie steal my glory. My parents have already commissioned a statue of me to be placed in the Night Manor gardens." I grinned. "I'm famous. And imagine how much more talk of me there'll be when they discover what I did – how I not only stole from the palace but escaped too. I'll be the greatest anti-hero ever known."

Ren gave me a smirk, pushing his hand into my hair and making my spine straighten at the overfamiliar touch. It was a very intimate thing to touch a Lioness's hair, but the way he did it made a purr rise in my chest.

"You are a raving lunatic," he said, and I pursed my lips. "And the most incredible creature I have ever encountered."

He leaned in for a kiss, but I stopped him by taking an envelope from my pocket and slapping it against his chest. "This is for you."

He frowned, plucking it from my fingers and peeling it open. He slid out the ticket I'd secured him for the ship leaving one hour from now from this very dock. A ticket to The Waning Lands.

"I made a name for myself, and I plan to run rings around the FIB across

Solaria, letting them chase my tail while I cause more chaos than they can imagine. I have never felt more alive than I do now. I'm actually looking forward to being on the run, my family will help keep me hidden, and they have ties with a Werewolf pack called the Oscuras who my father promises will help too. That's my calling. But it's not yours." Emotion welled in my throat, and he stared at the ticket in confusion, his shoulders dropping heavily.

"Thank you," he said. "For understanding."

"I got so wrapped up in chasing my own glory, I forgot to respect you chasing yours. You're right, Ren, you'll never be who you want to be in Solaria. I know that now. But you can rise to greatness in The Waning Lands. In fact, I want you to promise me that you will. And when the day comes that your name is hailed by the stars, I want you to write me. And I'll come."

"Swear it," he said gruffly, sliding his hand around the back of my neck and pulling me closer. "On the stars." His hand caught mine, fingers curling tight.

"I swear it," I vowed, and magic clapped between our palms.

My heart thundered with the loss of him, the inevitable parting that drew nearer by the second.

"An hour, you said?" he murmured.

I nodded, and his mouth claimed mine, marking it as his just like that.

"Then that will have to be long enough to ensure you remember me." He captured my hand, towing me back down the dock and adrenaline spiked in my veins as he led me onto a little sail boat that was definitely not ours.

He kicked in the door to the cabin and swept me into his arms as he carried me over the threshold, hitting his head on the lower doorframe.

I laughed, hooking my arms around his neck as he walked me to a table that sat between a ring of cushioned seats by the window. He placed me down and I fisted my hand in his shirt, pulling him after me as my back pressed to the cool wood, my fingers thumbing the buttons open to reveal his bronzed skin beneath and the deep cut of his muscular abs.

He shrugged it off and knocked my hands away from him, gazing down at me with the darkest of intentions.

"Focus on every touch of my skin to yours, bind it to your memory, and don't ever forget it," he commanded.

"I could never forget you," I said breathlessly as he reached down to pull my coat off, along with the yellow dress beneath. He made quick work of my underwear, exposing me to him and taking in my bare flesh with a carnal growl in his throat.

He raised his hand and cast a blindfold of woven leaves over my eyes. "Focus on how I feel. Do not forget me."

"I won't," I insisted.

He leaned down, his mouth pressing to my throat, the heat of it more like a brand than a kiss. I gasped, my back arching as his mouth dragged down to my collar bone, his fingers raking along the curve of my hip in time with the passage of his mouth. Every kiss was mimicked by his rough hands carving over a new area of my body, awakening it all just for him and scoring lines of fire across my skin. I writhed and purred for him, my hands balling tightly at my sides in a refusal to touch him back, letting him serve me and bathing in the sense of power that gave me.

His mouth found my right nipple and his teeth raked across the sensitive flesh as his fingers grazed my inner thigh. I moaned, arching into the touch as his other hand cupped my left breast and his thumb matched the rhythm of his tongue on my other nipple. Before I could get used to the intense bliss of that feeling, his fingers trailed over my clit and a cry left me, a jolt of pure ecstasy making me buck beneath him. He did it again, rolling his fingers over my clit followed by his knuckles, kneading and grinding in time with his mouth and other hand on my breasts.

I started to shiver as the first wave of release found me, Ren's steady rhythm bringing me to the edge of oblivion already, and just as I was about to fall, he slowed his pace, lightened his touch and left me suspended there, practically whimpering with need.

He stepped back, leaving my body bereft from his touch, but the sound of him removing his pants made my skin grow hot. I felt his legs pressing my thighs wide and his hand grasping my hip in a firm motion.

He slicked the tip of his cock in the wetness between my thighs and I gasped as a heady groan left him.

"Now you can come," he decided, sliding into me, the thickness of his length making me cry out as he stretched me.

His thumb rubbed my clit in soft, demanding circles and as he eased himself deeper and deeper into me, his cock bigger than any I had taken before, I started to fall apart.

I panted, grasping my own breasts and squeezing, but he shoved my hands from my body, replacing them with one of his own and dragging his thumb over my nipple as his other thumb worked my clit.

He thrust into me hard and I moaned and writhed, my body feeling like it was falling apart, scattering to pieces and cast into a whole other realm. It was like travelling through stardust, my mind lost to nothing but sparks of light and too much beauty to perceive all at once.

Ren started fucking me slow and deep, grazing my clit softer now that my flesh was on fire, but he never stopped, keeping me in a state of euphoria *that went beyond what I had ever thought was possible to experience with someone.*

He drew me mercilessly towards another orgasm, his hips grinding down on mine as he upped his pace a little, feeling me closing in, my walls tightening around his thick length and making a curse fall from his lips.

When I came a second time, it was more prolonged, shuddering through every inch of me and making me tingle with utter rapture. He had me in a state of nirvana and I was his now and always, this moment bound by starlight itself.

He grasped my thighs, hooking his arms beneath them and forcing my hips to lift so he could fuck me even deeper, his pace increasing as he reared over me and let me feel the true power of him. I didn't need to beg or ask for anything, he knew what I needed even before I did, the deep, hard drives of his hips making his cock strike a spot inside me that had me trembling.

He seized three more orgasms from me before he indulged in his own, his mouth coming down hard on mine and his fingers grasping my ass in tight fists, fucking me with the fury of a man who knew this might be the last time he had me in his hold. The hot spill of his seed filled me as he came with a roar, his body merged with mine and his hips still thrusting as he prolonged the bliss of his own release.

I was sore from the size of him, but it was the sweetest kind of ache as he fell over me, his weight crushing me to the table, our mouths coming together as he cast away my blindfold and let me see the blazing adoration in his eyes.

We eventually made it to the cushioned seats, me curled up on his body while the sunrise spilled in through the window and he painted pictures along my spine.

Then it was over. The hour drawing towards its inevitable conclusion, and we dressed in a haze of kisses and lingering touches that neither of us wanted to end.

Before I knew it, I was standing before the ship that Ren was ready to board, my hood drawn up so as not to draw the attention of any passers-by. And we shared one final kiss that heralded me as his from this day forth, and he as mine.

Before he could turn and board the ship that would steal him from me for who knew how long, I slipped the Scorpio music box into his pocket, a token to remind him of me.

I watched him board the ship with my heart cracking into shards and clattering down into the hollow space in my chest. And it felt like the most painful, perfect goodbye I would ever know.

"So that's it?" I asked, coming out of the memory, and finding Felisia looking at the mirror with a longing in her eyes. "What happened to the music boxes?"

"What happened to Ren?" Azriel asked as if that was the more pressing issue.

I wasn't sure I saw any value in having just witnessed Felisia fucking her best friend, but apparently, I'd had no choice in the matter. And I was still clueless as to where all the music boxes rested except the one the stars had shown me in the palace treasury. And if that was the only thing I had gleaned in all this time, then what use was her story at all?

"Dead king, you have such little patience for a love story, when I know well that you lived the most tragic one of all."

I ground my teeth together. "So Ren took the Scorpio box to The Waning Lands? And where did he put it?"

"In his castle," she said with a grin.

"Imai," Azriel said with a frown. "Yes, I've heard of them."

"A great and powerful family. Rulers in The Waning Lands," Felisia said with pride in her gaze.

"Did you see him again?" Azriel pushed.

"What happened to the other boxes? How did the Libra music box end up in the treasury of The Palace of Souls?" I asked.

"I gifted it to Wilbur," Felisia said. "And when he died after a long, good life, he laid out in his will that he wished for his prized possession to be passed to the Vegas and protected in the royal treasury. He asked that it was respected, left untouched and simply kept safe." She laughed. "Such a Wilbur thing to do. To sneak it back into the palace after all those years. He became quite the royalist during his time serving the Vegas, but he told me he wished to die with that little secret going to the grave with him."

"And what about the Sagittarius music box that the Acrux Dragon stole?" I asked.

She pouted. "That one was kept from me," she growled. "I discovered that Luxie Acrux took it to her treasure trove. A cave in the Havarian region. I attempted to steal it back once, but it was well guarded in those days. Now, I believe it lays forgotten, yet the magic remains intact that protects it. In a way, it was just another hiding place for one of my stones. I never *really* lost it."

Purrsy shot her a grin. "The Dragon was keeping it for you, right love?"

"Right," Felisia said, raising her chin.

"And the Cancer box which held the ruby Guild Stone…you put it back in King's Hollow," Azriel said in realisation. "That's where I found it."

"Yes, of all the hiding places I sought, none beat the Hollow in the end.

Not long before my death, I snuck back to Zodiac Academy to return it there. My legacy was kingdom-wide and had grown considerably after a long life of theft and trickery, and my enemies lurked around every corner. Many sought me and the gemstones I had taken from Queen Leondra. None found them."

"Then we have locations," Azriel said, hope brightening his expression. "Thank you, Felisia. Truly."

"She could have summarised the story," I muttered as Felisia's mates grouped around us, preparing to escort us out. But as I moved towards the cabin door in the large ship, I glanced back at the Lioness. "So what *did* happen to Ren?"

"I thought you had no care for my love story, dead king?" she taunted.

"I do not like loose ends, that is all," I said. "Loose ends are what torment the dead in this place." I glanced between her pride, acutely aware that Ren was not one of them. "He never summoned you, did he?"

Felisia scowled at the guess and Azriel glanced at me in warning as if it might be a bad idea to incur the ire of the cat queen. But I was a long dead Fae with little to lose.

"He summoned me, yes," she purred, stepping closer to me with delicate footsteps. "Ten years after that day. I had my pride by then, and he had a harem of his own. Yet our love still burned on as it once had. He was a great ruler in The Waning Lands, and I was overcome with joy at all he had achieved, and he felt the same in kind. Days we spent in each other's company, catching up on all the years lost, and between us, we came up with a way to love the other without leaving behind the worlds each of us were from. I would stardust to him and him to me over the years."

"All of us would sometimes," Purssy said with a filthy smirk on his lips that told me quite plainly that he and the rest of Felisia's pride had been more than happy to be a part of Felisia and Ren's love.

"So where is he now?" I pressed.

"He resides next door in his own grand palace. He visits often and I him," Felisia said. "We always needed separate worlds to rule, I think. Otherwise, we would have been in a tireless plight, trying to get the upper hand over the other. I loved him enough to let him go, to allow weeks or even months to slip between us at times, and he loved me just the same."

I nodded to her, respecting the weight of her love, and how both of them had honoured each other's need for power and position.

"Thank you," I said, and she laughed lightly.

"Have I earned the respect of the great dead king?"

"I shall leave it up for interpretation," I said, a smile quirking up the corner of my lips. "One last thing."

"Yes?"

"Did you ever work out how to remove the Guild Stones from the music boxes?"

Her throat rose and fell. "Beware the traps within," she rasped. "I lost a good friend to one, her determination to retrieve it for me a fool's path, one I begged her not to follow. There is no way that I know of to retrieve them. All who go in, never come out. And I have never met their souls here beyond The Veil either."

With that grim news, I let her pride guide me from the ship with Azriel at my side, glad of the information we had secured, yet how we would get it to our family, I did not know. Though I was certain Azriel had been working hard on finding a way to do so.

Merissa appeared from the stairway, running towards me with a thrill in her eyes.

"Fate is calling," she gasped.

Her hand found mine and we were tugged away towards the realm of the living, Merissa pushing hard against the barrier of The Veil and drawing me with her.

I found myself in my old treasury beneath The Palace of Souls, the familiarity of the place taking me by surprise. Gwendalina stood entranced with a Heart of Memoriae crystal in her hand, Lance Orion beside her, and the Untouchable Egg dashed to pieces at her feet.

"Did she...smash the Untouchable Egg?" Merissa gasped.

"Of course she damn well did. It was protected by Phoenix flames," I said in excitement.

Gwendalina's eyes glazed with the memories that were playing out before her, and I crept closer, desperate to know what she was *seeing*.

She relayed the memories to Lance and my heart sank. She had discovered many truths, but not what was needed to break the curse.

"The Imperial Star cursed them," Gwendalina said. "That's why all the Phoenixes died. And it's why Tory and I have failed time and again in this war. That old curse is still in place. We're fucked, Lance. Unless we can figure out what the broken promise is, we're never going to be free of the stars' wrath."

"Yes," I whispered heavily.

"If only we could tell her," Merissa said, moving to Gwendalina and pressing a hand to her arm.

"Azriel will find a way," I said in despair, but then time shifted, the vision of my daughter and her mate fading in and out before I latched onto them once more. But my attention wasn't on them, it was on Merissa as she moved to a shelf at Gwendalina's back, pointing to the gleaming music box which sat there so unassumingly. Yet now I knew what it was, a knot of dread formed in my gut.

"This is what the stars showed us," Merissa said.

"I have learned much about that box, and others of its kind from Felisia Night," I said. "It holds a Guild Stone."

Merissa's eyes widened with hope. "Then they must take it."

"No, we need to warn them," I said fearfully. "Whatever is in that box, it is danger embodied. Felisia may have hidden one of the Guild Stones within it, but a trap was formed with the power of the stones to protect it too. Fae have gone in and not returned."

Merissa's features skewed in worry. "Then how can they retrieve it?"

I looked to my daughter, knowing all she had faced, all she had endured and prevailed through. And I knew without a flicker of doubt in my heart, a simple music box would not be the end of her.

"This may be their only chance to find it," I said, and Merissa frowned as she realised what I was implying.

"We must trust her capabilities," she agreed, nodding firmly and I returned it.

Merissa reached for the music box once more, pushing hard against The Veil and I joined her in the act, our hands pushing and pushing just enough to move the box a little.

Lance shot over to it in an instant like that very movement had caught his attention and he took it from the shelf.

"Careful now, Lance," I warned. Not that he could hear me. In truth, I had not liked him very much at first. Alright, I had hated him in intensely. From his goading of my daughter, to his complete disrespect of his position of authority over her at Zodiac Academy. Eventually, in the strongest sense of the word, he had won me around. Witnessing his self-sacrifice, the loss of his career, and his dignity to protect my daughter had won me around a little. Not to mention his stint in Darkmore Penitentiary. Merissa and I had watched their Elysian Mating with disbelief and undeniable joy, but perhaps it wasn't until he had offered himself up to the Shadow Princess in payment for my daughter's curse that I had truly accepted him as a son.

"Now who's touching ancient artefacts?" Gwendalina taunted him.

His lips slanted up as he examined the circular box and the pair of weighing scales marked on its surface. "If you can't beat 'em…"

He popped the lid open and a miniscule, mechanical set of scales ascended on a little silver platform that resembled a miniature ballroom. A tiny girl made of wood stood on one side of the scales and she moved with delicate magic, leaping over to land in the other dish, then back and forth from one to the other, making the scales rock up and down as she danced. My fear for them grew.

"Prepare yourselves," Merissa urged.

A song curled up from the depths of the box, the voice haunting and feminine, that very same song I had heard in Felisia's memories.

"It's time to dance, to dice with chance, the scales they rise, and they fall now. Come to me, play with me, here in my lonely ballroom…"

Gwendalina and Lance reached for the girl, enchanted by the little dancer and my terror for them sharpened.

"Merissa." I looked to my wife in desperation.

"They can face this," she said fiercely, and I held onto her trust, using it to bolster my own as my daughter and Lance were swept away into the box, and the metal contraption hit the floor with a ringing noise.

Time shifted at that very moment, and I cried my daughter's name as we spun through the dark, clawing our way back to her. When we returned, I found the music box shuddering on the floor, a scream calling from within it that sent terror daggering through me.

But then Gwendalina and Lance were thrown out of the music box, landing in a heap on the floor of the treasury. My daughter held what seemed to be an arm bone in her grip and she tossed it away from her, looking to the music box in alarm. It began spinning on the floor, spitting out bones as they landed in the heaps of gold around them, and along with them, wailing souls poured into the air. The Veil snatched them away, their faces twisting into joy as they realised they were free at long last. Among them was the girl I had seen Birdie force into the music box at Zodiac Academy, tears of relief running down her cheeks as The Veil embraced her.

"By the stars," Merissa cursed, staring after them.

Gwendalina and Lance scrambled upright, backing away from the box, the magic deteriorating by the second and sending it into a frenzy as the last of the bones were ejected. Finally, the thing fell apart, pieces of metal and cogs scattering across the floor and among it all was a beautiful opal. The Libra Guild Stone.

"They did it," I laughed, running to Merissa and lifting her into the air.

She rested her hands on my shoulders, laughing too as we celebrated this victory, this fate we had had a hand in.

"So that's what you were for. You were keeping this safe." Lance moved forward, picking up the opal and admiring it in his palm.

"You'd best keep that away from Lionel," I warned him, placing Merissa down.

"And the shadow bitch," she muttered.

"Is it a Guild Stone?" Gwendalina asked hopefully.

"Feels like one," Lance said, running his thumb across it and the Guild Master mark on his arm suddenly flared to life, the sword shining along his forearm as it responded to finding this new stone. "Opal for Libra."

"Look at that," Merissa breathed, moving forward to touch her finger to the mark on his arm and I swear it glittered a little brighter at her touch. "He can really make this happen, Hail. It's his destiny."

"If he ever gets a chance," I sighed. "But this is a victory we cannot deny."

"Who do you think hid it in that creepy music box?" Gwendalina asked.

"Some long dead Fae who didn't want anyone stealing his treasure," Lance guessed with a shrug, then The Veil pulled us back and we didn't resist, our fingers intertwining while I smiled at Lance's assessment. *Yes, something like that. But not a man. A legendary Lioness.*

DARIUS

CHAPTER SIXTEEN

I stood by the edge of the river I had seen from the depths of Mordra's cavern, looking into the rushing water as it hurtled past, the screams of those it carried breaking through the air, time and again.

Hands clawed at the steep banks, limbs flailed in the tumultuous rush of water and hate-filled eyes glared up at me whenever they saw me standing vigil over their descent towards oblivion.

Downriver the Harrowed Gate stood, the darkness bleeding from the space beyond them like a stain that touched the golden light of The Veil. I wondered what suffering went on in there, what penance was demanded of those who found themselves within its barbed walls upon death. Would it be enough? Would the suffering awaiting my father there ever amount to enough to meet the cost of his malice and ambition?

I plucked a stone from the bank and tossed it into the rushing water, a foul hiss billowing up from it as it sank into the depths.

Could Mordra see me? Was my shadow cast above her hovel? Did she know the depths of my devotion to my cause?

As I stood there, my skin still alive with the echo of Roxy's touch, the scent of her clinging to me and life whispering my name like a taunting caress, I felt the beginnings of fear creeping in.

The Nymphs had offered her hope, but that was such a fickle, dangerous thing. And for my wife, it was precisely the motivation I knew she needed to push her into action. She wouldn't stop now. And though every part of me yearned to find my way back to her, the vow she had made upon the stars blazing through my soul too, I still feared what price she might pay, what sacrifices she might make in the name of seeing this done.

Roxanya Vega wouldn't take no for an answer when she set her mind on something she wanted, and the stars themselves should be trembling at the thought of her wrath turning their way.

"The Hydra bellows tomorrow," Radcliff called, drawing my attention to him where he loitered in the trees, keeping his distance from the careering waters before me.

A soul shrieked in defiance of his fate as he was swept past me.

"I visited the Heirs," I muttered, lost in my own thoughts. I spent every spare moment watching my loved ones from the privacy of my room in the Eternal Palace, staying as close to the living as I could while trying to focus on the efforts we were all making here too. "They're determined. The plans they're making seem solid-"

"Lionel's shifted fate," Radcliff interrupted gravely, the gravel in his tone forcing my gaze away from the water and back to him once more.

"What?" I demanded, stepping away from the bank, small stones cascading down into the water and hissing faintly as I stalked towards my murdered uncle. "Don't speak in riddles, spell it out to me."

Radcliff raised his chin as we came face to face, his spine straightening as he seemed to assess my height in comparison to his, his chest puffing out too.

"Merissa visited with Gabriel. He thrashes in the Royal Seer's Chamber, his brow furrowed with the destruction of his prophecy. He set your queen and the others on a path that is now destined to end in bloodshed."

"Where are they?" I barked, panic leaping through my chest as his garbled explanation came together within my mind. The prophecy Gabriel had given Roxy had set them on a path toward The Palace of Souls tonight. If fate had changed, then they could be walking into a trap, an ambush, anything, but clearly none of it was good.

"They're in their rooms, trying to get a message across the divide, hoping to warn-"

I broke into a sprint, not waiting for him to finish, charging back through the trees and running straight towards the only bit of open air here in the forest.

I called on the power of my Dragon as I ran, summoning it to the edges of my flesh, commanding it to shift with me and not part from my skin.

I wasn't sure if it was listening, a defiant roar rumbling through my chest as I took a running leap straight from the edge of the riverbank and sailed through the air above the rushing water.

Screams echoed up to me from below, arms lunging for me, hands grasping, the desperate, raging souls hungry to add more suffering to their own as I began to fall.

But the love I felt for the people now heading towards an ill fate in life wouldn't be denied. With an enormous roar, the golden Dragon within me burst free, my wings snapping out, fire blazing from my jaws.

The hazy sky beckoned me upward and I raced for it, wheeling toward the Eternal Palace, the windows along its side shifting and changing at the whims of those within, adjusting to the needs of the dead.

I didn't know which window belonged to Hail and Merissa, but the palace would provide what I needed.

I flew straight for it, flying fast and true, my wings beating hard as the closest window began to expand, opening wider and wider, becoming an archway large enough for a fully grown Dragon to sail right through.

I shifted as I passed within the building, the gathered souls who already stood within the dead royals' chambers all whirling toward me in surprise as I dropped to my feet, running several steps to counter the speed of my arrival.

The fine clothes and golden cloak tumbled across my flesh as I returned to my Fae form, and I glanced down at them in surprise.

"Makes a difference from having to stand around with my cock out," I muttered, taking in the strangeness of finding myself fully clothed without any effort at all.

"The Veil provides." Azriel nodded.

"Thank the stars," Hail added in an undertone.

"Yes, thank the heavens that you didn't have to see it and suffer the crippling inferiority complex brought on by the comparison," I quipped, strolling towards my mother who drew me into her arms with a fearful gasp.

"If you would like proof that no such thing is the case-" Hail began but Merissa waved him off.

"You can enjoy a dick comparison with your son-in-law later, Hail," Merissa snapped. "We need to try and shift Roxanya and the others from this path."

Hail grunted, his lips twitching with what I could have sworn was amusement and I pushed out of my mother's arms, moving to stand around a stone table which had appeared in the centre of the room, twisting smoke rolling over it. Azriel, Clara, Hail, Merissa, Hamish, and my mom already held a spot surrounding it and I elbowed the former king along so that I could look too.

"What is this?" I demanded, trying to make sense of the way the smoke shifted from place to place, revealing a mountain peak here, a tall spire there.

"It's a map of destiny," Azriel said.

"I thought they were a legend?"

"One that only seems to be real in death," Azriel agreed, sweeping a hand across a corner of the map, wafting the smoke away from a floating island that had been carved free of the land.

"We're going to attempt several approaches," Merissa explained. "We want to try and push them from this path. But failing that, maybe we can do something that will distract Lionel and move him towards another fate. So far as we can tell he doesn't actually know they're coming, but he has made plans which will send any who enter The Palace of Souls tonight towards a bloodstained destiny."

"Has anyone tried to warn Roxy or the others?" I barked, my attention fixed on R.U.M.P. castle while Azriel began clearing the smoke which covered other parts of the map.

"Warn them how?" Hail hissed. "We can't speak with them, can't even write them a note or do anything of consequence."

"Hail and I have deep connections to The Palace of Souls," Merissa explained. "We plan to head there and delve into the magic contained within the walls themselves, open pathways, hopefully steer them away from danger wherever we can while Azriel and Clara will attempt to rile the Nymphs who are stationed at the edge of the palace grounds."

"Rile them?" I questioned.

"I have a theory that I may be able to agitate the shadows with my inner power," Azriel replied. "Perhaps enough to set them off, start a fight...I don't know if it will work or if there's any chance of creating enough chaos to draw the Dragon King's attention but-"

"He's no king," I snarled. "Neither of those plans seem likely to change the course of fate enough to protect Roxy or the others from harm."

"I'm going to go to Lionel and see if I can discover more of his plans," Mom said softly. "Perhaps he will divulge something that can be of use."

"He grieves you?" I asked her, surprised that the monster who had sired me cared about her death at all after being the one to have caused it. I had felt the tug of his grief on my soul a few times as he thought of me, but the pull had been full of anger, and I knew he only really grieved what he wished he'd been able to mould me into. He was furious that I hadn't become the willing pawn he'd tried to craft me to become.

"He..." Mom glanced at Hamish who took her hand and squeezed softly. "He sometimes thinks of me when he is torturing his prisoners. He selects women who remind him of me and punishes them for how easily I escaped him, hating that I stole away into death rather than let him capture and punish me the way he had wished to."

Rage tore through me so potently that I almost shifted, my grip tightening on the edge of the table so hard that it was a wonder the thing didn't crack.

"You need to head to Roxanya. See if you can contact her – if any of us stands a chance then it is you," Hail commanded and for once I didn't balk at the order.

"Already gone," I replied, my wife's grief dancing across my flesh like soft fingertips. She'd been aching for me ever since leaving that clearing with the Nymphs, her heart torn open and bloody again.

I'd been avoiding her like the coward I was, my guilt over the pain I was causing her keeping me away. But it was little more than a thought to give in to her now.

The rest of the dead and the Eternal Palace faded away around me, my soul seeking hers out in the dark until I found myself in her chambers in R.U.M.P. castle.

It was dark in her room. The Book of Ether plus the four ancient tomes on the Elements were strewn across the bed and floor while she sat in the middle of the huge four-poster, her knees drawn up to her chest, hair falling forward to shield her face.

The only light came from the fire which was close to dying out in the hearth, its sound and her near silent sobs all there was in the space.

I moved to sit beside her, the bed not shifting as my weight joined hers, nothing in the mortal realm reacting to my presence, but as I wound my arm around her, she leaned into me, her head coming to rest between my collar bone and jaw, my fingers passing through her hair.

"Sometimes I think I feel you," she breathed to the silent room, her tears stalling, a rattling breath drawn into her lungs. "It's like you're just there, in the next room, about to walk in and ruin my life all over again. I wish you were. Or maybe I wish I'd never met you at all so I wouldn't have had to feel what it was to lose you."

"You haven't lost me," I replied firmly, focusing on the point of contact between us, pressing all that I was into the sensation of her flesh next to mine, my fingers in her hair, willing her to feel it, to feel me and know I would never truly leave her.

Roxy's head fell forward and she began to cry again, my presence as irrelevant as a gnat caught in a hurricane.

I growled, frustration burying its way into me as I fought to make her feel me, hear me, see me. But it was no good. Nothing I did made the slightest difference.

I threw my fist into the pillow in frustration, but I hit something hard beneath it, Roxy's Atlas tumbling free, her music app opening, illuminating brightly in the dim room. I blinked at it, shocked that I'd managed to affect it at all and quickly reached for it again, the songs scrolling beneath my touch, one name after another appearing, the device feeling my influence.

I glanced at the woman I'd pledged my soul to, seeing the way she was breaking in the dark and knowing exactly what she needed to bring her back out of it.

Roxanya Vega wasn't built to wallow and cower. At the depths of her fire-drenched soul, she was a warrior through and through. And she needed to get her heart back into the fight.

Cinderella's Dead by Emeline started up the moment I hit play and Roxy sucked in a sharp breath, whirling around to look at her Atlas in surprise, letting the words wrap themselves tight around her. Maybe she had forgotten she was a bad bitch like the song suggested, but now it was time for her to remember. Fate might have shifted but fuck that. This woman had chosen her own fate more than once before and I knew she wouldn't be guided by the stars alone.

I moved around her as the tears slowly dried on her cheeks, her jaw tightening as she listened to the song, her walls building back up, armour strapping itself tight around her fractured heart.

The Book of Ether was open to a page on breaking curses, none of it looking particularly helpful from my brief glance at the words. The curse which hung over her family was no petty hex. But the book seemed to call to me, whispering words of protection, of old ways for her to guard herself against death.

I reached for the book and flipped the pages. Roxy whipped around at the sound of them flicking over one by one, illustrations and text flashing by too fast to take any real note of until I jarred to a halt and slapped the page I'd been hunting for open hard enough to make the mattress bounce beneath it.

Roxy looked right at me then and for half a second I thought she could truly see me, but as she peered through me her eyes unfocused, I let my attention fall back to the book.

To Bind Oneself To Life

It is possible to cling to life beyond the point of otherwise natural demise through the use of soul bartering. A cursed soul who is bound to an eternity of torment can be lured to the edge of The Veil and trapped within the confines of a pure tigers eye crystal. The stone selected must be of highest quality and yet small enough to be housed beneath the flesh to the subject wishing to skirt death when needed.

First, a soul must be summoned by burning dill and lavender within the centre of a pentagram and speaking the power words listed at the foot of these instructions. Necromancy of this kind comes at a blood cost which can be paid by the sacrifice of a willing or unwilling subject. Or at a personal cost in the form of childhood memories which must be offered up in their entirety when claiming the soul from the confines of the Harrowed Gate.

It should be noted that reaching into death to claim such a soul is perilous indeed, the chances of failure increasing depending on how far the necromancer has to delve within The Veil to secure it. Further details of the incantations needed to capture the soul and bind it to the crystal are on the following page.

With the soul trapped within the crystal, it can be activated by using the word Vivere and calling on the ether, but this can only be done once the crystal has been driven beneath the flesh of the one wishing to claim its power.

The crystal will then keep death at bay by fooling The Veil itself, using the trapped soul as a barrier to hide the caster from the call of the beyond.

Note: this will not work in cases of decapitation, full dismemberment, or removal of the heart.

It should also be noted that the soul trapped within the crystal will perish once the power of the crystal has been used, the cost of wielding it their eternal existence.

One look at Roxy's face told me that she had no objection whatsoever to taking the risks involved with using that magic and I growled, leaving her there to continue reading, knowing already that she was planning to enact this spell. Which meant I needed to get a soul ready for her to claim. I was all in favour of her using ether to her advantage, but there was no denying the danger involved in it too, so anything I could do to ease that would need to be my highest priority.

I returned to the Eternal Palace, blinking as my eyes adjusted to the golden glow which never left this place and finding only Hail standing beside the map of destiny.

"Well?" he demanded, and I narrowed my eyes at his tone, but he knew far more about this place than I could hope to have learned in my short time here, so I gave him his answer.

"Roxy needs a soul," I told him. "To trap in a tigers eye crystal as part of a spell she learned from the Book of Ether. It will help her swerve death if it comes calling."

"So she continues to tread the path of dark magic?" he muttered, a note of fear and pride to his voice.

"The soul will perish eternally once the magic trapping it is broken," I added, not bothering to give the concern in his gaze my attention. She was on this path now and there was no turning her from it, so I was choosing to aid her instead.

"You mean to claim one from the beyond the Harrowed Gate?" Hail asked, stepping towards me, his cloak making the golden haze in the room shift.

"I assumed that was better than using a soul who had earned their way here," I agreed. "But the spell requires it to be from there anyway. So can you tell me how to do such a thing?"

"Not easily," he replied, sweeping past me so closely that his intention was clearly to make me move aside, but I simply set my feet and let his shoulder crash into mine, jerking him to face me, the two of us snarling at one another.

"You want to have this out with me?" I asked him in a low tone. "Right now? When she needs me to focus on this magic she's set on creating?"

Hail released a slow breath, his gaze matching with mine, violence dancing in the air. This was where we collided, but also where we held the most in common. Our love for his daughter was more powerful than any rivalry or pettiness which might have been between us, and we both knew it.

"I wasn't only referred to as the Savage King for the atrocities your father encouraged me into," he said. "And there was a damn good reason why Lionel never even thought to attempt fighting me one on one."

I stepped to him, my Dragon prowling beneath my skin, hungry for blood, though I pushed it back, ignoring the urge to give in to the temptation of the fight.

"I have no interest in fighting you, relic," I growled. "Because right now, my wife needs me and I made an oath to be her creature, to love and protect her into death and beyond. If you can help me then please do. If not, don't get in my way because the only thing that would cause me to waste time on warring with you in this moment would be that. But I assume we can agree that nothing matters more than helping her right now."

Hail eyed me for a long moment then grinned like a beast, clapping a hand on my shoulder.

"I can see why she picked you in the end, even if you had proven yourself to be a son of a bitch," he said, his grip tight, smile as savage as his reputation. "When it comes down to it, you'd burn the entire fucking world to ash for a single smile from her lips, wouldn't you?"

"Is there a problem with that?" I asked, uncertain if it was meant as a compliment or not.

Hail snorted. "I think heroes are supposed to put the good of all before their own selfishness. But you are selfish when it comes to her, utterly, unerringly selfish. She's the one and only thing you won't ever question, the one thing you put above all else. If the world had to end to see her safe, you'd light the fuse that blew it from existence."

"Damn right I would," I agreed, no element of doubt in my tone. "Besides, a hero is never going to be what it takes to bring my father down. He moulded me into a villain and so that's what I am. For her. For him. Damnation isn't good enough for that piece of shit. And heroics aren't good enough for her. So hand me the fuse, oh Savage King, because I'm ready to burn it all."

Hail grinned at me, no falseness to it, his grip on my shoulder turning to a push as he moved me towards the door, and I let him guide me along with him.

"Let's go get your queen a soul to destroy then, shall we?"

The door opened before us, letting us out onto the road which led up to the main entrance of the Eternal Palace, bypassing the halls entirely as if anticipating our need for urgency. The golden haze hanging around us was like balmy sunlight but the moment I looked for the Harrowed Gate and the lands of torment beyond, I spotted it lurking in the distance, a dark stain on this place of serenity.

"We can summon souls to the gates," Hail told me as we started up a quick pace along the stone road. "But only those who wronged us in life. If you wish to drag one of them through then the stronger your hatred for them, the more power you'll be able to claim over them here. It's part of their torment, to suffer whatever fate those who they hurt in life desire. Do you have anyone who you can think of who deserves total annihilation?"

I pursed my lips, thinking of my father and wishing that fate upon him before forcing my mind to shift to people I hated who were actually dead, and likely to have been damned and tossed into the river upon their arrival here.

"I'm sure a bunch of my uncles, cousins and the like were killed in the battle. All of them deserve a place in there and I hate them all plenty too," I said.

"Uncles on your mother's side?" Hail asked and I shrugged.

"My father's inner circle were always referred to as if they were blood relatives of ours. Some of them were actually cousins, second cousins or other distant relations, my mother's family were included too once she married in and secured their ties to him. But most of them held no blood with us."

"Lionel likes to spread the Acrux name like butter dripping across all who come close enough to touch it," Hail scoffed. "As if applying such a thing means anything at all in the face of true power. My parents only managed to carry one child to full term – me. After their death I was the only Vega left, but there was no part of me which wished to start tracking down old family relations and calling them Vega just to up the numbers. A name with power like ours shouldn't just be handed out at will. It is earned."

I glanced at him, noting the way he'd called the name ours and wondering if he'd intended to include me in that statement or not. I was a Vega now after all.

"Have I earned it then?" I asked, unwilling to let that comment pass.

Hail paused, his eyes rolling over me from head to toe, lips pursing. "I suppose we'll see."

I snorted dismissively, like his approval meant nothing to me. But maybe it did. Just a little. Maybe I wanted to be able to return to my wife and tell her that her father didn't despise the choice she'd made when picking me.

I pushed away the pointless thoughts, focusing instead on my destination while letting my mind drift to Roxy so I could see how far she had gotten in her preparations for the spell. She was on the roof of R.U.M.P. castle, drawing the pentagram on the floor, a perfect tigers eye crystal sitting ready beside her.

A growl spilled through my teeth as my mind snapped back into the folds of death and Hail arched an eyebrow at me.

"She's using another piece of my treasure," I grumbled, trying to push off the irritation I felt over her stealing from my hoard in favour of the thought of how it would help her, but it was fucking annoying. "I mean, surely there's plenty of other crystals she could have found. It's not like tigers eye is all that rare and all those rebels are desperate to please her, so I'm sure if she'd just bothered to ask them for one someone would have offered."

"I once stole a medallion straight off of Lionel's neck and tossed it in the lake at Zodiac Academy," Hail commented. "Never thought I'd see anyone throw such a bitch fit again in my lifetime, but it looks like you might be hoping to claim that title."

"Fuck off," I muttered, scowling at the enormous gates as we made it into their shadow. "That crystal is mine and she should know better."

Hail laughed and I resisted the urge to punch him in favour of looking to the wraith-like creature clad in black robes that moved to stand before the gates, barring the way onward.

Screams and pleas for mercy slipped between the iron bars where the darkness thickened beyond it. The creature didn't react to them, hooded eyes falling on me, a blue fire igniting in its irises. Its face was illuminated beneath the hood, slits in place of a nose, a mouth sewn shut, no ears and scars painted through those empty eye sockets which held nothing but those blue flames. It reminded me of the Nymphs that had bartered with Roxy for the information on the Damned Forest, but where they had held an ethereal beauty, this creature was nothing but horror wrapped in flesh.

"Who do you seek?" Its voice sounded within my skull, and I fought the

urge to flinch from it, a feeling like fingernails scraping against the inside of my head accompanying its words.

"I need a soul to cast to ash," I replied, uncertain whether this gatekeeper would allow such a thing, but somehow knowing that lies would get me nowhere here. "One deserving of it."

The creature cocked its head at me, curious, but not refusing.

"Such a fate can only be given to one deserving of it. One who has wronged you endlessly. One whose fate you have earned the right to decide in payment for all they did to you in life."

I frowned, my shoulders dropping as I considered the creature's words. "The man who deserves that fate from me still lives."

"There is another." The creature's gruesome lips curved upward as it lifted a hand and beckoned a soul from the shadows.

A figure approached, something about them familiar but before I could get a clear look at them, memories sprung up around me. Not memories of my own; these were seen through the eyes of a man who had long been an unwelcome presence in my life.

Jenkins smiled to himself as he let himself into my room, shuffling over to my desk which was littered with toys and half scribbled drawings. To one side of the room, the start of my very first Dragon treasure hoard lay. A collection of jewels and coins I'd earned either by impressing my father or had gotten as gifts at the elaborate sixth birthday party I'd been thrown the week before.

"I remember this," I growled, somehow knowing what he was going to do before he even did it, fury building in me as I watched that son of a bitch slip a gold coin from my Father's hoard in amongst my own.

The memory moved on and I was still watching Jenkins, his heart thumping excitedly, hands slick with perspiration and a sick thrill burning through him as my father found the coin and punched me so hard, he knocked me out.

All I could remember of that day were the screams of accusation and the blinding pain of that strike, followed by darkness. I'd never dared raise the subject of the coin with my father after I'd been healed and awoke in my bed, but I had assumed he'd been the one to place it there as some kind of test. Seeing the truth now, understanding the way Jenkins had set me up sent a trickle of bile rising in my throat. I'd been a fucking kid. What kind of sick bastard would get off on watching my father punish me like that?

More memories passed me by, times when I'd been accused of things I hadn't done, or times when my father had discovered secrets I'd been keeping from him. The first time Caleb had bitten me, my father had broken every single one of my ribs and I'd never known how he'd found out about it. Jenkins had been the one to tell him.

He'd hunted through every single bit of information the press published on me daily, reading everything from the Celestial Times to personal blogs, scouring the Faebook pages of people I went to school or the Academy with, hunting out any and every story which could be twisted against me or show me up. Then he'd gotten into the habit of laying them out for my father with his breakfast each morning, explaining how nothing I did ever passed him by and so many of the times I'd woken up to one of my father's brutal lessons.

There were countless memories of Jenkins either orchestrating or simply enjoying the treatment I suffered at my father's hands and smoke slipped between my teeth as I bore witness to more than enough evidence to damn that piece of shit.

Hail shifted at my side, clearly seeing these memories too and I caught his eye, warning him not to pity me with a single firm look. But no such thing entered his gaze, instead, a fiery hatred for my father's butler entered his eyes. He wanted vengeance for all Jenkins had done, I could see it plain and clear, and for a fleeting moment I imagined what it might have been like to know Hail Vega as Roxanya's father. He had not been given nearly long enough with his children, and it felt strange to be on the receiving end of his protectiveness when he'd had few opportunities to bestow it on those he truly cared for.

"Do you wish to claim this soul?" the creature offered, tossing him to the floor at my feet.

I snarled as I reached for Jenkins, taking hold of his collar, and yanking the asshole right up off the ground to look into my eyes.

"Oh, Jenkins, how did I almost forget about your pathetic excuse for an existence?" I asked, enjoying the fear that flashed in his eyes as he tried to fight his way free of me. But whatever magic had captured his soul stopped him from laying a hand on me while I was able to hold him tight and keep him exactly where I wanted him.

"Wait," Jenkins rasped, but none of us were listening.

"Reap justice from his unhallowed soul." The creature faded to nothing before us, and I turned to Hail with a savage smile.

"Let's go help Roxy cheat death."

Hail followed me as I headed to her, pushing against The Veil, a rooftop appearing around us where she stood in the centre of a pentagram following the words of the spell, drawing on the ether and turning her eyes towards death as she prepared to reach out for a soul to use in her dark magic.

"Please, there's been a mistake. I never did anything," Jenkins spluttered, the lies spilling from him making smoke pour through my teeth. But as my fist raised to silence him, Hail's got there first, knocking him flat on his back between us with a scream.

"I know worms like you. I have left one kicking in the living realm with a scar torn through his eye as a reminder of how easily I might have killed him once. I deeply regret leaving his heart beating, but I shall not regret tethering you to my daughter's dark power. I will let her harness you, break you, use up what little worth your soul has, then you shall be cast into nothing."

"I will never look back upon my memories of you, Jenkins," I said darkly. "None shall remember you. I shall score your name from the living world when I return to it, but first I shall score it from death."

"No – please – wait!" Jenkins screamed as Hail and I took hold of him, sharing a wicked smile.

The tigers eye crystal sat at the tip of the pentagram and as Roxy called on a soul to house in it, and Hail gripped Jenkins by his other arm and the two of us forced his screaming, pleading, pathetic soul inside it. The power snapped shut around him, securing his fate once and for all. And as I turned from him with my wife's father at my side, the two of us grinned like savages.

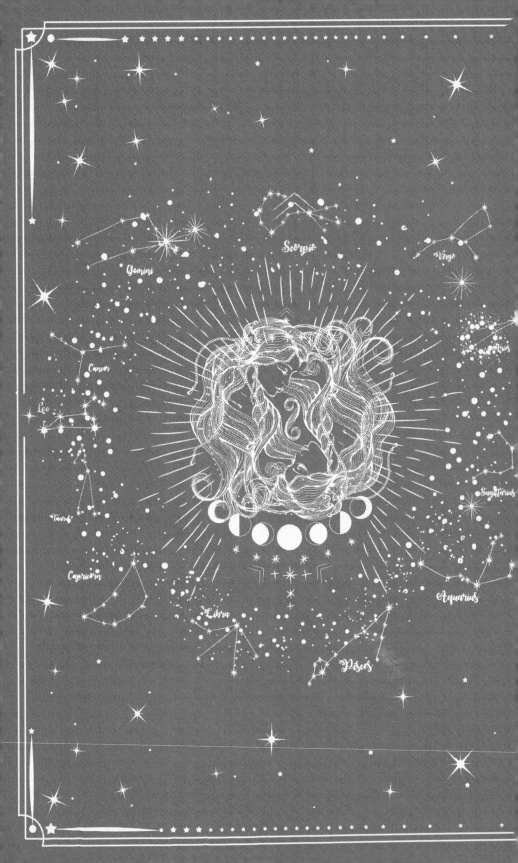

MERISSA

CHAPTER SEVENTEEN.

My form flickered between the realm of the living and the space beyond The Veil, my chambers rising up around me as I fought to stay closer to the other side where I knew I was needed most.

I closed my eyes, sagging against the throne in the Eternal Palace, breathing heavily though I knew I didn't have any real need of oxygen. But habits formed throughout a lifetime faded slowly even in death. I knew of some souls who never took a breath, never imagined their heart thumping in their chest, didn't experience the sensation of touch at all anymore. But I preferred to remember what it had been like to live, to continue experiencing my existence with those sensations.

The chamber was empty, the others all still set on their missions to change fate, but I'd visited with Gabriel, I'd held his hand while he lay strapped to the Royal Seer's chair, and I had seen the paths which lay before my daughters and their friends.

The door banged open and I looked up, finding Catalina there, her eyes wide with fear, long hair wild and tangling down her spine. She ran to me, Hamish Grus bounding into the room at her back in his Cerberus form, the roof raising to allow for the three headed beast.

"Did you find out anything about Lionel's plans?" I demanded. "Is he laying a trap? Were you able to change anything?"

"I made it to him, barely," Catalina replied, a frown furrowing her brow which spoke of nothing good. "He wasn't thinking of me but then Lavinia spoke of being his bride and for a brief moment, his thoughts turned my way. I slipped through a gap in the void and made it to his side."

Hamish growled softly, moving to stand closer to her, his huge leg brushing against her arm in a comforting gesture, but Catalina simply raised her chin, refusing to be shaken by the man she had once called her husband.

"I couldn't stay for long, but he was excited, hiding something from the Shadow Princess, talking about some big Dragon celebration he is due to host tonight during the Hydrids meteor shower."

"And?" I asked, terror for my children rolling through me.

Hamish shifted in a flash of movement, returning to his Fae form, drawing Catalina under his arm and smiling grimly.

"And my clever Kitty knew the scoundrel well enough to sniff out his lies like a snaffwaffer on the dawn," he said. "She hunted in his drawers and found a ledger he had secreted away like a squirrel with a nut too many for its gnawsome jaw."

"Meaning?" I prompted. Time was slipping by, the meteor shower fast approaching. I knew my daughter well enough to know that she would already be preparing to leave, to head to The Palace of Souls in search of her sister.

"He's been crafting a list of his most powerful and loyal supporters – meaning the Dragon Guild. I found an invitation stuffed in the back of his closet. The bastard never did know how to set a good enough concealment spell to outwit me," Catalina said. "The invitation was worded strangely. He was asking his Dragon Guild members to come to him and make the pledge they had agreed to. Hamish leant me some of his strength and together we managed to flip through the pages of the ledger within the confines of the closet. Merissa, I think Lionel plans to Guardian Bond every Dragon in the Guild, creating an army between him and any who try to end his reign."

I stilled at the thought of that. Countless bonded men willing to throw themselves between Lionel and death, a shield of flesh and blood that would strike back at all costs. The emotional toll that would take on both Lionel and those he bonded to was insane, and yet there was a kind of cunning brilliance to the plan. Lionel knew he couldn't win against the Vega princesses once they claimed their full power. Deep down he understood that, and this was his fear showing.

"He's afraid," I said, a slow smile building on my lips and Catalina echoed it, her grin a wicked thing.

"Yes. But not just of the Vega twins. I think he fears his new bride too. She wasn't cowering before him, and she wasn't simply bowing to his will either. There is a power struggle going on there and if Lionel thought he could crush it with brute force, then he would have attempted it already. The fact that he hasn't speaks volumes."

"And the fact that he has hidden these Guardian Bonding plans from her says even more," Hamish agreed. "He plans to do this tonight while she is otherwise engaged in some devilishly dastardly act we couldn't fathom. He wants that scaley army in place around him sooner rather than later, and as he said nothing of laying a trap or expecting an attack-"

"His plans are simply escalating because he's afraid. He wants that army there to protect him from Lavinia," I surmised.

We shared a look of conspiratorial victory. If Lionel was preoccupied with a threat from within his own palace, he wouldn't be looking for one headed in from the outside.

"Gabriel still foresees a great failure in tonight's plans for Roxanya and the Heirs," I said solemnly, breaking that sweet moment of victory to pieces. "But I've been working within the palace, joining with the magic I left there in my lifetime, finding the hidden ways, seeking out the Nymphs and Dragons posted throughout its hallways. With a bit of help and some extra power, I think I'll be able to form a safe path for them to travel."

"Just tell us what you need and it's yours," Catalina agreed, Hamish nodding too.

The doors burst open, and we all looked towards Azriel and Clara as they strode into the room.

"Did it work?" I demanded, that queenly authority colouring my tone.

"A little. The Nymphs started in fighting, but it was quelled quickly, the leaders among them keeping control. I don't think it's going to work," Azriel sighed.

"Well keep trying. We can't expect miracles but every little will help."

Azriel nodded and he and Clara headed away to continue their attempts with the Nymphs.

"So what now?" Catalina asked, looking to me for an answer I wished I could give. But we were out of time and this fate wasn't going to shift so we needed another option.

"We'll watch over them," I said firmly. "I'll bring you with me to The Palace of Souls and together with Hail and Darius we can unlock some of the magic hidden within its walls, guide them from danger as best we can and hopefully see them through this night, whatever horrors it may bring."

"Where is Darius?" Catalina asked, and her son materialised as if in answer to her question, my husband right along with him.

"Well?" I asked.

"Roxanya has summoned the power of ether once again. She has created a dark artefact which will help her stave off death if it comes calling for her."

"She succeeded in that?" I breathed fearfully, hope and fear mixing at the thought of Roxanya wielding such dangerous magic. But if the things Gabriel had *seen* about this night were even close to true, then I knew she was going to need every advantage she could get to survive it.

"She did," Hail confirmed, pride clear in his voice and Darius smiled darkly.

"Let's make sure it's enough," he said.

I quickly told them of Lionel's plan to bond the Dragons to himself, and Darius cursed furiously.

"Come, we must hurry," I urged, beckoning them all closer and they moved to me, taking hold of my hands and arms, gripping tightly as Hail and I focused on The Palace of Souls, the heart of our stronghold in the living realm, the place where our magic lived on most potently beyond our deaths.

Just as we were tugged toward it, Radcliff appeared, the Dragon shifter who had died before I'd ever even entered Hail's life charging after us as The Veil swept around us and tugged us towards the palace itself.

"I want in," Radcliff said as we arrived. "Call it vengeance if you must, but if there's a chance to get one up on Lame Lionel here then I want to grip it by the balls and pull."

"Charming," Catalina muttered, earning a grin from the man whose life Lionel had stolen.

"Now what?" Darius asked as we found ourselves in a dimly lit hallway, distant footsteps announcing the arrival of someone who shouldn't have been here.

"They're coming," I breathed, moving to the wall and pressing my palm flat against it, sighing as I felt the distant call of my own magic, the power which I had bound here all those years ago.

Hail placed his hand over mine and a distant rumble echoed through the walls as the palace awoke, greeting us like a waking house cat cracking open an eye and hoping for a belly rub.

"Xavier?" Catalina breathed and Darius took her hand as he felt the presence of those he loved drawing closer too.

"Max and Roxy are with him. How are they already here?" he asked.

"Time shifts to a beat of its own between here and there. A heartbeat for us can pass a week for them, sometimes more, sometimes less. The dead aren't constrained by the passage of time but that means time has no loyalty to us in turn," Radcliff replied solemnly.

"Meaning the path Gabriel foresaw is already in motion," Darius muttered.

"But we're here to open new passages for fate to select," I assured him. "We just need to know which ones to choose."

"They're hunting for Darcy and Lance," Darius said, looking from left to right as he tried to get his bearings. "Which path will they take?"

"That way." Hail jerked his chin to indicate the most direct path to the throne room, but a sense of dread stole through me the moment he did so.

"Lionel will have guards posted throughout these halls. We need to open up a path that avoids them," I said.

"Well wet my whiskers, why didn't you say? I shall go forth and assess the scoundrels myself." Hamish took off down the hallway Hail had indicated, and Radcliff took up the task too, taking a passage to the right.

"If we can lock down where the guards are stationed then we can lead them down a safer path – assuming our magic is powerful enough to do so," I said.

"It is," Hail growled, refusing to allow any other option.

Darius took off in the direction of Roxanya and the others, Catalina slipping through a closed door to our left and checking beyond it.

I closed my eyes and pushed my power into the walls themselves, Hail's magic merging with mine until I spilled into them and could feel the entire building as if it was an extension of my own flesh.

Lionel's followers lurked in some of the hallways, but most of them were beyond the palace walls, gathering in the amphitheatre for his ritual.

"There she is," Hail muttered, and I felt her too, our daughter striding towards us with purposeful steps.

I reached out for Gwendalina and found her in the throne room as expected, Lance beside her and a single guard stationed in the room to watch over them.

"Xavier and Max just entered the hidden passages and split from Roxanya," I murmured, flexing my power, feeling my way through the corridors surrounding us as our daughter drew closer still.

"Not this nelly way!" Hamish called and I could feel the cluster of Nymphs in the direction he'd taken.

"She's almost here, but she isn't focused on me," Darius said from somewhere close by as he returned. "I can't reach her."

"It's clear to the left!" Catalina called and I gritted my teeth as I delved deeper into the magic of the palace,

"I need more power," I snapped.

"How?" Darius barked in reply.

"Come here," Hail demanded and as Darius placed his hand against the wall beside mine, I felt the rush of his magic joining with ours.

I glanced at him, the determination in his eyes filling me with that same, undeniable need and as Catalina, Hamish and Radcliff all pressed their magic into the walls too, I found the strength I needed to take control of this ill-fated night.

"Go," Hail growled, taking control of the cocktail of power, his ties to The Palace of Souls the strongest, making it easiest for him to take the lead.

A flash of icy coldness raced through me as I stepped away from the wall, leaving him in charge of the palace and looking around just as Roxanya appeared looking ferocious with her sword in hand and her gaze burning with the desperate need to find her sister.

I could feel more guards headed this way, fate twisting to catch her out, but I would fight that destiny with all I had.

She sprinted towards me, heading straight for the route which held the most guards and I held up my hands, willing her to see me, to hear me as I cried out for her to stop.

She raced straight through my insubstantial form, utterly unaware of me, not so much as slowing her pace, the pain of that fact cutting into me as it always did, but I had no time to dwell in self-pity.

"Hail!" I yelled but he was already ahead of me, a cry of effort escaping him as he drew on the power of the palace and the doors to Roxanya's left flew open with a bang.

She whirled towards it, raising her sword in anticipation of an attack but when she found no one there, her thoughts fell to me. The memory of the last time I'd sent her a message in this Palace made her think of me and like a guiding star, I latched onto the grief she felt.

The power of that pang of longing gave me the extra strength I needed and I ran to the door, willing my power into the floor beneath my feet, shimmering silver footsteps appearing on the flagstones, guiding her after me.

Roxanya didn't hesitate, darting through the door which Hail slammed behind her right before the guards I'd felt coming appeared around the next corner.

They didn't see me as I scowled at them, cursing them for setting foot in our home and hoping the dark fate that had been prophesised for this night would fall on them instead.

I raced away from them, chasing my daughter as the others ran after her too, Hail opening another door which I sped through, leaving a trail of footsteps once more, guiding Roxanya through the palace as safely as possible.

Hamish, Radcliff, Darius, and Catalina called out warnings whenever they spotted more Nymphs and we skirted them time and again, leading her to the throne room without once coming into contact with any of her enemies.

Eventually, Roxanya made it to the throne room and we all fell still, panting with the effort it had required to affect the living realm so much. Each of us hoping with quiet desperation that she might be able to find a way to rescue Gwendalina and her mate now that she was here. But between Lance's Death

Bond and Gwendalina's shadow curse, I feared what could be done to save them.

Roxanya moved to the throne room doors, reaching out to break the magic Lionel had placed upon them and Catalina caught my arm.

"Xavier is in need," she gasped, her eyes fearful and I looked to Hail who nodded once, feeling his way towards her son through his connection with the palace.

"Gabriel is at risk too," I added. "Seth, Geraldine and Caleb are hunting for him."

"We can't do any more to help Roxanya here," Hail said, though I could tell he didn't want to leave her. "Darius can stay to watch over her. If we want to help Xavier and Max, it will take both of us. Are Gabriel and the others safe for now?"

"Yes. So far as I can tell," I agreed and Hail nodded, my word on it more than enough for him.

Darius looked to Hail in surprise, the weight of the trust he was placing upon him leaving him stunned.

"Save my brother," he said firmly, his own heart clearly torn on where he should be, but we needed Hail's connection to the palace if we were going to help Xavier. And Roxanya's keen grief over Darius made him the best choice to help her here. If anyone could, then it would be him.

"Those are my daughters in there, son," Hail growled, gripping his shoulder as he met Darius's tempestuous gaze. "Don't fail them."

"I won't," Darius swore, gripping Hail's shoulder in return, a powerful energy rippling between them which set the hairs standing along the back of my neck.

And with that we left him there, a single knight guarding his queen as we fell into darkness and raced towards another soul in need of our help to survive this cursed night.

DARIUS

CHAPTER EIGHTEEN ·

Roxy shattered the spells my father had placed on the door to the throne room, throwing up a silencing bubble to hide all sound of what she was doing and capturing the Fae my father had left there to guard Darcy and Lance.

I narrowed my eyes at the Dragon Shifter as he whirled toward the door. He was a distant cousin, ugly bastard with a fondness for bait games where he pitted magical creatures against one another for the amusement of assholes like him. He had a taste for inflicting suffering. My father had taken me to watch one once when I was around fourteen and I'd openly sneered at the whole thing, calling the men who took pleasure from gambling on such cruelty pathetic and questioning their so-called manhood.

Father had predictably punished me, and this motherfucker had offered up his training cane for the lesson. I'd taken every strike of it without flinching then broken the cages of all the poor beasts in the place and set them free the moment it was done, ignoring my own wounds in favour of their freedom.

Father had smiled then, using stardust to spirit me away from this piece of shit while he'd started raging and screaming about his lost profits. I'd expected a worse punishment on our return to the manor, but I'd gotten praise instead.

A man of substance won't ever retract his word.

Father's proud smile still lingered in my memory. Blood had dripped from the wounds he'd given me to stain the rug, pain throbbing through my flesh, but in that moment, my chest had swelled at gaining his approval.

What a poor, broken creature I'd been. Whipped and kicked and still desperate for his validation. Shame coloured my memory of that day now. I'd been starting to fight back, to hold my own and show my grit and yet he'd claimed that as his achievement too. Even in defiance I'd been his pet, his prize, his protégé. The Heir with the crooked crown.

I watched as the Dragon threw an air shield up around himself, trying to recall his name.

It had been something like Trevor. Or Terrance. Or-

Roxy hurled her power at him, a bird of blue and red phoenix fire erupting from her outstretched palms, tearing across the throne room and shattering his shield in the blink of an eye.

Tony maybe?

Roxy charged for him, sword raised, lips parted in a feral challenge.

Tim. Tim the Dragon…no, that didn't seem right, it was more like Tilbert, or-

The Dragon threw his arm out to cast at my wife and a snarl escaped me, but she was too fast for him, her sword striking with savage precision, his arm severed before he could even call on the magic he needed.

Tommy screamed at the wound, the pain slowing him, stealing his last chance to fight back before she whipped around and slit his throat wide open.

Blood sprayed and I stared at that beautiful, wild creature of mine as she stepped away from the falling Dragon Shifter, his eyes wide with the panic of death.

The Veil whipped and thrashed around me, and I stumbled as I fought to maintain my place in it, a violent ricochet snapping through it as Toto's soul was wrenched through and hurled onto this side of death.

The Palace of Souls faded, that golden glow taking its place as we were transported deeper within the grasp of The Veil, and I cursed as I lost sight of Roxy.

The river appeared before me, Turnip standing between it and me, blinking in alarm, looking all around and grasping at his throat as though searching for the wound that had killed him.

"D…Darius?" he stuttered, taking me in as I loomed over him, smoke trailing from my lips. "Am I dead? Is this the promised beauty of the beyond?"

"No, Tiger," I growled, my hand curling into a fist as I narrowed my eyes at the piece of shit who had been standing watch over my best friend and sweet little Gwen while they rotted in that cage. Who had tried to throw magic at my fucking wife. "This, is the river of the damned."

I punched him so hard that he was thrown clean off of his feet, his scream echoing all throughout The Veil as he tumbled towards that rushing water, the arms of other cursed and desperate souls reaching for him greedily as his final words rang out for all to hear.

"My name is Toooooodd!"

"Oh, right." I shrugged, figuring I'd been close enough and turned away the moment the river swallowed him in a ferocious splash, fixing my attention back on my wife whose pain was slicing into me.

Roxy must have been reuniting with her sister and Lance, and my chest ached with the truth they were breaking to her, the reality that Lance was trapped there thanks to the deal he'd made with Lavinia.

I forced my way back to them, their pain like an anchor that drove me on, Lance's grief for me sharp as he took in what the loss of me had done to my wife.

I stumbled as I made it back to the throne room, moving to stand with them even though they couldn't see me there.

The Death Bond clung to Lance like a wraith sitting on his back, the stench of it choking me, the weight of it pressing in around me and making panic rise sharply within me. So many of the people I loved were caught on this line, dancing with death, The Veil whispering their names as it felt them edging closer.

I slipped out into the corridors surrounding the throne room, hunting for signs of more guards, but the palace was oddly quiet. No doubt most of them had been summoned outside to take part in my father's ritual, the knowledge of what he planned to do out there itching at me. I hated the Guardian Bond magic with a passion, and I could only hope that there was some cost involved in using it on such a scale. Maybe being linked to so many would drive him mad with need for all of them and it would turn out to be a good thing after all. Though somehow I doubted fate would be so kind.

I moved back into the throne room, pausing as I noticed the tension in Roxy's posture, her pain biting into me as her grief sharpened. One look at Lance and Gwen let me know that they'd told her, the defiant set of Gwen's shoulders making it clear she wasn't going to leave Lance here either.

"I'm dangerous," Gwen breathed, looking to Roxy with sorrow in her eyes. "The beast inside of me is volatile, and I can't always control it. I'm no good to you or the rebels, I'd just be putting you in danger."

"Fuck danger," Roxy spat, her hand curling into a fist so tight that it had to hurt. "All I want is you."

Her words were fierce, defiant, but I knew her well enough to see the pain in them, the utter agony of what this rejection was doing to her. She had come all this way to reclaim the other half of her soul, the one person who might be able to help her find her way back to herself from the pit of grief that had consumed her since my death. She needed her twin more than she needed air to breathe and if Gwen didn't go with her now, then I knew it was going to break her more thoroughly than she could ever recover from.

She wasn't the savage princess who stood before them, bloodstained and ready for war, she was a broken girl in desperate need and if Gwen turned her back on her now then I knew there would be no undoing the damage it caused.

"Don't do this to her," I breathed, imploring, hating myself for the words, knowing Lance needed her too. But Roxy was already on the edge, she had been fighting to hold herself together for nothing other than the girl standing before her and if she lost her too then I feared what would come of it.

But as my fear for what this would do to Roxy grew, I noticed a look which passed between her and Lance, a decision they made which Gwen missed, one that would only cause more pain and hurt, but might be their only choice.

"You need to leave, Tory," Gwen started, but before she could go on, Orion snapped his hand out and struck her in the temple.

He caught her as she sagged to the floor, her eyes widening at the betrayal as she passed out.

I cursed, seeing nothing but more devastation coming from that choice, but it was already done.

A pained sob escaped Roxy as she dropped to her knees, brushing the shadowy strands of hair from her sister's face.

"I'll keep her safe," she swore to Lance, her hand squeezing his in both thanks and apology.

"I'll hold you to that," Lance snarled, and Roxy threw her arms around his neck, pinning Gwen between them as the weight of this reality fell over them, both of them accepting what had to be done while hating it at once. She'd come all this way to rescue him, only to have to leave him behind.

"I'm sorry," Roxy breathed.

"Don't be," Lance growled. "Never be sorry for protecting her. That's something the two of us will always put above everything else."

I stilled as a rumble moved throughout the room, something deep and dark shifting within the air, the sensation putting me on edge, though neither Roxy nor Lance seemed to notice it.

A pounding sounded wildly within my skull as I hunted for the source of the gathering dark and my attention fell to Gwen in horror as she began to fall apart in her sister's arms, shadows stealing her away, transforming her and waking her from the forced slumber Orion had inflicted.

The two of them scrambled away from one another as Gwen shifted, a beast out of legend appearing in her place, feral eyes swinging towards the girl she loved above all others, no hint of recognition forming as she bared sharp teeth and growled ferociously.

"Run!" Lance roared, his word echoing mine, but Roxy didn't move, her eyes widening in horror at what she was seeing and her feet remaining stubbornly in place as she stood to face the monster that had been born of her sister's flesh.

Of course she didn't run. That woman had been created without the capability to flee. She didn't back down from a fight and certainly not from one which involved her sister. I loved her, but in that moment all of the fire and raw fury which held her spine so rigidly in defiance of the world was the most terrifying thing I'd ever encountered.

Darcy swiped at her with an enormous paw, claws slamming into her air shield and flinging her across the room, making me curse. Roxy used her control over the air magic to whirl out of the way before landing on her feet behind the throne, but one look at the monstrous creature which had taken her sister's place made it clear that this fight wouldn't be won easily. And that was assuming Roxy would fight.

"Darcy," she barked, irritation in her tone where there should have been terror. "You know me, you hairy asshole."

If Gwen understood her at all it didn't show and she roared, charging again, forcing Roxy to retreat around the throne, using it as a barrier between them.

"I don't think insulting her is helping," Lance called from the cage where he was still chained to the wall by the shadows, and Roxy flipped him off as she darted away again.

I looked to my best friend, my own uselessness carving its way through me as I ran to him, leaving Roxy to play cat and mouse with a monster as she used her air magic to keep out of reach of the Shadow Beast's claws.

"Lance," I barked, punching him in the bicep when he didn't so much as blink in my direction, willing him to see me, uncertain if he could even do anything to help, but I had to hope he could.

I wrapped my hands around the chains of shadow which bound him in place, an icy cold washing into me with a spike of agony which stole my breath away.

The Veil cracked like thunder around me, darkness rushing in, screams filling my ears as the weight of the tainted shadows bucked and thrashed against my hold, the touch of death an unwelcome intrusion into their realm.

But I couldn't let go.

The throne room, Lance, the Shadow Beast and Roxy all fell away as I crumbled from the force of the vibrations which tore into me, my soul becoming little more than a bridge between two places which should never collide.

I felt the souls of the Nymphs who had been consumed by that darkness, the desperation they felt at being trapped within it for so, so long.

Terror dug its claws into me, my fists locked tight around the chain of shadows, my feet anchored beyond The Veil and those empty, desperate souls all rushing for me as one, an army of the lost and ruined victims of the shadow realm.

If there had been enough left of me to scream then I would have, the weight of them charging for me so horrifying that there was nothing which could possibly stop them. They'd devour me in their passage to that brighter realm and from there they'd continue in their destruction, ripping through The Veil, destroying the souls who were harboured within it, stealing their essence, and changing the path of the stars beyond all hopes of repair.

I fought with all I had, trying to release my hold on that darkness, my soul full of sorrow and love for those I was failing, the frantic lashing of what power I could still claim seeming like nothing more than a teardrop splashing into an ocean.

But just as I found myself staring into the empty eyes of those screaming souls, a hand found me in the darkness, fingernails biting into my skin, pain blossoming through my flesh as they ripped me away, freeing me and closing that door, stopping the passage of those desperate souls before they could destroy everything in their path.

I fell at the foot of the large rock which sat in the centre of Mordra's cavern, panting and shaking, the dim light hurting my eyes. I tried to take in where I was, what was happening and-

"The shadows won't help you, boy," she sneered, her voice echoing around the chamber, no body visible to accompany it.

I was staring up at the river from beneath once more, screaming souls tearing past, the flood thicker than it had been the last time I'd looked upon it.

"How did you break me free of their hold?" I asked, unable to summon the energy to rise, the panic which had chained me sluggish to fall away.

"Your mind is warped by the way of the stars, the path of the zodiac colouring your outlook on the world. But what if we weren't all travelling down pathways which lead in a single direction from birth to death? What if our choices affected far more than our simple lives and who or what we become? Perhaps instead of pathways we are simply tethered to strings which are tangled like a ball of yarn. Perhaps those strings need cutting from time to time if we are to have any hope of removing the knots?"

I pushed myself upright, hunting the shadows for some sign of her and finding a shimmering silhouette perched at the very top of the boulder, looking

down at me with what I could have sworn was pity.

"The stars are the knots?" I guessed and her smile appeared in full, a laugh hissing off the walls which surrounded me.

"Do you really think so?"

Mordra cocked her head at me, eyes with yellow shot through the whites blinking slowly.

"Do you hear that?" she breathed before I could answer her.

I could hear it. A rushing, thundering beat which sounded strangely like...

"Wings," I muttered, my head snapping up to look at a large shape as it passed overhead, blotting out the light, moving over the river. "Is that a boat?" I asked the beating of those wings growing fiercer, the pounding echoing through my chest. I knew that sound, I knew it...

"A raft," Mordra replied simply. "He feels a death oncoming. One worthy of his attention for the passage."

"Roxy," I gasped, realising whose wings I could hear beating, whose soul was moving too close to this place, whose power would rouse the interest of the ferryman.

Mordra grinned at me, but she was already fading, Roxy's screams ripping into me as I rushed towards the realm of the living. I felt her agony, the Shadow Beast's teeth and claws ripping through her flesh, her power locked down, her deepest love destroying her from within a cursed body.

I crashed into the throne room in The Palace of Souls, a cry of utter despair escaping me as I found her beneath the Shadow Beast, so much blood spilled that it was hard to believe she could still be alive. But she was thrashing beneath her attacker, trying to push at the monster with nothing but her own physical strength. It was no good; her power was locked down by its bite and the shadows were racing for her thundering heart.

"Roxy!" I bellowed, charging for her, throwing myself between her and the Shadow Beast, my body falling apart until nothing but the essence of my soul remained so that I could hurl every drop of my remaining power into her.

Her pain pierced my flesh, every slice and bite and break resounding through me so I could feel all of it too and I latched onto it, drawing it away from her, offering what help I could while The Veil still held me in its clutches.

"The crystal!" I roared, my hand locking around hers as it fell limp to the flagstones, willing her to find the strength she needed to keep fighting, just a little longer, just long enough.

Roxy blinked and for a moment I could have sworn she saw me, that she felt that surge of power as she thrust her hand into her pocket and ripped the crystal free.

Jenkins was screaming from within the tigers eye, howling for a freedom he would never again possess.

"That's it, baby, fight it. Fight this fucked up fate and choose your own destiny," I snarled, willing her to do it.

More blood spilled across the flagstones, too much fucking blood. No one could survive this. Not for much longer. The space between her heartbeats was thick with the weight of The Veil, and I knew she was almost out of time. If she crossed over, she'd be with me again. But there wasn't even a selfish part of me that could wish for that. Not for her. She was so full of life that I refused to even consider the option of death stealing her away.

I gave her all I had, and she took that strength, binding it to her own and shoving the crystal into her side with a grunt of pain, the cold stone sinking beneath flesh.

"Vivere," Roxy choked out.

Ether stirred the air around her and relief practically suffocated me as I felt it answering her call.

Jenkins screamed as he watched the memories Roxy sacrificed for the magic. Two little girls shivering in a bed together, wondering if their foster parents would come home tonight.

I watched with a festering hatred, feeling the fear of those small children. They were hungry because there were locks on the kitchen cupboards and their foster parents had left them alone all day, not specifying when they'd be back. The house was cold, and darkness had fallen beyond the curtains. Roxy's jaw was locked tight with a fury I knew all too well, that stubborn determination to survive so bright in her even then.

She had been a princess lost to a world that didn't understand her but now she was back, and I knew there would be no stopping her again.

The memory was devoured in payment for the magic, the ether swallowing it whole and locking Jenkins's soul into the crystal, his dark taint shadowing her bright glow, shielding her from the eyes of death itself.

The Veil fluttered around her, uncertain now of where the lines between life and death fell, unable to reach out for her soul while the rotting stench of Jenkins covered it. To The Veil she appeared dead already, but I could feel her there, her heart still beating but only weakly.

The Shadow Beast continued to savage her, and I cried out, knowing this magic could only work for so long, seeking help in whatever form I could find it.

There were so many points of light rushing closer, so many of my loved ones fighting. Lance was roaring his defiance of this act and somewhere, and further away I felt another soul who was so in tune with my own that he felt like an extension of myself.

Caleb was coming. Caleb was almost here.

"Hold on, baby," I growled, the words a command as I gave her all I had, my hand tightening around hers, willing her to feel me there.

The ruby necklace she still wore for me heated between us as our souls reached for one another and I pushed everything I had into it, offering it to her, willing her to keep fighting even after she fell from consciousness.

"Just a little longer," I demanded, looking to the door, feeling that piece of my soul rushing to us.

The doors crashed open and there Caleb was, Lance crying out to him as his wild eyes took in what was happening.

Caleb launched himself onto the Shadow Beast's back, yanking its fur hard enough to draw its full focus.

I couldn't afford to give the fight my attention as I continued to pour my strength into the love of my life, the pauses between her heartbeats a terrifying reality which took up all of my focus.

"Get her out of here," Lance growled and suddenly Caleb was there, drawing her up and into his arms, healing magic flooding from him into her while he struggled to combat the work of the shadows. Each beat of her heart was stronger than the one before it, each breath she heaved in a little fuller than the last.

"Run, Caleb," Lance urged. "Please, you can't stay. And I won't leave Darcy." He looked to the dome of earth which Caleb had used to contain the Shadow Beast. It shuddered and cracked, its power almost breaking through it already.

"I'm not leaving you," Caleb replied. "You're my sanguis frater. I can't walk away from you now that I've found you."

"I made a Death Bond with Lavinia, Caleb," Lance revealed and the pain I felt over the failure that had befallen my loved ones this night almost consumed me, the call of The Veil beckoning me back, but I refused it. I couldn't leave her until I knew she was safe. I wouldn't.

Their words grew distant, the light around me flickering but I stayed with her, pouring all that there was of me into the ruby at her throat, offering up anything she might be able to grasp as she teetered too close to death.

Caleb finally accepted the truth of the situation and raced for freedom, and I went with him, stealing through The Palace of Souls and escaping into the dark of the night. Roxy needed to heal from the venom in her blood, but I knew they had what she required back at R.U.M.P. castle so that was all I could hope for.

Failure may have claimed this night, but Roxy's heart was still beating.

HAIL

CHAPTER NINETEEN

I took in Lionel's freshly made army of Bonded Men where they fought with the rebels in the amphitheatre. Merissa and I shared a look of horror then I lunged forward instinctively as fire bloomed our way from the jaws of an ugly brown brute of a Dragon passing overhead. The flames swept through us, the two of us untouchable of course, but I realised my hands had been raised in defence despite the fact my Elements were long lost to me.

I glanced back at Merissa but found her running away across the sand on Catalina's heels, the two of them reaching Xavier Acrux just as Radcliff materialised beside him too.

Lionel's son fought with a ferocity that spoke of the injustice and pain he had faced at the hands of these Dragons, his hatred spilling freely out of him as he took on one of the bonded men in their Fae form.

"That's it," Radcliff whooped at Xavier. "Back straighter, shoulders squared. Never let him get you on the back foot."

In a blink, I joined them, pushing against The Veil to remain there while Catalina watched on in terror.

"You are a stain on your father's name, you should be ashamed of yourself, you little runt," Xavier's opponent spat at him, fire blasting from his hands again, but Catalina's son sent his own fire back at him that was twice as hot. "He should have drowned you at birth."

"You bastard, Cyril, I always despised you," Catalina snarled, diving forward and swinging her fist at him, even though it sailed straight through without touching him.

Hamish materialised beside Catalina as if he had sensed her anguish, bracing her and looking to Xavier in terror.

"Oh Kitty," he breathed. "Never fear. Your boy has the heart of a walrus."

My eye caught on Max Rigel standing on a pillar of air and firing flaming arrows at anyone who got in his way. His mother, Serenity, watched from below, her eyes brimming with pride as she cheered him on, though he couldn't hear her any more than the rest of the living could hear us.

Xavier's flames curled around Cyril's head, blinding him for a moment and he quickly pressed his advantage, tugging his metal Pegasus horn free of his pocket. It seemed as though he were about to strike Cyrus, but he hesitated, his features pinched in turmoil.

"It's okay, Xavier." Catalina moved up behind him, resting a hand on his shoulder. "Death is justice for men like this."

Before Cyril could escape Xavier's flames, he made his decision, plunging the horn deep into Cyril's chest, a shout of effort leaving him.

"Woohoo!" Radcliff cried, leaping forward and clapping Xavier on the arm. "Did you see that, Cat?" He elbowed Catalina. "Your boy's a man now."

"He was a man long before this moment," Catalina said, raising her chin.

Cyril spluttered, blood splashing over Xavier from his parted lips as his fire died out, leaving them staring eye to eye with one another.

"I'm no runt," Xavier snarled, twisting the horn.

Cyril tried to summon his magic, but death was moving forward on silent wings. I felt The Veil opening for him, his soul hovering at the edges of his body as he fought to live. But Xavier was showing no mercy, his teeth bared, his gaze full of so many years of abuse it didn't bear thinking about.

Merissa smiled at Catalina, moving to her and together they watched Xavier secure his kill.

"This is for them," Xavier hissed, love and loss tearing through his words and Catalina released a shuddering breath, knowing he meant her and Darius. "And you won't be the last."

He yanked the metal horn from Cyril's chest, setting fire to his body as he fell.

Cyril came tearing through The Veil and Catalina pounced like an alley cat, kicking out the backs of his legs so he hit the ground beneath her. She gripped his hair in her fist, her foot slamming down on his spine to hold him there as she spoke in his ear, "Hello, Cyril."

He turned his head, taking her in with wide eyes, lips quivering. "Wh- where am I?"

Hamish stepped forward, crouching low and glaring like a heathen. "This is the deep, dark yonder, you sandy flan of a fellow."

"Crucia is calling you," Catalina growled, rising to her feet and dragging Cyril along by the hair. "I'll take you to the Harrowed Gate myself."

Radcliff booted Cyril in the ass before The Veil could steal the three of them away. "Never liked him. Big ego, tiny Dragon."

The Veil shivered around us and I lost sight of the battle, my hand finding Merissa's as we pushed back against the barrier, seeking out our children and leaving Radcliff behind.

We found Gabriel first, bound in chains while Vard dragged him through the palace, our son unable to use magic.

"Let go of him," Merissa snarled, pressing forcefully against The Veil to try and claw at Vard's face. But he passed right through her, tugging Gabriel after him, his head hung low in defeat. It was so unlike him, and I feared this misfortune would be the thing to finally break him.

"It wasn't Gabriel's fault," I snarled. "How was he to tell his loved ones that fate had changed when he is trapped here?"

"He will not forgive himself so easily," Merissa said in despair, reaching for our son.

Time rippled again and I found us deeper within the palace where Vard still shoved Gabriel along.

"Quiet now, aren't you?" Vard chuckled. "By the end of this war, you will likely have no one left. No wife, no kid. All your disgusting rebel family good and dead where they belong."

Gabriel roared in defiance, lunging at Vard but the Cyclops blasted flames at him, sending him stumbling backwards with fire scorching his arms.

"Get away from him!" Merissa screamed.

Vard closed in on Gabriel and the palace rumbled right down to its core as the magic of old called to us. The useless Seer didn't seem to notice as his fire sizzled out and he closed in on Gabriel with a sneer, but our boy glanced up at the ceiling like he could sense the power brewing in the stone.

"Maybe I'll melt your lips shut and your eyes too. I can get into your mind anyway, that's all we need of you," Vard threatened, and my Hydra bellowed from deeper beyond The Veil, flying this way as rage scored a line through my chest. This rage in me was murderous, the kind that would have seen a hundred dead had I still possessed my crown in the living realm.

I stalked up behind Vard, but Merissa got there first, throwing her power into the door to his right and making it fly open so violently that it nearly came off the hinges. It slammed right into the Cyclops, sending him tumbling backwards down the corridor like a ragdoll.

Gabriel's eyebrows rose in surprise, and he looked right at Merissa where she stood by the door, squinting as if trying to see her.

Vard sat upright with blood streaming from his shattered nose and he quickly healed it, swiping at the blood and releasing a small murmur of fear. He glanced left and right, hunting for who had opened that door, and I prowled towards him, the walls trembling and the lights flickering overhead.

"Wh-who's there?" he stammered. "Show yourself!"

"I think you would piss yourself if you could see me now, worm," I hissed, my boots striking the tiles with such power that he could hear the pound of them in the living realm.

"Wh-who is that?" Vard raised his hands, fire flashing in them.

"I think my mother and father are close," Gabriel whispered, his eyes roaming, still seeking us out.

"I'm here, my love," Merissa called to him, but he didn't hear her.

"Nonsense," Vard spat, trying to get to his feet, but I stamped down hard on the tiles and crack shot along them, making him scream in fright. The shockwave rocked through the hall and sent him falling back onto his ass.

I couldn't do any more than that, but the terror in his good eye was enough. He knew what would find him in death, and so help him when he walked through The Veil. For Merissa and I would be waiting.

The power in the palace ebbed away and I felt suddenly drained, the strength it had taken to do so much leaving me exhausted. Not in any physical way, but like a tap had been left running on the energy of my soul. Merissa came to me, looking as weary as I, but her presence gave me some strength to hold onto.

Gabriel had renewed hope in his eyes, and I was sure our efforts had not been for nothing. The Veil swept us back, but Max's mother Serenity burst into view between a haze of golden mist and the vague view of The Palace of Souls hovered beyond her.

"Hail, Merissa, I need you. My son and Xavier Acrux are cornered. I cannot wield the palace as you can. Please. You must help them escape." Serenity gripped Merissa's arm and we moved with her in an instant.

Before we reached them, a piercing song blasted through the air, making me wince from the power of it. I clapped my hands over my ears and the others did the same, the song so terrible it cut through into The Veil, forcing us back.

I dug my heels in while Serenity pulled us nearer, and the tune of death and destruction roared ever louder.

"What is that?" I yelled.

"My son's Dread Song," Serenity said, looking to me with a fierce smile.

As we made it closer, The Veil thinned and souls came spilling through, each still kicking, screaming and thrashing against the monstrous song that had caused their end. They remained unaware of their death for a few seconds more before The Veil snatched them away, many no doubt being sent straight to the river and the Harrowed Gate.

We reached the room where Max was holding off the Dragons with his song, while Xavier hunted for a way out from the dead end, carefully holding a set of Pegasus wings in his arms. I couldn't believe he had found them, and prayed to the stars they were still salvageable.

Catalina and Hamish had returned, and Radcliff was grappling with an iron candle stick on the wall which he seemed convinced was the answer to their problems.

"Surely this ugly thing must have a purpose!" Radcliff cried. "An entrance to a secret tunnel or a panic room perhaps. Why else would someone have such a hideous thing hung on their wall?"

"That was my grandmother's," I snapped, shoving him away from it and Radcliff wrinkled his nose.

"You mean to say someone bought that because they were fond of it?" he balked.

"This is not the time!" Serenity shouted over the piercing song that was still puncturing the air.

"There must be a bunny run, or a wibble wander way, perhaps a jolly man's jiffy hole?" Hamish looked to me in desperation. "Where is the jiffy hole, my king?"

"If you mean the passage, it is over here." I marched past him.

"There's nothing here," Xavier mouthed to Max from within his silencing bubble, and Max nodded in understanding, thinking there was no way out. But there was, I just wasn't sure I had the strength to open it.

I hurried to the wall where the door was hidden and Merissa joined me, the two of us throwing all we had into opening that door.

"Come on, old palace friend. Remember me?" I said through my teeth.

"Good palace. Daddy Hail is here," Radcliff said, placing a hand on my shoulder and lending me his strength. "Now open your door nice and wide for him."

"Stop that," Merissa clipped, and Radcliff laughed, clearly loving the chaos of all this.

"Please hurry," Serenity begged, placing her hand on Merissa's arm to give her strength while Hamish and Catalina did the same.

"I shall give you my deepest seed of power, oh great Vegas," Hamish called over the wailing song and Max blasted the doors apart, clearly intending to leave. "I will summon it from my banded balls."

"*Stop talking*," I gritted out, trying to focus and Radcliff laughed harder.

The clash of magic and roar of that song was so loud it began to drown out everything and my vision flickered a little at the power channelling through me and fresh souls tearing away into The Veil around us.

Max and Xavier left the room and I cursed, changing tact, and launching us all into the secret passage I was trying to access, dragging the souls of my friends and wife with me. We spun along through the darkness, becoming formless and swirling together into one single ball of power. All of them were yelling a battle cry in my ears, except Radcliff who was still laughing like a madman, and then I drove us into the hidden door further along the corridor where Max and Xavier must have been.

It flew open with so much force that it banged against the wall and all of us went tumbling across the ice-covered floor, splitting apart as our souls reformed. My hand found Merissa's and I pulled her close, lifting my head to find Xavier and Max racing down the path we'd offered them.

Fae were strewn across the floor, either still trapped by the Dread Song or long dead, laying in a pool of cooling blood.

Merissa drew me to my feet, and we chased after Serenity, Catalina, Hamish and Radcliff as they followed the boys into the dark.

The roar of more Dragons drew closer, and we forced the door to slam shut as we made it into the corridor, locking it tight.

Max's Dread Song finally faltered, and I let out a breath of relief, realising my power had been affected by it too, all of us weakened by the immensity of the magic.

Max grabbed one of Xavier's wings from him, casting away his silencing bubble.

"We need to get out of here!" Xavier cried.

"Which way?" Catalina looked back at us, and Merissa hurried to keep pace with Max and Xavier, ready to try and guide their path.

"I will mount your heads on spikes at my gates when I finish ripping you apart, traitors!" Lionel's voice boomed through the air, a spell making it resound across the entire palace.

"Get fucked, Lame Lionel!" Radcliff cried.

Max and Xavier made it to the far side of the ballroom, and I raced to catch Merissa, throwing our strength into the huge set of double doors there. They flew open and silvery footprints appeared beneath Merissa's feet as she moved ahead of them, summoning them after her down a small, concealed passage ahead.

Max and Xavier chased after her, thankfully trusting the guidance which led them to a narrow staircase that circled down out of sight.

The sound of shattering glass reached us from the ballroom and a Dragon's roar split the air apart.

"Nobble goblins," Hamish cursed.

"They need to move faster," Catalina said in fear.

"Follow my lead," Xavier commanded, elbowing Max aside and throwing one of his glittering wings down onto the steps before leaping onto it and pushing himself off.

He began to slide, and the iridescent sheen which sparkled across the rainbow feathers seemed to light the stairwell. He picked up pace quickly and disappeared with a whinny that made Radcliff smile.

"That's my boy," Radcliff said.

"He's *my* boy," Catalina growled, and Radcliff raised his hands in innocence, backing off.

As Max set up the other wing for his own descent, Merissa rushed off ahead of him and we all took chase once more. The Veil drew in around us, depositing us at the base of the stairs just as Xavier skidded to a halt there and jumped up, tucking his wing under his arm once more.

Merissa set more footprints out for them, and Serenity hurried towards Max as he shot out the bottom of the stairwell. She reached for his arm as if helping him up, and I swear he moved a little faster than he might have done alone.

Max scooped up the other Pegasus wing, and the two of them sprinted after Merissa as she left another trail of silver prints in her wake.

I ran ahead of her with Catalina on my heels, and together we commanded a hidden doorway to open, holding it wide for them.

"Thank you," she exhaled, and I nodded to her.

"Your hearts are pure and bound in steel. You'll find safe passage here," Merissa called to them as they passed into the tunnel and her voice carried beyond this realm into the next, echoing out and making Max snap his head around to hunt for the source.

"He heard you," Serenity gasped. "Wait, you must him tell him something!"

"I cannot do it again, it was not by choice," Merissa said sadly.

I sealed the door shut with Catalina's help, securing them safe passage out of here.

"Please, you must try." Serenity tugged her towards the hidden door. "He needs to know about-"

The Veil parted us, dragging us away and I reached for Merissa in the dark, our fingers intertwining and locking tight.

We arrived in The Room of Knowledge, but our feet barely touched the ground before we reached for our daughters, hunting them out in the land of the living.

I fought the fear daggering through my chest at what I might find, and as we reached Gwendalina, it seemed my fears were well founded.

She stood in the form of the Shadow Beast in a huge hall in front of over thirty Dragon Shifters. They surrounded the beastly form of Lionel Acrux in his luxurious blue robes, and hatred spewed into my gut at the sight of him.

Lance stood with Gwendalina, his hand against her shoulder, his fingers knotting in her fur. She seemed to have hold of her mind, her eyes full of clarity instead of violence, and I had to be glad of that.

"I don't like this," Merissa said thickly, glancing around like she could sense some dark fate drawing close.

"You did not consult me about this!" Lavinia screeched at Lionel, and I was satisfied at least to witness the severing of their alliance. Lionel had done the unthinkable to protect himself from the Shadow Princess, and with any luck it would start a bloody fight that would end in one of their deaths.

The shadows danced in Lavinia's hands threateningly and the Dragons grouped closer to Lionel with protective growls.

My fear for my daughter deepened as I realised Lavinia might wield her in an attack against these Dragons, and I did not know if the shadows could win against so many at once.

"I am the king," Lionel said calmly. "I do not need to consult anyone on my plans, nor do I see why you would have any reason to object to them."

Lavinia gnashed her teeth together near one of Lionel's Dragon guards and he raised his chin, a flicker of fear in his eyes, but he didn't back down.

"I have ensured that I am safe from all enemies," Lionel said smugly. "I cannot be touched."

Lavinia flicked her finger and Lionel's shadow hand lifted, latching tight around his own throat and making my eyebrows lift. At once, several Dragons ran to his aid, their combined strength dragging the shadow hand back from his neck and freeing him from Lavinia's control.

"Damn," I exhaled.

"That would be too easy," Merissa said, stepping closer to Gwendalina.

I noted Lance's magic blocking cuffs had been removed and wondered how much power he was privy to right now. My skin prickled protectively as I moved to place myself between Lionel Acrux and my daughter, pressing my power into the palace and hoping it might play a part in defending her and her mate if it came to a fight.

Lavinia shrieked, raising up on a plinth of shadow and wailing furiously at Lionel.

"You dare do this on the night when I have worked so tirelessly to birth you a worthy heir!?" she demanded.

"What?" Merissa hissed, our eyes meeting and revulsion stirring my gut at Lionel laying with this creature of shadow.

"Then where is this heir?" Lionel demanded. "Bring him to me at once, my Queen, if you have fulfilled the promise you made."

Lavinia released a high-pitched noise that made Gwendalina flatten her ears and growl in discomfort. A thump sounded in the room above us, the ceiling trembling from the weight of whatever had just landed on it.

Lionel frowned, peering up at the ceiling as heavy footfalls travelled overhead.

"That does not sound good," I muttered.

"He has likely found some bodies to devour in the wake of your little party," Lavinia said bitterly.

"Party?" Lionel spat. "An entire wing of the palace has nearly been obliterated, I have lost around thirty Dragons, and the amphitheatre lays in ruins. I may have emerged victorious this night, but the rebels will pay for their insolence in trying to assassinate the King of Solaria."

"You will be the one to pay," Merissa said icily. "And that payment is long overdue."

"I do love when you get bloodthirsty, Daddy," Lavinia crooned, her voice becoming honey sweet and sickening.

The thumping carried down the stairway beyond the room and the door swung slowly open, revealing no one beyond it, but the darkness of whatever was out there seeped toward us.

A grotesque creature arrived, scuttling across the ceiling, its features sharp among the shadow it was made of. Its hulking form fell from the ceiling and landed with a thump at Lavinia's side. The shadows sank into the thing's skin, a man slowly appearing from the darkness, his face handsome yet wicked. A sinister smile curved his lips and his eyes were hollow, depthless things. He was naked, his powerful body marked with scars of shadow which pulsed against his skin. Worst of all, was what lay beneath his exterior in the living realm. Where we stood beyond The Veil, four screaming souls could be seen, bound within this creature's flesh, writhing and thrashing with a desperation to get free. But the darkness of this monster was devouring the good in them bite by bite, latching onto the sins of their essence and leaving the rest to rot.

"By the stars," Merissa gasped, backing up towards me. "What is that?"

"Hello, Father," the monster purred at Lionel.

The Dragons all shifted protectively in front of their Dragon king, closing ranks, their eyes taking in this new, terrifying arrival.

Gwendalina growled, assuring me she still held her own mind and Lance's fingers knotted tighter in her fur. If it came to a fight, I knew they would be ready, but their odds in such a battle terrified me.

"I named him Tharix," Lavinia cooed, reaching up to brush her fingertips along her new son's jaw. "It means prince in the language of old. Isn't he perfect? Come closer, Daddy, say hello to your son."

Lionel lifted his head, eyeing the monster with caution, but with a hint of intrigue too. "He does appear to be a powerful specimen," he observed, his eyes roaming over every inch of Tharix's body with approval, and I noted some similarities between them too, this impossible union of their DNA, all packaged up and ready to fight for them.

"But is he Dragon born?" Lionel added sceptically.

"He is of his father's seed," Lavinia replied proudly. "He is just as pure-blooded as you, my King, and he is gifted with all four Elements. Though I will admit, he is blessed with the gift of the shadows too."

"This will change fate," Merissa said in terror. "And this thing cannot be *seen* by Gabriel or any Seer alive. It will be utterly unpredictable to the rebels."

"Perhaps it is not so strong," I said hopefully. "Our daughters are more than a match for a monster."

"Show me," Lionel demanded, and Lavinia gave Tharix a curt nod, ushering Lance and Gwendalina back to make room for him.

Tharix remained entirely still, and the Dragon Guardians all tensed as they stayed in place surrounding Lionel, ready for an attack. But none came.

Instead, Tharix leapt forward with a feline pounce that became a shift so abruptly that even I expected an attack.

A Dragon burst from his body, its scales a matte obsidian which seemed to suck all of the light from the room, making it near impossible to define any details beyond his immense size and poised wings. Within that Dragon, the four damned souls screamed louder, wailing into an abyss that none could come back from.

The Guardians closed ranks around Lionel, magic glimmering in the air as they threw shields into place.

"Oh my," Mildred Canopus gasped, the awful woman fanning herself as if she was flustered by the display.

Tharix reared back, roaring so loud it made the palace shudder, and screams broke out as servants and guards were terrorised by the horrible noise which spilled from him. But that was nothing compared to the shadows pouring from those deadly jaws, spewing from his mouth in vicious strikes.

"That will do, sweet pea," Lavinia purred, shooting closer to the enormous beast and trailing a hand along his flank.

Tharix quieted, shifting back into his Fae form – if that was what you could call it. Because from where I was standing, I could see the souls trapped within, though Tharix did not possess his own.

"Magnificent," Lionel breathed, stepping forward, causing his Guardians to scatter and make room for him. "Will he do as I say?"

"He is entirely obedient to your whims, my King," Lavinia promised. "Try it out."

"Break three of the Vampire's ribs," Lionel commanded, and Gwendalina roared as Tharix closed in on Lance.

"Don't fight when he breaks your ribs, pet," Lavinia commanded lightly and Lance tensed in preparation of attack the monster closing in on him. "This will count as part of my torture."

Lance snarled the same moment I did, and Gwendalina swung around to protect him, placing her body between him and Tharix.

The terrible creature lowered to the floor in a crouch, scuttling beneath her and leaping to his feet again. Lavinia cast a leash around Gwendalina's throat before she could catch him, yanking her back.

"Get your filthy shadows away from her," Merissa cried at the Shadow Princess.

I tried to throw my power into the palace again, to force it to help, to do something to protect my daughter's mate. But it did not answer my call. Perhaps I had used too much of my strength already, or perhaps it knew there was no fight here that could be won.

Tharix casually prowled into Lance's personal space then reached out and gripped his sides, his dark eyes alight with glee. He broke his ribs one at a time and I launched myself at Tharix, trying to tear him away from this man who had stood firm beside my daughter for so long, who had suffered too much in the hands of these bastards already.

"Get away from him," I barked.

The Veil tugged at me, a firm command for Merissa and I to leave. We had spent far too long here already, and the stars were turning their attention our way.

"No," Merissa growled, holding onto me, the two of us fighting to remain with our daughter.

Lance cast a blade of ice in his hand and slammed it into the monster's temple with a roar of defiance and I gasped in shock, looking to Tharix who hit the floor with a loud bang, blackish blood spilling from the wound.

"Ha," Merissa said in delight, and we shared a relieved smile.

I looked to the dead beast, wondering if the souls trapped inside it might break free and cross the barrier of The Veil, or if any sorry piece of its existence might make it here too. But all was still, perhaps no soul intact enough to make the journey beyond The Veil.

"Who released you from your cuffs?!" Lavinia screamed. "Come here this instant and do not cast a single spell more or I will cut off your pretty little Vega's fingers and toes tonight."

Lance stalked over to her, darkness in his eyes while glaring defiantly at Lavinia, and The Veil tugged on us harder.

"Just a little longer," Merissa demanded, gazing at Gwendalina with a longing I felt right through to my core.

Horror filled me as Tharix twitched then began to move, death somehow having spared him as he slowly recovered, pulling the ice blade from his temple with a jolt before tossing it to the floor and returning to his feet.

"He is no Fae. He is death itself," I said, throat thick.

The Veil wrapped around us tighter, and this time we had no choice but to let it take us, the barrier tearing us away into the beyond where we could no longer see our beloved daughter. Though we would rush to The Room of Knowledge to watch over her and Roxanya as soon as we could.

The horror of Tharix's presence still thumped through me, and I knew without a doubt that the creature was set on a path of devastation. Because it was a weapon forged of shadow and death itself.

DARIUS

CHAPTER TWENTY

I stood at the foot of the tower which led up to the Halls of Fate, the one place within the confines of The Veil which stood close enough to the stars for the souls here to be able to speak with them directly.

Its shadow stretched out across the landscape before me, shrouding me within it, coating my skin in its darkness. I craned my neck to look up at the impossibly tall tower, turning over the knowledge I'd gained from those who had been in death far longer than me. Few souls were powerful enough to make the climb to the top of that tower, let alone gain any answers from the celestial beings who lingered there.

A patch of the sky directly above the tip of the tower was filled with a dark space coated in twinkling stars. How beautiful they seemed from down here. I supposed that was part of their power.

But I knew the answers I sought didn't lay in starlight.

"The highest hope for the twins lies with the Guild Stones," Azriel Orion said softly from behind me. "Any and all prophecies which have pointed to their victory in this war include the formation of the Zodiac Guild – the rise of a new dawn."

I nodded. I'd listened to them recounting the tales of the Guild Stones, I'd taken note of the locations of those which remained unfound in the living realm and had sat through Azriel's tales about the Guild and the power its formation could bring. Since the failure at the Palace of Souls and the revelation of my father's new twisted shadow son, the souls trapped here in death had been frantically plotting, planning, and trying to think of anything and everything possible to help those we loved who still lived beyond The Veil. I'd listened to it all in silence. The only hope I could find among the devastating information we had gathered was that we had several ideas on how the living might survive the plague of my father's rule. But that was of little consequence in the light of our situation. We couldn't tell them any of that, and without the knowledge we had gained here, the rebels' chances were dwindling.

"The rest of us are meeting to discuss ways in which we can help the living discover the knowledge we have unfurled," he went on, but I cut him off.

"I'm done, Azriel," I said, the truth heavy in my chest. "Done playing these games you all toil at. I can't remain here in death and claim victory in things so little as turning the page of a book or playing a song. I can't watch the people I love from a distance anymore. I know I'm not the first Fae to find myself trapped in death before my time, but I plan to be the first to find a way back from it and seize a second chance."

"Darius," Azriel sighed. "Part of the process you will experience here beyond The Veil includes this denial you are going through, and I know how incredibly hard the end of your own mortality is to come to terms with."

I snorted, shaking my head and turning from the Halls of Fate, the impossibly tall tower placed firmly at my back.

"The problem is that we have spent far too long following the path of the stars," I said to him. "Letting fate and prophecy take choice from our hands. But I met a girl who took one look at fate and said fuck you. She found her own path. She told me no when the stars gave us our one and only chance at being mated then told *them* no when they tried to keep us apart against her will. She stood before the wings of fate and told them to get fucked and she was right. Because why should the circumstances of our birth or upbringing define all we are and all we ever can be? Why shouldn't we all get to pick precisely who and what we want to be and tell destiny, providence, or circumstance to step aside so that we can make our own fates? Roxanya Vega taught me to defy the stars in all things and I have never once regretted it when I followed her advice. So no, I won't simply walk this path into my demise and stay put like a good boy. And no, I won't be climbing that tower to beg for some deal or promise or desperate hope from them. There is power in this world which doesn't simply belong to them. There is power in the truth of my heart and the knowledge of who and what I am and who I want to be. Death has come knocking for Roxy time and again and she has told it to fuck off. Now it's my turn to do the same."

"You plan to go to Mordra?" Azriel asked, concern pinching his brow.

"The last times I have visited her she's given me little more than riddles and half-truths. This time, I plan on demanding all there is."

Azriel frowned but nodded in understanding. "Then try. If it is what you need to do, and I hope with all my heart that you succeed."

I made to walk away from him then paused, turning back, and offering him my hand. "I'm sorry," I said as he took it, his eyebrows raising in surprise.

"What for?"

"For hating you when I was a kid. And for all the fucked up shit my family caused yours."

"Tell Lance," he began hesitantly. "Tell him I am forever with him. That I love him and that I know he is worthy of the position he is yet to rise to. Tell him I will be watching him through every moment of it and that I couldn't hold more pride in my heart if I tried. And tell Darcy how grateful I am for all she has done for my boy, and that I will be celebrating with all the lost souls who adore her when she seizes her crown."

"So now you think I might succeed?" I teased and he quirked a smile.

"I've always believed that all things in this world are possible given the right use of power. So, despite my doubts, I do believe that if anyone might have a chance to succeed in this endeavour, it will be you and your queen."

He bowed his head to me and released my hand and despite my general aversion to physical displays of affection, I followed my gut and drew him into my arms, holding him tightly for a brief moment.

"Lance is the man he is because of you," I told him. "His love for you has always given him the strength he needed in the darkest of times. Thank you for creating one of the most important people in my life. Lance was one of the few bright points in my existence for a very long time and he has that brightness because of you."

Azriel squeezed me in his arms, a choked sob lodging in his throat as he nodded in acceptance of those words before releasing me.

"Go," he urged. "I'll see what I can do to distract the attention of the stars for a while."

I nodded, clapping him on the back before turning and stalking away from him, striding towards the perfect harmony beneath the trees in the forest that bordered the lands of the dead.

I passed through dappled sunlight, my destination clear in my mind as I strode straight for Mordra's cavern, ready to at last claim the destiny I had sworn to retrieve.

I could feel Roxy like a tug against my soul, her grief sharp after the failure they'd suffered at The Palace of Souls and her mind on me. I could almost hear an echo of the oath she'd sworn, the curse she'd promised the

303

stars, the words whispered by the leaves of the trees overhead. Her focus was shifting, fixing on that promise and I was shadowing her footsteps from beyond The Veil.

I found the entrance to Mordra's cavern easily, slipping through the dark passage until I came upon the space beneath the river of the dead, her boulder perched in the centre of it. Mordra's insubstantial form rested on a space near the foot of the jagged rock, a bony hand caressing a cluster of coat buttons which sat in the small space beside her.

"Ether doesn't follow the rules you were bound to in life," she breathed, not turning toward me, simply speaking into the silence. "It is alive in a way, dead in others, a conduit for the power of the world itself. Accessing it is akin to turning a key in a lock, but once that door has been cracked open, it is impossibly hard to turn from what you will find within."

"Is that a warning or a promise?" I asked, earning a breath of laughter from her.

"Neither. Both. Who can say? You are the only one who knows the fullness of your own heart and the strength of your desires. But ether like all things comes at a cost, you may wish to dance the line of death, but to cross through it will host a steep price indeed."

"Why speak in riddles? Tell me plainly what it will cost," I demanded, the light flickering as souls passed through the river overhead, momentarily blocking the sun.

A hand closed on my shoulder, broken fingernails digging into the skin as I turned my head to meet Mordra's haunting gaze.

"If you want that answer, you will have to prove yourself worthy of it," she replied, a deep rumble sounding through the cavern, its vibrations rattling through me.

A crack appeared in the wall to my left, a soft, grey glow resonating from within it, the path that was revealed following the direction of the river which raced on by overhead.

Chilled air crept from that crevice, a coldness that went beyond mortal feeling, like the icy breath of a creature which held nothing but darkness in its heart. It swept around me, through me, into the depths of my being and beyond, like it was tasting the very essence of my soul.

"If you hope to bend the laws of death to your will, then you will need to gain mastery over The Veil itself. You will need to face the truth of what rules us here and break its hold on you," Mordra purred, her hand slipping down my spine, making a shudder rise in me.

"I have fought all manner of monsters, curses and injustices," I said dismissively, refusing to cower before the weight of what lay inside that crevice. "I have known and conquered endless fears. I will conquer this too."

"Go ahead then, Dragon prince, test your mettle against the laws of life itself."

Mordra's hand collided with my spine, and she shoved me towards the jagged gash in the wall like a sacrifice she was offering up to a foul god.

But if she thought to make me a sacrifice in some plot of her own then she would soon find out the true worth of the man who had fought to claim Roxanya Vega for his bride, and she'd learn the depths I'd fall to in pursuit of my desire.

I prowled into the crevice without looking back, the damned dead who rushed along in the current of the river overhead my only companions as I delved into the dark and began my descent. For better or worse, I was on this path now and no power in this world would turn me from my fate.

Each step I took created a ripple in the air around me, that coldness reaching out and clawing its way into my limbs.

The darkness grew down here in the dark but above, the river still raced on, the light refracting through it and casting shifting shadows against the grey rock walls.

Roxy's grief was a sharp tug in my chest, and I let myself turn to her as I continued my descent, The Veil rippling, allowing me to push through once again, to see her even as I continued my trek into the darkness beyond Mordra's cavern.

She was in her room in R.U.M.P. castle, alone with Rosalie Oscura, the two of them sitting on her bed. I watched as the Wolf girl took the Book of Earth and placed it into Roxy's lap, some keenly painful truth hanging between them.

"Moon Wolves are gifted foresight and intuition not governed by the stars because the moon herself is a celestial being all of her own variety," Rosalie said, and I felt a truth in her words which went beyond what they were talking about. The moon wasn't a star. It was a force of its own, governed by its own set of rules. It didn't bow to their power and its magic belonged to no other, born of the nature of the world itself. Did that mean it was charged with ether then? That the magic of the moon was its own potent cocktail of raw power?

"There are many other gifts I am rumoured to have, some of which I've proven true or false, others I may yet discover, it's hard to say," Rosalie continued. "But I can always tell when two souls are destined to be with one another. Or sometimes even more than two."

"What do you-" Roxy asked, but Rosalie went on.

"I have never felt anything like the connection I felt between you and Darius Acrux," she breathed, and the mention of my name like that held a power I had never given any notice to before. It was a summons, an incantation, a call. "The power of your love and hatred burned hotter than the sun, the constant tug and pull, a war unending and a passion unyielding. You were two stars always set to collide and cast the world on fire because fuck the consequences."

"Why are you telling me this now?" Roxy asked, her voice weak, her need for me bordering on desperation and of course I went to her.

I dropped onto the bed on her other side, summoning my power and pushing it into the necklace she still wore for me, urging it to heat, to let her know I was here. I brushed my fingers through her hair, laying my cheek against hers, as I leaned in to press a kiss on her neck.

"Because that fire hasn't gone out yet," Rosalie breathed, taking a lock of Roxy's hair from between my fingers and winding it around her own until it pulled tight, her gaze shifting to mine for the briefest of moments and I could have sworn she saw me there, or at least felt me. "I feel a chord of it straining to remain in place. And I think it's time you tugged on it."

"Can you see me?" I asked Rosalie, but her focus was on Roxy again, though there was a twitch to her lips as she gave Roxy's hair a sharp tug which I almost could have sworn was meant for me.

Rosalie stood, backing away towards the door as though making to leave and I frowned in confusion, looking between her and Roxy, wondering if I'd imagined it or if she really did know I was here. But then why would she leave if she knew? Why not say anything or try to help me?

"That's it?" Roxy asked, frowning in confusion as Rosalie moved towards the door.

"Segui il fuoco," Rosalie replied. *Follow the fire.* Roxy frowned in confusion, clearly not understanding her, but I did. I knew enough Faetalian to understand her perfectly and as her gaze shifted to me once more, I sucked in a sharp breath. Was that message for me?

"Follow it where?" I demanded, but Rosalie was talking to Roxy again, no longer looking at me.

"I'm horny and my pack have been begging to fuck me for a full week now. I usually prefer the efforts of a real Alpha, but they're in desperately short supply around here. I'd ask you to take a tumble with me, but your heart will always be with him, and I don't want any part of anyone else's love story."

I snarled angrily at the suggestion of her fucking my wife, pushing to my feet and placing myself between them. Rosalie's eyes brightened with amusement like she could feel my anger and jealousy, but Roxy didn't seem to notice.

"I thought the army was crawling with Alphas?" Roxy asked.

"Plenty of Betas like to think they're all Alpha, amica, but it's a sad reality that far too many of them fall flat when put to the test." Rosalie sighed.

"So, you'll just have a pack orgy and hope for the best?" Roxy teased and Rosalie grinned.

"I can always get myself off if I have to – but Jessibel has been dying to get between my thighs and Andre has been sending me dick pics for two weeks straight. So, I might as well let them shoot their shot. Who knows, maybe I'll like it."

"Enjoy," Roxy called as she left.

"Wait," I added, taking a step closer to the Wolf girl whose eyes swum with secrets. Rosalie's smile widened, her gaze locking on mine, and I *knew* she could at least sense me there. But she said nothing, turning away and sauntering off like she was a queen in her own right.

"Rosalie," I growled, stalking after her out of the room.

Roxy called out to her as she gave her attention to the book Rosalie had placed in her lap, but she ignored that too.

"Are you going to pretend you can't hear me?" I snarled.

Rosalie tossed her hair and laughed. "You're welcome!" she called back to Roxy, but as she turned her head, she looked straight at me again. "You should pay more attention, stronzo," she said.

"To what?" I demanded and she cocked her head, making me wonder if she could actually hear me or not.

She moved to look out of a window which held a picturesque view of the full moon, her lips lifting into a knowing smile as she pushed it open with a sigh of pleasure then began to unbutton her pants and kicked off her boots.

"Your loved ones are listening to the whispers of the moon as she toys with Venus," she breathed, her eyes falling closed as she tipped her head back, bathing in the moonlight, her skin glimmering with its light. "Maybe you should listen too."

Before I could ask her what she meant by that or try to confirm that her words really were for me, she pulled her shirt over her head, dropped her pants, and shifted so fast that barely an inch of skin was exposed.

She leapt out of the window in a blur of silver fur, her tail swiping right through me like I wasn't there at all. A howl burst from her lips as she pounced from tower to turret, navigating her way down from the castle roofs with far too little effort considering the sheer walls and steep drops. Her howl was answered by every Wolf on the floating island, and I watched as she tore away into the night, wondering if I'd imagined that or if she really had been able to sense me there.

I headed back to Roxy, finding her engrossed in the book Rosalie had opened for her, my gut tightening as I leaned over her shoulder to read what had captured her attention so powerfully.

To Raise the Trees of the Damned.
Once the blood of the intended is added to the seed, the essence of the caster's soul must be leashed to its roots. The light of the moon helps raise the shadows to assist in the growth of the sapling, and the longer the bone chant continues, the larger and more powerful the tree itself shall grow.

The page held all manner of gruesome pictures of bloodletting and sacrifices of small children, along with a particularly disturbing explanation of how to harvest a seed if you were looking to curse a family line with it but the information Roxy fixed on was at the foot of the page. Directions to the Damned Forest where all of the cursed trees grew, the clue the Nymph witches had given her leading to this.

To reach the Damned Forest you must drink a dose of wolfsbane mixed with larkspur from a chalice scrawled with the runes halgalaz and raido, and carve the name of your deepest desire into your flesh, then follow the ache of your heart before it gives out on life itself.

One look at Roxy made it clear to me that she was at the point of no return. She was going to risk this in pursuit of me. She'd drink poison from a cup marked with the runes linked to trials and travel, carve my name into her flesh, and follow this dark magic to the Damned Forest.

Shit.

She got to her feet and started packing, my words of warning falling on deaf ears as she focused on her plan, no longer hunting for signs of me in the world around her. And I knew with all certainty that she was going to tread that path, no matter the cost it bore. Ether didn't work like deals with the stars; only those wielding it or directly offered to it in sacrifice could pay the price it asked, meaning Roxy knew no harm would come to any of those she loved for this. All of the risk was on her. And she was clearly beyond the point of caring about her own survival if it meant continuing without me by her side.

I frowned, letting The Veil draw me back, the stone beneath my feet hardening as I continued down the passageway hidden within Mordra's cavern. My mind was a jumble of thoughts and fears, but Roxy wasn't the only one who was willing to risk it all for this choice.

My pace stayed steady as I delved into the dark, that cloying cold reaching up to wrap itself around my throat and threatening to end me.

Whatever awaited me at the bottom of this path couldn't be good, but I'd face it just as I'd face any other blockade between myself and life because the time had come for us to make good on our promise.

The darkness pressed in, pressure building as the air grew thin. My chest heaved with the effort of drawing enough breath, my feet faltering as I coughed against the ache in my lungs.

I stumbled again, my hand crashing against the sharp rocks as I steadied myself, pain slicing through my skin, blood spilling over the stone.

Whatever lay before me shifted in the darkness, an inhale sucking what little oxygen remained in the space away, leaving me utterly without air.

I cursed, lungs burning as I dropped to one knee, my chest heaving as I fought to get enough oxygen.

Dark spots blossomed across my vision, a ringing building in my ears.

I couldn't breathe.

The dark was closing in around me, the screams of the souls who were being torn along in the current of the river above growing louder as I came closer to the limits of my mortality, death whispering my name and-

I blinked.

Death had already come calling and I had stepped into its embrace, willingly or not.

I had no need for air, my lungs not even a functioning part of what I was now.

This was some trick, some test brought on by the thing which writhed in the darkness ahead of me.

I stood slowly, looking to my hand, the blood which pulsed from the jagged wound there growing still, dripping against the rocks by my feet once, twice. The third drop fell but never hit the ground, fading away, the deep knowledge of my death banishing it.

My chest remained entirely still, the screams quieting again as I focused on the lack of sound my body created. No pulse. No rush of breath in and out. Nothing.

The darkness snarled in the distance, and I lifted my chin as I stalked towards it.

The jagged gash in the stones grew wider, my body no longer working to replicate the acts it had once needed for survival. I wasn't flesh and blood any longer. I was a malignant spirit, restless in death, hunting for an alternative to my damnation.

The cold grew more potent the further I went, my skin coated in goosebumps, shivers driving themselves so deep within me that I felt like my bones themselves were rattling, the cold threatening to steal me away before I

ever found what waited at the foot of this path.

My mind grew thick with the cloying cold but as I focused on it, I realised the wrongness of that too. My body wasn't affected by the cold any more than it would be by anything else. My body wasn't even my body. And even if it was then the cold never would have affected me as such in life. I was born to fire and had been gifted mastery over ice as well. The Dragon in me was bathed in flame and I was more prone to burning than freezing.

With a growl worthy of the beast which shared my soul, I burst into flames, the illusion of my body falling away along with the sensation of cold which had tried to fool me.

The darkness grew as I hovered there, nothing but a ball of flame in the pitch black, shaking off all mortal shackles.

Then, and only then, did it come for me.

A flash of teeth and blazing white eyes, ruin and chaos combined, came tearing toward me at a furious pace. I ducked aside, feeling the brush of those fangs against the edges of my flames, the fire extinguished as soon as it met with them. Something beyond pain ripped through me as that fire went out, an end looming which held no ever after. The thing which lurked in this place held no sway with the Destined Door that tried to beckon the dead closer to their final resting place. Whatever this was only held hunger, the need to destroy, to consume, and it was coming for me, hunting, snapping, salivating at the thought of my destruction.

I flinched aside, dancing this way and that in the dark, the enormity of the beast too much to comprehend, its jaws snapping shut closer and closer to me with every strike.

It was impossible to fathom, so big I couldn't comprehend it, my annihilation so certain that I could count the time remaining to me in seconds alone.

A roar burst from me at that thought, at the failure which loomed, the oath I wouldn't be able to keep if I succumbed to this end.

Fire exploded from me, the flames building as I thought of Roxy, of Xavier, of Caleb, Max and Seth. I thought of Lance, Darcy, Geraldine, my friends from school, my mom who had died to try and buy more life for her children. And with every piece of my heart that swelled for those I loved, the flames of my soul expanded.

A shriek broke the darkness as the creature's jaws finally snapped shut on the fire which made up my being, but instead of devouring me, it found itself burned by the power of my magic.

Not elemental power, or even ether, but the purest, most undeniable force in any of the realms known to Fae and man alike. Love had brought me back from the brink of darkness. The people I cared for far more than my own miserable existence made the flames grow bigger and bigger, consuming anything it could find, *everything* it could find.

With an explosion of power and a scream which rattled the skies themselves, the creature which had tried to trap me in the confines of death fell back. And I broke free, spilling into the space between spaces and spiralling into the depths of death itself.

DARIUS

CHAPTER TWENTY ONE

Tumbling, rioting, thrashing. I lost my place in the world as the flames grew beyond my control, all that I was cast aside and forgotten, the person I'd been shattering as I descended into the chaos of my basest nature.

The blazing light and heat became all there was of me, this tremendous force unchecked and unbalanced, no desire beyond destruction, no form beyond the flames.

I was lost.

But some part of me fought the burn, some thundering bass in the furthest reaches of my soul was screaming to return to something.

I almost lost myself to the violent blaze of the flames, but before I could fall fully into fire, I felt them. All the souls which were tethered to mine, all the love I had in me for them, all the time we'd had stolen from us.

The fire grew hotter and hotter, the flames becoming a writhing pathway which led in two directions. One sang to me of power untold, of an end beyond endings, a temptation so potent it was hard to look away from it. But the other was like a cool breeze on the back of my neck, a whisper of something I knew I didn't want to leave behind.

I had chosen to discard the visage of flesh which had been housing my soul since my arrival into death, and I could choose to reclaim it too.

The fire popped and blazed, a roar of pure power tearing from the flames as I drew on them, calling them back to the core of me.

I turned, looking along that flickering pathway, hungering for what still waited there. *Follow the flames.*

I rushed towards it, consuming the flames as I went, drawing them back into me and bellowing through the pain of holding so much. But it was all mine to begin with, my power, my energy, my destiny.

I fell back into the illusion of my body and slammed into The Veil hard enough to make it bend around me, letting me look back to the realm of the living, returning me to Roxy's room in the R.U.M.P. castle.

I stumbled as I found myself at the foot of her bed, panting from the force of my arrival and looking around, expecting to see her.

But Roxy wasn't here. She'd already left to seek out the Damned Forest. In her place I found Caleb and Seth, the two of them seemingly in the middle of some kind of spat.

Seth stalked across the room towards the bed and whipped the covers off with an "Ah-ha!" before staring blankly down at the empty sheets.

"Where is she then?" he asked.

I sighed, the pieces of myself slotting back together as I found myself with my brothers, one of the few places in this world that had always held such sanctuary for me.

"Who?" Caleb asked.

"Where's Max?" I muttered, but obviously neither of them could hear me, their conversation continuing without any acknowledgment of my words.

"Tory, obviously," Seth growled, and I took a seat on the edge of the bed. "Is she moisturising her perfect tits or lubricating her vag or doing something equally feminine somewhere?"

"That's a weird set of fucking questions," I growled, the jealous beast in me rising to the bait of his words about my wife, and I narrowed my eyes on Seth as he glared at Cal. I had to assume Caleb had eaten something Seth had had his eye on or some shit because he usually only got this pissy over food.

"She's gone," Caleb explained. "I dunno when she'll be back." He retrieved a note scribbled in Roxy's handwriting and I snorted in amusement as I leaned closer to Seth to read what it said.

I've reached my limit with this shit, so I've gone to take my destiny back from the stars. Gerry, I love you – lead the rebels against the Court of Solaria like you suggested. Make that scaley bastard pay. The rest of you, try not to cry too much if I don't make it back, I was a mean bitch anyway. x

"That's pretty funny," I commented. "But if either of you calls her a mean bitch, I'll break your nose."

"She can't just take off," Seth snarled, crumpling the note in his fist and tossing it aside.

"Who can stop her?" Caleb asked and my brows rose at the suggestion in those words because either one of them should have been able to do just that, but my girl wasn't the untrained novice who had arrived at our academy all those months ago, she'd come into her own, a true queen, and I doubted there was any who could stand in her way now.

"We should have welcomed them home with open arms," I said, wishing they could hear me, hoping they were starting to see that too, that they understood the way fate needed to turn now. It had taken my death for me to fully appreciate it, but the throne wasn't meant for the four of us anymore. It never had been really.

Seth shook his head suddenly. "I need to go," he muttered, stalking towards the door, his shoulder slamming into Caleb's as he went, knocking him aside.

I frowned at the two of them. Seth didn't often get pissed like this. I was missing something. I doubted even snack theft of the most delicious treats would have him this angry. So *what* was I missing?

Caleb whirled on him, a snarl building in his throat which almost certainly equalled a fight. I glanced to my right, half expecting to see Max there so that the two of us could place our bets on who would win this time, but he wasn't there, and I guessed I wasn't either.

I sighed, hating this, being with my brothers and yet not being there at all.

"There's been a lot of shit going down beyond The Veil," I told them, knowing it was pointless really, but just wanting to hang out with my best friends the way I always had. "We've been tracking down the Guild Stones and-"

"You got the tattoo," Caleb said, drawing my focus to the two of them where they stood by the door, Seth glancing over his shoulder with one hand on the doorknob, the position showing off the new ink between his shoulder blades.

"No fucking way." I grinned, getting up and moving to stand beside Cal so that I could take a closer look. "The detail on this is sick," I commented, studying the crescent moon with a wolf perched upon the curve at its base while a bat hung from the curve above. Within the moon was a clock with no hands, only a ring of numbers and shattered cogs spilling out beneath it. "Never thought you'd actually bite the bullet and break your tattoo virginity."

"Yeah," Seth grunted, replying to Caleb who was just kind of staring at it, giving no real comment at all because this wasn't his bag. This was all me and dammit, I needed Seth to hear my fucking opinion.

"You added stuff to it," Caleb said.

"Whose work is this?" I demanded, but Seth only answered Cal.

"Yeah," he said.

"What does it mean?" Caleb asked.

"It means he's gonna get a Dragon next in memory of me, asshole," I muttered, looking to Seth like he might laugh at the joke but no, still nothing for me.

Seth shrugged, saying no more. Knowing him he'd just gotten it because it looked cool because the longing in the eyes of that Wolf on his skin wasn't something Seth was even interested in feeling for one person.

Caleb shot closer to him, coming to a halt right behind him and reaching out to trace the lines of ink with his fingertips.

"It's beautiful," Caleb murmured, and I rolled my eyes.

"Fucking poetic, that is. Point out how badass that shading is and look at the linework around the moon's craters. I need to know who did this piece. Ask him that. Ask him how long he sat for it. Ask him if he howled like a little bitch while getting it done." I tried elbowing Caleb to get some reaction from him, hoping he might ask at least one relevant question, but my elbow just sailed straight through his arm, bringing a huff of irritation to my lips.

"Stop," Seth growled.

"Why?" Cal asked.

"Because you're stroking him like he's a pet cat and it's fucking weird, man," I pointed out, arching an eyebrow at Caleb and wondering if he was thirsty or something because he was being a bit of a lurker, and touchy-feely wasn't usually his thing.

Caleb started to move his hand again, but Seth whirled on him, snatching his wrist into his grasp and throwing him back against the wall, pinning him there with a feral snarl.

I barked a laugh. "Told you, you were being weird," I pointed out, almost feeling like I was a part of this little hang out, back with my boys again. "Can one of you call Max?" I asked but they still didn't react to me.

"I said stop," Seth snarled.

I leaned against the wall, watching the show, deciding to place my money on Seth winning this little spat because whatever had started it, the Wolf in him looked near feral with pent up anger.

"And I asked why," Caleb bit back.

Seth growled a little, staying where he was, pinning Caleb to the wall. It was kinda weird that Cal hadn't pushed him off yet. Unless…he had a plan. Huh, maybe I was gonna put my money on Caleb instead.

"Max, where are you?" I yelled, wanting his input, but he wasn't here. Probably off with Grus. I sighed, but hanging out with two of my bros was better than none.

"You were an asshole tonight," Caleb said, sounding all kinds of butt hurt and I arched a brow at him.

"Why the fuck are you whining like a little bitch? Just slap him with a boulder and let me see if I win the bet or not," I urged, not sure why I was bothering because I was still nothing to them here.

"I'm an asshole every night, Cal, you just like to forget that when it suits you or when it isn't aimed your way," Seth replied.

"Truth," I agreed.

"Does the mixture of the moon and Venus make you think you're some kind of sex guru then?" Caleb bit out. "Because you seemed all too keen to tell me how much better you think you can fuck than me, and then you went on to try and convince others of the same thing. Were you going to join in with Rosalie's pack once you got done telling them how to fuck too?"

"Seriously?" I barked a laugh. "You're having this argument over which one of you can fuck better? I know it's tempting to try and claim the crown from me, but it ain't happening, assholes."

"What if I was?" Seth shrugged, pushing away from Caleb and prowling across the room, his back firmly to his best friend.

"Shit, Cal, are you just gonna let him turn his back on you like that? Slap him with some vines or set his hair on fire already!" I called.

"You didn't seem up for the challenge I gave you, so why not get my kicks elsewhere?" Seth said, leaving me lost again because I had no idea what they were talking about but apparently that was the insult required to make Caleb snap at last and I whooped as he finally started the fight.

Caleb shot towards Seth with a snarl, his fangs snapping out as he went for him, but he instantly collided with an air shield, the force of the impact breaking his damn nose as he hit it at full speed and stumbled back.

"Oh shit," I laughed, knowing that if he could have heard me, he'd be coming for me next but come on, asshole, that was a rookie mistake.

A vine snapped around Caleb's ankle and threw him across the room onto the bed, blood pissing down his face from his broken nose.

"Oooh," I cringed on Cal's behalf as Seth handed his ass to him, watching as Seth snarled like a beast and pounced on him. He caught Caleb's wrists in his hands, pinning them above his head as he straddled him, snarling like a heathen.

"That was embarrassing, man," I told Caleb, crossing the room to the bed, and dropping down beside them to look at him. "Are you just gonna lie there and take that?"

"You look good down there, Caleb," Seth taunted. "Wanna know how good it can feel subbing for me too?"

Weird choice of taunt, but okay.

Caleb bared his fangs, trying to buck Seth off, but he still wasn't using his magic to try and fight back.

"Are you tapped out, man?" I asked him, tilting my head to assess him. "I'd offer you a bite but I'm kinda lacking in a body right now." I snorted at my own joke which really was pathetic when I thought about it. Here I was lingering on the fringes of life, hanging out with my friends who couldn't even tell I was here, making jokes about my own demise which neither of them could appreciate and laughing to myself.

"I think subbing suits *you* better," Caleb hissed, yanking on his arms which Seth had secured with vines now too. "You practically melted for me when I called you a good pup."

"I thought I was your perfect dom fantasy, Seth?" I joked. "Have you really moved on already? I feel like you could have picked Dante or someone a bit more rugged though – Cal is too pretty to really pull off the daddy vibes, don't you think?"

Seth scoffed darkly, his eyes flashing, not seeming to find any amusement in Caleb's teasing or my joke – which, okay, he couldn't hear, but it still pissed me off.

"Nah, I just let you think that. I wanted you to feel good about yourself as the big, bad Vampire, but really, when it comes down to it, you're just a scared little boy, aren't you, Caleb? You thought you'd play with the Wolf and see if you liked it, but now you're in over your head, wondering if it's safer to go crawling back to your ex and her tits and-"

"Why the fuck are you so obsessed with Tory's tits?" Caleb snapped.

"Where the hell did that come from?" I barked, my amusement shattering and a snarl rolling up the back of my throat which drowned out whatever the fuck they were saying to each other as the possessive Dragon in me fought to break free of my flesh. "Don't talk about my wife like that you assholes. Her tits are none of your fucking business."

Caleb jerked on the vines restraining him, snapping them with his Vampire strength then flipping the two of them over, the fight breaking out at last and I snarled at them, wishing I could throw a few punches too and give them a good kicking for that comment.

Except they weren't punching each other; Caleb tried to pin Seth beneath him, but the Werewolf flipped them again, his hand locking around Caleb's throat, shoving his head back and-

"What the fuck is this?" I roared, leaping to my feet as my two best friends started kissing each other with the force of a wrecking ball, the tension in the room shattering around them as they devoured each other's mouths like the stars would fall from the heavens and set the whole world alight if they didn't.

"Prove it," Seth growled against Caleb's mouth, biting his bottom lip and making him groan as they ground against each other.

"Prove what?" I demanded, backing up a step and glancing towards the walls as if they might part for me and draw me back away into the embrace of The Veil, but no, if anything they seemed more solid than ever before as I stood in a room with two of my best friends in the world while they kissed each other in a way that said in no uncertain terms that this had happened before.

"When did this start?" I snapped at them. "How long have you been lying to me and Max? When were you planning on telling us that the two of you were-" My eyes bounced between the two of them as Caleb broke their kiss, a look passing between them which was so heated that I was surprised he hadn't set fire to the damn bed. My wife's damn bed.

Caleb dropped back against the pillows, lifting his chin and I just fucking gaped at him as he bared his throat to the Wolf who loomed over him.

"Are you...what is this?" I demanded. "Ah shit, Seth, please don't go all Wolf kink while I'm right here watching. If I have to see you do that nipple thing in the flesh, I'm gonna come back to life simply to kick your hairy ass."

Seth lunged forward, driving his teeth into Caleb's throat and I was gifted the wholly unappealing sound of hearing him moan and curse with pleasure, the two of them grinding against each other, and the mood descending fast into debauchery.

I gaped at them as Seth began to unhook the buttons of Caleb's shirt. This was actually happening. I was standing in the afterlife, haunting two of my closest friends in the world, watching as they shattered all the parameters I thought had existed within their friendship and-

Oh for fuck's sake, I did *not* need to see Caleb's cock.

I turned away, heading towards the door, but my foot hit something which lay discarded on the floor, and I looked down at it instead.

Was that...oh hell no.

I crouched down to get a better look at the box on the floor. Was that an old photo of me? My mouth fell open as I looked from the photo to the product it was advertising, a full set of sex toys based on my cock in both Fae and Dragon form stared back at me in dazzling gold plastic.

"Why the hell have you got this?" I demanded, looking back to the bed right in time to watch as Seth finished jerking Caleb off, making him come all over his own chest.

"Gah!" I fell backwards as cum shot towards my fucking face, managing to avoid it before remembering that I was a ghost, and it would have sailed straight through me anyway.

Either way, that was a fuck no from me.

"Good boy," Seth purred, scooping some of Caleb's cum onto his fingers before sucking them clean. There was a mental image which was going to haunt me for the rest of time. "But don't go thinking I'm done with you yet. You wanna learn from the big, bad, Wolf? Then I'm going to make sure you get a really thorough lesson."

"Seth," Caleb growled.

"You want to learn this lesson or not, pretty boy?" Seth taunted, grabbing Caleb's hair.

"Not," I barked. "He's all good. Maybe find a cloth or something for him and fuck off out of my wife's bed though, yeah?"

"You look like you want to hurt me," Caleb said and one look at Seth did kinda confirm that, but I officially didn't want to know any more about this. I'd seen enough to have discovered their sneaky secret and I planned to give them hell for lying to us about it if I ever made it back to life myself, but right here and now, I was good to leave. I just needed to figure out how the fuck I was supposed to do that.

"Are you gonna tell me why you're so pissed at me or are you just looking to hate fuck it out of your system?" Caleb demanded.

"I could never hate you, Cal," Seth muttered.

"I'm angry too," Caleb replied. "Angry at the whole fucking world. For Lionel, our fate, for our terrible fucking luck. For Darius-"

"Don't bring me into this shit," I snapped because they had already done that, hadn't they?

"-for everything. But I don't feel like that when I'm with you. You make me forget, even if it's only for a little while."

"You make me forget too," Seth said, shadows passing behind his eyes and I felt their grief, guilt tearing at me as the depth of the pain they felt over losing me rose between them. I was glad they'd found something good in each other, especially if it was helping them deal with that pain, but I did not need to see any more of the show. There were a lot of things I'd enjoyed discovering from the afterlife but snooping on my friends' sex lives was not one of them.

"Good." Caleb kissed him and I groaned because it wasn't over. Of course it wasn't fucking over.

I shoved against The Veil, snarling furiously as it refused to welcome me back into its embrace.

"Help!" I yelled, wondering if some spirit might take pity on me and pull me back. Every time I'd done this before it had happened so naturally that I couldn't pinpoint what specifically had drawn me away to replicate it.

Seth and Caleb were moving on the bed, and I was looking pretty much

320

anywhere but at them, blocking out their heated words, pretending I did not hear Caleb ask Seth to show him how he liked it because I didn't want to know. I. Did. Not. Want. To. Know.

"Merissa?" I yelled, wondering if she might be able to help pull me back. She'd been dead far longer than me, so she had to know how to reach me.

"Yes?" Merissa asked as she appeared before me, and I groaned as Hail materialised at her back.

I tried to move between them and the two Heirs who were now half naked and- yeah, Caleb was basically choking on Seth's dick, so that was fucking peachy.

"Did you just summon your mother-in-law to watch your friends fucking?" Hail asked in outrage, and I groaned, trying to block Merissa's view of the bed while she made no attempt at all to look away, a laugh falling from her lips.

"No," I snapped. "I was calling for help because they won't stop doing... *that*." I waved my hand in their general direction upping my voice to try and cover Seth's as he cried out in ecstasy behind me.

"Shit, Caleb, I can't keep holding back," Seth panted.

"And I can't leave," I added loudly, pretending not to hear Caleb's reply.

"Then stop holding back," he commanded, and we all heard him. Me, my mother-in-law and my father-in-law. Brilliant.

"Why can't you leave?" Hail demanded and I scowled at him.

"I don't know, that's why I called for help."

There was a lot of groaning and moaning and out of the corner of my eye I could see a lot of thrusting going on and I really needed to get the fuck out of here.

Seth howled loud enough to rattle the damn walls as he came, Caleb groaning as he fucking swallowed and I was caught holding eye contact with Hail motherfucking Vega the entire time.

There was a beat of silence that followed where we all tried to think of the appropriate thing to say but luckily Seth filled that with yet another filthy declaration of just how long this experience was set to last.

"Stop," he panted. "I'm the only one making you come tonight. So keep your fucking hands to yourself or on me."

The bed slammed into the wall as Caleb lunged at him and for some unknown reason I looked around at the noise, gaining a view of him biting Seth, the two of them near naked, smeared with cum, still in my wife's star damned bed, in full view of Roxy's parents.

"By the stars, where is the lube when we fucking need it?" Seth hissed.

"Get me out of here," I begged, looking back to Merissa who seemed for too amused by my predicament.

"You just have to want to leave," she replied.

"That's a lie," I snarled just as Caleb spoke again.

"There's some here," he said, and as one, all of us looked to the box of unlicensed sex toys which sat on the floor between us and the bed.

"How would you know that?" Seth growled, his Wolf rising in his expression.

"Because I found this earlier." Caleb leaned down and grabbed the box from the floor, ripping it open.

An enormous, golden Dragon dick vibrator fell out and smacked Seth on the chest, followed by the rest of the contents which tumbled onto the bed beside them.

"Is that your face on the side of that box?" Hail asked, stepping closer.

"No," I snapped but it obviously *was* me and Merissa pressed her lips into a flat line as she fought a laugh. "It's not licensed," I protested.

"Oooh, blind bag!" Seth cooed, and Caleb knocked the Dragon dick vibrator from the bed, causing it to fly straight through Hail's ass. My lips parted, but honestly, what the fuck was I supposed to say when a golden Dragon cock had accidentally penetrated him?

"How vanilla are you feeling, Altair?" Seth purred, licking a fucking butt plug and I was done. I was *done*.

"Get me out of here," I snarled as Merissa gave up on holding back and started laughing loudly.

She offered me her hand and I took it, The Veil finally showing me mercy and hauling me away from the realm of the living. For once, I was glad to leave it behind.

I was gifted one last glimpse of two of my best friends in the world fucking each other like it wasn't the biggest secret either of them had kept and I scowled at them. When I got back to life, I was going to make them pay for keeping this from me and for doing it on Roxy's bed too. Oh yes, I was going to have a lot of fun with my best friends when I saw them again, and they would rue the day they used unlicensed sex toys with my face on them.

CATALINA

CHAPTER TWENTY TWO

I rested my head against Hamish's shoulder as we lay curled together in a hammock, tethered between two palm trees on our little private beach in our rooms. The sea lapped calmly against the shore, and I found such peace in my husband's arms, his fingers trailing up and down my spine so soothing that I almost fell asleep. We had created something of a honeymoon resort for our space in the Eternal Palace, a vacation we had never had a chance to take together in life.

A knock came at the door in the wooden cabin behind us and Hamish mumbled sleepily, "Who the devil is dancing on our doorstep?"

"I'll go see," I said, placing a kiss on his lips then climbing out of the hammock and adjusting my rose pink bikini before heading inside.

My body was mine now. And nothing about my skin felt tainted by *him* anymore. Even my mind was lighter, the dark memories of Lionel's insidious touch lessening with each day I was here. Perhaps The Veil was designed to help you find peace, or maybe I was just able to let go of it all at last. Hamish made it easy for me to just be me. He had never once made a derisive comment about me, belittled me, or made feel anything less than the person I was. It was like coming home after years of being shut out in the cold.

I moved through our summer cabin, covering myself in a silken white robe with nothing but a thought. I opened the door, finding Radcliff there in his golden clothes, looking slightly sheepish.

"Ah, hello," he said. "May I come in?"

"If you like." I stepped aside and he moved into the cabin, looking around it with intrigue.

Hamish appeared beyond the open doors that led onto the sandy beach, snapping the band of his swimming trunks against his hips. "Radcliff, you old tripper trapper. Fancy a dip?"

"Not just now, Hamish," he said. "In a moment perhaps. I would like a word with Catalina."

"Say no more. I shall wet my whipper and meet you in the depths of the orry ocean for a splish and a splash when you are ready for the merriment."

Hamish summoned a snorkel and bright pink flippers onto his body then went tromping out into the sea with such keenness that it brought a smile to my lips.

"Everything alright?" I asked Radcliff, my gaze creeping over his features that were an echo of Lionel's. Radcliff's were softer, more handsome in a pretty boy kind of way, but he reminded me enough of him that it unsettled me some. I'd never really spared much thought for this man whose life had been cut short many years ago, and only when it had come out that Lionel had murdered him had I realised how long my ex-husband had been destroying people's lives. Of course, I'd pitied Radcliff at that revelation, but I had never once imagined myself face to face with him beyond The Veil.

"The thing is…well…" Radcliff scored a hand down the back of his neck. "I've known you quite some time actually, Catalina. I've been watching Lionel all these years, scorning him as I do. His mind turns to me more often than you would imagine, thinking of his victory over me."

"He thinks of me too," I said bitterly. "Not in ways I like to dwell on."

"No, but that's the thing, isn't it? We are doomed to dwell, lest we take the Destined Door and move on into the after."

"I will dwell on the lives of my children, that is all." Sadness touched my words at the thought of Darius, how I should have been watching over him in the living realm now just like I was Xavier. But instead, he was here too. Of all the things Lionel had done, to me, that was the worst of all.

"Yes, it's best to hold on to the good," Radcliff said, nodding seriously. "Which is why I wanted to speak with you. You see, when I first came to The Veil, I harboured a lot of rage, a lot of resentment and vitriol towards my brother. Still do, in fact. But for a time, all I could see of my life was my death. Nothing I had achieved leading up to it registered anymore. I never let my thoughts drift to the good parts, never relived the memories which were full of light. Instead, I spiralled into replaying my death from every angle and all the moments leading up to it, trying to see where I might have made better choices that could have led to me surviving that night. I'd hear the buzzing of that norian wasp everywhere I went. The incessant bzz bzz haunting me. At times, I still hear it." His head snapped sideways as if he could hear it then, his shoulders becoming rigid, then he sighed. "Our deaths can become our greatest traumas, and all the events leading up to them. But I wanted to tell you that I have watched all that has happened to you, witnessed the way your mind was stolen, your emotions locked away...how you so deeply loved your sons and yet could rarely express it. But I knew how much you wanted to."

A tight ball formed in my throat as I nodded, unable to form any words in response, sure I would break if I thought on it too long.

Radcliff stepped closer, reaching out to squeeze my upper arm. "Catalina, you are a good person who became the victim of an abusive monster. You would have done everything right by your children given the chance, and before my brother got into your head with dark magic, you had so many wonderful moments. Think of those, replay them over and over. Remind yourself of who you were before Lionel got his claws in you, and don't ever blame yourself for what happened."

I released a slow breath, then moved forward and wrapped Radcliff in my arms. "You are nothing like your brother," I whispered, and his shoulders dropped.

"I know it to be so, yet it is always good to hear it."

I felt the tug of Xavier calling to me and I went to him, pulling Radcliff with me until we found ourselves standing on top of a sun-drenched hill. Xavier was in his beautiful lilac Pegasus form, his wings reattached and flexing against his spine.

I gasped, running to him with joy sweeping across my heart, reaching out to stroke the soft feathers.

"Well dingle my dongle." Washer sprang up from a patch of long grass to our left in a tiny Speedo, leaving three naked Fae cuddling each other in the fronds. "Your mighty wings have been restored!"

I grimaced as he strode towards my boy, and thankfully Tyler was there to intervene.

"He needs some time to prepare for a flight," he said in a tone that told Washer to back off.

I had been delighted to witness Xavier's union with his herd members, his love for both Sofia and Tyler, and theirs for him, making me so very happy. They were good for him after so long kept hidden away from other Fae. They accepted him as he was, and there was no greater gift than that from the people who loved you.

"Well say no more, my boy," Washer said, moving in front of Xavier, clearly not taking the hint. "Follow my arm movements with your wings, young Xavier. I am an expert in the bendings of the body. A little flexing and jangling should get them in ship shape order."

He began squatting, stretching his arms either side of him and flapping them like a bird with every squat he did. "Hup, then down. Hup, then down."

Radcliff jogged up beside him and started mimicking his workout. "Oof, to be fair, that really does open up the hip flexors."

I snorted a laugh, wondering what Brian Washer would think if he knew who was copying him right now.

Darius appeared beside me so abruptly that I gasped, then broke a smile as I embraced him. "Xavier has restored his wings and is about to take his first flight!"

"Let's see him shine then." He squeezed me tight, keeping his arm around me as we looked to Xavier.

Washer was drawing the attention of the rebels at the bottom of the hill and a crowd began to form when they realised Xavier's wings were back in place. I brimmed with pride at the hope and excitement in people's eyes as they gazed upon him in all his glittery glory.

"Go on, Xavier!" a young girl called to him, her eyes bright as her mom swept her into her arms so she could see better.

A cheer went up and I cried out with them. Xavier's cheeks turned pink from the attention, and I reached out to pinch one of them with a grin.

"Don't be a coward, just go for it," Darius called, and I shoved and elbow into his ribs.

Xavier started flapping his wings, mimicking Washer's movements and Sofia and Tyler gave in, joining him in the grass, doing the squats and wing flaps too while Radcliff gave all his energy to it as well.

Xavier whinnied a laugh at them, glitter tumbling from his mane and his wings flashing in the sunlight.

"Go on, baby!" I cried.

"Come on, Xavier," Darius called.

An oooh broke out from the crowd, their cheers growing louder, more and more people showing up to join in.

"Let's hope he doesn't make a tit of himself, eh?" Radcliff called. "He has a track record of doing that."

"Nonsense," I clipped. "He'll be great."

"At least he's out there making a grand tit of himself. You're stuck here titless for all eternity," Darius said with a smirk and Radcliff blew out a line of smoke in annoyance.

Tyler whipped out his Atlas, aiming it at Xavier and starting to record. "Today, Xavier Acrux has had his wings restored after they were viciously torn from his back by his cruel father, the asshole king. Lame Lionel displayed them on his wall like a trophy and Xavier seized them back in a daring act. Prepare for your mind to be blown, because I'll be sharing his memories from that wild night in the next article of The Daily Solaria. Long live the Vega Queens!" Tyler shot Xavier a thumbs up and my son dragged his front hoof across the grass, readying to take off.

"I've got you if you fall, bro!" Seth Capella pushed his way to the front of the crowd, and Max and Geraldine muscled their way through too.

"Oh my dear, Pego-brother!" Geraldine squealed. "Fly to the clouds and into the yonder. Leave a merry trail of colour in the sky and neigh so loud it stirs your ancestors beyond The Veil." She wiped a tear from her eye, and I lifted my chin, my chest expanding at all the encouragement.

"You can do it," Sofia whispered, moving forward to kiss Xavier's nose and I smiled at them, my heart bathed in happiness. "I believe in you." She stepped aside and Xavier looked a little nervous as he prepared for his flight.

"You've got this, baby. Just focus," I told him.

"Yah!" Washer cried, slapping him on the rump and Xavier whinnied in alarm, taking off at speed down the hill.

I wanted to kick Washer for that move, but was too focused on my son, nervous and hopeful for him. His wings flapped and he released a neigh of delight just as the wind swept under them and he climbed towards the sky.

I whooped, jumping up and down with Darius, joined by Radcliff who stood with his hands on his hips, admiring the glimmering form of my son wheeling through the air above.

"Big, isn't he?" Radcliff said cheerily. "He would probably be almost as big as me if I had been a Pegasus."

"Nah, he'd be bigger by far," Darius said, earning himself a glare from Radcliff.

I shoved my son's arm with a laugh then went running down the hill, leaping up and letting the shift ripple down my spine. I burst into my Dragon form, chasing Xavier into the sky and roaring to him in encouragement, his ears flicking like he might just have heard that.

Tyler and Sofia came to join us in the clouds and Radcliff took off too, flying up and doing a somersault above me in his Dragon form. Darius joined us next, his beautiful golden Dragon bursting from his flesh as he fully shifted and followed us into the sky, letting out a bellow that shook the heavens.

Glitter tumbled from the coats and manes of Xavier and his herd, creating trails of light and colour everywhere they went, making the crowd cheer even louder.

Darius swooped along beside me, his right wing brushing against mine, a roar bursting from him in encouragement of his brother.

Xavier was looking our way, a neigh leaving him that said perhaps he knew we were here, celebrating this win with him. And as we twisted and soared through the air, I felt sure that Xavier's victory was bolstering the hearts of the rebels below. And after so many failures, it was just what they all needed to find it in their hearts to keep fighting.

AZRIEL

CHAPTER TWENTY THREE

I circled a paragraph in the book I had borrowed from the Archive of Yore that resided here beyond The Veil, swatting a loose lock of black hair away from my face. This was one of the oldest tomes in existence. The problem was, it was written in riddles. Some of the words readable, while others were written in a language so old it was impossible to decipher. If only I still had access to my linguistics compendium, I might have had a better chance at understanding it.

Though I may have been able to sneak a few things through The Veil from the deal I'd struck with Mordra long before I'd died, I could not have sent the entirety of my book collection. I had contacted her through the means of a magic so dark, it had required a heavy price of blood, and not just mine.

Once the deal had been made, I stowed my artefacts in the pockets of Fae I sent directly to her in death, and she had snatched the items from them during their passing down the river. Not all had been seized, but enough had made it here, waiting for me when I arrived. And of course, I'd placed trinkets in their pockets for Mordra to grab and keep as her own.

I had only killed those who belonged in the fields of chaos, who I had felt no guilt for in using them as sacrifice. Murderers, rapists, those who lurked in the underbelly of society and who deserved the death I had handed them.

My own death had been plotted intricately, and when it had been time to take my life and hide the Imperial Star in my crypt for the Vega twins and my son to find, Ling Astrum had been there to see me out of this world. The last

Guild Master. Eventually, when the rest of the Guild lay dead too, our pact to protect the Imperial Star solidified, and we bought a precious chance for Solaria from the stars. An opportunity for a fresh Zodiac Guild to rise with the Vega twins, and bring on a new dawn in Solaria.

My gaze tracked over the intriguing passage in the book again.

Starlight bright and dark the other.
Wielded, both can rip asunder.
In the Grawl where the light one sings.
Blood and bone, the ether brings.

I circled the word *Grawl* and started thumbing through the notebook I had managed to bring here that contained translations of some of the old words.

"Grawl... what could you mean? Do you have roots in the word grawvern?" I sighed, not finding what I needed. I was on another dead-end path, seeking answers in places they did not lie.

"Azriel?" Serenity stepped through the door. "I knocked but there was no answer."

"Forgive me, I would not hear the chiming of the bells of the apocalypse when I am engrossed in my studies. Crucia could be standing at my back come to burn my soul to ash and I would still be questioning my latest hypothesis as I went into oblivion."

Serenity laughed, moving closer and resting a hand on my seat, taking a glance at my work. Her fingers brushed my spine and I straightened a little, glancing up at her and taking in the soft curve of her cheekbone, her large brown eyes keenly poring over my work.

I cleared my throat, pushing out of my seat and knocking her back a little in the process.

"I didn't mean to pry," she said. "Well, alright, I did. But I am quite fascinated with your work."

"You're welcome to pry," I said, smoothing back my hair. "I... ah, here." I plucked a piece of paper off my desk and held it out to her. "It's something of a plan to get a message to your son. Excuse the scrawling handwriting, and the er, scribbles in the corner, oh and that small diagram I crossed out. In fact-" I scrunched it up in my fist before she could take it. "I'll write it out clearer."

"I really don't care whether it's written in perfect calligraphy or scrawled there in Griffin shit, Azriel. All I want is a plan, and your plans are the best I've seen. Methodical, genius really."

"That is a grand word for an average mind, I assure you."

"It is the exact word I would choose, and I refuse to retract it," she said, and

I couldn't help the swell I felt in my chest.

I rooted around in the drawer of my desk, taking out a little vial of crushed bloodsvein root along with a fire crystal. This plan was not just for her benefit of course. If it worked, I could contact Lancelot and tell him the locations of the Guild Stones, and so much more. So much hinged on my attempts to reach them, that it made me hesitant to try it and fail. But that was the nature of science. The problem was, this time, a lot more was riding on it than my simple curiosities. I would test it first with Serenity, then if it was a success I would go to my son at once.

"Well then, let's give it a try. Reach for Tiberius," I said.

Serenity closed her eyes to focus and she took my hand, guiding me with her to him, her palm sitting inside mine and her fingers squeezing tight. We arrived on the shore of the rebel island where Tiberius was training some Fae for war, putting them through drills and barking orders. He looked ferocious, like a commander of bloodshed, his shirt off and gleaming with sweat from working alongside the rebel recruits.

Serenity watched him with a sad sort of smile on her face.

"Do you miss him?" I asked, unsure why the question came to me when the answer was certain anyway.

"Yes, I miss him. But so much time has passed. His grief for me is always there, but it's no longer raw. I was so bitter when I first came here, furious, and distraught over what Linda had taken from us. I wanted Tiberius to pine for me, to wait for me. But what use is there in waiting for the dead? We are the ones who must wait, and could I ever say I loved him if I demanded he grieve me forever? He has many years of life to live, and I hope love finds him again. He deserves that."

"Do *you* deserve that?" Again, the rogue question left me. Unfounded. Not carefully picked over and deliberated as it should have been.

Serenity looked to me in surprise, and I held her gaze, unsure quite what I was truly asking here, only that I very much wished to hear the answer.

"There can be no true life for the dead," she said miserably. "We're just spirits wishing for more time."

"I do not believe that to be so," I said thoughtfully. "Though I can see the reasoning in the idea. However, I have come to see death a little differently."

"In what way?" she asked, ever curious. I liked that about her, how she was open to possibilities. She may have held that opinion, but she was willing to indulge me in mine, to see if it might hold some merit.

"Death is a doorway in which we must stand, yes, waiting for those we love to join us, or to find peace in knowing they live on. Either way, it is not our final destination. It is a place between the here and there. What the *there* is, I do not know. But the here, I believe, is an opportunity to find harmony. A harmony, perhaps, we did not manage to find in life."

"That is an interesting theory," she said, thinking on it. "So you believe it is not wrong to seek joy here? Happiness even?"

"I think we must else we will fall into madness. My work keeps me sane. Without it, I would be adrift."

"It makes you happy?" she questioned, and I was suddenly tipped sideways by the truth that rose in me.

"Not happy exactly," I said slowly. "It satisfies me. It is an addiction, in a way. It gives me purpose."

"So where does your joy lie?"

"With my children."

She smiled. "That is my focus too. Watching Max becoming a man, righting his wrongs, finding love. Oh Azriel, there is nothing like it."

"Truly there isn't," I agreed, thinking of Lance and Darcy and all I had seen them go through to be together. How strong Lance had become, how Darcy had given him reason to fight again, to thrive.

"But he is not the only one I watch," Serenity said sullenly, looking to Tiberius and I knew of what she spoke, the weight of that burden clear in her eyes.

"Then let us try to help," I said, laying the crystal on the ground beside Tiberius and shaking out the vial of bloodsvein root in a circle around it. "This should act as a conduit for your voice once the crystal ignites the bloodsvein. Speak into it clearly. You may only have a moment, seconds, a minute at most, I cannot be sure."

"Alright," she said, dropping to her knees, preparing to speak into the fire crystal. "Ready."

I touched the crystal and it burst into flames, the powder catching light quickly and burning brightest pink.

"Tiberius!" Serenity cried and Tiberius looked around in fright, her voice carrying right to him.

"It worked," I gasped, thinking of my son and how swiftly I must go to him to try this very thing. To tell him everything he needed to set him on the right path.

"You must seek-" Serenity started but I felt a change in the air. The Veil slammed into us, forcing us back and snuffing out the fire in an ethereal wind that swept violently around us. I battled to keep us there, grasping Serenity's arm as we pushed against The Veil with all our strength.

The crystal burst back alight, but this time the fire was roaring and full of starlight. It threw itself against us and the heat of it blasted against our souls.

"This fate is not for you to decide, seeker of knowledge," the stars bellowed inside my mind, their fury clear. *"The voices of the dead do not belong in the ears of the living. You shall not attempt this twice, or our wrath shall befall you and all those you hold dear."*

I tugged Serenity against my chest, shielding her from them and turning from the fire, letting The Veil have us, guiding us back to my rooms. It spat us out on the bed, and I rolled over, checking she was alright.

"The stars won't let us," she croaked, shoving out of the bed, and knotting her fingers in her hair.

"Maybe they have a path we cannot see yet," I said heavily, disappointment crashing down on me. I could not reach Lancelot with this magic, could not tell him of the Guild Stones. And I realised how deeply I had pinned my hopes on this plan.

She hung her head, walking to the door. "Or maybe they never intend for this truth to be unveiled."

"I will find another way," I called to her, but she was gone, leaving me with my failure to burrow into the core of me. I had to focus. I would work tirelessly until I found another solution, even if the stars wished to deny me of this path. I would forge on regardless and damn the consequences.

The door swung slowly open revealing a dark-haired woman standing there, peering into my room uncertainly. "Excuse me, Mr Orion? Can I have a word?"

I pushed to my feet, opening the door wider.

"Francesca," I said heavily. "I have been meaning to find you."

"I've come to apologise for failing your son," she said, misery filling her eyes.

"You did no such thing," I said powerfully. "The information contained in your memory loop has rattled the foundations of Lionel's dictatorship. Lance will see that as a remarkable win in the war."

She lifted her chin. "I suppose it has helped, a little."

"Thank you for trying to free him. I am sorry it was not to be, but you showed such bravery in what you did for him," I said, avoiding the declaration of love she had shown him, having been there to witness it all myself. I did not wish to remind her of that painful rejection.

"Thank you," she said. "It's hard to accept all that's happened. I think my head is still in the living world, like death hasn't really happened to me yet, you know?"

"That happens for a time, then it passes," I said. "Once you have found acceptance, it is best to seek all the answers you ached for in life. It is the only way to find peace."

She nodded glumly. "You said you had been meaning to find me…"

"Ah yes, well I am on the hunt for the lost Guild Stones, and I have tracked one down to the FIB impound. It is of great importance that Lance and the Vegas discover these stones, every last one of them. And I wondered if you might know of a way they could gain access to such a place undetected."

Her eyebrows rose at the news, and she thought on it for a moment. "I believe everything they need to access it is contained in my memory loop. If they know to look for that stone in the FIB impound, perhaps it will occur to them to search my memories?"

"Mm, the trouble lies in them knowing to look for the stone there." I frowned. "No matter, we will forge on and find a way. Would you like to come in for coffee? The illusion of it is quite real."

"Thank you, but my mom's waiting for me in The Room of Knowledge. Plus, I suppose it would be strange to have coffee with me after everything."

"Strange?" I questioned.

"Well, Lance and I were a thing for a while. I could have been your daughter in law." She laughed and I squinted at her, trying to remember a time I had seen my son have such inclinations towards her. It had seemed he had made himself quite clear in his final words with her that he had never desired her as such.

"Not once Darcy arrived of course," she went on. "But in another life, perhaps. Where he hadn't met his Elysian Mate."

"If the Vega twins had not come to Solaria, I think then he might have ended up with Darius Acrux. The two always seemed so well suited to one another, always tussling and laughing together, bound by their cause against Lionel. But it does not surprise me that each of them fell for a Vega twin. How could they not fall for their power, their passion, their fire? It is rather poetic, I feel, that they would be made family in that way."

"Well, if Darius had not been in the mix, it could have been me," she laughed, though the laughter was more strained this time.

"Yes, perhaps. Although, I do believe my son had some serious interest from a Lion Shifter once – Leon Night, do you know him? He licked Lance, which in the Lion world means he is his apparently. But again, it was not to be. Another life though, like you say."

"Yes, or perhaps I-"

"Then there is Gabriel Nox, of course. My son drank a love potion once and fell head over heels for him. I thought that might be the start of something wonderful, as they seemed to get on so well and were so very fond of one another. Yes, they would have been a fine match too, but I am overjoyed that it is Darcy. I truly love her, I do. I wish I could meet her, to bathe in that light of hers for a moment which my son adores so deeply. It is clear as day why he has fallen for her, why she of all people could pull him from the dark."

"Well I'd...best be going," Francesca said and I smiled, waving her goodbye.

I was stood there hardly a moment before a tug in my chest told me my son was in need and I went to him, finding Hail and Merissa Vega materialising with me in a dimly lit stone chamber.

A large tank full of blood sat at the centre of it beyond Stella, and as I turned, I found Lance and Darcy chained to wooden racks, him just waking while she remained unconscious.

I cursed in shock.

"What is she doing to them?" Hail snarled and I ran to the table full of potions where a book lay open on its surface, anxious to discover that answer for myself.

Merissa joined me, reading the dark spell laid out before us involving blood magic and the coven bonds of old.

"By the moon," I breathed, unable to believe Stella had really found an answer. "She is trying to alter Lance's Death Bond."

"This does not appear to be for their good, are you sure Azriel?" Hail demanded.

"I cannot be certain," I said, hurriedly reading through the spell again.

"She has them tied up," Merissa said, looking to her daughter in fear. "What if she means to hurt Gwendalina?"

I ran my finger along the line that required sacrifice for a transference of the Death Bond. Stella was going to place it on another soul, and my throat thickened as I looked to Darcy, her inky hair swirling around her. Surely she wouldn't...

"Azriel?" Hail prompted, following my gaze, and I anxiously deliberated over what Stella's intentions were.

"What is this?" Lance rasped at Stella, waking fully from whatever spell or potion she had used to make him sleep.

Stella moved towards Darcy, and Lance bucked against his restraints.

"Stay back!" Merissa cried at Stella, pushing her power out into the walls, but something about this chamber felt different. It was cloaked in dark magic, and I wasn't sure if the Vega king and queen could affect it while it was so.

"Get the fuck away from her," Lance snapped, and time tipped and tilted, lurching us through it until Stella was standing beside Darcy with a curved blade in her hand that resembled a Vampire fang. I knew that knife, it was a possession of the Barbarian Queen, a blade famed for slitting a thousand Fae throats, their blood drained for the supply of the royal coven.

"What are you thinking?" I growled at Stella.

"Don't touch her!" Lance roared in terror. "You stay the fuck away from her or I'll make you pay. I'll rip every organ from your worthless body and keep you alive until I claim the last one."

"Royal blood is so very powerful," Stella whispered, ignoring him, and carving a long slit down Darcy's forearm where it was bound in place above her.

"No!" Lance yelled, jerking harder against my restraints, his voice echoed by Merissa's.

Fear clung to my heart and I worked through answers in my mind, one after another, trying to find a way to help her.

"Azriel." Hail fisted his hand in my robes. "You must do something. The palace isn't responding to my power. I must protect Gwendalina."

Time shifted again and I fought to remain in this place, terror for Lance and his mate binding me in agony.

Stella was now covered in blood from an apparent dip in the tank, and she held a potion in her grip, forcing it against Lance's lips.

"Drink," she commanded, and she eventually got him to do so, making him give in.

"Fuck. You," he panted as she released him.

Stella gazed at Lance woefully through the blood staining her face. "It's the only way."

"The only way for what?" Lance demanded.

"She's going to try and remove his Death Bond and hand it to another," I rasped.

"Gwendalina," Merissa said in horror, running to her daughter and standing before her like she could shield her from this fate.

Hail tried to call on the palace, desperate to strike at Stella from the beyond, but I could see it was no use.

I had to think, find a way out of this. Form a plan.

"Long ago, our kind ruled the world," Stella breathed. "Blood holds untold power, Lance. But these powers cannot be fully unlocked unless we embrace the Vampire ways of our ancestors."

"Get your filthy fucking hand off of me," Lance hissed, but his pupils dilated with hunger, the potion she had given him certainly driving it.

"Here, baby." Stella raised her wrist, offering it to Lance's mouth and his fangs snapped out and within moments, he bit her.

"No!" I roared.

"Yes," Stella gasped.

Time rippled once more and I felt the power of their coven bond forming, spanning between them and latching tight.

"Why?" Lance demanded, regaining clarity and realising what she had done. "You had no right."

"I love you so much," she said, her eyes watery. "Trust me, baby, it's for your own good."

"Prove your love for him," I hissed. "You will not harm his mate if you know anything of true love. It will kill him more surely than death would."

Time bounced and skipped, and I found Darcy awake with Stella standing before her.

"A lover's promise made in solemn silence," Stella murmured, and I recognised the words from the spell. She cast a silencing bubble around herself and Darcy, and I ran forward, stepping through it and hearing the words that Lance no longer could. Merissa and Hail did the same, their shoulders pressing to mine.

"Get away from me," Darcy hissed.

"Listen, I'm not going to hurt you," Stella said, and I met Merissa's gaze, hope passing between us.

Hail's posture loosened, but he still had the glint of a demon in his gaze. "Your wife was always a decent liar."

"Yes," I agreed, hunting Stella's face. "But something tells me this is not a lie."

"What is this all for?" Darcy demanded.

"I'm going to break Lance's Death Bond," Stella vowed, and Darcy's eyes flashed towards my son in desperation.

"Don't listen to her," Lance called, not hearing a word of this, and I realised why Stella was keeping it from him, putting it all together from the spell and the notes she had jotted in the margin. "She's a liar, a fucking manipulator. Anything that comes out of her mouth is dirt."

Stella cast an illusion over her mouth so Lance couldn't lip read any of her words. "I swear I will do everything in my power to save him, but I need you to work with me."

Darcy eyed her uncertainly. "Do you really think you can break the bond?"

"I know so," Stella said passionately, tears brimming in her eyes. "I know I've been a bad mother, but I can make it up to him. I swear I can. I just need you to work with me."

Darcy fell quiet and Hail and Merissa shared an intense look that said they weren't sure if they trusted Stella. I may have felt that way too had I not known my wife so well. This was remorse in all its brutality, eating its way out of her and guiding her actions at long last.

"I really think she is telling the truth," I said. "She does not intend to hurt her."

"How can you be sure?" Merissa growled. "It could be some trick."

"She has Darcy chained and at her mercy, she could harm her now if that was her intention. But then that means…" I studied Stella's face, piecing her plan together and finding the answer so shocking that it was difficult to believe that was really the path she had chosen.

"When it is done, you will have a chance to run and take him far from here," Stella said. "Lionel is at the Court of Solaria with his Dragon Guild and will not be back for some time. So do I have your word that you will help me?"

"Alright," Darcy said, clearly seeing what I saw in Stella then, or perhaps she was simply willing to risk it all for her mate, as always. "What do you want me to do?"

Time fluttered forward like the wings of a giant bird were beating either side of me and I threw my power against The Veil to get back to that chamber, finding Darcy hovering above the tank of blood in the grasp of Stella's air magic, slowly lowering into it.

"I love you," Darcy breathed.

"Blue!" Lance bellowed.

Merissa ran to the tank in desperation, but time ebbed and flowed and everything swirled before we found our way back to them once more. The air was humming with an almighty power, the Death Bond clashing in the air.

"Matrem consanguinitate religatam et ultra. Filii mei vinculis mortis suscipio," Stella whispered, and I repeated the words, looking to Hail and Merissa to encourage them to do the same. They laid their trust in me, echoing them back into the atmosphere and the power of the words whipped across the boundary of our worlds to fuse with Stella's.

"I am his blood, his kin, his coven!" Stella tipped her head back, the words pouring from her and tainting the air. "Eius vinculum meum est!"

"Eius vinculum meum est!" I yelled alongside Merissa and Hail.

A sound like thunder tore through the room and all at once, everything went dark.

"Ab ipso peto nunc et semper – his bond is *mine*," Stella panted, and a flash of red light exploded between her palm and our son's.

She was blasted away from him by the rebound of the magic and the aftershock shattered the glass tank Darcy was trapped in, washing her out of it on a tide of blood. She coughed and spluttered, pushing to her hands and knees. Merissa patted her back to try and help, no matter if she couldn't really reach her.

"It's okay, my little darling," Hail said, dropping to his knees beside her. "We've got you."

Stella rose above us with air magic and her entire body began to glow with the crimson light of the Death Bond. But it was no longer tied to my son, instead, that terrible power was bound to her. I knew in my heart what was coming next, but wondered if she was truly brave enough to go through with it.

Stella lifted a hand, tears running down her cheeks and carving lines through the blood staining her face. She flicked her fingers and brought the fang-like dagger flying across the room, catching it in her grip. I moved to stand with her, my chest tight and my thoughts dark. The stars were drawing closer, sensing the importance of what was coming.

"Why?" Lance gasped as Stella angled the blade towards her own heart.

"Because I am your mother. And I love you more than life itself," she exhaled then drove the dagger into her chest.

A scream left her as she used the strength of her Order to carve her heart from the cavity of her ribs and yanked it out of her own body, skewered on the blade as she held it before her. I staggered back, unblinking and taking in the choice she had made, the sacrifice that was so powerful it sent a tremor through the atmosphere.

"By the light of the moon," Merissa gasped, her hand falling on Hail's arm.

"She's given herself to the Death Bond," he breathed in disbelief.

A single moment of life remained in Stella's eyes and her soul balanced on the edges of her skin. In her final breath, she flicked her fingers and released Lance from the chains that held him to the rack.

In the next second, she was dead, collapsing in a pool of blood, her body broken and the bloody knife sitting upright beside her where it was sunk deep into her heart.

Stella's soul came quietly into The Veil, her death a presence that hushed all words on my tongue. She stepped towards me, blinking in surprise, but no fear crossed her expression. She had chosen this after all.

"Azriel," she said, moving closer then noticing the Savage King and his queen.

Her throat bobbed, her eyes moving between us all and shame colouring her features.

"Have you come to punish me?" she whispered.

Merissa moved forward, striking Stella across the face. "That is for all your poor choices." She swept closer and kissed the place she had hit Stella's cheek. "And that is for the good ones you made in the end."

"Forgive me," Stella croaked.

"It is not my forgiveness you need now," Merissa said coolly, sweeping past her towards Darcy and Lance where they were embracing on the floor.

Hail nodded curtly to Stella, and I doubted she would get more from him than that. He moved to join his family and Stella was left eye to eye with me. Her long dead husband. A man she had thought of more times than she would likely ever admit. But I had felt the pull of her often enough, the regret, the shame. Yes, she had grieved me, but not in the way a wife should have grieved their husband. Most of her grief had been rooted in guilt.

"Azriel…" She inched closer. "What you must think of me."

"It is quite telling that The Veil has not swept you away from here into the river that would deliver you to the Harrowed Gate," I said cuttingly.

She shivered at the thought of it, wrapping her arms around herself. "I'm sorry."

"Apologies are for the living," I said. "Your story is written. Your actions speak your truth now."

"And what to do *you* say of my truth?"

I deliberated that, thinking on all the devastation she had caused through her choices, yet in the end, she had come through for Lance when he needed her most. And as my son was one of my most cherished loves, I could not help but be grateful for that. Still…when all things were measured and considered, it was impossible to forget the bad she had done.

"I am thankful for your final act, and for the times you helped pull Lance from the dark. But I can never forgive the acts of the past. I will, however, lay them to rest. I will not harbour hatred towards you, nor demand you suffer here in penance for those sins. I believe sitting here with your regrets will likely be enough payment for it all."

She bowed her head to me, then moved to scuttle by, slipping away towards the Eternal Palace. I felt Clara drawing near and as she ran to embrace Stella with a look of grief mixed with joy, a small smile lifted the corner of my lips. Clara would forgive her, and I wanted Stella to find peace for her daughter's sake.

I left them to it and turned my attention back to my son, that small moment of joy crushed away as Darcy Vega began to scream. The shadows poured from her, tearing from her skin and I cried out to her alongside her parents and her mate, terror crushing my heart.

Every last scrap of the shadows left her body and she hit the floor, collapsing there in a heap, looking up at the monster who was no longer one with her, the huge creature standing there across the chamber.

The Shadow Beast seemed momentarily dazed, sniffing the air, and gaining its bearings. Darcy pushed to her knees and Lance shot towards her, looking her over in concern, but she seemed impossibly well.

"What happened?" Hail rasped, closing in on Darcy and I noticed his hands were shaking.

"Her blood was my blood," Lance said to his mate. "She paid the price of your curse in her death. You're free."

"By the sun, it's true," Merissa said in sheer happiness, flinging herself at Hail and hugging him tight.

Our delight was short-lived relief as the Shadow Beast came charging towards Lance and Darcy, feral and full of rage, and I knew this bloody night was far from over.

DARIUS

CHAPTER TWENTY FOUR

The walk back to Mordra's cavern seemed longer this time, the path taking more turns, the trees thicker in the woodland. Even the golden glow appeared to shift more sluggishly, the light dripping through the canopy overhead instead of spilling through it.

But I didn't delay. I kept my destination firmly in mind, cursing this place for the effort it was going to to keep me from what I wanted, and eventually, I found the clearing where her cave was secreted between the trees.

I stalked inside without slowing, no hesitation in my steps as I prowled into her den.

I could feel Roxy's grief like a living beast beside me, her pain over our separation edging into a desperation which frightened me. But it only made my steps more solid, only confirmed exactly why I needed to be here and what I had come for, so I focused on my task and resisted the urge to go to her despite how deeply it hurt me to do so.

"You think there's freedom in hiding away down here like a worm skulking in the shadow of a blackbird?" I called as I stepped into the wide opening which held the boulder she favoured for a perch. "You think hiding from the stars negates their power?"

Mordra hissed angrily, appearing at my back, yellowed claws slicing through the air as she swiped an animalistic paw at me.

I growled in reply, her claws sliding right through me, making no contact at all with the illusion of a body I wore, and she hurtled past, settling on her rock once more.

"I see you have released one of your desperate hooks into life," she spat, her edges forming then dissolving, no features adorning her hollow skull.

"I faced the creature you sent me to and escaped it, if that's what you mean," I replied bitterly.

"You have to face your death to stand a chance of mastering your death," Mordra chuckled. "Only once you accept the truth of what you are – and aren't – will you be able to claim mastery over your destiny once more."

"Well, I faced my mortality, or lack of it, and came out swinging. So will you tell me now what I must do to return to the realm of the living?" I demanded.

A flash of stained teeth and bloodshot eyes. Mordra clucked her tongue.

"Took me too long to learn," she muttered. "Too long to understand what the answer to that riddle was. And by the time I figured it out, I could not pay the price."

"What price?"

"Grief burns, does it not? It festers and rots, then somehow it blazes and takes on a new form. The pain dulls, the sweetness lingers. There's power in that."

"Stop speaking in riddles and spell it out plainly," I snarled.

"Look closer at your sweet queen." Mordra clicked her fingers and The Veil shattered around me.

I found myself standing before Roxy who was fighting to stay on her feet, something horribly wrong with her which made her soul slip far too close to The Veil.

My name had been carved into her arm, blood dripping to the floor at her feet and I took in the discarded chalice she'd clearly used to poison herself already.

"Fuck, baby girl, you never do things by halves, do you?" I breathed while she fumbled with the pouch of stardust in her hands.

Her soul brightened beneath her skin, one step separating her from death. I moved to her, cupping her cheek, pressing my power into the heart of the ruby pendant which she always wore for me.

"Come on, faster," I growled, knowing it was too late for her to turn back now. She had to go on, see this through.

Something was screaming within her, and it took me a moment to realise it was Jenkins's cursed soul, locked in that tigers eye crystal which was still buried in her side, burning with agony as he was forced to anchor her to life.

I leaned in and pressed my mouth to Roxy's, willing her to feel me there, urging her to take what strength she needed from me.

Roxy threw the stardust as she leaned into the kiss, her heart dictating the destination, my fingers locking with hers but closing on nothing when she was whipped away.

I stumbled back, Mordra's cavern forming around me once more, her jagged teeth bared in a grin.

"Do you see yet?" she whispered. "Have you found the path?"

"What path?" I snapped. "All I see when I press close to The Veil are the people I love suffering."

"Yes, yes. Love is so powerful, isn't it? It draws you close, lets you see. Sometimes you can touch – but why? Why?"

"I don't know," I snapped.

I stumbled back again, The Veil thrashing against me before I arrived in a forest of horrors, trees with pitch black leaves and bone white trunks spreading endlessly out around me. The lack of life in this place was so potent that it choked me.

My wife was dying in the dirt between trees, panting over a pool of her own vomit, her body succumbing to the toxins she'd ingested.

She was trying to pull something from her pocket, the sight of her fighting to do something so simple while dancing the line of faceplanting her own vomit had me breaking.

A laugh spilled from my lips, amused, bitter, broken. I didn't even know what the fuck was wrong with me, but somehow the sight of her reduced to this in the name of saving me after all she'd been through to get here had hysteria bubbling through my chest.

"Fight," I commanded.

Roxy tried to pull something from her pocket again, her soul all too visible through her skin.

Finally, she managed it, and I cried out at her victory as she retrieved a vial which must have contained the antidote she needed, only for her to drop it in the dirt where it promptly rolled away from her.

"Fuck that for fate," I growled, dropping down to press my hand to her back as she rolled onto her front, her body almost giving out entirely now. "Come on, it's only a few inches away. You can do it, baby."

Roxy started pushing herself across the ground inch by inch, little more than one foot working now as she closed in on the little vial of Basilisk Venom which would save her.

Jenkins was screaming so loudly that I couldn't even pick out her heartbeat, the magic binding him to the crystal in her side starting to come apart beneath the pressure of holding her away from death.

I dropped down as her eyes fell closed, taking her hand in mine, the vial so near to her.

I squeezed her palm, urging her to feel me, offering what power I could.

"Come on, beautiful. You didn't survive all the shit life has thrown at you just to give up here in this lifeless place. You're the strongest person I've ever known. And this isn't your end."

Her eyes flickered beneath their lids, her toe pushing into the dirt once more and I reached for the vial of antivenom, shoving it with all I had, encouraging it to roll just a little. I yelled out in triumph as it did, meeting her lips.

Roxy snatched it into her mouth, shattering the little vial between her teeth, the dose of Basilisk Venom washing into her body just before it could give up on life.

Jenkins roared as the last of his power was consumed by the crystal, forced to anchor her in life for the final few seconds she needed to see the poison vanish from her veins.

The Veil broke open for him as he was ripped free of the crystal, and he screamed to all hell as he was flung through that door. But there was no afterlife waiting for him on this side anymore. The Veil screamed as it met with the lingering remnants of his soul and with a blinding flash of light, he was obliterated, the price paid for the magic she had needed to stave off death and any festering pieces of that son-of-a-bitch destroyed once and for all. If anything, he'd gotten off lightly.

I looked into Roxy's eyes as she teetered on the precipice of death, her lips parting in awe for half a heartbeat before that opening snapped shut, hurling her back into life where the tigers eye crystal fell from her skin, its magic spent.

"Do you see it yet?" Mordra cooed, her wet lips brushing my ear and I jerked around, finding myself in her cavern once more.

"See what?" I demanded, but she simply grinned that broken toothed smile in reply.

DARIUS

CHAPTER TWENTY FIVE

"What am I searching for?" I demanded.

Mordra tiptoed from her rock, her wraith-like body undulating like a flickering flame as she began to circle me, a finger pressed to her withered lips.

"The answers you seek slip closer," she breathed.

I opened my mouth to demand them again, but her hand landed on my chest, the force of her shove enough to shatter bone if I'd had a body left to break. I gasped as she flung me against The Veil once more.

"Eyes open, wits sharp," Mordra hissed, nothing but a voice among the endless forest I found myself in.

I hunted for Roxy between the stillness of the Damned Forest, the bone white bark of the trees creating pockets of utter darkness between them, the black leafed canopy overhead impossible to see beyond.

"Roxy?!" I yelled, taking a step forward and something caught on the toe of my boot.

I crouched down, inspecting the ruby necklace which lay there on the utterly barren earth, the only spot of colour in this entire place.

Something felt different here, The Veil seeming thinner than ever before. The power of the winter solstice mixing with the dark presence of the cursed trees lured me towards life in a way that felt so easily surmountable, yet something still rooted me in death.

The screams of a child set a chill racing down my spine and I jerked around, looking through the woodland for any sign of them, or of my wife whose presence seemed shrouded in shadow.

I tried to take a step, but I couldn't move beyond the ruby pendant, its power anchoring me here while those screams rattled on.

I cursed, lurching back towards Mordra's cavern, whirling on her where she perched on the tip of her boulder once more.

"Enough with these games. I came here for an answer. I fought off the shackles of death and accepted what I am here and now. So tell me how I return."

Mordra sighed, waving a hand. I found myself stumbling as I pressed against The Veil once more, my friends and family appearing before me one after another, various perils closing in on them.

"The door opens for one thing only," Mordra whispered. "And your power swells for the love of those you cherish."

"So what?" I barked.

"Ether is a balance. A push and a pull. A transaction. So what do all transactions require?" she purred, her fingers trailing down my cheek as she appeared before me, those hollow eyes scouring my soul.

"Payment," I breathed, an icy sensation dripping through my veins.

The Damned Forest appeared around me again, my breath catching in my lungs as I found Roxy there, racing for me as fast as she could run, panic blazing in her eyes as something hounded her steps from behind.

I couldn't make sense of what it was, its shape twisting and flickering between the trunks of the trees which separated her from it, but its malignance tainted the air itself as it gave chase.

"Run!" I bellowed, reaching for my wife. Still, she sprinted for me, her eyes on the ruby pendant which still lay in the dirt at my feet.

I dropped to my knees once more, placing my hand over it, lending it what power I could, and urging her closer as that terrible force closed in. The truth of Mordra's words were sinking into me, the pain of their truth shattering every last drop of hope I'd been clinging to. I felt Roxy closer than I had since the moment of my death, The Veil so thin here I could almost believe it didn't exist at all.

She threw herself towards me, snatching the ruby pendant from the ground, hurrying to fasten it around her throat, our connection deepening as she did.

My presence thickened as that connection to her was restored, my power flooding across the divide between realms like a breath of wind stirring the air around her.

I reached for her, running my hand down her arm, taking hold of her wrist and tightening my grip. I willed her to feel it, willed her to realise what was racing ever closer at her back.

She shut her eyes, leaning into me like she could feel me there, the seconds slipping past while she wasted them on a man who was already dead and gone.

"Come on, Roxy," I growled, using my power to try and tug on her arm, encouraging her to move.

"*Run*," I hissed.

Her eyes snapped open, and she spun around, whipping her sword from her sheath just as the horrors behind her converged, becoming a young girl who just had to be Roxy herself.

The child version of my wife stood between two of the towering trunks, a bright scar ringing her throat, blood dripping down to stain her white nightgown.

"You killed him," the girl snarled in accusation. "You were the reason he fought in that battle. You were the reason he was so desperate to defeat his father. He'd been planning to challenge him long before you came and uprooted his entire life. He'd been waiting until he was ready to win. You made him strike too soon. You. Killed. Him."

"No," I snapped, reaching for Roxy again, willing her to feel the lies in those words, to know the truth. Nothing would have kept me from that battle, nothing would have changed this fate. It was on me, not her.

Roxy began to tremble, those words cutting her deeply as she failed to see the truth of it.

"I didn't kill him," she whispered raising her sword slowly again and pride swelled within me as she fought off the despair and came out swinging like always. "But I will keep my promise to avenge him."

The thing that appeared as a girl widened her eyes the second Roxy charged her, her arms widening, almost accepting of this end. She did nothing to avoid Roxy's blade which pierced her heart, a crack resounding throughout the entire forest as her body split and sundered.

Roxy jerked her blade back, watching as the scars on the child's skin began to glow with an inner light, the corners of her lips lifting at her demise.

Roxy threw a hand up to shield her face, the thing that appeared as a child exploding into blazing light, golden flames arcing from her before splitting apart and dispersing, fading into nothing and leaving us in the silence of the forest once more.

Roxy was panting, trembling, and clearly exhausted, but there was no sign of her slowing down as she raised her chin and began to hunt for her bag.

"You see it, don't you?" Mordra hissed in my ear. "How closely she tiptoes near death, how thin The Veil is around her, how easily you could reach across and pull-"

"No," I barked, the truth she'd been hiding becoming all too clear.

"So after swearing on all you were to return to the land of the living, you balk at the price which needs paying?" Mordra scoffed. "Love fades. It is only useful while it's potent. Took me too long to realise. I had none left who cared for me enough by the time I did. But you have her. Or if not her, so many others…"

I saw them again, the Heirs, my brother, Lance, everyone I cared for. I could *see* fates spiralling before them which offered death, and I could *see* how I might reach out and tug them closer to it, wedging my foot between the door which opened in The Veil as I did so, forcing it to part so that I might slip back through.

"It would take just one of their deaths in exchange for your soul's return to the land of the living," she purred.

"Never," I spat, swiping a hand which banished all of them from my view, expelling Mordra with them and leaving me in the Damned Forest with the warrior who I had taken for my bride.

Roxy closed her fist around the scar which bound her to the promise she'd made to change our fate, and the pain that rose in me at the motion was more than I could bear.

"I'm coming," she told me, somehow knowing I was close, as she strode to the tree she'd been using for the next part of her plan and summoned fire to ignite on her fingertip.

"Roxy," I breathed, that word a broken plea.

I moved up beside her, trying to take her hand, but she didn't feel me there anymore, her focus too fixed on her destination, the truth of what lay before her too hard to accept.

The tree screamed as she used her flames to carve the Elemental symbol for water into its bark followed by a flame and a Dragon. The one greatest desire of her heart.

It broke me to know that. That I had her heart so completely in my grasp and that our time together had been so painfully short.

My lips parted on all the things I wanted to say to her, on all the reasons why she should stop heading down this path, on warnings over what I'd learned, the truth of it too hard to ignore.

The price of a life was a death. And perhaps I could have chosen that path if I could have chosen a soul worthy of death to take my place. But to pick between the ones I loved? To use the power of their love and grief for me to force a trade in our places? It was an impossible choice, and one I could never even consider making. I wouldn't be the man she'd fallen in love with if I was capable of that. But not being capable of it meant this divide between us was eternal for however long she had in the living realm.

What if Radcliff was right? What if she found love with another? What would become of me if I was forced to watch that unfold? Or would it be worse if she never did? If her love for me never faded and she was in this pain for the rest of her life instead?

A rumble started up in the ground beneath our feet the moment Roxy slit the scar on her palm open with her dagger, blood trickling between her fingers as she called on ether and it rose to her summons.

The power she invoked was incredible, stirring the essence of the world, offering up her own blood in payment for its cooperation.

Roxy slammed her bloody palm against the bone white trunk of the still screaming tree, and the power which erupted from her sent a shockwave tumbling out into the forest as the tree was ripped from the ground.

I threw all that I was around Roxy, trying to protect her from the vile magic of the damned tree as it fell, its screams piercing the air. A groan loud enough to be heard for miles around followed before the echoing boom of it crashing to the forest floor consumed all else.

The tree's screams cut off sharply and Roxy threw her arms up to shield her face. The curse which had been bound to it shattered, the ether vibrating with the power of its end.

Roxy stood on the smooth bark of the fallen tree trunk, her Bridge to the Beyond stretching out ahead of her, leading her towards me. She was coming. She was going to walk into death and there was no stopping her, the force of her power too immense for even the stars to refuse.

"I'll be waiting, baby," I swore to her, pain scoring through my chest. Because I knew I wouldn't be waiting to return to her anymore. I couldn't pay the price required to do so, no matter how desperately I wished I could. So I would simply wait for her to come to me then I would give her the goodbye she deserved.

Roxy started walking, her gaze fixed ahead as whispers started up either side of the tree, the passage she'd created between the realms making her vulnerable to all manner of foul things, but she never once looked their way.

I stayed in her shadow, snarling at any who moved too close to her, warning them off with fire and fury. Then I hounded her closer to death, knowing she would find a way to cross over, but that I had no way to cross back.

"A soul for a soul," Mordra urged, her voice my bane.

"I won't," I growled.

"Then you shall be cursed just like the rest of us," she spat furiously. "There is only one way to truly cross The Veil and that is in death. All other passages are fleeting, ghosts at best, no bodies to house them. It all awaits you and yet you scorn the gift you might claim."

"I scorn nothing but the stars," I replied bitterly. "And you're no better than them."

HAIL

CHAPTER TWENTY SIX

Merissa and I watched on while Gwendalina fought with the Shadow Beast hand to hand in the palace armoury, no magic to aid her. The father in me wanted to intervene, my fear for her so great that it burned, but another part of me wanted to watch her ferocity spill out in furious swipes of her mother's sword. She had been caged too long, a wild creature all of her own, chained and kept subdued, but now she was free it was a sight to behold.

Lance was in a furious battle with Tharix, the monstrous Acrux heir taking hits time and again, only to heal with the power of the shadows that lived in his flesh.

Gwendalina was climbing the rack of weapons on the far wall to escape the powerful jaws of the Shadow Beast and Merissa stayed close to her, calling out in encouragement. "Strike for the heart! Cut it down – yes!" she cried as our daughter struck a blow against the beast and I hollered in encouragement.

Lance was in a bind, his back against the wall and Azriel kept close to him, watching every move he made. Tharix closed in, the heinous creature on a hunt for blood, but Lance was putting up one hell of a battle. It almost felt like blood was thundering through my veins in response to the fight, the old instinct in me for war coming back in full force. What I'd give to fight at Lance and my daughter's sides now, casting blows of my own and bathing in the victory of bloodshed. It was a thrill like no other, and even though they were in peril here in the fray, their Fae nature was thriving, and I knew them capable of defeating their enemies. They had suffered long enough, and had been waiting for this very moment to unleash their fury over their imprisonment.

"Go on, son!" I roared to Lance. "Give him hell!"

"Son?" Azriel hooked an eyebrow up at me.

"He is that to me, Azriel," I said fiercely and he moved closer, grasping my arm.

"And Gwendalina is a daughter to me," he said, the two of us sharing a brief smile before we turned back to watch the fight.

Lance blasted the shadowy form of Tharix away from him with a torrent of air, and the monster shifted back into his corporeal form, landing on a wooden table across the room.

Lance turned his attention to the weapons hanging across the walls in racks, raising his hand to summon one to him. I shoved my power into his own, making him select my own sword and Azriel gave me a surprised look. By the stars, I had missed that blade, the metal obsidian, a twin to the white sword that had belonged to Merissa and was now in our daughter's possession. We had forged these blades ourselves in the Mountain of Ignolia with the help of the most famed blacksmith in the land. They were imbued with our power, touched by the magic of our Order gifts too, and my chest swelled at the sight of Lance taking mine into his hand.

"You never even let *me* wield that blade," Azriel pointed out and I shrugged, tossing him a grin.

"Touch the Hydra constellation to ignite the fire," I called to Lance, and as if he had heard me, he did just that, purple fire bursting to life along its edge.

I groaned with longing to wield that blade just once more, possessiveness rising in me. But if it had to be wielded by other hands, Lance would have been high on my list.

"Cast him to nothing," I encouraged, smiling in a mirror of Lance's sinister grin.

"You'd better be watching, sir. Because this fight is for the Vegas," Lance said, making my heart lurch, those words meant for me. He knew I was here, or at least suspected it and I moved to stand at his back, placing my hand on his shoulder to lend him what power I could.

"Oh, I'm watching alright, good choice," I said with a dark laugh and Azriel moved to lend him power too, gazing at me with a soppy ass look. "Now remind me why the stars selected you as a match for my daughter."

"Go on, Lancelot!" Azriel bayed.

Lance charged into the fight with a keen hunger, but I only managed to watch a couple of blows land before time swept me up and threw me forward into it, leaving Azriel with Lance.

A blur of images swirled around me of Gwendalina fighting the Shadow Beast out in a corridor above the armoury, her bravery boundless in her feat to destroy the monster that had kept her captive so long. I cheered her on alongside my wife, and when she plunged Merissa's sword deep into the creature's chest, I stood in awe of my daughter and her victory.

Before I could pause to question what might happen next, magic poured from the near-dead beast, and suddenly Gwendalina's Elements were returned to her in an explosion of power that knocked her from her feet.

"She's done it," Merissa said, emotion thick in her words.

I moved to my wife, wrapping an arm around her, feeling sparks of my daughter's supreme power make it here to us to dance against our skin.

When a beautiful Phoenix bird flew from that gaping wound in the Shadow Beast's chest, and swept down into Gwendalina's body, I all but broke with the joy of it. Her Order was restored, the power in her veins so tumultuous that the Palace of Souls was trembling with it.

When she regained her feet, she moved to finish the Shadow Beast and I urged her on, slinking closer at her back.

"Strike true, my little darling," I growled.

But instead, Gwendalina noticed a collar of shadow bound around its neck and cut it loose.

"It was Lavinia's prisoner too," Merissa gasped in realisation.

"It is a monster," I said in disbelief. "Kill it while you have the chance, Gwendalina!"

Time lurched again, throwing us into another room entirely and we arrived with Gabriel in the Royal Seer's Chamber. Lance and Darcy ran to free him, and I urged them on, hoping beyond all hope that they could escape Lionel and Lavinia's clutches this very day. Azriel materialised, following his son here and Merissa quickly told him of how Gwendalina had restored her power, leaving him speechless with happiness.

Gabriel reached up and clasped Gwendalina's cheek, a smile lifting his lips and knowledge filling his gaze. "You did it."

"She did," Merissa sighed, and her relief brought a fresh smile to my lips.

"I did it," Gwendalina confirmed with a grin, pulling Gabriel to his feet. "And now we've gotta go."

"Yes, and you must make haste now," I growled.

"No detours, just get out of here," Azriel urged.

The Shadow Beast bounded into view and grunted in greeting, making a curse leave me.

"By the fucking stars," Gabriel breathed as Lance moved to break him out of his magic restraining cuffs.

"It's okay. He's on our side now. I think," Gwendalina said, and dammit the girl had always had a fondness for wild creatures. I had taken the twins to the Celestia Zoo once and she'd been crying like the hounds of death were coming for her. She had only stopped when she'd caught the eye of the biggest, scariest beast in that place with so many claws and fangs, it could have murdered her in a hundred different ways, but she sat in my arms cooing at it like it was a puppy. "Or maybe it's a girl. I don't really know," my daughter said.

"It's not coming with us," Lance muttered, and Gwendalina arched a brow at him.

"Firstly, do not boss her around," I growled. "Secondly, you have a point."

"It seems friendly enough," Merissa said, moving closer to it and reaching out to pet its side despite the fact it couldn't feel her.

"It is," Gwendalina said simply and Azriel chuckled, clearly not disturbed by the idea of them adopting the thing. I was hardly surprised, considering he had found the darkest of creatures fascinating in life.

They argued on and the Shadow Beast turned to smoke, though now it was a pale grey colour instead of inky dark, and it moved to hover by Gwendalina's shoulder.

"No," Lance growled.

"Yes," she retorted, and Gabriel got up, stepping between them.

"Ah, Gabriel will see sense," I said.

"This really isn't the time for marital bickering," he warned.

"It's not marital if we're not married," Gwendalina pointed out.

"We will be married," Lance said in a growl, and Merissa let out a small squeal while Azriel shot her widest grin.

"Oh Hail! Think of the wedding. The bridesmaids all in deepest blue, an ice sculpture in the shape of a Phoenix," Merissa gushed.

"They could hire a jazz band," Azriel said excitedly, and I gave both of them a dry look.

"Says who?" Gwendalina balked.

"She clearly doesn't want to be married," I said.

"Says me," Lance snapped and I rounded on him.

"Watch your tone, boy," I snarled.

"I will wed you the moment this war is over," Lance said, and I had a mind to clip him around the ear.

"He's possessive. Now who does that remind me of?" Merissa sung and Azriel nodded, looking at me.

"Oh you will, will you?" Gwendalina narrowed her eyes at Lance. "We're already mated, why would we get married too?"

"Again," Gabriel cut in. "Really not the time. We need to go."

Time shivered and we found ourselves following them out of the Royal Seer's chamber.

"What will their wedding song be, do you think?" Merissa whispered to me.

"He hasn't even proposed to her," I scoffed. "There will be no wedding if she does not wish it. Besides, he hasn't asked our permission."

"And how is he meant to ask the permission of two dead Fae?" Merissa asked dryly. "Honestly Hail, you were just as uppity over this when Roxanya married Darius."

"Don't remind me," I muttered. "Or I will think twice on letting that go. I would like to think that Lance would at least make an effort. Hold a séance perhaps."

"You're ridiculous," Merissa said.

Lance spoke in a low voice to Gwendalina. "You *will* marry me."

"You know, people usually ask someone if they want to marry them, not just command it," she whispered.

"You're already mated to me by the stars, what's there to ask?" Lance demanded.

"Just because we're mated doesn't mean you get to skip a proposal." Gwendalina shot him a sharp look and I smirked. *Give him hell, little darling.* "So you'd better ask really, really nicely the next time you bring this up. And I am making no promises that I'll say yes."

"Or that I'll agree to it," Gabriel tossed back over his shoulder, and I barked a laugh.

"Good boy," I said.

"He's so protective of his sisters." Merissa smiled serenely, though apparently me being protective made me ridiculous.

"And since when do I have to ask your permission?" Lance asked in shock, and I revelled in that look while Azriel chuckled, simply enjoying the back and forth.

"I second that question," Gwendalina called to him.

"Since I'm your brother, it's my duty to look out for you," Gabriel replied, taking a sharp left down a short hallway and they hurried after him with us in their stead.

Gwendalina scoffed.

"Darius didn't ask your permission to marry Tory," Lance said.

"That boy doesn't know the meaning of respect, that's why," I muttered.

"I don't recall you asking my father for my hand in marriage. Actually, I recall you kidnapping me to Solaria," Merissa said, shooting me a look and I shrugged innocently. "All this asking is outdated anyway, I say. It's down to Gwendalina whether she wishes to marry him or not, and the only person Lance need ask is her."

"I know. And I'll be taking it up with him beyond the Veil, but as we're currently on two different planes, and I don't plan on dying anytime soon, he'll have to wait for the ass kicking I plan on presenting him with in the afterlife," Gabriel said to Lance. "You, however, don't get to escape me via death, so you'd better be nice as pie to me if you're determined to marry my sister."

"Ha." I beamed at his stance on the matter, then time shifted, and my smile died a quick death at what I found waiting for us.

Gwendalina was in a furious battle with Lavinia, while Lance and Gabriel were locked in a fight with too many Nymphs to count, and Azriel kept with his son, calling to him in fear. Merissa and I flitted between watching our daughter and our son, the two of them separated and in so much danger it left me desperate and terrified once more.

Gwendalina fought with a skill that far outmatched Lavinia, but the power of the shadows was so great, she was a deadly opponent indeed.

My soul flashed into view before Gabriel while Merissa stayed with our daughter, and I spotted Lance hurtling between the trees, driving my sword into the hearts of countless Nymphs.

"Use the Hydra power in the sword!" I bellowed to him.

"He does not know how," Azriel said anxiously.

Gabriel spread his wings, flying after Lance while Azriel and I took chase, keeping up with him by simply willing it to be so.

"Go on, Gabriel!" I cried, and I swear those words crossed the boundary to reach him, his jaw tightening with determination.

"Orio!" Gabriel called, and Lance glanced over as he slowed to drive his sword between the shoulder blades of a Nymph.

It turned to ash before him and my son landed at his side, catching his breath and bracing his hand on Lance's shoulder. But lingering there for even that small measure of time allowed too many Nymphs to surround them, the rattles in their chests locking down their magic.

"Hurry," Azriel begged in fear.

"Give that to me." Gabriel snatched the sword from Lance's grip.

Lance bared his fangs, turning to our enemies, ready to rip their throats out with nothing but his teeth.

"Stay close," Gabriel warned.

"Ignite the Hydra fire within," I demanded. "You must move it just so, let The Sight show you how."

"Come on, come on," Azriel urged.

Time flickered and Gabriel's eyes flashed with knowledge as we made it back to him. He twisted the sword through the air in the right movement and I hollered my encouragement as purple fire raced down the length of it in a spiral.

"Yes!" Azriel shouted.

Time jolted again, but I clung to Gabriel, standing next to him, and turning my gaze on his enemies. "Destroy them," I breathed.

Purple fire exploded away from the sword in every direction, and Gabriel yanked Lance against his side to make sure it didn't hurt him. The tornado of savage flames carved through their enemies, turning the first rows of them to soot while the others ran for their lives, screeches of terror rising into the air all around us.

"Watch over them, I must go to my daughter," I said.

"Of course," Azriel vowed.

With their win secured, I turned my mind to Gwendalina, letting my soul dart away to join Merissa's.

Gwendalina had Lavinia trapped on a hill beside the palace in a flaming orb of Phoenix fire. The Shadow Princess screamed from within, and my daughter spoke the words of a powerful spell, the magic of it cracking through the air like a whip.

"She's cutting her off from the shadows," Merissa told me, her eyes bright with hope. "Are Gabriel and Lance well?"

"For now," I said, watching Gwendalina in reverence.

She and Roxanya were so much more powerful than even I could ever have claimed to be. It rattled the foundations of the kingdom. And if they could defeat the monsters who had to play dirty to get the upper hand in this war, then it would change the whole world. I did not want them on the throne simply because they were of my blood; they had earned it, had proven themselves worthy of it time and again. There were no truer queens than them.

Time shuddered and a horrid, shrieking roar pierced the air as Tharix joined the fight in his Dragon form, chasing after Gabriel and Lance. I tried to get closer to Gabriel, but time jolted once more and he and Lance burst from the trees, riding on the back of the Shadow Beast, leaving me speechless.

"Do you wish she had killed it now?" Merissa asked and I blew out a breath, unsure what to think.

Tharix tore after them in the sky, black wings descending.

"Adiuro te. Fores claudo. Adiuro te. Fores claudo," Gwendalina spoke her spell louder, the power building and snapping through the atmosphere, and I swear the hairs raised on my arms as the colossal magic swept around us.

"*No*," Lavinia sobbed from within that sphere of fire, the spell binding itself to her and shutting her off from all shadows which were not already contained within her flesh.

"Finish her," Merissa urged, eyes darkening with the oncoming death of the Shadow Princess, and hope blossomed within me at the prospect. "Make her suffer."

A Dragon's roar sounded off in the distance, and I turned to look towards the gates of the Palace of Souls, a glint of jade green scales in the distance telling me all I needed to know. Lionel and his bonded men had returned.

"Fuck," I spat. "They have to go. Now!"

"Darcy!" Lance's voice cut through the air.

The Shadow Beast bounded up the hill toward her with Lance and Gabriel on its back, and Gwendalina's lips parted in surprise. I could see another soul sitting astride that beast too, Azriel Orion behind his son, his expression a mixture of wonderment and concern.

Tharix was in their wake, gliding along on dark wings with shadows flourishing from his mouth. Gwendalina raised a hand to fight and time skipped, bouncing us along and making me cry out in alarm.

We had to get back. We couldn't leave them now.

When we managed to return, the Shadow Princess was gone along with Tharix, and a hoard of Nymphs were charging from the trees towards our family where Gwendalina sat on the Shadow Beast in front of her brother.

"The Dragons are here," Gabriel gasped. "Go!"

Gwendalina used a whip of air to summon the dagger Lavinia had dropped on the ground, her thumb brushing the crimson garnet gemstone in its hilt before she tucked it into her waistband, cutting a hole in her shorts so the blade stuck through. I knew that blade; Merissa had gifted it to me long ago, and only now did I consider the possible value in the gemstone gleaming in its hilt. It had always felt so powerful, yet never once had I considered it might be a Guild Stone until now.

"Get to the perimeter, turn the Shadow Beast around," Lance demanded.

"There's no time," Gwendalina said decisively, turning the Shadow Beast towards the palace where two ornate silver doors stood.

"You need to open them!" Azriel called to us.

Merissa ran to the doors and I chased after her as fast as I could move.

We threw our power against them, forcing the palace to bend to our will. They flew wide and the moment our loved ones were through, we locked them tight to buy them more time.

The Shadow Beast carried them down the hallways and we raced along beside them, gliding along just as fast and slamming the window shutters closed as we went. It was all we could do to keep them safe, and I swear the palace wanted that too, the whole place groaning and answering the call of our power but most of all Gwendalina's, the shutters and doors and windows locking down across the entirety of the place. My daughter's strength called out to us, bolstering our own power. The palace was alive with it, making the walls hum and buzz, this ancient place relishing the chance to worship her.

"That's it," Azriel cried, lending us his own power as it spilled from his soul into the walls.

They took a passage in the direction of Lionel's bedchamber – which was just a guest room thanks to the palace, my wife and I keeping him firmly out of mine and Merissa's rooms.

With the Nymphs left far behind and their magic returned, Gabriel and Lance took a moment to heal themselves, my son's wing cracking as the break in it fixed and Merissa hissed between her teeth at the thought of the pain it must have caused him.

Gabriel healed Gwendalina next as she urged the Shadow Beast onward.

A clamour of Dragon roars sounded beyond the building, and as the beast reached the next landing, a flash of green scales beyond the vast window ahead made my heart judder.

Gwendalina cast an air shield just as the window shattered and Merissa and I sped forward, forcing the shutters to slam tight to keep him out. Magic rumbled through the palace walls, securing those shutters with a power that would only answer the call of my daughter now, and Lionel roared in anger as he found himself unable to break through.

They took another stairway, climbing ever higher and time threw Merissa, Azriel and I forward once more. The palace was angry now, like it was a beast of its own, and I swear Gwendalina had brought on a wrath in it that would not allow Lionel back between its walls. The magic was ancient and so thick in the air, it was like feeling the touch of my ancestors at my back, my power merging with theirs and making it mine to command.

"You shall not return to this palace, Lionel Acrux!" I bellowed, the words ricocheting through the walls.

They made it to Lionel's bedchamber, and Merissa threw the door wide for them, the Shadow Beast moving so fast that it crashed into the four-poster bed, breaking it to pieces and sending the three of them flying from its back, while Azriel landed lightly on his feet, unaffected by their fall.

Gwendalina scrambled upright, immediately hunting through Lionel's things.

"Stardust," she called to the others and Lance nodded, shooting around the room with his speed and throwing every drawer out until he stopped before her again with a pouch in his hand and a grin on his lips.

369

"Why didn't you say so sooner, beautiful?" Lance said.

"Show off," Azriel smirked.

Gwendalina cracked a laugh, but it was lost as Lionel collided with the side of the building, his talons tearing through the stone wall so the whole structure shuddered.

"Get off of my palace, asshole," I cursed, but more Dragons threw themselves against the walls to try and gain entry.

The palace groaned and I felt another blast of power roll through it, lending my strength to it too. One glimpse out the window showed Lionel's servants and prisoners alike being tossed out of windows here, there, and everywhere by the magic of the palace. My soul quivered with the power of it all, starting to feel drained by how much of myself I'd given, and as I met Merissa's gaze, I could tell she was exhausted too.

"Just hold on," she demanded, and I nodded once.

"No force in this world will take me from them now. We will see them free this very day," I growled.

"They are so very close to freedom, I can taste it," Azriel breathed.

"Here!" Gabriel called, and I turned, finding him pointing to the wall. "There's a hidden passage, it will lead us to the roof," he said, his eyes glimmering with The Sight. "We have a chance to get to the wards above. But we have to go now."

Gwendalina opened the passage Gabriel had *seen* there without needing our help, looking back at the Shadow Beast.

"Come on, beastie. Do the smoke thing," she encouraged, and it quickly obeyed her, turning into a cloud of grey at her back.

"Remember it's dangerous," I called to her in concern, but she had clearly adopted the damn thing. And considering how it had helped them, perhaps she had made a decent choice, though it still worried me after I had witnessed the violence of that creature.

Time blurred, and suddenly we were in the sky, watching Gabriel and Gwendalina fly with the wings of their Orders while Lance was carried in Gabriel's arms. They were fleeing for the wards high above the palace, and Lionel was on the ground, blasted there by a recent attack while his bonded Dragons flew to avenge him.

"Faster!" Merissa screamed, our hands locking as we chased them from beneath.

"Keep going!" Azriel roared.

Gwendalina cut through the wards with a boom that splintered through the sky and Lance tossed the stardust over their heads as Lionel roared in utter fury below us.

The palace was locked up tight and before they disappeared, Gwendalina cast a flaming Phoenix bird out of her fire, sending it down to fly above the Palace of Souls, singing their victory and perching on the roof in a mark of defiance. Then they were gone, stolen away into the safe embrace of the stars and The Veil dragged us back.

The three of us cheered, hugging each other and I kissed Merissa between breaths.

"They made it," I said in utter relief, my feet landing in our rooms back in the Eternal Palace.

"I will go and tell Clara of their victory," Azriel said eagerly, disappearing in a flash.

Merissa leaned into me, and we stood in the wake of all that power, the exhaustion lessening quickly now that we were back where we belonged.

"Our children are so remarkable, I wish I could tell them so myself," Merissa whispered, and I kissed her forehead, not needing to say I felt the same, because she knew it to be true.

A tremor ran through the Eternal Palace, and I frowned as my mind turned to Roxanya, sensing something wasn't right even before I looked for her. I couldn't see her, couldn't find her at all in the living realm, my soul remaining firmly rooted here.

"What's going on?" Merissa murmured as she felt it too.

"*A savage flame draws closer,*" the stars whispered, something about the way they spoke making me think they might be startled. Though I had never once sensed emotion in the way they uttered things before now.

The whispers grew thicker, carrying everywhere across The Veil, but they spoke in a language too old for me to understand. The hiss and spit of their words was enough to tell me of their rage though.

Darius burst through the door, eyes wild. "Roxy is coming! She has made it to the ferryman, but she lives still. I need your help."

"How can this be?" I said, confounded, but then the air shivered and we were thrown into the grand hall in the Eternal Palace as if the stars had shoved us there themselves.

"*Mother and father of the flames, a doorway parts, the souls of the dead will rush as one to seek the land of the living. If they cannot be stopped, all shall fall,*" the stars hissed.

"And this our responsibility how?" I barked.

"*Your daughter breaks the laws of old, bends the rules long ago set in place by the Origin as she walks here not in death, but alive with her heart still beating. You must thwart her in her path. Stop her from stepping through The Veil. This is your duty, do not defy it.*"

371

"How has she done this?" Merissa questioned in dismay, but I held no answer for her.

"You must also hold the dead where they belong, or ruin shall come. A bodiless mass of hungry souls will unbalance what is so finely balanced."

"We can't let them get through to the living realm," Merissa said, her eyes flickering in a way that said the stars had just shown her something terrible. I felt the stars turn their attention elsewhere, no longer focused on us while they no doubt looked upon Roxanya.

"Roxy is going to be here any moment," Darius said urgently. "She wishes to try and break me out of death and return me to life, but I followed that path and learned the truth of it. For me to live again, someone I love must die, and I will never choose that fate."

I looked to Merissa in shock then back to Darius. "Then what is it you wish for now?"

"A moment, that is all. To speak with her and tell her I cannot return with her. And to…give her the goodbye we never got in life," he said thickly, heartbreak tearing through his eyes.

"Oh Darius," Merissa croaked. "I'm so sorry. Of course we will buy you that moment."

I gripped his arm, our decision made. "You *will* speak with her. Remain here and we shall forge a path to bring her to you."

"You'll be defying the stars' orders," Darius reminded me darkly.

"I am the Savage King. No one gives me orders."

"What's happening?" Radcliff appeared alongside Catalina and Hamish.

"Is Gabriel well?" Marcel murmured, arriving too in a glimmer of light, his form seeming far less corporeal than the last time I had seen him.

"He is, and he needs your help Marcel," Merissa said urgently. "All of our help."

"One of my daughters has made a passage here like the stubborn girl she is," I told them all. "A door to the living will open. The dead will rush for it, and the entire world shall be unbalanced if we do not stop them."

"Will your daughter get back to the living?" Marcel asked in concern.

"She will," Darius answered. "I will make sure of it."

"Then perhaps she might tell Gabriel to think of me from time to time?" Marcel asked imploringly.

"It's not the time for this," I barked, looking to Darius and placing a hand on his shoulder, unsure what might happen next, only knowing that now was the time to speak any unspoken words between us. "Darius…I shed you of the Acrux name."

"Already happened," he said. "When I married your-"

"I shed you of the Acrux name," I repeated louder. "I am proud to call you a Vega."

His next retort died on his lips, and I gave him a tight smile. "Say hello to my daughter from me."

"And make sure she gets home safe," Merissa demanded, moving forward to embrace Darius and place a kiss on his cheek. "We are so very proud to have you in our family. She has chosen well."

"Now you're just blowing smoke up his ass," Radcliff commented.

"He has enough smoke to blow up his own ass," I said, but Darius didn't seem to be listening, a heaviness hanging over him that tugged at my heart.

I frowned, moving closer to him. "I am sorry you could not find a path back to life."

"We would have given anything to see you return to her," Merissa added, sadness burning in her eyes.

"Thank you for...trying to help me," Darius said to her, hanging his head in desolation.

Catalina ran forward to hug him, kissing his temple, his forehead, his hair.

"Mom," Darius complained, though he didn't pull away.

"Just be careful," she fussed.

"I will," he vowed.

"I love you more than the moon and the stars combined," she said.

"You were a dastardly duck upon our meeting, now you've shed your feathers, and oh how jolly proud I am to see the great Fae you have become," Hamish gushed, knocking his knuckles against Darius's cheek. "Revel in your moment with your beloved quail, then return to us as swiftly as a goose with its tail on fire."

"I will." Darius squeezed Hamish's arm.

The Eternal Palace trembled, and the stars focused on us all again, sweeping us away and leaving Darius behind before we could say more. I was deposited in a hazy golden field, nothing here but mist and too-still grass. The sky above was dark, the stars glittering angrily from above.

More souls glittered into existence; Azriel, Serenity, and Florence.

"What ho?" Florence gasped. "The stars have wangled a worm in my ears, speaking of a dastardly door. They wish for me to don my armour and fight like a fair lady!"

"Then you shall, dear Florry. We shall fight together like peas born in a pod." Hamish nodded to us all and gleaming golden armour fell over us, cladding tight to my chest, a helmet slamming down on my head.

"Fucking stars." I looked up at them but as a glittering golden sword appeared in my hand, I felt slightly less angry at them.

"Each strike cast by the celestial swords will make a soul fall into slumber," the stars hissed to us all. *"Strike many. Strike all."*

More chosen souls appeared around us, Felisia and her pride along with old kings, queens, ancient warriors and hundreds of other souls the stars apparently deemed trustworthy in taking up this fight.

Radcliff spun his sword in his grip, shooting me a fierce look. "Good to be back in the game, eh?"

Azriel moved to join me, eyes alight. "I have waited many years to fight alongside you again, Hail."

"And you, dear friend." I smiled, looking to my wife, taking in the way the armour hugged her curves and her eyes lit with a ruthless hunger for the fight. The stars were stoking the flames of our hearts, wanting us to want this. But I didn't need their encouragement. I would fight as a Fae in the company of his kin, for family and the world we had long left behind.

The moment Roxanya arrived here, I would fight for her to have time with Darius too, forgoing the commands of the stars. One wordless look with Merissa told me she was ready to forge a path for her the second we got the chance, but we did not dare voice our plan again while the stars watched us so closely.

A dark Pegasus came galloping across the field with Reth and Clara Orion riding it, a line of mares following at their back. Armour clad them just like ours and the Pegasus reared up before us in a show of glitter and bravado before planting its hooves.

"A door opens as it once did long ago!" Reth yelled. "Follow my lead. And keep your eyes from the gateway to the living once it parts. Resist its call, it is stronger than you can ever imagine."

"You're not in charge here," I barked, and he turned a smile on me.

"Oh, but Savage King, I am the man who almost lived," he said like that was supposed to mean something, then he cried, "Yah!" and charged away down the line of warriors.

"She's almost here," Merissa exhaled and a gasp left me at the tumultuous power that roared at my back.

As one, we turned to look, the air peeling apart behind us and revealing a rip right through the atmosphere, creating a gateway between worlds. Blinding light poured from that gateway and its call was so potent, I nearly dropped my sword and ran for its beckoning glow, but Merissa caught my hand, squeezing and reminding me where my feet belonged.

"You and I have fought many fights together," she said as I met her gaze, my love for her so fierce that the temptation at my back dwindled to nothing. "Let us fight this one for all those we left behind."

There was nothing for me beyond that door anymore, no body awaiting my soul, no place for me to reclaim. If I crossed through, I didn't know what I would become but I knew I could never again be what I once was.

The ground quaked and I dragged my attention away from the captivating creature before me, finding the entire horizon blazing with the shimmer of thousands of souls. They came as a blur, souls colliding with other souls in their haste to reach that door and it took everything I had to ignore the call of it too.

"Ready?!" I bellowed to the warriors around me.

"Ready, sire!" Hamish cried, and the answer was echoed by the rest of them. "Into the baked blundercake we go!"

"We'll buy them their moment the second she arrives," Merissa murmured to me.

I nodded, and as one we moved, running to meet our enemies, swords raised and battle cries tearing from our throats.

The first souls spilled against us, and I swung my sword, casting five of them into slumber at once, their souls sparking away to some unknown palace within The Veil. Azriel took down four more and Merissa's wings burst to life as she took off, slicing the sword through the crowd and taking out a whole hoard of desperate souls in one go.

My Hydra bellowed, descending from the dark sky above and starlight ran over it before fire billowed from its jaws. It was no longer purple as it should have been, but purest gold, not harming the swathes of souls it seized, but sending them all into a star-bound sleep.

Florence, swung her sword in a wide circle and she spun with it, spinning and spinning like a tornado as she took out soul after soul with her mildly crazy yet entirely effective attack.

Marcel's form seemed more solid as he fought with renewed purpose, flying after Merissa as they carved down the souls in droves.

"Radcliff – summon your Dragon!" I yelled, turning to look for him.

My gut lurched as I found him facing away from the battle, sword loose in his grip as he stared at the gateway to the living.

"Radcliff!" I bellowed, slashing my sword through another line of souls.

He started walking, feet dragging at first then moving faster, his sword slipping from his fingers entirely.

I cursed, turning from the fight and sprinting after him as he made a bid for the door.

"Radcliff – stop!" I roared.

"Just one more day," he cried. "Or a week perhaps. A month even. I never had long enough there; I'm owed it!"

I ran faster, powering towards him, reminded of my Pitball days as I prepared to take him down.

He was a fast motherfucker, but I was gaining on him. He put on a burst of speed, hand outstretched, not looking back as the glow of the doorway lit him in purest white light.

I slammed into him, the two of us rolling across the grass before I managed to pin him beneath me. Then I slapped him across the face, and he blinked hard.

"You do not get another chance at life," I growled.

"It was seized from me too soon - I never got to leave my mark like you did!" he bellowed, fighting me, and I shoved my weight down on him, but he was damn large and his fist crashed into my side.

I grabbed his face in my hands, forcing him to look me in the eye. "We are lost men. Life is not ours to claim. But you can make your mark here." I forced him to look at the surge of souls, the endless tide of them slamming into the line of warriors. Some were slipping past the line, and Merissa swept down on them fast, swiping her sword through their souls.

"We need you. Your Dragon could give us the upper hand," I implored. "You can be the hero of the living world, even if they never learn of what you did here this day. But you must make the choice, Radcliff."

He glanced towards the door, a groan of longing leaving him.

"I feel it too," I swore. "I want to go back there more than you can ever imagine. My family has lived their lives without me, and I wish every day for more time with them. But we do not belong out there, dear friend."

His throat bobbed and slowly, agonisingly, he pulled his gaze from it.

His Dragon bellowed in the heavens and came diving from the sky. Its fire was touched by starlight as it opened its jaws and let all hell loose on the souls, scattering them from this field and sending them away to sleep.

I shoved to my feet, pulling him after me and clapping him bracingly on the shoulder. Together, we ran back to the fight and Radcliff picked up his sword before launching himself into the fray.

I hefted my own blade higher, preparing to re-join the battle, but then my gaze hooked on a figure appearing within the light of the holy door across the field. And I knew in my heart it was Roxanya. Just steps away from making it beyond The Veil.

"Merissa!" I bellowed, and she landed beside me in the next moment, gazing towards our daughter as the battle raged on at our backs.

"I want to go to her," I said in pain, taking a step forward. "Just for a moment."

Merissa stepped after me. "I want that too, Hail, more than anything. But the stars won't allow this for long, and she may only have time enough to spend with one Fae here. It should be with Darius."

I growled, knowing it to be so and my Hydra roared in the sky at the pain that truth caused me.

"Then let us forge a path for her that the stars cannot touch," I breathed, our hands interlinking as always.

Our power burst from us, tearing away in a flare of golden light that collied with the door and started threading a path for our daughter. It was a tunnel built of love and light, and the moment she stepped into it, the stars screamed, and the ground bucked beneath us.

I gripped Merissa's hand tighter, watching as Roxanya travelled along the path we built for her, taking her all the way up into the sky and on towards the Eternal Palace where her true love awaited her.

Tears glinted on Merissa's cheeks and dripped to the ground, and I realised one had escaped me too. Our pain bound with our love, and no matter how deeply this angered the stars, they didn't come for us. Our magic was too great, our love too pure. But it was more than that, it was our sacrifice that truly kept them at bay. Our vow not to go to our daughter ourselves, and we paid the price of this act against the stars in the terrible ache that burned deep through our chests. We were one in that moment, Merissa and I, two parents making an atonement to the stars in our suffering, which could not be denied by them or any other.

The two of us turned to take up our places in the battle once more, to keep these souls away from the door and the passage we had made for our daughter.

Whatever Roxanya had done to reach this place, I prayed it had not cost her too much. But I knew The Veil would not get its chance to seize her yet, because Darius Vega would not let it be so.

DARIUS

CHAPTER TWENTY SEVEN

My soul shook as that beautiful, powerful, unstoppable mate of mine stepped through the barrier between life and death like it was any other door which she refused to leave closed.

She was here.

I reached out towards the table, a bottle of bourbon appearing between my fingers at the mere thought of it just before I poured myself a glass. My hand was trembling. I could feel every step she took within this place, like ripples in a pond signalling to all who dwelled here that something was coming. Something which didn't belong.

I'd helped clear that route for her, what power I still possessed currently pressing out of me, widening the way, keeping all other souls from her path while her parents, my mother, Hamish Grus, Azriel Orion and many others fought to keep them at bay too, helping to buy us this time.

Death was endless. The beauty of the Eternal Palace which I currently sat in beyond compare, the gilded streets outside it filled with countless bounties, and the Harrowed Gate past that marking the path to immortal pain.

Her footsteps drew closer, that bond between us yanking tight and drawing her to me, every strike of her boots on the marble floor like an echo of a heartbeat which thundered through my still chest.

The room I had been gifted here was beautiful, ornate, perfect, and yet there was little which really spoke of me the way I'd seen the rooms that others here did. I knew why. Because none of what mattered most to me was here. Nothing that made me feel alive resided in this place and no substitution of the reality which I'd lost would ever suffice.

I swallowed the rich mouthful of bourbon, the taste so reminiscent of Orion that I could almost see him standing there, a single eyebrow raised as if to say, "Aren't you going to get up?"

But I wasn't. I couldn't. The impossible had come to pass and she was striding straight towards me while I waited here like a coward, knowing I could never give her what she needed, never fulfil that yearning in her shattered heart.

I'd seen it all, every moment of suffering and heartache she had endured. I'd watched her become the creature she needed to be to make this journey, watched her bleed for every sacrifice and felt the agony she had taken upon herself in this pointless hunt.

But I'd been to The Room of Knowledge and looked out of the great orb, at the world through the eyes of the stars themselves, and I knew the truth when I beheld it there. I'd confirmed what Mordra had forced me to learn. It had destroyed me, that understanding had broken the last rays of hope I held for a solution to our situation, but I knew that this would break me more. To steal a moment in her arms, to hold her close and know how fleeting it would be. Because she couldn't stay here, no matter how selfish I wanted to be over that desire, I knew it couldn't be. She had a world waiting for her and a destiny so great that even the stars weren't certain of it yet. She'd been born to topple mountains and make the stars quake; she'd been born to ruin and rise.

I stood and looked into the shimmering wall behind me, my own personal view of all those I loved who remained among the living, the only way I'd ever be able to be with them again now.

Her footsteps drew closer like the ticking hands of a clock, and I swallowed the lump in my throat as I took a step towards the tall, double doors then stopped.

She was here. And that meant I was going to have to face the consequences of my failure in their fullest at last.

I couldn't make myself move from that spot, the sunshine beaming in from the windows, casting one side of my face in the light while the other was left in shadow. Like the two parts of my soul; the man I was when I was hers, burning bright and hot and full of life, and the one I had been in all the years before her, festering in a need for vengeance, drowning in my own failures.

I wasn't sure which of those men I had become in the end, though I supposed I would always be some mixture of both.

The doors flung themselves wide as she reached them, banging against the walls either side of the frame and leaving us there, staring at one another, tension crackling in the space which divided us just as it always had.

And of course, there was no smile there, of course she wasn't pleased to see me in that fairy tale perfect way that most people would have dreamed up for this scenario. She was fury given breath, her green eyes flashing with a deep and resounding rage. Her full lips pursed with anger as she took me in, standing before a chair which could have been a throne, waiting for her to come to me.

"Hello, Roxy," I said, my voice rough, my gaze drinking her in.

She was bloody and battered, the price of her passage into this place weighing heavily upon her shoulders, and the runes she had painted on her flesh glowing slightly, like they were warding off the press of death which ached to have a taste of her.

Those lips parted, a thousand kisses burning through my memory as I watched them, waiting, wondering if after all of it she might still think I was worthy of her.

No words escaped her, not a single one and I almost smiled at that. Roxanya Vega left speechless, no venom left to spit, no rage left to break from her. I thought I'd never see the day.

She took a step towards me, then another. Every inch she closed between us awakening that desperate need in me for her. She was mine, my one good thing, the keeper of my heart and the shackles surrounding my soul.

I'd broken over her grief for me. I'd shattered watching her fall apart. Yet here she was, striding through the barriers of death itself to come for me. Her. Only ever her.

Roxy's eyes moved over me slowly, the doors banging shut behind her as she kept coming for me, taking in the opalescent sheen of my shirt, the golden cloak which was pinned over my shoulders. I'd been hailed a true warrior in the moment of my arrival here, a circlet placed upon my brow in honour of the sacrifice I'd made fighting for those I loved. I appeared as such now, but I felt anything but valiant beneath that penetrating gaze of hers.

She drew closer, the air between us growing thin as I took her in, this beautiful, broken, queen of mine.

Roxanya Vega fell still with less than a foot dividing us, her face turned up to look at me, her eyes telling me that she feared this was some trick, that I might vanish again at any moment, ripping the last of her hope from her and destroying what little strength she'd clung to.

I wanted to reach for her, kiss her, tell her...all the things that words could never encompass. But there was something I needed to do for her before I could attempt any of that.

I drew the glimmering sword from my hip in a fluid movement before placing its tip against the ground between us and dropping to one knee in front of her. A tremor rumbled through The Veil as my knee hit the ground and I clasped the pommel of my sword as I bowed my head before her, my limbs trembling with the magnitude of this action, of what I had known and should have admitted for a long time now.

"I pledge myself and all that I am to you, my Queen," I breathed, emotion wracking my core as those words tumbled from me at last, my place in this world somehow fixing there as if I had found the truth of my own destiny, and all that I had ever needed to be. "I would be your sword to fight your enemies, your shield to protect your people, your monster to own and to wield. I would be yours in any and all of the ways I could be, and I should have told you that a long, long time ago. I am your creature, your servant…yours."

Silence followed my words, and I didn't dare move, didn't dare look at her to gauge the way that promise had been received, even knowing it had come far too late to matter now.

"You once told me that you would never bow," she said, her fingers brushing my jaw in the lightest of touches which set my entire body quaking beneath her. "You told me, that I would have to break you, just as you once tried to break me, and you laughed at the idea of it."

My lips parted, but I had no words. We'd promised each other no more apologies for the time that came before us, but I'd struggled with that oath every day since making it. The memories I had of hurting her tortured me always, and as if my mere thoughts on the subject had summoned them, I heard my own cruel laughter ringing out from behind me. The wall I'd used to watch my loved ones still fighting in the realm of the living reminding us both of all the damage I had done when we'd met.

I dared to look up at her, needing to know, needing to see what hurt still lined her beautiful features as the worst of me was presented to her once more, as she was reminded of all that I'd done to her.

But she wasn't looking at the wall, her green eyes were entirely fixed on me, and there was so much love there that it cut me apart to look at it. To know how unworthy I was of it.

"My father," I rasped but she shook her head, ebony hair tumbling over one shoulder from the movement and taking the edge from that warrior's visage so that I could see the girl she was beneath it. My girl.

"He has no place here," she said firmly. "And he is not your father. He bears no responsibility for the man you became despite him. He can't have a single piece of credit for that. He can't even have your name anymore."

"My name?" I asked, a frown furrowing my brow and she nodded as she traced the back of her hand along my cheek, the metal of her wedding ring brushing my skin and filling my chest with more pride and love than I had thought anyone capable of.

"You're Darius Vega now. And you weren't built to bow to anyone."

The words I'd once spoken to her resounded through me as she fisted my shirt in her hand and yanked me to my feet.

The sword fell from my grip as I stood for her, and her mouth captured mine as she hauled me to her.

My hands came around her waist as my lips parted for her and I drew every piece of her flush against me, the world fading to less than nothing beyond us as she claimed me right there, in the heart of death, like it meant nothing at all that she had ripped her way into this place to come for me.

She didn't release her hold on my shirt as she pulled me against her, kissing me like everything that made up the entire universe began and ended with the two of us.

That kiss was hello and goodbye, a bittersweet reunion, and a promise of everything we should have had. It was a breath of life into the silent cavity of my chest, a wordless plea for me to return to her, for the world to somehow make sense again purely because we were together.

But it was a lie.

Even as I felt the heat of her skin against mine, there was no denying the coolness that came from me. Even as my lips devoured hers and she released a sound so full of love and hurt that it burnt me, there was something still dividing us. I inhaled her air, and she consumed my soul, but that line remained. It remained, and it grew until our kiss broke apart and we were left staring at each other, facing the fact of our reality.

I opened my mouth to say the words, but she shook her head fiercely, tears gilding those stunning eyes as they saw right through me. Like they'd always seen right through me.

I kept my silence. Just for a little longer. Because I could see that she knew now anyway. She had felt that divide, had realised what still parted us, even with her fighting her way through the doors of death to come for me. Because I couldn't step back into life. There was no path leading that way, not for me.

I knew I needed to tell her so many things. About the Guild Stones, Lionel's plans, everything me and the others had seen from this side of death, but I just couldn't give any of it my attention while I held her in my arms, knowing each second was precious, each moment fleeting.

Until I Found You by Stephen Sanchez started playing at little more than a thought from me and I offered her my hand. One more song. The wedding dance we should have had. The beginning we'd been denied.

Roxy hesitated as she looked at my hand and I knew that she knew. One song. A few minutes stolen before it would be over. Before we had to face this goodbye and I would go back to waiting for her while she returned to the life she still needed to live.

She swallowed thickly and her hand slid into mine as she let me steal this moment, like she couldn't bring herself to deny me this one request.

"Roxy," I rasped, the feel of her so hauntingly perfect as I drew her into my arms, the warmth of her fire breathing the echoes of life into my lungs as if it were real, as if we might truly have been standing on the precipice of a future together.

"I hate it when you call me that," she whispered, her eyes tilting up to meet mine as I drew her against my chest, the world blurring around us.

Rose petals fell from the sky, dropping against her skin and coating her in them until she was clad entirely in their blood red colour, her wedding dress appearing on her as I was gifted a moment reliving that unreal memory when she had given herself to me entirely, beyond all reason, utterly mine, no matter how little I had deserved it.

"No, you don't," I growled, feeling the tremor in my flesh as it passed into hers, our souls connecting, tangling, weaving themselves back together as if we had never been ripped apart at all. "From the first moment I called you by that name, you looked at me and you knew me. You knew yourself. We just spent too long lying about the truth of that destiny."

"I'm done with destiny," she hissed, the light around us shuddering as her power flared, pushing against the will of the stars themselves while she used the raw magic she owned to deny them. The foundations of this place and everything beyond us rattled as she shook the heavens for this stolen moment, and I wondered how I had ever tried to deny the strength in her.

The song continued to play around us, and we both knew that its end would be the end of this too. We couldn't keep stealing time that had never been intended for us.

"You shouldn't have come here," I breathed though I couldn't mean it, not really. Not while she was there in my arms, real, and raw, and beautiful, her heart thrumming with all the life we should have lived together, the thump of it against my hollow chest almost making me feel like my own heart still pounded within me, the way it always had for her. "You know I can't leave this place."

"You can," she said fiercely, trying to pull back, but I held her tightly, refusing to let go. Our moments were slipping by one by one, and I knew as well as she did that there was no after. The song would end and so would this, the two of us slipping apart like grains of sand divided by an ocean. There was no power on earth – even one as great as hers – which could deny the laws of

all.

"Fuck, I wish I could," I swore to her, drawing her tight against me and inhaling the summer and winter scent of her. It was all things and nothing at all. This essence of immeasurable power which hummed with so much of everything that I was little more than a mortal kneeling before a goddess. "I wish I could come back with you more than any man has ever wished for any fate in all the history of all the world. I'm yours, Roxy, heart and soul and everything beyond, I'm yours. But even that can't free me from this place. What I lost can't be returned. There is no healing the body I once owned and there is no returning through The Veil now that it has closed at my back."

The walls trembled again, the truth she wanted to deny rushing up on us as the song played on and I looked into her green eyes, trying to show her what she was to me, what she had been. My salvation. I would have died a thousand deaths to be gifted this moment in her arms, to look at this perfect creation and see so much love for me burning within her. She had tried to deny death itself for me.

There was only her.

It had been no false declaration. She was my light when I had been so lost in the dark. She was the mirror she made me face, the truth I needed to see. And still she'd loved me. She'd been the only one who ever could have looked at all of the darkness in me, who could have seen beyond what I had done and found something worth loving within it. She'd been forged for me by something so much more powerful than fate. And the only regret I had in death was that I had broken her heart in the end. I hadn't been able to keep my promise. And though I'd tried, I'd fought to get back to her with all I had from the moment I'd found myself here, I knew that there was no going back.

This was goodbye.

And the song was ending.

"I love you, Roxanya Vega, and I wish I could have been worthy of you."

DARIUS

CHAPTER TWENTY EIGHT

I opened my mouth, all the things I needed to tell Roxy rushing to my tongue as silence fell, marking the end of the song and the end of the time we'd stolen far too soon.

But before I could utter a single word, a clash of power exploded throughout The Veil, a deafening boom making the foundations of the Eternal Palace rock beneath us, and Roxy stumbled back a step.

I caught her hand, the pain of our separation rising in me as I tried to capture everything about the way she looked and felt, wanting to keep every moment with her captured in my heart for the endless time which would follow on without her.

My grip tightened as a force started pressing against her, an impossible weight of power which tried to drive her back the way she'd come, back to a world without me in it.

"No," Roxy gasped, her fingers locking tight around mine.

The world flickered and blurred, my hand losing substance before materialising again, my grip firming once more.

"I'll wait for you," I swore to her, seeing the panic in her eyes and needing to comfort her in whatever way I could. "Right here. I'll wait for you for as long as it takes. And I'll watch over you, Roxy. I'll be there even though you won't see me. I'll never truly leave you. I swear it. I'll wait for you even if eternity passes me by while I do. I won't ever leave you."

"It's not enough," she choked out, tears gilding those bright green eyes, her pain mirroring my own. "I won't leave without you."

I wanted to hold on, I wanted to give in and go with her, I wanted so much with her which we couldn't possibly claim, and I had no idea how to let go of her now that she was here.

The walls splintered with cracks as she refused to leave and I fought to hold on too, not knowing where this could lead, but knowing I couldn't simply release her.

"Roxy," I began. "You need to find the Guild Stones and reform the Zodiac Guild. Your mother and Azriel have seen a turn in the tide of this war if you can do it. Three of them are hidden in music boxes-" my words cut off as I realised she couldn't hear me, The Veil thrashing so wildly that it was stealing my words, keeping the information she so desperately needed from her. I tried to call her name, but she wasn't trying to listen to me, her focus had moved on, and she drew a sun steel dagger from her hip which sent a chill of utter terror through my soul.

That blade had been the thing to steal my life from me, the dagger which had pierced my heart and ripped me away from her once and for all, making certain my body couldn't heal.

"Don't!" I roared as I took in the blade, the intent in her wild green eyes. She was going to end it all, sacrifice herself so that she might stay with me and no matter how much the most selfish parts of me yearned for that, I couldn't allow it. She had too much to live for, too much to achieve.

Her grip on my hand became insubstantial again but she refused to let go, instead latching on to that thread which connected our souls, that unbreakable link between us that nothing could rip apart.

The sky beyond the windows flashed purple and orange, a storm of pure magic thrashing against the confines of The Veil as her presence here threatened the stability of it all.

In the distance the clash of blades and a roar of raised voices sounded, letting me know that the people we loved fought on, buying us this time, keeping back the dead who were rushing for the gap she'd torn in The Veil. They couldn't pass back into life, not truly, but whatever might get through could cause chaos unknown and we couldn't risk that happening, no matter how tempting the call of life might be.

"Don't let go," Roxy snarled.

I blinked at the raw power in her voice, realisation dawning on me as I looked at this dark goddess who had given herself to me. She wasn't succumbing to death. No, she was telling fate to get fucked all over again. And if there was any chance at all of her making it listen then I was right there with her for the ride.

I nodded in agreement, not even fully understanding what she was doing. But I knew my wife. I knew she didn't have it in her to back down and with a flash of desperate hope, I realised she wasn't going to give in this time either.

"You are going to fight this," she ordered me. "You will fight it with all you have and if the price of that fight is the end of us both then I will gladly take that over death or life without you."

My jaw locked as I took in her command, the oath I'd just made to her singing in my soul. I was her creature to command in all ways and if this was what my queen demanded of me then she would have it.

"I'll give you all I have," I swore.

My fingers gripped hers tight enough to bruise, the full might of my magic building within me until a roar powerful enough to shake the stars in the sky erupted from my chest and my Dragon burst from my flesh, clawing its way free of me and moving to beat a path around us with its immense wings.

Roxy gasped, looking between the beast and me, taking in the insanity of seeing us as two separate beings.

She burst into flames, bronze wings tearing from her back before beating once and taking off, leaving her Fae body behind as a bird of flame and fury raced to join the Dragon.

We were surrounded by our beasts, the creatures who resided alongside our souls fighting off the laws of magic for us as we stood between them in an orb of potent power, our hands still locked as one while a wild wind tore at our clothes and hair, almost knocking us from our feet.

The roof of the Eternal Palace splintered overhead before hurtling away like it had been caught in the fist of a giant, and we looked up at the spiteful stars as they looked right back, their almighty power washing over us, promising their wrath if Roxy didn't stop.

She smiled at them, a savage, beautiful smile that stole the breath from my lungs. She slit her arm open, the blood of a true royal spilling from the wound.

Roxy reached for me, fisting my shirt right over the place where my heart should have been and ripping the fabric open to reveal the inked skin there.

"Roxy," I growled, catching her wrist as she raised two bloodstained fingers, my fear for her overriding my need to let this go further. I had to know what price she was paying to make this happen, what expense this great and terrible magic came at. "What will this cost you?"

"No cost is greater than the loss of you," she replied as the world hissed, the acidic whispers of the stars closing in on us.

Stealer of life.

Twister of destiny.

Beware the cost.

Turn from this path.

Stop before you unbalance the scales.

His ascension will bear a price.

"I don't care," she snarled, and the truth of her words silenced them instantly.

There was no denying her now.

I released her wrist, and she threw herself into the dark power of ether as she summoned it from the ground itself, the air, the flames, the distant rain, all of it flooding towards her and answering her call without so much as a hint of starlight among it.

That magic filled her up, making her skin glimmer with it, sparks of power crackling across her limbs.

Roxy released it like a whip, lashing at the sky far above and battering the stars themselves with a many-tailed attack.

They screamed as the ether tore into them and she smiled grimly, finally able to fulfil the curse she'd sworn against them.

Talons of ether cut into their power and with a flood of her will, she stole a piece of magic from each and every one of them. She took what they refused to give willingly, and ignored their horrified screams which rattled the sky as she twisted their will to her own and forced them to fuel her magic.

Roxy's legs gave out, but I caught her, holding her upright so she could keep going, so she could exact the vengeance she was owed and claim back what was rightfully hers.

Roxy hissed in pain as she began to paint a rune over the place where my heart should have been, but she didn't slow.

"My soul is his," she said, her words thick with magic as the declaration became an undeniable truth, like it was written into the fabric of the world just as any other law of nature might be. "My heart is his."

I gasped as I felt the weight of her power crashing into me, my knees almost buckling. I stumbled towards her, but she was there, waiting to catch me and I caught her too, both of us holding the other up. I clasped her face between my hands, my forehead pressing to hers and we held each other there like matching pillars of stone, each unable to fall while they had the other, stronger together.

"Let them beat as one," she choked out, the power almost too much for her body to bear, but I tightened my grip on her, lending what strength I had. "Let them *be* one," she demanded, painting another line on my skin, the rune unlike any I'd ever seen or studied, the power of it biting through my flesh and sinking into the essence of me.

"My life is bound to his. His death bound to mine. One heart...." Roxy panted heavily, her legs caving and nothing but my grip on her holding me upright. I wasn't going to let her fall; I wouldn't let her fail after coming so far. "One life... One path. Together," she hissed, a slash of her finger completed the rune and a scream of unimaginable pain burst from her lips as she finished it.

"No!" I bellowed, my gaze falling from her face, finding the sun steel blade now piercing her chest, mirroring the wound which had ripped me from life, the echo of its agony resounding through my chest in reply to what she was feeling.

Her eyes fell closed, hope abandoning me as I drew her into my arms, a roar burning from my throat, all of our combined magic thrashing and writhing, demanding the spell she'd cast to take hold.

Roxy's eyes snapped open meeting my terrified gaze, but she shook her head in denial.

She hadn't bound us in death. She'd bound us in life and the stars were simply trying to deny her.

Power exploded out of her, ricocheting across the sky itself, time warping and shifting around us as she refused their call again, denying them as she had been doing for so long already, refusing them even in the matter of death.

With that explosion of power, they fell back, the sun steel blade no longer piercing her heart but gripped tight in her fist.

Roxy summoned the power of her Phoenix to her fist and the blade turned molten, a puddle of silver dripping to the floor between us as it was destroyed, and the power of our binding sank in.

Roxy gripped my forearms where I still held her and met my eyes as the most astounding thump began to pound within my chest. One heart. Hers and mine. Bound in endless rhythm with one another, beating again, defying death.

"There is only him," she swore and with that vow, her power broke, crashing from her, through me and into the very heart of death itself. She tightened her grip on me and wrenched me back towards the blazing light of the living realm.

I caught a glimpse of the dead who battled to buy us this chance as we raced past them, Hamish waving wildly with a whoop of, "Tallyho, my son! Give that dastardly Dragoon what for!"

Hail's Hydra bellowed, joined by the ferocious roar of Radcliff's Dragon, the beasts singing their farewell to my own golden reptile before it collided with me, sinking back into my being where it belonged.

"Raise the Zodiac Guild!" Azriel hollered.

"Fate is shifting. My daughters can rise, Darius. Tell them that – tell them we await their call at the final gate and even hell shall bow to the voice of the true queens!" Merissa called.

Time seemed to slow as I passed by my mother last of all, her hand reaching out to claim mine, her eyes glistening with tears of pride, love, and happiness.

"Live long, live well, and love fiercely, my brave boy. I will watch over you both in every day that is to come."

"I love you," I choked out. "I'm so sorry for all we missed. I love you, Mom. I love you-"

The Veil snapped shut between us as the one true love of my life hurled us back into the land of the living and I crashed into a body preserved in ice, a heart which never should have been able to beat again coming alive once more, pounding to the tune of my wife's own love.

I sucked in a sharp breath as the fire at my core heated me through, the ice melting away and revealing the picturesque edge of a mountain where I was born into life again. I let that breath roll into me as I stared up at the dark sky, the winter solstice coming to an end above me and the stars all peering back with furious, vengeful gazes.

A slow smile grew across my lips as I stared right back at them, the rioting defiance in my heart all for them. If it was a fight they wanted, then they could have it, because I had just reclaimed my destiny from their clutches and I wouldn't be relinquishing it for anything.

HAIL

CHAPTER TWENTY NINE

Darius passed on into the land of the living, and all of our souls were tugged sharply towards him and Roxanya. There was so much light, and time flickered like a candle flame, ever changing. I felt my daughter's presence more profoundly than I ever had since my death and it made my form feel more solid, almost as though I could step right after her into the Fae realm. It was a temptation that crushed me inside. I wished to spend just one day in the sun with my children as grown Fae and tell them how endlessly proud I was to be their father. But it was not our path, no matter how much I ached for it to be.

We were thrown back onto the battlefield where the gateway to the living sealed up fast, and the hordes of desperate souls staggered to a halt, seeming confused, sad, lost. In droves, they swept away, returning to their rooms in the Eternal Palace, or perhaps elsewhere, leaving only us warriors on the field of golden mist and ever-watching stars.

I pulled Merissa into my arms, and suddenly I was in the middle of a group hug as Radcliff, Azriel, Hamish, Florence, Catalina, Marcel, and many more joined the embrace. A cry of victory went up and we broke apart, echoing it too.

Merissa's cheeks were damp with tears, and I swiped them away.

"I'm happy," she said, quieting my worries. "Hail, Roxanya has her mate back. Darius has returned. It's impossible."

"Remarkable," I agreed, a smile lifting my lips.

"It's a cause for a ham-pam-jamdy indeed!" Hamish cried.

"We can have ugg cake and joggle-slosh!" Florence squealed.

"Will there be sandwiches?" Marcel asked hopefully.

"Every kind, dear boy!" Hamish said in excitement, turning to Catalina, but she came rushing towards Merissa and I, grasping each of our hands.

"They're together where they belong once more," she said, emotion blazing in her eyes. "Your daughter has saved him in all the ways he needed, and now she has saved him from death itself." She hugged Merissa tight then threw herself at me.

I held her close, a light laugh leaving me. "My children have a tendency toward surprising us."

Music started up and I noticed Felisia and her pride had summoned instruments, drumming up a fast beat that spoke of our victory. I spotted Ren standing close to her, a little older than he had been in the memories I'd seen of him with a gruff line of stubble on his jaw. He watched Felisia dance, eyes alight and a hunger there that told me he would be laying a claim on her just as soon as he got a chance.

Catalina released me and ran to Hamish with a squeak, leaping into the air and he caught her in his arms, their mouths coming together as he spun her around in a wild dance. He threw her into the air, the man so big, he acted as though she weighed nothing, catching her against his chest before tossing her up once more. Catalina laughed in delight and Radcliff ran to grab Florence, whirling her around in a dance. She shed her armour with nothing but a thought and an unnecessary hip thrust, fully naked for a moment before donning herself in a flowing white dress. Radcliff twirled her under his arm, but it was soon clear Florence had no intention of letting him lead, kicking him in the ankle every time he tried to do so until he succumbed to her demands.

Azriel offered Serenity his hand and her eyebrows rose before she nodded and the two of them moved close in a dance that reminded me of the grand balls I had held at The Palace of Souls long ago.

Merissa shrugged, tossing her helmet away so it turned to glittering dust before she did the same with mine. A gold dress tumbled over her form in place of the armour, hugging her curves so perfectly that I groaned.

I caught her waist, tugging her close and we danced like we had long lives ahead of us and eternal paths laid at our feet.

The field around us faded away along with our armour and weapons, our entire cohort of warriors all transported to The Room of Knowledge as one where more souls joined our celebrations. Even the Remnants seemed to flash with a little more life from their seats up in the stands, and one in particular, who always seemed to be looking for someone called Bob, actually rose from his seat and rocked in time with the music.

Felisia was playing a banjo like she had been born to play it, and she ran over to me, opening her mouth to sing as she nudged me with her elbow.

"The Savage King was the oldest thing,

And he had a black soul too-oo-oo.

But the best thing about him was his wife.

And the fact he looked like a poo-oo-oo."

A roar of laughter carried from the souls around me and I looked down, realising she had forced an illusion over me to make me look like a shit dressed in golden robes.

I cast it away and she managed a small smile from me but a lot more laughter from Merissa. Seemingly satisfied, Felisia moved on to roast Hamish with her improvised song.

"Hamish Grus was as big as a walrus,

And he kinda looked like one too-oo-oo.

But the best thing about him was his fine moustache,

And the fact he only had one shoe-oo-oo."

Hamish looked down at his feet in confusion and Felisia swatted him over the head with the shoe she had somehow stolen from his foot. He fell into a fit of laughter, clutching his sides at the joke which had been funny, but perhaps not *that* funny.

"Do me next!" Radcliff jumped into Felisia's path.

"The dead Acrux didn't achieve so much,

And his brother was bigger too-oo-oo."

"Actually, don't do me," Radcliff grumbled, but Felisia sang on.

"But the best thing about him was he wasn't lame.

And the fact he was hotter too-oo-oo."

"Oh." Radcliff beamed. "On second thoughts, I rather liked that – but Lame Lionel isn't bigger than me!" he called after her as she pranced away.

"Yes, he is," she sang back.

"No, he isn't," Radcliff snarled.

"Yes, he isssss," she sang louder, strumming her banjo wildly to drown him out.

The party went on so long, it must have been a day or so before we stopped, no aching feet or tiredness finding any of us since we were long dead. The crowd grew in size with every moment that passed, the souls who had been sent into slumber during the battle re-joining us as either the stars woke them or perhaps the power wore off.

Some souls grew irritable as they fought to watch their loved ones in the great orb, especially when Florence climbed up on top of it and did a bare-footed jig while Felisia played the banjo as fast as she possibly could.

We were all drinking our favourite alcohol, our glasses refilling in our hands, mine an ale which Merissa had brewed under my own name during our lifetime, while she sipped on a glass of Arusco red wine. The haze of drunkenness swum through my head, but the moment I wanted to return to full clarity, all I needed to do was decide it. It was all an illusion, but one I fell into easily after everything that had happened.

"Mother and father of the flames," the stars' whispered inside my head and I looked to Merissa, confirming she had heard it too. *"You led the warrior souls well, and though you scorned us with your choice to let your daughter walk through into the realm of the dead, your sacrifice was acknowledged. You may have one ask of us in return for the preservation of The Veil. Speak it now and we shall deliberate upon its viability. You cannot ask for life, nor the death of those who live."*

The party quieted around us like a bubble had been placed between us and them. I felt the weight of this moment right down to the root of me, and knew what it was we had to ask. What Darius had walked out of here not knowing, what could only be told from the stars themselves now. If only I had thought to tell him sooner, there would be no need to ask for it now.

"The Vega curse," Merissa stated.

I nodded, looking to the ring of darkness above the great orb where the stars twinkled with intrigue.

"Tell our daughters of Clydinius," I called. "Give them the chance they need to break the curse of their ancestors."

A hiss of whispers in an old tongue ran through my mind, the discussion between ancient beings setting my skin prickling. This was immeasurably important, a gift from them so rare it could only be to balance out what we had offered them in return.

"It is done," the stars' purred, then a flash of light exploded through the great orb, and I gasped at what the celestial beings showed every Fae soul in The Room of Knowledge.

Our daughters stood on the grounds of Zodiac Academy in the heart of the Howling Meadow, surrounded by hundreds of Fae. Before them knelt the four Heirs; Caleb Altair, Seth Capella, Max Rigel, and Darius Acrux himself.

Everyone began to bow with them, dropping to their knees and my eyes caught on Gabriel and Lance as they dropped down with smiles on their lips and a weight of reverence about them.

"By the stars," I gasped, taking Merissa's hand, my chest swelling with what I was witnessing.

"Long live the true Queens!" Geraldine Grus bayed.

"That's my daughter!" Florence shrieked. "There, right there! That's my babble bug!"

Geraldine's words were echoed by everyone just as the sun crested the horizon and the entire crowd in the meadow was lit in amber light.

The stars crackled with power, acknowledging our daughters, and every dead soul around me watched on, captivated by this moment which was so important that there was utter silence around me now.

The stars pulled on my soul, stealing Merissa and I away and placing us before our daughters in the living realm, The Veil so thin that I could almost feel the wind against my cheeks.

I stared out at the bowing crowd, the weight of this action pressing down on all of us as fate shifted and our daughters finally rose to the position they should have held from birth but had now earned in action.

"Crown the new queens, and weave a new path into existence, mother and father of the flames," the stars encouraged.

Pride made my chest swell beyond measure, my daughters stepping up and claiming their places at last.

I brushed my hand across Roxanya's cheek the same moment Merissa pressed a kiss to Gwendalina's brow, my throat thickening with the magnitude of what was happening. Then with a roiling burst of power gifted to us by the stars, a crown formed in my hands, mine brightest red while Merissa's burned hottest blue.

I placed the crown upon Roxanya's head and Merissa placed hers on Gwendalina's, the flames igniting there in the living realm for all to see.

The magic surrounding them was fuelled by the stars themselves, humming and purring like they were drawn to the power of our daughters, recognising their strength, their unity as one.

"Your request shall now be answered," the stars whispered, just for Merissa and I.

The Imperial Star that hung from a chain around Roxanya's neck began to glow, ready to be used by the true queens, proof beyond doubt that they were prepared to rule.

The stars forced us back beyond The Veil and we arrived in The Room of Knowledge again, a wild cheer going up from the souls there who had witnessed it all.

Azriel slapped a hand against my back, smiling from ear to ear. "They have ascended at last! Now all they need are the Guild Stones, and perhaps this war can be won."

Before I could answer, a flash of light flared across the great orb, then burst through the room with such power that it threw several souls from their feet. Cries of alarm carried across the space, and I blinked through the hazy glow before the light fell away and all that remained in the orb was a blackness so thick it was impenetrable.

"What's happening, old bubkin?" Hamish asked me.

"I'm not sure…" I moved closer to the great orb.

"Has anyone seen Bob?" a Remnant swept down from behind me, flitting into my way and I wafted him aside. The power in the air was rousing them all from their seats, their forms becoming more tangible as they were drawn to witness this vital moment in time.

"Wait…I *am* Bob!" the confused Remnant cried. "All this time I was seeking Bob, and I was he! Rejoice! Rejoice! Bob is me and I am he!"

Merissa pressed her hand against the smooth glass of the great orb and the darkness rippled at her touch. She inhaled a little. "Oh, I *saw* something."

"What is it?" I asked urgently. "Are they well?"

"They are. The stars have taken them away, to speak with them about Clydinius's curse." She turned to me in delight.

We waited as mutters broke out across the room, souls anxiously watching on and waiting for our view of the living to reappear. At last, the blackness lifted just enough to reveal Gwendalina and Roxanya hovering within it.

"We've been cursed this whole time because of that fucking star," Roxanya said fiercely. "I say we use the Imperial Star to kill Lionel, Lavinia and all their screwed-up followers. We're not bringing some psycho star into the world to walk around, and cause fuck knows what havoc."

"If they use it, it will curse them deeper," I swore. "That is not the answer!" I yelled.

"But what is?" Merissa breathed. "The only alternative doesn't bear thinking about."

"There must be an answer…" I had thought on this long and hard, knowing the Imperial Star had to be returned to Clydinius to end the Vega curse. But what then? That had always been the problem. It would raise him into Fae form, the stars had told me it was so, and they had warned me of the dangers that posed. Unthinkable dangers.

Gwendalina shook her head in refusal of Roxanya's words. "We can't wield it. Look what happened to our dad. What happened to all the Phoenixes who tried to use it. It never works out well. Why don't we destroy it instead?"

"Exactly," I said.

"Maybe they could just use it briefly," Radcliff said hopefully. "To smite my brother."

"If they wield it at all, I fear the curse will worsen," I said. After all I had gone through because of the Imperial Star, I shuddered to think of my daughters falling to a similar fate.

"We use it first, then we destroy it," Roxanya suggested.

"No, darling," Merissa called. "It's too risky."

"I don't think we should ever use it," Gwendalina objected. "It could make everything so much worse. When I watched those memories play out in the crystal, the Phoenixes were all killed off. They were consumed by their own flames, turned to ash."

"I'll risk it," Roxanya said stubbornly, and Gwendalina grabbed her hand, pulling it away from the star.

"This was a mistake," I rasped.

"No," Merissa said firmly. "If she will listen to anyone, it is Gwendalina."

"I don't want to risk *you*," Gwendalina replied firmly, and Roxanya's gaze softened at that.

"I suppose using this lump of rock to kill Lionel might make it seem like we couldn't crush him without it," Roxanya admitted, releasing her hold on the amulet and laughter rippled out around the room, though I was too tense to find the amusement in it right now. "And I really am looking forward to seeing the look on his face when I cut his head off and prove just how much more powerful than him I am."

"We could return it, break our curse and destroy Clydinius the second he materialises," Gwendalina suggested, and Roxanya's eyes widened.

The stars screamed at that idea, knowing the moment they returned the Imperial Star to Clydinius, he would rise to walk upon the earth. They had told me of that time and again when I had begged them to relinquish this knowledge to my daughters, but it was the only answer to the curse. Perhaps they had expected our daughters to wield the Imperial Star instead, tempted by its power, but here they were surprising them again, fates unpredictable.

Still…destroying the star once it had risen seemed like a terrifying prospect. One I had not considered.

"Reckless madness, that is what my daughters know best," I said in fear, carving my fingers through my hair.

"Perhaps Gwendalina's idea is not so mad. Think of all they have achieved, perhaps they are strong enough to do this," Merissa said with hope.

"I do not wish to doubt them," I said slowly, thinking over everything I had witnessed them succeed at.

"Kill a star?" Roxanya murmured, a smirk lifting her lips at the idea.

Of course it appealed to her. Together, they were trouble embodied.

"If we pull it off, we'll be free of the curse, free of fucking Clyde and-" Gwendalina said excitedly and the stars shrieked louder, making some souls clap their hands over their ears.

"And nothing will stand in our way when we attack Lionel and his army," Roxanya finished for me.

"Your daughters are as mad as you Savage King," Felisia called to me, and laughter rippled out in response. "I rather like them for it. They have your wild heart, Merissa."

My wife smiled, lifting her chin. "Well, if any Fae can destroy a star, it is my children."

"Here, here!" Hamish yelled.

The stars screamed so loud the ground beneath our feet trembled. But they could not affect this decision, it wasn't theirs to make. They had given our daughters the choice, and they would not take the easy path. Whatever they had hoped for had not come to pass, or perhaps they had no better answer themselves, but once this truth was relinquished in payment for our sacrifice, there was little they could do. The stars were all about balance, and perhaps their hands had been tied to offer us this gift.

The darkness swirled around our daughters, rivers of colour spilling into it until they were travelling through a swathe of starlight.

They were thrown into the jungle at the foot of the Palace of Flames, but before we could see their next move, time flitted within the great orb and the scene changed before everyone's eyes.

We were looking into a cavern now where light danced across the ceiling, the large, glimmering star humming eagerly as it felt the Imperial Star approaching.

"Return the heart," Clydinius whispered, golden light pulsing and flickering through the air.

Roxanya took the chain from her neck, holding the Imperial Star in her fist. She broke it out of the amulet, removing the concealment spells that had been placed on it too, then moved towards the hole in the star's glittering surface.

Gwendalina slid her hand around Roxanya's, the two of them sharing this moment, ensuring the act was committed as one.

"Ready?" Roxanya whispered.

"What's that saying the Oscuras use? A morte…"

"E ritorno," Roxanya finished, and they thrust the heart of the star into the hole, fixing it back in place to the sound of a hundred Oscura Wolf souls howling around us in The Room of Knowledge, excited to get a mention.

"Creatia," Gwendalina spoke the power word for creation which would wield the Imperial Star.

Light blazed from the hole in the star, threading between their fingers and Merissa and I moved closer to one another, breaths baited as we waited to see how this might play out.

My wife was right, they could destroy a star. They were more powerful than I, more powerful perhaps than any Fae who had come before them. I would not doubt them, but still, fear bloomed inside me.

Time flickered again and I cried out in a command for it to steady itself and let us watch.

The light of Clydinius fizzled away, revealing two women in the image of Roxanya and Gwendalina, flames flickering between their fingers.

"Hail," Merissa whispered in fright. "Why is it mimicking them?"

I shook my head, having no answer but my fear drove deeper.

"I am Fae," the false Gwendalina spoke in reverence, her voice perfectly mimicked by the star.

"True freedom is mine," the fake Roxanya finished.

Our true daughters charged into battle to meet them, but as I prepared for the bloody fight to come, Clydinius's two new forms shimmered and disappeared from the cavern, trapping them there alone.

In the wake of Clydinius's departure, words rang out around us in the voice of the stars, a new fate knitted into existence in response to what our daughters had done, and those same words resounded out through the air here beyond The Veil.

When all hope hinges on a promise forged of lies,
Beware the threaded minds of blood and chaos.
Unlikely friends and broken bonds may shift the tide,
Cleave open the walls of the lost in the depths of the unholy night.
Unleash the souls tethered in the tainted dark,
Unite the rising twelve and toll the bells of fate.

"What does it mean?" I begged of Merissa, but she had no answer, and the silence that fell in The Room of Knowledge was so thick, that it seemed no one had an answer. "What does it mean!?" I roared to the stars, but they were quiet now, their new fate set.

And whatever path was coming for those I loved, I feared it would be draped in peril.

HAIL

EPILOGUE

I sat up in the stands that ringed the great orb in The Room of Knowledge, speaking with my wife over all we had witnessed while the masses chattered on about everything they had seen too.

With our daughters trapped in that cavern and Clydinius out in the Fae world causing unknown destruction, my mood over their ascension had been replaced by a sombre heaviness.

"Why is it that any time my daughters get ahead in life, they fast find themselves in a bind once more. The Vega curse is broken, why does their bad luck persist?"

"It could be worse," Merissa said. "They could be dead."

"True," I conceded. Clydinius had let them live, and we had chewed over the reasons for that.

Was he afraid he might be defeated in a fight against them? That was a high hope indeed, but a possibility all the same. Another possibility was that he didn't see them as a threat at all, inconsequential to his plans of world domination. He had taken their form, and perhaps had been arrogant enough to believe they would perish in that cavern without him having to lift a finger. I had hoped the twins would find a way to break free swiftly, but so far, they were still trapped, and I was starting to worry they really would have trouble escaping.

I ran a palm over my face, the stress making me feel older than I had ever been in life.

Merissa placed her hand on my knee and squeezed. "This is not the end."

"No, but it is the beginning of some fresh new hell," I sighed, kicking the seat in front of mine.

The seat trembled then the ground rumbled beneath me, and I frowned, wondering if I had caused it. But the rumbling deepened, the walls shook, the arches which swept overhead began rattling and the stars released a horrible, tell-tale wailing noise which could only mean one thing.

Cries of alarm carried around The Room of Knowledge and someone pointed to the dark circle of sky above the orb.

Merissa and I shot from our seats, gazing up at the stars there which grew brighter, hotter, burning, blazing, blinding. Then among them all, one began to move, ripping a fissure through the sky that left a fiery trail in its wake.

"Hold onto your nellies!" Hamish yelled from somewhere in the crowd.

The falling star was blasted away from here, out of the sky, out of our sight entirely and the stars whispered words that carried all throughout The Veil.

"Our kin falls. Their time is done. Pay your respects to the fallen star."

Someone's arm shot up in the air, the keen asshole splaying their hand out wide then curling it into a fist and repeating the motion again and again while the rest of the crowd joined him. It was a salute to the fallen star, and as the pressure built around me, the magic of the stars zapping against my skin, I raised my hand too, offering up a moment of respect.

The palace shook violently, then all fell quiet and still.

"Let's watch where it falls," Merissa said curiously and we moved down from the stands, reaching the railing at the edge of the great orb.

Azriel joined us, his shoulder brushing against mine. "Where do you think it'll strike? I doubt this one is bound for Solaria after the last one fell there."

"It depends where it chooses to fall," Merissa said and we looked to the swirling view within the orb to find the answer, asking it to give us the knowledge we sought.

We were shown a rocky mountain in a barren landscape, nothing but grass and stone for miles around.

"This is Solaria," I said in surprise.

"Perhaps the falling star favours this land," Merissa said, intrigued.

The sky lit up as the star came tumbling from the heavens, the trail of fire in its wake telling every Fae in a hundred-mile radius of its demise. The wind stirring the grass on the mountainside fell still as if nature itself was pausing to witness the star's fall, and an energy crackled within the rocks as if in anticipation of its arrival.

With an impact that shook the entire mountain, the star slammed into the face of it, carving out a wide, burning fissure in the stone and sending huge slabs cascading down the steep slopes.

The wind picked up again, roaring and blasting this way and that with far more vigour than it had had before. The storm crashed against the mountain as if trying to touch the molten stone that glowed with heat from the star's impact, and I gasped at the majesty in it all. The burning rocks hissed as the air struck them and the stone slowly cooled, leaving a gaping cavern that looked half melted, frozen in time.

Starlight glimmered from within, the pulsing silvery essence of that holy being sending waves of energy out into the air around it. I waited with bated breath for it to release its energy into the world, fuelling the Elemental power that lived in the blood of Fae. This was our truest gift from the stars, their death an offering of power to our kind. It was a law as old as time, and Clydinius's thwarting of that law was what had caused such chaos in our kingdom for so long. Too long.

A glimmer of light caught my eye lower down on the mountainside and my gut clenched as Lionel, his shadow queen, Tharix and Vard appeared via stardust swiftly followed by his cohort of bonded Dragons.

"By the sun, what are they doing here?" Merissa hissed.

"They must have been close enough to see it fall," I said. "Perhaps Lionel wishes to witness a Donum Magicae."

It was one of the rarest events to ever be witnessed by our kind, after all. And Lionel tended to covet all things rare. Though I scorned him of the privilege.

At least he looked in no fit state. His fine clothes were unkempt as if he had not changed them in a day or more, and there was a tightness to his expression that told me of the stress he was under. I wondered if he even knew of our daughters' ascension yet.

With a thought, the great orb showed us Lionel and his minions up close, and Lavinia swept closer to him, gripping his hand. "I can do this, Daddy. Just give me the chance."

Lionel frowned, looking from her to Tharix then the Dragons at his back as if doing a mental count of his Guardians. They were still a powerful bunch of assholes, but they were on the back foot now, and the hint of worry in Lionel's eyes told me he was desperate.

"You mustn't die," Lionel hissed, and Lavinia cooed, moving in to kiss him.

When she pulled away again, I could tell he had said the words not out of any sentiment for the monster, but his need for her. He couldn't risk losing one of his dwindling allies. Especially not one so fierce as her.

407

"Come with me, Daddy." Lavinia stepped onto an animal track that led higher up the mountain, bare toes pressing into the dirt.

"For the love of the moon, will she ever stop calling him that?" Merissa cringed.

"Her mind cracked long ago," Azriel said. "She is but fragments of the past, clinging to a shattered soul."

I didn't mention the fact that Lavinia had likely claimed the term daddy from her time joined with Clara's soul. The poor bastard didn't need the reminder of his daughter's infatuation with Lionel. At least she was past that now, and I knew she had enough regrets to last her an eternity in this place when it came to that Dragon.

"No, I will wait h-" Lionel started, but Lavinia's shadows grabbed hold of him and dragged him after her up the path.

Vard hurried after them, but Tharix stepped into his way, the beastly creature wetting his lips with hunger. Vard staggered backwards with a murmur of fear, scurrying into the masses of the Dragon Shifters, and they all waited for their master to return.

The view through the great orb moved after Lionel and Lavinia, taking us with them into the deep cavern where the glittering star lay, about to release its power.

"What is Lavinia planning?" I murmured, unsettled.

"What can she do?" Azriel said.

"Surely nothing," Merissa replied, but there was a note of doubt in her voice that drove my worries deeper.

Lavinia pulled Lionel close to her, the whip of shadows around his waist releasing him, and he straightened as his gaze fell on the star.

"Celestial heavens above," he breathed. "It is truly something..." He crept towards it, his hand outstretched with the arrogance of a Fae who had never been denied anything in life. The want in his eyes was clear, the possessiveness of a Dragon rising in him.

Lavinia slapped his hand down, keeping him back. "It's dangerous, my king. We mustn't touch it. Not with our hands anyway."

My throat tightened, her plan clear as she raised her palms and shadows slid out of her, four tendrils of darkness slinking carefully closer to the star.

The celestial creature hummed with building power, the buzz and drone of it speaking of how much magic was twisting around the two of them from that star.

Lavinia's shadows slipped closer, hovering above the star's shining surface, and the giant being pulsed and hummed faster, urgently preparing to release its power before the shadows could touch it.

The stars began to whisper around us, a rush of frantic, fearful voices telling me this ploy of Lavinia's was not so foolish after all and concern gripped me too.

With a clash of power, the shadows lunged at the star, snaring it and spreading over its gleaming surface like ink spilling over a boulder.

The star screamed, the noise a high-pitched cry for help that made the stars above shriek in horror.

"No!" Merissa cried, her hand touching the orb, her eyes flashing with glimpses of futures untold.

The stars were wild and furious, their laws thwarted once again and this, it seemed, was the final straw as a giant crack burst up the centre of the great orb. Shards of crystal shot out of it and the souls in the room scattered with cries of terror.

Azriel pulled me back by the shoulder and I caught Merissa's hand, tugging her with us.

"They don't want us to watch any longer," Azriel hissed, but my eyes remained riveted to the scene before me, certain the star would break free at any moment.

Lavinia stepped closer to it, power pouring from her in droves, her shadows smothering the star and trapping all of its power in its core.

"I can feel it," Lavinia gasped, a moan leaving her as the shadowy coils of power that threaded between her and the star lit up with glimmers of light, all trailing back into her body. "I can feel it all."

A sickening smile lifted Lionel's lips while the room around us tremored violently, the archway overhead cracking, a chunk of rock crashing down close beside us. The stars shrieked louder, demanding we leave, and I let Azriel haul me away, towing Merissa after us.

My fingers tightened on my wife's hand, and the horrors I perceived in her eyes told me all I needed to know about what she had managed to *see* of the future. She looked hopeless, desolate, and my heart fractured, certain that fate had twisted against our children once again.

"What can we do?" I pleaded, but she shook her head, eyes wide and full of endless sorrow.

"Nothing, Hail. Nothing but watch and pray."

AUTHOR'S NOTE

Here we are, on the precipice of death, and the final book in the Zodiac Academy series which will be coming very soon. This has been one hell of a ride for us, our little budding idea of an academy series set in a world filled with all the chaos of the zodiac has made it through eleven of the star signs and hangs on the cusp of number twelve.

Did you enjoy this little venture into the beyond? Was walking through The Veil as traumatic as clinging to life by the tips of your toes like so many of our characters do day by day? I'd say not. All in all, I think death tasted pretty sweet compared to life in Solaria, and maybe that means that those fucked up stars need to think about their behaviour.

(Caroline and I take no responsibility for the actions of the stars so don't come looking over here for your answers to that little nugget of shit.)

So here we stand, awaiting the end, and as I may know a thing or two about the trauma-filled, anxiety inducing, twist-stuffed chaos that is to come, I salute you for your bravery as you stand on the front lines and beg the stars to be merciful at this final moment.

Will they be?

Well…probably not.

Thank you all so much for venturing into the beyond with Darius and all those who were lost along the way, thank you for reading our words and for taking the pain with the Pegasus farts, all wrapped up in a paper crafted bow just desperate to claim your tears.

If you want to come talk to like-minded lovers of all things dark and Fae, then come join our legion of tear donors in our Facebook group. And if you want to be up to date with all the latest from our writing cave then make sure you sign up for our newsletter too.

We love and appreciate all of you dream makers so much, and so in parting I will give you this gift of a hint to the happenings of Zodiac Academy book 9:

Beware the words on the page, for darkness follows the readers who dance along their lines of ink.

Love you, Susanne and Caroline XOXO

ALSO BY
CAROLINE PECKHAM
&
SUSANNE VALENTI

Brutal Boys of Everlake Prep
(Complete Reverse Harem Bully Romance Contemporary Series)

Kings of Quarantine

Kings of Lockdown

Kings of Anarchy

Queen of Quarantine

**

Dead Men Walking
(Reverse Harem Dark Romance Contemporary Series)

The Death Club

Society of Psychos

**

The Harlequin Crew
(Reverse Harem Mafia Romance Contemporary Series)

Sinners Playground

Dead Man's Isle

Carnival Hill

Paradise Lagoon

Harlequinn Crew Novellas

Devil's Pass

**

Dark Empire

(Dark Mafia Contemporary Standalones)

Beautiful Carnage

Beautiful Savage

**

The Ruthless Boys of the Zodiac

(Reverse Harem Paranormal Romance Series - Set in the world of Solaria)

Dark Fae

Savage Fae

Vicious Fae

Broken Fae

Warrior Fae

Zodiac Academy

(M/F Bully Romance Series- Set in the world of Solaria, five years after Dark

Fae)

The Awakening

Ruthless Fae

The Reckoning

Shadow Princess

Cursed Fates

Fated Thrones

Heartless Sky

Sorrow and Starlight

Beyond the Veil

The Awakening - As told by the Boys

Zodiac Academy Novellas

Origins of an Academy Bully

The Big A.S.S. Party

Darkmore Penitentiary

(Reverse Harem Paranormal Romance Series - Set in the world of Solaria, ten years after Dark Fae)

Caged Wolf

Alpha Wolf

Feral Wolf

**

The Age of Vampires

(Complete M/F Paranormal Romance/Dystopian Series)

Eternal Reign

Eternal Shade

Eternal Curse

Eternal Vow

Eternal Night

Eternal Love

**

Cage of Lies

(M/F Dystopian Series)

Rebel Rising

**

Tainted Earth

(M/F Dystopian Series)

Afflicted

Altered

Adapted

Advanced

**

The Vampire Games

(Complete M/F Paranormal Romance Trilogy)

V Games

V Games: Fresh From The Grave

V Games: Dead Before Dawn

*

The Vampire Games: Season Two

(Complete M/F Paranormal Romance Trilogy)

Wolf Games

Wolf Games: Island of Shade

Wolf Games: Severed Fates

*

The Vampire Games: Season Three

Hunter Trials

*

The Vampire Games Novellas

A Game of Vampires

**

The Rise of Issac

(Complete YA Fantasy Series)

Creeping Shadow

Bleeding Snow

Turning Tide

Weeping Sky

Failing Light

Made in United States
Orlando, FL
04 July 2024

48568092R10248